I0594584

Painted Words 2021

Painted WORDS 2021

AN ANTHOLOGY PUBLISHED BY
BENDIGO TAFE'S PROFESSIONAL WRITING
AND EDITING PROGRAMME.

© Bendigo TAFE 2021
All rights reserved.
Bendigo TAFE
136 McCrae Street,
Bendigo VIC 3550
Telephone: 1300 554 248
www.bendigotafe.edu.au

Copyright is retained by individual authors. The moral rights of the authors have been asserted. All rights reserved. Without limiting the rights under copyright reserved above, no part of this publication may be reproduced, stored in or introduced into a retrieval system, or transmitted, in any form or by any means (electronic, mechanical, photocopying, recording or otherwise), without the prior permission of both the copyright owner and the publisher of this book.

The Australian Copyright Act 1968 (the Act) allows a maximum of one chapter or ten per cent of this book, whichever is greater, to be photocopied by any educational institution for its educational purposes provided that the educational institution (or body that administers it) has given a remuneration notice to Copyright Agency Limited (CAL) under the Act.

This book is an anthology of fiction, non-fiction and poetry. Except where indicated, names, characters, places, and incidents either are the products of the author's imagination or are used fictitiously. Any resemblance to actual persons, living or dead, businesses, companies, events, or locales is entirely coincidental.

First published in Australia in 2021

Printed by:
IngramSpark
http://www.ingramspark.com/

ISBN: 978-0-646-84878-5

Cover design—Peter Wiseman, *Regeneration*, digital illustration, 2021.
Book design, typography and layout—Peter Wiseman

Foreword to Painted Words 2021: Aftermath and Regeneration

Signs of Regeneration?

This year's Painted Words journal has been assembled under conditions not dissimilar to our 2020 Pandemic Edition. Victoria, indeed most of the south-eastern seaboard of Australia, has been in lockdown for the bulk of Semester 2 – though PWE program teachers did manage to deliver most of Semester 1's classes face-to-face. Readers might think it was overly optimistic of us to label this year's edition 'The Regeneration Edition' (and terms like 're-emergence', 'renewal', 'resuscitation', 'recovery' and 'resurrection' also come to mind) given we are suffering (at time of writing) the highest infection rates of the entire pandemic across Victoria, and a stringent lockdown remains in place across metropolitan Melbourne and many other parts of the state. Also, daily deaths and hospitalisations are again rising. Similarly, the virus once again circles Bendigo - as it did for much of last year - like a hungry shark. It would be easy to change the name of this year's journal to "Pandemic 2" (suggesting in the process the subject matter of ghoulish B-Grade Disaster and Post-Apocalyptic movies) and overthink the likely impact of approaching COVID-19 variants, especially when one of them is called 'the Doomsday Variant'.

*   *   *

A closer look at the reality around us, however, suggests that our theme for this year's edition, The Regeneration Edition, is indeed accurate … at least for now! As I write, I note new data from the University of Melbourne suggesting that the mass vaccination programmes introduced across Victoria and NSW are working, not only in reducing infection rates, but also in preventing hospitalisation and death. The virus has not gone away, but for those who are willing and able to be double vaccinated the 'spectres' of: a) getting infected; b) requiring hospitalisation (once infected); and c) dying from COVID have receded significantly. As I write, NSW has just recorded its lowest infection rate in months – largely due to ever-increasing vaccine coverage - and consequently that state is starting to re-open. Victoria is on a similar trajectory. These are clear signs of 'regeneration', 'resuscitation', 'recovery', 'renewal' and 're-emergence' from "The Great Pandemic of 2020-21".

*   *   *

For many years I've believed that most creative acts in the cultural realm are, in essence, optimistic life-affirming attempts to regenerate self and society. The argument is easy to make for the so called 'Literatures of Awe', e.g. speculative fiction genres like SF, Fantasy, Magical Realism and Quantum Fiction which are, quite often, inspired by 'love of life'; a quest/journey where the protagonist experiences 'awe and adventure'; or a desire to try on and recommend to others 'best possible futures'. But there is even something optimistic in gloomy and cathartic works of literature and art – yes, even in the 'poetry (and fiction) of witness' which often digs up and explores the personal and social traumas of the past. The impulse in such works is often to make sure the traumas, alienation, injustices, etc. explored 'never happen again', which is to say such works offer a warning, and thus represent acts of cultural inoculation/vaccination.

*   *   *

The situation currently faced by Australian society - these strange 'in between days/weeks/months' as we await vaccine-driven 'herd immunity', these days before a promised 'opening up', before

'Freedom Day' (as it was somewhat hubristically labelled in the UK) - seem to me to evoke two apparently antagonistic states of being: a state of pregnant excitement and a state of apprehensive/anxious waiting. Such times are, potentially, immensely creative. They usually demand deep reflection – both personal and collective. We ask: 'What has changed from the time before all this happened?' 'How will we be able to live after the pandemic ends (what is possible in the aftermath)?' 'What did we learn about ourselves and each other during the traumatic times?' There is also perhaps the most important question of all: 'How should we live in the New Reality (are there new possibilities on offer)?' These are the searching questions we must ask in the time of Regeneration … otherwise the fragile green shoots of recovery can wilt or become trampled underfoot. I think good writers are in the permanent business of 'Regeneration', and the most diligent of us will be working busily to respond to the above questions, as well as others that crop up as the species-wide recovery/renewal (for surely this has been an experience of collective trauma) proceeds into 2022. I like to think that we are already in the time of Regeneration – new growth, new life, new possibilities blossom all around us.

Endurance: Learning About Writing and Editing at Bendigo TAFE in 2021

My optimistic stance should not obscure the very real difficulties PWE students and staff endured this year, particularly in the second half of the year. As with 2020, staff were forced back online to teach, out of safety concerns, especially from the middle of the year on. Though many students coped okay with this altered learning environment, it was difficult for many – especially as we entered the second year of the pandemic, and most people's psychological resources were already running low due to the many life stresses thrown up by the pandemic. It was not an easy second semester for many students!

*   *   *

Peter, Honeytree and I did our very best to keep the show rolling along each week, with regular Zoom sessions and online content and exercises posts. Given the Writing and Editing Industry is largely digital these days, PWE students sampled (in the second half of the year, in particular) the contemporary work-place environment experienced by many workers in our industry. Put simply: the industry demands self-motivated workers (not easily distracted, even when working alone at home); a good computer with appropriate programmes and back-up protocols, and world wide web connectivity involving the ability to work remotely using industry-standard multimedia technologies/software (e.g. Zoom, Learning Platforms, etc.). Although not ideal from an educational perspective, the second half of the year was useful preparation for the industry realities students will encounter in today's highly digitised writing and editing industry.

*   *   *

This year's journal is, once again, a stunning achievement. As usual, the journal features creations birthed in various Cert IV and Diploma of Professional Writing and Editing classes. Readers will encounter high quality poems, short stories, nonfiction pieces, etc. that were written and structurally edited in PWE classes this year. Congratulations to all the students who went through the process of selecting, polishing and then submitting work to the journal this year.

*   *   *

Given the size of this year's edition, it is important to acknowledge the prodigious amount of work put in by our Diploma level Project Management/Advanced Editing class of 2021. These students launched and oversaw the submission process, liaised with authors to copyedit incoming work, assisted with design, printing and production decisions, and also helped plan and carry out the launch event – ably assisted this year by Peter, Honeytree and Jan. Together the staff and students working on the project were an awesome team! This crucial work took place in a difficult, online setting – so all kudos to those involved in bringing *Painted Words 2021* to fruition under such testing circumstances. The cover to this year's journal looks incredible and the writing is explorative, interesting, experimental and deeply reflective – whether exploring fantastic, visionary worlds of the imagination or dealing with the everyday realities of modern life.

*   *   *

Finally, just before I close, this year we lost (hopefully only temporarily) a wonderful long-term PWE teacher from the program – Tru Dowling. Tru taught Short Fiction and other units across our program for many years. Her vast store of industry knowledge, as well as her finely-honed skills as a writer, poet, editor and teacher were missed this year. Thank you, Tru, for all the effort you've put in over the years!

*   *   *

The poster that Peter and the students developed to advertise this year's journal depicts a green hand surrounded by healthy young plants. The hand and plants are tentatively emerging from soil infested with the COVID-19 virus. Two butterflies are perched on the tips of the hand's fingers – depicting, I think, the fragile nature of the regenerative process, but also symbolising hope. Many of the stories and poems in the Regeneration section of the journal capture the precarious mood of our current species moment – a moment of anxious waiting, deep reflection and hopeful excitement. Likewise, given all creative activities are, metaphorically speaking, perched like butterflies on the fingertips of a perpetually forward-striving life force, we might suggest that perhaps *Painted Words 2021* is itself a kind of humble Object of Regeneration for people wearied and tested by the events of the last 20 months.

*   *   *

Open the cover … then read, absorb, reflect and dream. Hopefully, you'll imbibe small energy-packets of psychic and spiritual renewal/ regeneration/hope from the marvellous poems, stories and articles offered up by students enrolled in our incredible "Class of 2021"!

Dr Ian Irvine
October, 2021.

Contents

Flash Fiction

Flash Non-Fiction

Short Stories

Poetry

Regeneration

The Painted Words Team Zooming…

Preface

The anthology you now hold in your hands, *Painted Words,* was written, collated and edited by Bendigo TAFE's Professional Writing and Editing students during the second year of the global pandemic. It is a compilation of short stories, novel extracts, poetry and non-fiction works – our way to share our collective and creative experience.

Painted Words celebrates the diverse talents of writers and visual artists within the Bendigo TAFE community. Under the stewardship of Peter Wiseman, Honeytree Thomas, and Dr Ian Irvine, with support from Jan Bayliss, we gathered our resources, planned our approach and brought this book into the world.

> "I always marvel at the range of ages, occupations, ethnicities, life experiences, and education I see every year in the PWE course."
>
> P Wiseman.

Our experience in creating *Painted Words* has been one of enormous personal growth and development. Together we created an environment of welcome and inclusion, which allowed us to openly express our ideas, inspirations and explore new opportunities.

The theme for this year's edition of *Painted Words* is regeneration. We asked ourselves - what does it mean to regenerate? Is it merely the renewal of a thing back to its initial state? Or does it describe an evolution, an improvement, an emergence of something new and unique to the world?

For even if yesterday's normal is forever gone, tomorrow's normal could still be something better.

This theme has been addressed in unique ways within the various works submitted, representative of the diversity among the student group.

> "The quality of the work is extremely high with a multitude of both fiction and non-fiction pieces maintaining interesting and complex narratives which express interesting and unique ideas in an entertaining way."
>
> C Irvine-Kingsmith.

For readers who are seeking escapism, and yearning for a 'break from reality', you will find within these pages romantic tales of kings and queens in elaborate fantasy realms. You will have intriguing encounters in mythical forests, meet a range of magical beings, werewolves, dragons and monsters. You will find disturbing stories of dystopian futures or augmented realities; tales of alien invasions and jealous ghosts. Fairy weddings. Detached brains. Vengeful vegetables and demonic cats.

> "Humour was a hallmark of many pieces – perhaps an antidote in difficult times."
>
> M Irwin.

But escapism was of course not our only response to the difficult year behind us. We also selected honest, emotional, and heartbreaking works that examine the loss of community and human connectedness. Stories that explore grief and personal tragedy, and of family and self-reflection. These pieces provide powerful imagery in a world where our emotions are too often hidden behind a mask – a world without smiles.

> "Writing is a catalyst for healing and self-exploration."
>
> S James

You will also find within these pages in-depth discussions addressing issues of racism, oppression and injustice as we challenge the divisions in our society, question our political leadership, defend the bullied and give minorities a voice. We have delved into the online world, explored the impacts of virtual-realities and addressed social media's influence, propaganda and censorship.

"The last two years have given everyone a lot to think about when it comes to societal issues and that comes out in the works that have been submitted."

D Cornwall.

The global pandemic and its prolonged impact on our society has weighed heavily as the world continues to battle the spread of COVID-19. As students, we have navigated wave after wave of fluctuating lockdowns and restrictions. Yet driven by our passion for the written word, we have supported each other, cared for each other, and guided each other throughout the year.

Inspired by the opportunity to create, we have banded together to create something, we think, quite magical.

"It has been made easier by the fact that, this year, we have an awesome team of hard-working, quality writers and editors."

MJ. Douven.

"It's been really hard – but through everything that's going on, I found encouragement in the knowledge that we were going to create something. Actually, achieve something during this tough time."

S Pratt.

We hope you enjoy the remarkable visions and voices of the Bendigo TAFE community in our regenerative *Painted Words* anthology.

The Painted Words Team
October, 2021

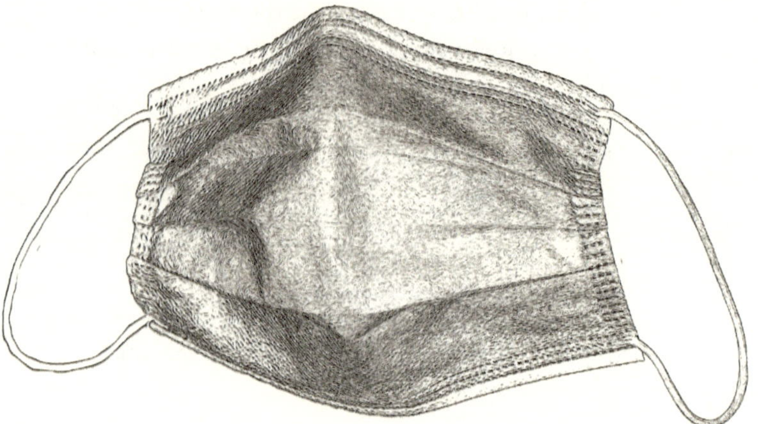

FLASH FICTION

Nourish

Rhys Allen

S ian ignored the harsh discomfort of her pressure suit and set her tired brain to the task of breaking up the hard baked stuff that passed for soil here, 20,000 light years from Earth. Ben was gone, and so was Jep. Even Suze, with her broad grin and mopped red hair. Gone. Sian breathed heavily and attacked the ground once again, breaking up the cold grey sod in preparation for the last of her viable seeds.

The sky flashed in violent purple: the evening storm was rolling in. Sian quickly finished her work. Plough, scrape, plant, water – and breathe.

Hope.

Would it be enough? It couldn't possibly be enough, could it?

None of the crops had ever thrived.

Nothing grows on this fucking planet!

No. No, this time would be different.

She laid her gloved hand gently upon the broken soil; upon her lost crewmates, inches below.

"Thank you," she said.

As the first fat drops of water began to fall from the sky, Sian picked up her spade, and returned to the empty shelter.

Little Hero

DD Woods

Little Jimmy wriggled the door handle under the stairs as he walked along the passage. To his surprise, the door opened. He turned on the light and ventured through; little sister Sarah followed. Once away from the entrance door, the thick walls, and low ceiling, created a cave-like feeling. Jimmy pretended that it was the centre of the earth down the rough concrete steps to 'Aladdin's cave'. The walls were stacked high with dusty tea chests and storage cartons. Old steel frames raised the storage boxes off the bluestone floor. The children found toys they hadn't used for ages as they explored in and around the stored cartons. They shrieked with delight with each 'new' toy they discovered.

"Aladdin kept these toys for us Sarah."

"I love this bug catcher. I had it full of praying mantis; they're fun to feed and to watch," said Jimmy

"And look at my toy cap gun Sarah, it made a big bang when I fired like this," he continued as he played with the toy.

"Let's play hide and seek, Jimmy, me first," giggled Sarah, "so wait til I ready."

Jimmy waited for Sarah to find a hiding place. "Five, four, three, two, one. Ready or not, here I come," laughed five-year-old Jimmy. His little sister covered her eyes and held her breath. She hid around the corner but not secretly enough to trick Jimmy. At two and a half, she thought she was hiding if she couldn't see you; that usually meant her hands were over her eyes, but her body was in full view. They both squealed with delight when he found her.

*   *   *

A heavy rain band descended over the city. The wind howled, and the streets were awash. Water started to trickle over the bluestone floor. It was fun for the children to splash in the water, but the basement was dark and scary when the lights went out. Jimmy turned on the large torch he found, but it wasn't bright enough. The storm had caused a blackout—no power for the city or the basement pump.

"I scared Jimmy, and I don't like dark. Too much water, my socks are wet, Mummy will be cross," cried Sarah.

"Now I wet everywhere, Jimmy. I scared. I want my Mummy, MUMMA!"

"Don't cry, Sarah, we can go back to our room. You follow me this way."

He turned to lead the way. Sarah screamed. A tea chest fell as she moved between them and pinned her arm to the bluestone floor. Jimmy tried to help, but the tea chest was too heavy to lift. They both screamed in terror as the water level rose quickly. They cried, shouted, huddled together as the water rushed around them; the basement stifled their cries. When the water level increased, the tea chest floated and lifted slightly. Jimmy saw his chance and tugged her again. Sarah was free! He wrapped himself around her and guided her to the trapdoor and safety. He would not leave her—Jimmy was her little hero.

Faded Friends

Brandon Kelly

Gerald looked out the window as the Counsellor asked him, "How are you feeling these days?"

Gerald replied, "Terrible; my friends keep fading when I get close to them."

"How do you mean?"

"Every time I ask them to go out with me, they fade from the feet to the head until I can't see them at all."

"And do you ever see them again?"

"Yes, they're different somehow, sometimes they're smaller, other times they'll have a sort of rainbow-tinge over them." "I can't see them properly, the only time I can fully see them is on web chat." "I can see them crystal clear then, but I can never interact with them."

Gerald turned from the window to face the Counsellor; he could see that she was disappearing into nothingness.

The fading image of the Counsellor staring at Gerald whispered, "Is there something wrong Gerald?"

Gerald said quietly, "I guess I have touched you also, I can't see you anymore."

Gerald left the empty room; he knew that he would have to start all over again

Into the Light

A L Fraser

What some people do just to see their favourite actor! Charlie grumbled to herself as she filled a bucket with hot soapy water to wash the car. A vehicle that was supposed to be white but right now was a dreary kind of grey.

She had a deal. If she cleaned the car, her father would take her to see Russell Crowe in his latest movie. However, looking at the front of the vehicle, Charlie realised her dad was getting the better end of the deal.

Two hours later, her arms ached, and her knees hurt from kneeling and scrubbing away the mangled corpses of what had to be a new and special breed of suicide insect. But at least the car was clean.

On the way home Charlie was unamused to see hundreds of kamikaze insects just dying to be splattered over the grill and windscreen she had so meticulously cleaned.

"Oh, get lost!" she said.

"Pardon?" her father asked.

"Those insects! I spent the morning cleaning their mangled bodies off the grill, and now look!" Charlie pointed at the little glowing bodies zipping by in the headlights.

"They're attracted to the light, Charlie. They're not doing it to piss you off."

"They are pissing me off," she retorted.

"They're just going toward the light," he repeated.

"Well, doesn't that make a mockery of what happens when we die? Going into the light only to be splattered all over God's new Saab," she said.

"No, God wouldn't drive a Saab. He'd drive a Mercedes Benz."

"How do you figure that one, Daddy?"

Charlie's father burst into song, "Oh Lord, won't you buy me a Mercedes Benz?" He turned toward his daughter, "If someone is asking *Him* for a Mercedes, *He* must be an expert."

"Okay, Daddy, very clever."

"Thank you, Charlie." He kept humming the tune as Charlie closed her eyes.

Two sets of headlights suddenly appeared in the distance. They were still some length away, but her father dipped his lights as their car bumped onto the bridge across the river flowing through town.

"Oh God, he's passing that car!" her father cried. Charlie was frozen to her seat as the second car, with no regard for approaching traffic, passed the first car, switched beams from low to high and headed toward them as though they weren't there. Her father jerked the steering wheel and their car tore through the bridge railings .

*   *   *

Charlie opened her eyes; she was floating above their crumpled car, which was cloaked beneath the dark water.

Her father was beside her, watching emergency vehicles crowding up to the splintered railing.

"They're too late, Charlie," her dad said.

"I know, Daddy," Charlie answered. "What now?"

As she asked the question, a portal opened in the sky above them and from it poured a beckoning light. It was irresistible. Her father floated calmly toward the opening, and Charlie couldn't help it as she followed her father into the light.

Then it happened; Charlie should have known it was coming. It really shouldn't have been a surprise. The light faded until the only thing visible was the numberplate GOD 01 on the Lord's brand new BMW; she was shocked for the three seconds before impact.

Red Flowers in August

Tenzin Castleman

I always think of you when I travel out here to the country house by the lake. Skin as soft as forget-me-nots and a smile as sweet as honey. I wish to know your love warm as the summer sun again, but the honeysuckles here grow with streaks of red.

Footsteps in the Forest

Jessie Mayflower

The forest was always quiet during this time of year; a blanket of fog carpeting the pine-needle-covered floor, muffling the sounds of the forest. The only sounds audible to the traveller as he trudged along the deer path to the town beyond were his own footsteps echoing back at him through the fog and the distant bird-calls of alarm.

The quiet left the traveller uneasy. The traveller quickened his pace in attempt to leave the forest behind. For a moment, as the traveller broke his rhythmic stride for the first time since he entered the forest, the traveller swore he could hear another set of footsteps behind him. The traveller came to a halt to better listen.

The soft shuffle of footsteps continued for a moment even after the traveller had stopped, before they too fell silent.

For a few seconds, the traveller could only hear the rapid beating of his own heart, his own shallow breaths as he stood there, still as a statue but for the rise and fall of his chest. He listened, straining his ears for any sounds at all in the heavy stillness. When he could not hear anything, he shook his head and scoffed. He was being foolish!

But then footsteps started up once again. Only this time, they were running.

The traveller did not think. He was moving before his brain knew it.

Suddenly the world was full of sound, his footsteps pounded the dirt of the trail as another set followed close behind. His breathing was loud in his ears, along with the calls of alarm from the birds in the trees lining the path.

The traveller sprinted until he broke through the trees, when the sounds of footsteps behind him once again stopped.

Against his better judgment, the traveller turned back to see what had chased him.

For a moment, he couldn't see anything. Then his caught the tiniest movement – a patch of green that stood out against the forest leaves.

Standing among the trees, shrouded in shadow, was a lone figure. The shadows were too deep for the traveller to see its face, but he could see that the figure was dressed in worn, brown trousers, a jade green tunic and leather vest.

The traveller looked down at his own worn brown trousers, green tunic and leather vest, eyes widening before he quickly looked up again.

But the figure had gone.

Heart racing, the traveller looked long and hard at the tree line but the figure had disappeared back into the forest from which it came.

When the traveller reached the town his first order of business was a new set of clothes. Dressed in an ill-fitting outfit he had scavenged from unattended laundry lines; the traveller burnt his clothes until nothing remained but ash.

Years later the traveller could not shake the unease he felt whenever he thought of the forest and the thing that lived in it. On his bad nights, he would have nightmares about looking back at the forest and seeing a monster with a mouth filled with sharp jagged teeth and wild fur. On his worst nights he dreamed he was looking back at the forest and seeing a mirror image of himself.

FLASH NON-FICTION

Possum Mania

Sha James

Headlines in the local newspaper read, 'New Residents in Town.' A family of possums had recently taken over the Botanic Gardens. The community was divided. Some of the locals were delighted and welcomed the new arrivals. It added another dimension to their beloved communal meeting place. Others were concerned about the havoc they would wreak on trees and other wildlife that had previously set up residence in the gardens; cherished members of this natural wonderland who established themselves earlier with minimal fuss.

Regardless of which side of the debate you were on, it spiced things up a little in this sleepy regional town. Eventually, over time, the furry migrants became an accepted part of the community and the furore died down. Despite attempts to stop the possums' climbing trees, with plastic strips wrapped around tree trunks, they were here to stay.

One balmy summer evening, I was racking my brain for something to do to entertain my grandson. He was only three years of age at the time. It was far too hot to sleep after four consecutive 45+ degree days. Then it occurred to me, in a light bulb moment, let's go to the park and feed the possums.

We went into the kitchen to search for food. Uncertain what

exactly possums like to eat, we settled on fruit. After chopping bananas and sweet juicy brown pears into bite-size pieces, we packed them into two snap-lock bags and drove to the park. My grandson did not know what to expect when we arrived at the Botanic Gardens. It was the first time he had seen a possum. But he was always ready for an adventure.

It was very dark that night with no moonlight to help us locate the furry critters. We gently meandered around the pathways looking for signs of possums. Then we spied two little red eyes peering at us from the canopy above. As we opened the bags of fruit, the possum scurried to the ground in eager anticipation of receiving a tasty morsel.

My comrade-in-arms squealed with delight as the possum took food from our hands. I had to remind him to talk softly and tread gently so that the possum did not run away. They were clearly familiar with this routine for this adorable marsupial showed incredible trust. It was easy to see why the locals were compelled to feed them nightly. The sheer delight on my grandson's face said it all. My heart melted with joy as I added another memorable moment to my collection of priceless treasures. How could I not welcome these precious creatures who needed a safe place to live? I too was a migrant once upon a time.

The Gift
Meredith Adams

We had just spent six hours submerged in the hypnotic opera *Einstein on the Beach*. Back on the darkened street we look for somewhere to eat.

There is a patch of light; we head towards it.

We sit in the middle of a brightly lit space filled with happy, elegant diners.

Our mains arrive. A nearby couple stand up.

"Tonight is the owner's birthday." They gesture towards the man in the chef's uniform. "As a gift for staying open for us every night we played for the past year, these duets are for you."

They are Anthony Warlow and Marina Prior. We stop eating. We are sitting amid the cast of

The Phantom of the Opera!

The couple sing perfectly. Their voices hold the attention of the room.

An hour and a half later, we erupt into exuberant applause.

Our meals are stone cold. A small price to pay for an exquisite experience!

The Trip
Meredith Adams

"Meredith!"

I spin around. "Petra!"

She flings her arms around me. "My favourite nerd. You made it!"

*   *   *

Somewhat disappointed, Petra had cancelled her thirtieth birthday party last June due to COVID.

Bang! An invite arrives through Facebook. Petra's Belated Thirtieth: Sunday the fourteenth of March, Royal Botanical Gardens near the Shrine of Remembrance. Noon to three o'clock.

Fantastic! I clicked the coming button and logged out. *Cool, I know where the shrine is!*

Stepping onto a train for the first time in over twelve months feels strange. The smooth plastic walls, the greenish fluorescent light. Passengers, heads down, so absorbed in their own world they hardly notice anyone getting on at Kyneton. Doors close with a pneumatic hiss. Carriages clank together and we roll forward leaving the station behind. Outside, hill after hill of rolling lush fields and lines of pine trees criss-cross the countryside. An endless blue of sky arches overhead. I haven't seen this much open space in a long time.

Beige and grey Colourbond fences sever farmland from city sprawl. Gone are the open spaces! Stations, shops, hospitals, and houses flash past as we tear down the track. I am engrossed in the ever-changing scenery as grey factories, rust-brown shunting yards and herds of dockland cranes appear, and we rattle over the Maribyrnong River.

Our train glides into Southern Cross Station; the city skyline towers over me. I feel like an ant. The train stops with a jerk. Passengers spring to life, talking, gathering belongings, squeezing into the aisle anxiously trying to get out. The platform becomes buried under trampling feet as people surge towards the ticket gates. I am one of the last off the train, and amble towards the station exit.

The city rush hits me face first. Speeding cars, trams clanging within inches of the curb, people pushing, jostling to get to the crossing first.

Swept up in a crush of people, I reach the other side of the road.

The shrine! How do I get there? A tremble starts in the back of my legs.

The traffic pauses in front of me; I look up. A fast-food delivery driver, hot box on the back of his bike, is holding his hand out gesturing me to cross to the tram stop. I nod, smile, mouth "thank you", then scuttle across.

Looking at the mass of coloured lines on the map, any tram passing near Flinders Street station will do; then change to another route heading towards St Kilda.

Disembark near the Shrine.

Simple.

But how am I going to find Petra? Anxiety fidgets down my arms and shuffles my feet. My throat tightens. *What am I going to do?* The clanging and revving of the city crashes down on me. My fingers, white, clutching the handrail.

Crossing the Yarra River, I can see the Shrine. I let out a sigh. Prying my fingers off the handrail, I alight from the tram.

The forecourt of the Shrine is semi-deserted. Peering into the park, I can't see anything like a party going on.

Someone yells my name; I spin around. "Petra!" We hug. I finally breathe out.

"Yep, I made it. So good to see you!"

"You know, everyone's getting lost," she said, "I should've put a map on the invite."

Twice Saved

Sha James

On the morning of April 10th in the year 1968, our taxi pulled into the school driveway. In a flash, the cab door flew open, and before I knew what was happening I was being propelled across the field like a hovercraft. My nine-year-old feet never even had a chance to touch the ground as I sailed through the air like a paper plane, only to find myself pancaked against the fence with torso and limbs immovably pinned to the wire. I began to panic. The rain lashed at my face so hard I could barely catch a breath.

Then I felt two strong hands peeling me off the fence. The taxi driver leaned into the wind as he carried me back to the cab. Cold, saturated, and sporting two horizontal gashes to my forehead, I begged the driver, "Please take us home." I could hear my sisters crying in the background but noticed how visibly relieved they were that their older sister was now safely seated in the backseat of the cab. We sat in silence, listening to the windscreen wipers flapping rhythmically as we headed for home. Every now and then the taxi jolted and shuddered from another windy blast.

Later that day while huddled together watching the Wahine disaster unfold on TV, the reporter confirmed people's worst fears. The ship was capsized just off the coast of Wellington and rescue attempts were being hampered by the weather. Fifty-one lives were lost that day, with many more passengers stranded on the listing vessel.

Despite feeling dazed and saddened, a wave of relief washed over me. "It's a good thing you cancelled your booking on the Interisland Ferry, mum. That could have been you!" Shock set in as we realised the enormity of our near misses.

Virtual Sticks and Stones

Cyber Bullying, Keyboard Warriors, and the Online Community

MJ Douven

"It's not worth it unless it hurts someone."

– recently said by a player widely known as a bully on the server of a popular online game.

In the current online climate, hurting people is easy. Too easy. It's possible now to become a bully as simply as clicking a button or swiping a finger across a phone screen.

Bullies hunt the game-servers in packs made up of the most powerful players, harassing anyone who dares to stand up to them. Victims either rage-quit or join the wolves to survive. Those who continue to resist are hounded repeatedly, day after day, night after night. Wars are fought on those virtual plains as fiercely as any real-life war, even if the blood and damage are only imaginary.

Or are they? Being under such emotional siege, even if only "in a game", can take an enormous toll, as can the accompanying propaganda and vitriol. Prominent female players have crude comments directed at them repeatedly. Players who refuse to waste resources and choose defense over pointless, impossible battles get called cowards and "chicken." One player even got told by another, "Why don't you go hang yourself?"

The anonymity afforded to online players leaves keyboard warriors free to say whatever they want to whoever they want, and to say things they would never dare to say to someone's face. When confronted, the bullies either defend their actions with "it's just a game" or worse, they change their in-game identity and start it all over again under a different name. Such behaviour can create a paranoia that sweeps across a server in a matter of hours, as accusations of spying for another alliance or of cheating the system, are hurled against multiple players.

Meanwhile some players just get the popcorn, sit back, and watch the show. Others add to the chaos, making comments that push their own agenda purely for the thrill of watching the server burn. Still others take the ostrich approach and ignore the entire chat function of the game.

With so much of our lives being online these days and with whole communities forced to resort to virtual connections rather than physical ones, more stringent moderation is called for. We protect our children from being bullied at school. We protect our friends, family, and coworkers from being bullied in their jobs. But who protects the online community? Who protects the innocent from the virtual sticks and stones?

SHORT STORIES

Number 43

MJ Douven

"43."

She shuffled forward. Eyes ahead. Body straight, lined up at a ninety-degree angle to the machine's blood red eye. No longer flinching when the scanning beam ran over her. Controlling the urge to twitch as her naked skin tingled.

The Eye blinked green. She'd passed the first scan.

Plastiglass doors in front of her swished open, and she stepped into the cubicle. There was a metallic whirr overhead, and the pulsating cascade of chemicals began.

She kept her eyes open, turning her face up into the shower. Welcoming the first few seconds of pain, of feeling, as the chemicals stung her retinas. Before the numbness descended.

*   *   *

Numbers filing past the plastiglass, one-way screen. Numbers in their naked, shivering, pallid bodies standing in front of The Eye. Numbers exiting the chemical showers on the other side, numb, vacant, pulling on grey formless coveralls like automatons.

Numbers. Everywhere he looked, he only saw numbers. Not people with names and families and pasts. Just the numbers assigned to them.

He hated them. He hated them all. They were the scum of

society, an ever-growing blight, filling up reprogramming centres as fast as they were built, using up funds that should be spent on those who actually deserved it. On the hardworking, contributing members of society, not on these mindless less-than-animals *scum*.

People like them shouldn't even have been born. Not when ISA was capable of scanning embryos for genetic defects. How much more of a step would it be for the computer to scan them for low brain function and IQ? Then the pregnancy could simply be terminated. Why bring a child into the world when it was only going to be a drain on state funds?

They should be dealt with. Not medicated and fed and safe. He'd be more than happy to do it too.

Guard 5. ISA's metallic voice addressed him.

He started guiltily. The light on the camera of his small cubicle had started blinking angrily at him. He had gotten so involved watching the numbers file past, stewing over the waste of it all, that he had forgotten his part in this machine.

He hurriedly slammed his hand down on the palm scanner that unlocked the second set of doors. Trying to cover his mistake and cursing under his breath when the scanner bleeped its displeasure loudly.

Error. He should have known that ISA missed nothing. *Please explain your failure to fulfill your designated task.*

Guard 5 swallowed, his mouth suddenly dry. "I was distracted."

Your function here is to fulfill your designated task. If you are incapable of doing so, a replacement will be ordered.

He straightened in his chair. "It will not happen again. I promise."

ISA was silent for several agonising seconds. *Proceed.*

He slowly let out the breath he had been holding. Conscious of being watched even more closely than usual, he placed his palm on the scanner again. This time the scanner read his imprint, the light above the doors turned green, and the numbers began filing out of the shower block.

A moment later, just when his heartrate had started to slow, ISA spoke again, her precise voice somehow more chilling than ever. *Notification: This error has been logged in your file, and your file has been flagged for review. At the end of your rotation, please submit to Psych Evaluation Room 1 on Floor 19.*

He swallowed hard but nodded obediently. There was nothing else for him to do but nod. No one questioned ISA.

*   *   *

He emerged from the psych evaluation room, sweating and shaking. He hadn't gone through one since he'd been assigned to guard duty. He'd managed to push to the back of his mind just how terrifying they could be. He remembered now. He staggered and just barely managed to steady himself against the wall.

The sensory stimulant the technician had given him when he entered was still buzzing through his system. His head was buzzing too with the hoard of images and sounds he had been bombarded with during the session. The stimulant kept him hyper-alert, kept him from hiding his responses.

Squinting to read the fuzzy-edged numbers on the nearest screen, he realized that he had been in for almost twelve hours. He could have sworn it was no more than three or four hours. How much of what had been done to him did he not recall? Worse, what had he said or done during that time?

He didn't have the time to think about it, though, as his next rotation was due to start any minute. ISA did not tolerate lateness. Another black mark to his name, and he would be terminated.

A film of sweat broke out on his forehead at the thought. No one talked about what went on at the termination centres in every major city. No one talked about those who disappeared. But they all knew.

He entered the guard cubicle and came to a stop. On every screen, from every angle, from all the eyes in the corridors and rooms, was displayed the same images – swarms of numbers in their grey formless coveralls filing down into the feeding hall.

In that moment their vacuous, blank expressions incensed him in a way he had never felt before. It was because of them that he had been forced to undergo such a painful session. They were everything that was wrong in his world. They should be terminated. Not the good, hard-working people like him.

Blind rage overcame him. Turning sharply, he headed out of the cubicle, ignoring the startled exclamation of Guard 4. Stimulants still buzzed in his system, making him not care that everything he did was observed and recorded.

It was easy, shockingly easy, to slip into Medical Storage and swipe a vial of something. He didn't know what it was, but it was on the shelf labelled Hazardous so had to be something good.

From there, it was a short walk down a flight of stairs and into Dispensary. Kitchen workers were loading tubs of nutritional supplement into the machine. He sidled up to one of the tubs and emptied the vial into it. It was the work of two seconds. So easy.

And then he was back in the hallway, panting as though he had been running, feeling both terrified and exhilarated at the same time.

After a moment, he pushed away from the wall and sauntered back down the hallway, back toward his guard post. No one had seen him. He had gotten away with it.

He rounded a corner and froze. Two of the elite nameless, numberless guards stood there, their ominous black uniforms reminding him of the unofficial name the residents called them – Reapers.

One of them stepped forward and placed a bony hand on his shoulder. "Your offense has been recorded and forwarded to ISA for judgment." The guard's emotionless drone was even more chilling than his uniform. "You are to be transported to Termination Centre Alpha to await her decision."

He did not resist. He did not fight them. No one resisted ISA. It had been a mistake to even try.

*   *   *

Grey. The numbness had receded to a grey swirl of formless shapes.

Nothing felt real, like she was somewhere outside herself, watching herself through a cloudy glass screen. Screaming, beating against the glass, her cries a slowly dwindling murmur.

She trudged forward, following the shape in front of her. Dragged along like a leaf on the wind.

She barely remembered what leaves were. Or wind. The images were faded sepia in her mind, like old pictures, too blurry to focus.

From far away, she watched herself shuffle forward to the nutritional dispenser. Her hand lifted to the contact spot, and the machine attached itself to the tube implanted in her wrist. Her eyes drifted shut as she waited for the warm buzz to start.

Instead, what flowed into her veins was liquid fire. Scorching, burning, like electricity sparking along her nervous system. Burning away the numbness.

Screaming, she dropped to the ground, clawing at her wrist, yanking out the tendrils of the machine. She was burning from the inside out. From far away came more screams from around her as the room turned into chaos.

Lights went out in the splintering smash of glass, plunging her into total blackness. The wail of an alarm started up somewhere close by, harsh, discordant, pulsating through her whole body.

She had to get away. That single thought burned in her head.

Blind, she scrambled on hands and knees. Just trying to get away from the screech of the alarm. Crawling over or around the bodies in her path, some of them still numb and inert, others flailing and screaming like she had been. Hands grabbed at her but she clawed them away.

She did not know where she was going. She just kept crawling until she hit a wall, and then followed the wall blindly. The only thing that mattered was that the screeching alarm had started to fade away behind her, even slightly.

Her brain was still on fire. The sensations battering her from every direction made it hard to think, to focus on anything. In that moment, she would have welcomed the numbness, would have welcomed the grey cocoon of warmth she'd been wrapped in for almost as long as she could remember.

Her groping fingers brushed cool ridges of metal, a change from the smooth concrete walls. Metal ridges surrounded by a smoother metal square – it seemed familiar, but it took a few minutes for her to access the name. A vent?

Hands shaking, she felt along the edges. The vent was loose – she did not stop to ask why. She pulled it off the wall, letting it fall to the cold floor with a clang, and crawled blindly into the dark space behind.

Behind lay a tunnel just wide enough for her. She crawled for an interminable length of time, through the endless blackness. Every so often, she had to stop to wipe her hands, damp and slick from the tunnel floor, on herself.

The burning – the hyper-sensitivity of her entire body – had started to cool. Instead, she just felt immensely tired. Strange, unfamiliar words – half-formed, mixed-up memories – her mind was a jumble. *Too much.*

She kept going on sheer instinct, on fear of being found and dragged back. It was inevitable. Everything was watched. Everything was recorded. No one escaped.

Gradually, she became aware that the tunnel around her had grown lighter. She could now see a short distance ahead of her, could just make out the grey, shapeless walls. The floor slanted down up ahead, rivulets of water running down the slimy shale.

The water stung on the raw skin on her hands and knees, scratched and bloody from crawling so far. She was starting to shiver, her coveralls soaked through with sweat and damp.

It was getting harder to keep going. Her hands kept slipping, and the pain was so bad that it brought tears to her eyes. She pressed the backs of her hands to her cheeks and realized that she had been crying silently for a while now. She didn't know why. Every breath felt like it was torn from her in a ragged, gasping sob.

She slipped and fell hard, scraping her chin on a piece of jagged rock. Her teeth clacked together so hard that she bit her tongue, and blood filled her mouth.

She picked herself up, only to fall again. This time, however, she was unable to stop herself, and the incline of the tunnel floor sent her sliding downward at a rapidly increasing rate. She flung her hands out, trying to stop herself, but just tearing her nails on the wall. Crying out as her body slammed into rocks on the way down.

As she slid, she caught sight of bright light up ahead, rapidly getting closer – the tunnel mouth. But she did not have time to react.

She reached the tunnel mouth, and her momentum launched her through the opening. Into open air.

She fell. No time to even cry out. No time to do anything, not even to see how far down she was falling.

She landed with a splash in ice-cold water and sank immediately. Instinctively sucking in a breath and getting a lungful of freezing salt water.

No strength to try to swim. Unable to breathe. Gray, cold, fuzzy numbness expanding around her, wrapping her in familiar oblivion.

Hands, seizing her shoulders, pulling her to the surface. She struggled blindly, weakly, against the hands. She didn't want to go back to the harsh, bright world. She didn't want to go back to be watched and measured and kept. She preferred to sink.

She was dragged up out of the water, and then just lay there, too cold, tired and miserable to move. The sand was coarse, sharp under her fingers.

Slowly, she became aware of warmth beating down on her shoulders – sunshine? She rolled over slowly and pried open her grit-caked eyelashes. People stood all around her, looming over her and looking down at her. The guy who had pulled her out of the water – at least, she assumed it was him, since he was the only one dripping wet – was on one knee beside her.

"You're the first one ever to make it."

His words didn't make sense. Nor did the fact that they weren't immediately slapping restraints on her or jabbing her with something. None of them were in uniform either. None of them had numbers.

"Do you still remember? Anything?"

She blinked up at the faces surrounding her, crowding her. They were all throwing questions at her, but half of their words were lost in the blur. They wanted something specific from her. She didn't know what.

"They called me 43." Her voice was harsh from disuse, and the words tasted strange on her swollen tongue. The effort it took to pull the coherent thoughts out made her head hurt. "But my name is Shay."

Was I The Monster?

Faith Dam

Was I turning into a monster?

Yellow eyes stared at me from where my green eyes should have been. Ginger fur crawled up my arms where white, pale skin should have been. Claws like daggers where there should have been small nails. I lifted my hands to my face and dragged them down my cheeks, feeling the cuts open as the claws tore my skin.

It was too much to take in.

Clutching my stomach, I fell forward as my body heaved, my insides churning. Bones popped and cracked – my shoulders rising and falling with each progressing inhuman breath.

Painful. Pain. Such a horrible pain – worse than any I had felt before. A pain so strong it left you on the ground curled up in a ball. You couldn't cry or get air because it hurt you so much.

*   *   *

Back in the Grounds, the festivities froze as the Chief signalled for silence. A hush fell across the nervous crowd. Silence apart from the crackling fire and the breeze that stirred the trees. Darkness apart from the harvest moon. They muttered to each other as they peered into the shadows of the forest. What was it? Maybe a bird? Or perhaps an animal? A fox screeching into the night? The Tribe waited with bated breath, anxiously listening out for it again.

Just beyond the forest, Nova pushed Hamish away, a grin fading from her face. Hamish threw out a protective arm as he pulled Nova behind him. Sick of his protective behaviour, she stomped on his foot, pulling a dagger from her boot. Stifling back a cry of pain, Hamish surrendered. Nova rushed forward, her hand poised with the dagger. Hamish quickly grabbed her outstretched hand. He held it tight as Nova relaxed, comforted by Hamish's firm grip.

"That sounded like Charlotte…" Nova said. "We shouldn't have left her".

*   *   *

Teeth. Pale, white, and sharp enough to tear flesh from bone, pierced my gums. A low shuddering growl rumbled in the back of my throat. It was all too painful. I looked up to the sky and to the moon. A Harvest Moon. A full moon. A Wolf Moon.

"Charlotte! It's Nova! Where are you?"

Ah…sweet Nova. I could recognise her voice anywhere. I wanted to cry out. I wanted her to find me – to hold me tightly in her arms and tell me everything was okay. But it wasn't.

"Charlotte! Are you alright?"

I didn't respond. I couldn't respond. Her shouts echoed through the night and rang louder in my ears.

Was I a wolf? Or was I still human? I had forgotten who or what I was. I wanted to cry, but all I could feel was anger. I could feel it. The beast. It was taking over – taking hold of my mind, fighting for control.

I gasped as my vertebrae shifted – my hands and eyes clasping shut at the intense pain.

A presence was growing in my mind, pushing me down as it tried to reveal itself. A darkness, an evil. Something I had never felt before. Something trying to destroy my humanity. It was like being drowned as I fought for control of my own mind.

I remembered a time when I was younger. A sweeter time when I didn't have to worry about anything. I had insisted my parents take me down to the stream that ran through the camp and the forest surrounds. It was the beginning of a new spring. The sun was at its peak in the late afternoon. Cicadas created a chorus in the trees as I ran ahead of my parents, through the dry undergrowth, my feet bare, my face flushed and warm. Desperate to reach the coolness of the stream, I leapt without looking. The water was freezing. I heard my parents scream. I tried to scream, but the water filled my lungs and I gasped for breath as I tried to reach the surface. I was drowning. My father plunged through the icy depths, and I felt his strong hands reached under my arms as he pulled me to the bank. My mother held me tight against her warm body. I was safe now. I could breathe again. But there wasn't anyone to pull me out now, no one to hold me tight. No one to save me.

I pushed the memory back, desperate to keep my mind sane and maintain control over my body.

I needed to breathe. I needed to swim to the surface and breathe again. I gasped.

I was gone. I had lost control – and now the beast had taken over.

Broken Mirror

Rhys Allen

I have simulated myself.

I watch him with the help of my VR headset. He is sitting at his desk studying his computer. As far as I can tell he has no idea that he is a simulation. He wouldn't care if he knew. I am quite pleased. I didn't think it would this easy.

I'm going to be honest: I sort of cheated. Rather than simulate just myself, I simply simulated all of it. You may not think that is easy, but trust me, I can show my program a simple action – say, a ball dropping from a height – and the computer program see this and extrapolates a rule of physics. There's more: if I utilise Leifer's principles of retro-causality in quantum calculations, I can ensure all the required calculations are done tomorrow and sent back to today by way of – well let's call it space-time quantum magic. I don't know, it's weird, but it works. I set a problem for the quantum computer and – hey presto – I have the answer. Even if the calculations take billions of years, they each come racing back to the initial point of query thus solving the equation almost before I even send it! Sort of. Don't worry about it, it's fine, have a cup of tea and read on.

My VR headset is comfortable, and I watch my counterpart tick-tocking on his (our) silly keyboard. I am tallying the differences between his world and mine. He is using the same computer, the same interface as I am, so presumably he is now looking at his own simulation of himself. I know what you're thinking: I could also be a simulation. Obviously, this has occurred to me. But if I am, and if you are reading this, then you too are part of the simulation in which I write. Are you bothered? No? Yes? What possible difference can it make to you? The answer is none at all.

My counterpart is wearing the same clothes, I think. Except – no wait – if I look carefully, he's chosen the red tie today! I chose the blue. Fascinating – I wonder what effect this will have on his universe. Or mine. Probably no effect if we're honest – these small discrepancies usually iron themselves out with no real cause for alarm. Well, theoretically speaking of course.

OK, now this is a bit weird – his phone is ringing. I had thought we were synced time-wise, but apparently not. He's moving differently to me, but that's understandable. His environment – his reality – is subtly different since he selected a different tie – an extra second here or there – probably to undo the knot in the tie. I wasn't bothered, so I chose the blue. Why didn't he choose the blue tie too?

My phone isn't ringing though. This suggests a much bigger difference, because whoever is calling him isn't calling me, and that suggests the outside world for him is radically different from the outside world for me. He pulls off his VR headset and he picks up the phone.

I can't hear him talking. I was so excited to begin the experiment that I forgot to set up the audio. But I can see him. He's not happy, his face has suddenly fallen. He has lost all animation. Is that really what I look like? I should shave, I think. He's hung up the phone now. In his chair, he's slumped over and – crying? Unbelievable, I didn't even know I had tear ducts it's been so long since I've –

OK, I'm getting a bit creeped out now. Why would I be –

He's digging through his drawers – my drawers. I know what's in there, what should be in there, at least. I'm right – a note pad, yes, and a Sharpie. He's writing a note now. Oh shit, it's – He's holding it up, pointing it straight at me. It reads:

PETER – RESTART SIM FROM 24 HOURS AGO. MAGGIE HIT BY BUS. DEAD.

Maggie? But she was right here — she's — oh God, has this happened? Is this happening? Why hasn't anyone called me then?

The tie! He would have taken longer with the tie. I could wind back and see, but he may have been late getting out of the door, late getting into the car. I had a dream-run through the traffic lights this morning, but maybe he didn't. That's it: Maggie late to school — Maggie dead!

I should restart the sim: of course I should. I can feel my own tears now, on his behalf. Maggie is dead — except — only for him. This is an opportunity, isn't it? How would my life look now with her — gone?

He's only a sim. Only a sim. I keep saying it but I know it isn't true. He is me, just there, instead of here.

He's writing again, holding up a new sign.

PLEASE!! GODDAMN IT, PETER,
YOU CAN FIX THIS!

Alright, alright. Fine. I do it, I stop the sim, I rewind it back to the morning, to the tie. I watch him and he chooses the red tie. NO. Stop, restart, re-run — red tie. I don't know how to communicate with him, it can't work in that direction. I can't hold a sign to him.

I set the computer on a loop. It's watching for that change, for that moment when he selects the blue tie. It has been running now for minutes, he has been created and un-created a thousand or more times now, as has Maggie and everything else. And every simple time he chooses the fucking red tie.

I'm going to stop it. I have to stop — this is crazy. I —

*   *   *

I've just noticed my phone. Seventeen missed calls, all from Maggie's school. I had it on silent this whole time. How did I — it doesn't matter now. I turn off the simulation and open the drawer of my desk. I know what's in there.

The Demon Cat
Meg Irwin

I roused from my cosy reveries when the master came home. "Tabitha," he called, "I've brought you a friend."

I was struck by a ghastly, fermenting foulness. I shook my head to clear it from my nostrils. It was the acetone stench of starvation, overlain by the grime of city drains and the half-rotten flesh on which the "friend" must have dined.

I saw a lean, matted thing, which could barely stand. His head lolled. His colour was indeterminate, a dirty mixture. But when I beheld his face, I had to look away. His eyes burned with intelligence and limitless greed. His whiskers flared out, fierce and strong.

I walked over and tried to clean the worst of the filth off the newcomer. Flecks of white, brown and yellow began to show in the dark coat. And there was ginger that matched his glowing eyes.

He arrived tiny and weak, but rapidly became robust and strong, under my and the master's care. I kept him clean and tried to teach him how to behave in human company. After the first year, he had grown into a massive cat, the largest I have ever seen.

*   *   *

Once mature, Wilmore did not observe curfews. At sunset he was indoors for his food, but as soon as the master slept, he slipped out through the slightly open window.

Night after night, I heard Wilmore's howls of lust as he consorted with one female after another. The sounds of hoses jetting and objects being thrown added to the night music. Each morning before dawn, Wilmore swept in, and resumed his place. How could the master miss the stink of sex and all the other cats? Wilmore never cleaned himself. He luxuriated in the rankness of his nocturnal liaisons.

*   *   *

Mr Lennox from the flat below came one morning .

"I had no sleep again last night," he said to the master, "they were at it all night, and this one," he said, pointing at Wilmore, "is the trouble maker."

"But he was inside," said the master.

"Check tonight," said the neighbour, "He's always out."

But the master, as usual, slept soundly and did not hear the noises that regularly woke the rest of us.

So, next morning, Mr Lennox was back.

The master nodded towards Wilmore. "He's been here all night. It must be another cat. He is very dark."

"OK," said Mr Lennox, "Tonight I'll try to catch him."

All night, came the same loud cries, and, just before dawn, Wilmore high-tailed in as usual. Mr Lennox had not caught him. Mr Lennox was in hospital, having fallen down the concrete stairs at 10 pm, and fractured some ribs and vertebrae.

*   *   *

A week later, another neighbour came. This time, it was Lucinda from the ground floor.

"Ah that's the one. I thought so," she said looking carefully at Wilmore. "He's been spraying around my door for weeks and making such a stink. I can't get rid of it."

"But he doesn't do that here," said the master quizzically. (Surely, he must have noticed! The smell was everywhere.)

"I don't know how to stop it. I've tried 'Puss off'' and other sprays but nothing works. Actually, the whole stairwell stinks of him."

Then something snapped in the master. I smelt his stress and belligerence. I took action, rubbing hard against him and calming him. It doesn't do to argue with the neighbours. I noticed Wilmore watching. He was in the habit of ignoring me, but this time, he approved.

From the top landing, you could see right to the bottom of the stairs. Though I did not range far from the apartment, preferring my own cushion and comforts in my senior years, sometimes I sat out there to keep an eye on what used to be my territory. The morning after Lucinda's visit, I was sitting there just before dawn. (Yes, sometimes I also took advantage of that open window . Just before dawn is the best time of day.) Lucinda is an early riser, and was already moving around. She opened her door. "Whew!" she cried, and disappeared inside. She was out again in a moment with spray bottles and rags, mumbling curses as she scrubbed impotently at her front step. "Right!" I heard her say, "I don't care how early it is" and she started up the stairs, still carrying her cleaning equipment.

As she reached the second flight, I saw something large and dark streak across in front of her. Up the stairwell, rose the distinctive scent of Wilmore. He had hit his mark. Down she fell, the steps becoming marked with blood from repeated contact with her cranium, until Lucinda lay at the bottom, not moving.

I kept my place and watched. Wilmore darted down after her. With his tail up, he circumambulated her inert form; one, two, three times before darting up and inside through the open window.

I had to follow quickly as dawn was already breaking. Inside the flat, there was a disturbing odour of blood; Lucinda's blood. Wilmore was licking his paws, but not to clean them. He was relishing the taste.

*   *   *

"No, you must not bring mice in here" the master was saying some weeks later. (Wilmore must have loved the master. He brought him the fattest mice. But the master never accepted them. He put them in the bin and they went off each week with the garbage.)

"My God, that cat's a killer", moaned Ruth, the master's adult daughter, who was visiting.

"He was orphaned very young," said the master proudly. "He's a survivor."

"It's revolting," said Ruth. "What is this?" Carefully she picked up the chewed and staggering small yellow bird. "That's a pardalote!" she stormed. "They're native and they're protected. That cat's got to go! You won't be able to break that habit." I rubbed against her. "Don't bother, Tabitha," she spat, "You've got the same genes. You're just too old now."

I looked at Wilmore. He was watching, eyes flaring. No, I thought, not the daughter. It was definitely not politic to go for the daughter. But how could I convince Wilmore? He never heeded me.

That day, when the daughter left, I walked her down the stairs, rubbing her legs, impeding her, so that she had to watch each step and move slowly. She got to the bottom safely. Wilmore stood on the landing watching our descent. When I reached him again, for the first time, he hissed at me.

*   *   *

The day came when Ruth visited again. I was asleep on my cushion in the sun. The cleaner was scrubbing the stairs and there was a high wind. I did not hear Wilmore leave. I woke to a cry and the metallic vibration of the bannisters. Then came a distant crack. I sprang up, but by the time I reached ground level, everything was over. Wilmore was marching around his prone victim. I saw him stoop and lap up the blood from her shattered skull.

It was the master who found her. His smell, and everything about him, changed forever that day. He barely left the flat. We had to call incessantly to get our food. Our litter boxes were never emptied and we could no longer use them.

Artificially scented men-strangers visited; funeral directors, real estate agents, and police. There was a young policeman, a go-getter, keen to impress his superiors. I observed him looking at the kitchen window, and another day, at the floor and furniture near our beds. I knew what he had seen. I tried licking, but it was dried-in, that blood that Wilmore had carried inside on his paws. Then, the young policeman arrived again with three other men and they took the master away.

From then on, we had to make our own way. Another neighbour took me in. She gave me a cushion in the sun, just as the master had. But Wilmore went away.

*   *   *

I have heard that he is huge now; the size of a panther. On clear nights, when sound travels well, I think I hear him in the mountains, yowling, lonely for his master, perhaps even for me, and frustrated that his plans all went wrong .

Puddle

Meredith Adams

Jamie is three. The world is a fascinating place as he runs down the steaming path after the rain. The silver flash up ahead has caught his eye. He races ahead of his mother down the path that winds through the park.

"I beat you! I beat you!" he yells out standing next to the puddle. Now it's not silver; it's blue with patches of white clouds sailing across it.

Crouching down in front of the puddle, he rocks back and forth on his heels watching his reflection bob in and out of the clouds. *What would it be like to be the boy in the puddle?*

He rocks too far forward and falls head-first into the puddle.

There are two choices:

One: He hits his head and gets wet.

Two: He finds himself in the puddle.

One: He sprawls on the concrete footpath face down, eyes screwed shut, mouth open bawling. Water and spit dribble down his face. The front of his shirt is wet.

His mother scurries over to him, leaving the stroller behind. Bending over him, she scoops him up in her arms cuddling him to her chest. She strokes the back of his head and presses her cool cheek against his, cooing in his ear, "You're alright; you're alright."

Kissing him on the top of his head, she gently rocks him back and forth as she walks back towards the stroller. Her dress swishes around her legs, and the soft click of her heels envelop him.

Jamie has a small scrape on the tip of his nose.

Two: He finds himself crouching in front of a puddle that shows no reflection. He stops rocking. Putting his finger in the water, bands of light and dark radiate out from his finger to the edge of the puddle. He hears running footsteps behind him. Jaime turns his head and sees a little boy that looks just like him, running towards him. The little boy runs straight into Jaime, hitting him on the nose and pushing him backwards into the puddle.

There are two choices:

One: He hits his head and gets wet.

Two: He finds himself in the puddle.

One: He sprawls on his back on the foot path, eyes screwed shut, mouth wide open bawling. Water and spit gurgle in his mouth. The back of his shirt is wet.

His mother hurriedly pushes the stroller over to him. Bending over him, she pulls him up to his feet by his arm, pressing him against her legs. Her dove grey skirt makes a hushing sound as he crushes against it. She strokes the top of his head and coos in his ear, "You're alright; you're alright."

She crouches down to him and takes a tissue out of her pocket. Folding it in half, she carefully wipes his face dry. Scooping him up, she gently places him in the stroller and rocks him back and forth.

Jamie has a small scrape on the tip of his nose and a bump on the back of his head.

Two: He crouches down in front of a puddle. Rocking back and forth on his heels, he wonders, *what would it be like to be the boy in the puddle?* He puts his finger in the puddle, and the water ripples. He is fascinated. His face breaks into band of light and dark concentric circles radiating out from his finger.

His mother smiles at him and casually pushes the stroller over to where Jamie squats. He doesn't hear her. She quietly crouches down and says, "BOO!" in his ear.

There are two choices:

One: He hits his head and gets wet.

Two: He finds himself in the puddle.

One: He clumsily lurches sideways, landing face first in the water. Blowing bubbles as he bawls. Water splashing.

Her arms dive under him, scraping the shaking child onto her lap. His face is bright red and his lashes leave wet marks on the bodice of her dress. His saliva strings across his face. Her arms enfold him, rocking him back and forth.

"I'm sorry; I'm sorry." She repeats over and over again. "I didn't mean to frighten you." Holding the back of his head, cooing in his ear, "You're alright; you're alright."

Her dress crushes against her under his weight. The edge of her skirt trailing in the water.

Jamie has a scrape on his nose and scratches on his forehead.

"It stings! It stings!" he wails.

Two: Jamie finds himself crouching in front of a blank puddle.

"Do you really want to know what it's like to me?"

Jamie looks around and slowly stands up to face the boy who looks like him.

"Don't you want to push me back?"

Jamie shakes his head again.

"How come you look like me?" says Jamie.

"I don't. You look like me!"

Jamie shakes his head again. His eyes tear up. His bottom lip trembles.

The boy that looks like Jamie pushes him.

Jamie whimpers, "Don't."

The boy pushes Jamie again.

"Don't!" Jamie cries.

The boy pushes him harder.

"Stop it!" Jamie screams. He throws a punch, then another. This time Jamie cries out in pain and cradles his hand. Through his tears he sees the other boy holding his mouth, red seeping between the boy's fingers and trickling onto his striped shirt. He is backing away. Jamie runs at him, pushing the boy backwards into the puddle.

The boy disappears. Jamie's eyes widen. His mouth hangs open. His fingers tug at his bottom lip.

Jamie sees his mother in the water with the boy who looks like him. She is hugging him to her chest. Her hand wipes the wet hair out of the child's eyes. She is placing him in Jamie's stroller. She is wiping his face with a folded tissue. She takes something out of a bag. She plays the aeroplane game with him and finally pops it in the child's mouth.

Jamie explodes. "My treats! Mine!"

His feet throb as he stamps the ground. Throwing himself down, he bangs his head on the concrete. Eyes screwed shut, mouth open, his face red and gasping.

"Mum, mum, mum, mum, mum." He gurgles. "Mum, mum, mum."

Saliva dribbles off his chin.

No one comes.

Legs folding under him, he sits up. His light blue shorts are dark with water and stick to him. He rubs his face on his stripy shirt.

His red gritty eyes sting as he watches his mother strap his reflection into his stroller. He watches as she smiles lovingly at the reflection and casually pushes the stroller away.

Jamie leans as close to the surface of the puddle as he can. He sees his mother pushing his stroller further and further away across the park. The twilight is falling and the street lights are coming on.

A Cat Thing

Sheree Pratt

Sooty's sleek black form scaled the fence as it had every night since we moved into this neighbourhood. His long cat-tail swished as he tried to steady himself. It was always the last thing I saw as he disappeared into the night.

I scratched my long silky ear then sniffed along the fence-line. My white fountain-like tail curled in a question mark, as I searched for a clue. I sighed. I should've retreated to my gel-bed on the deck.

Instead, I continued to sniff. *Where did he go?*

The 'good-dog' in me was gone. Curiosity took over. My white paws began frantically digging. I broke through the hard dry surface into soft damp soil, taking in its fresh scent and settled into a relaxed rhythm.

The simple feeling of cool mud under my claws made it too good to stop. I didn't notice myself getting tired, or the sun rising, or the sweet song of birds that I usually loved waking up to. I only noticed the fence shaking above my head, the thud of paws bigger than mine landing on the ground and Sooty's laboured growl as he landed.

"Oh you're home!" Hitting my head on the fence as I pulled out of my half-dug trench, I yelped.

"What are you doing, Sampson?" Sooty asked. His yellow eyes were fixed on my muddy snout. I met his glare with my brown button-like eyes.

"Looking for you." My ears pricked up.

"Sooty! Sampson! Wet-food time! Come and get it!"

Sooty nimbly bounded off, scaled the garden's rocky edge and cut through the freshly mowed lawn. I leaped behind him, nipping at his hind legs and tripping over rocks to keep up. We skidded to a stop in front of his freshly-filled bowl on the neatly paved back deck. I nearly landed on top of him.

The aroma of beef casserole and gravy tickled my whiskers. I peered into Sooty's bowl and saw the 'wet-food' the humans served up – diced muck and a thin layer of gravy. I inspected my own bowl. It was the same muck. *Maybe later,* I thought and circled back to Sooty's bowl. He was diving enthusiastically into it. The fur around his shoulder blades stood on end and his tail swished.

"Go eat your own food!" he growled.

"Okay, okay!" I backed away. *Why was he so protective? It's just muck.*

But if he's enjoying it, it must be alright. I returned to my bowl and tentatively licked the gravy off and started on the chunks of meat.

By the time I finished, Sooty was already fully immersed in his after-dinner grooming ritual, cleaning his whiskers with his front paws and then cleaning his paws with his tongue. I watched him work down his whole body, leaving a velvety smooth sheen over his coat. He pointed his back paw to the sky as he began to clean the base of his tail. I approached him with an offer to help and began cleaning the top of his head.

"I said no!" he growled, and followed it with a slap. Five knife-like claws nearly sliced my eyelid.

I backed away quickly. "Ouch!" I yelped. I wiped my face with my paw to check for blood. There was none, I shook away the sting and shock and crawled onto my gel-bed. "I was only trying to help."

I pawed at my blanket, turned two circles and curled up on the bed. I rested my head on my paws to watch Sooty finish his ritual.

He glanced around with wide eyes, like he expected something to jump out and attack him. Or was he scanning the yard for prey? I wasn't sure. Then he stalked across the wooden deck to join me on the bed. His purr was a comforting sign that his agitated mood was subsiding. He began to knead the blanket before settling into a small loaf, tucking his paws beneath him.

Then he closed his eyes.

"Where do you go?" I asked.

His head popped up and his eyes snapped open. "What?"

"When you jump the fence at night, where do you go?"

Sooty rolled onto his side towards me but refused to meet my intense gaze.

"Hunting." His tail thumped the bed to mark the end of our discussion and I knew not to continue. Again, he laid his head down and closed his eyes. I watched him until I, too, succumbed to sleep.

Later that night, I waited for him to clear the fence and resumed work on my hole. I ignored the rush of damp soil. This time I was determined not to lose focus. Soon I could squeeze my whole body under the fence. I shimmied under with ease, tasting freedom.

I found Sooty's scent at the base of a hedge. I scanned the quiet dimly-lit street of fences, houses, caravans and parked shiny cars. I followed Sooty's scent along the hedge. As I neared the nature strip, the cars and caravans towered above me. Thankfully, none of them moved.

The road disappeared in the distance behind a cloud of fog. I put my nose to the ground and smelled Sooty's scent going up that road.

Every scent was exhilarating; scents of other dogs in the street and of rubber and asphalt. I marked trees, fence-posts and hub-caps every few steps to ensure I could find my way back. With my nose locked on Sooty's scent, I wandered to the middle of the road.

Screech! The smell of burning tyres, blinding headlights and the driver shouting, "Get off the road, mutt!"

Exhaust fumes burned my nose, making me sneeze. I bolted, almost tripping on my tail between my legs. I didn't stop until I was further up the road. I shook to calm down. I would explore the world beyond the fog and, more importantly, find Sooty.

I was panting. Where the road ended, I was surrounded by large shadowy trees where the familiar scent of Sooty mixed with that of many other cats. Through the bush, I zig-zagged, still sniffing and marking. Leaves crackled under my now black paws. I followed Sooty's trail between the trees. His scent grew stronger the further I went into the bush. I ignored the claw-like twigs that snagged in my woolly coat and scratched my skin.

Aah-OWW – the familiar growl sliced through the otherwise silent night.

Aw-EEEE-Oww! Another cat's yowl interrupted Sooty's. It came from deep in the bush.

My ears jerked upwards. *Sooty's in trouble!* I quickly marked a nearby tree and bolted in the direction of the sound.

I froze when I reached a clearing by a small creek. A large group of cats were gathered in a semi-circle. Their tails swished in relish at the action.

Two cats crouched by the water's edge. Their fur was standing on end and their tails were violently swinging.

One cat's coat was long, scruffy and tabby-brown with a crisp white chest and muzzle. The large tabby towered over his sleek black opponent – Sooty.

As the tabby edged closer, Sooty backed into cold water lapping the rocks. His tail skimmed the water's surface and he jumped from the shock. He locked eyes with the bigger cat.

OWWW! Sooty screeched. The other cats made no move to assist.

"I'm coming, Sooty!" I barked as I ran into the ring of cats. They scattered, leaving Sooty to face his opponent alone.

I jumped between them, baring my teeth at the tabby. "Back off, you big bully! Leave my friend alone!"

On either side, the cats sat. Their yellow eyes burned into my flesh.

"Does *this* belong to you?" the tabby asked.

"Yes," Sooty muttered. He turned his face away.

"You were *supposed* to come alone," the tabby growled at Sooty. "Now we'll have to rematch tomorrow night."

The tabby followed the rest of the cats into the shadows.

"The hell you *will!*" I snarled after him.

Sooty turned to me, his pupils still round. "What are you doing here? You embarrassed me!"

"I could ask you the same thing, considering I just saved your hide," I said earnestly. But he smacked my nose. I yelped and backed off.

"Thanks," he snarled as he turned away. There was no hint of gratitude. "We'd better get home before sunrise."

Without another word, he stalked expertly through the bush and I followed him out to the road.

"You're welcome by the way!" I called after him.

"Humph!" He launched into a trot. "Keep up!"

The only sound we heard was the clinking of our name-tags on our collars, as we trotted down the road.

He broke into a run as we neared home and effortlessly cleared the fence into our yard.

I scurried under the fence through the hole I'd made.

"What was that, anyway?" I asked, as I followed him back to his biscuit-filled bowl on the deck.

"It's a cat thing," he muttered in between crunches. "You wouldn't understand."

Flatmates

Deanna Troy

The first house is marketed as "rent free" in Melbourne. It's a sparkling three-bedroom house. The photos are crisp on the webpage. The lighting and clarity of each stark-white room is professional, the empty spaces cold and uninhabited. The house belongs on a real estate agent's portfolio. The bedroom on offer has grey carpet, a built-in robe, and plain cream curtains. There's a lovely outdoor patio area with a fireplace and television mounted onto the surrounding brick, perfect for snobby get-togethers.

One image sticks out like a sore thumb, a square among the rectangles. It was taken by a phone camera. A scruffy rough-haired Jack Russell lies on a bed staring up at whoever is holding the phone. The cute dog is a positive selling point for potential renters.

The profile image of the homeowner shows a wispy-haired bloke with a scruffy beard and tattoo sleeves. His frame and skin indicate someone in their early thirties, but his clothing style is obnoxiously hip, like a man-child. His sunglasses obscure his gaze, which seem to be directed toward something in the bottom left corner of the frame. The house doesn't match its owner – a hospital-white family home, occupied by a tattooed, hipster-chic thirty-year-old. It's hard to determine whether he's just trying to give off a certain vibe to attract renters or if he's really like that.

CHAT OPEN

Hello, are you interested in my home?
:)

It looks good! I'd like to know a little more.

Rent is free. No bond, either.

Sounds too good to be true!

Would I be paying bills?

Nope! Totally rent free.

How long is the "lease"?

As long as you can keep cooking and cleaning.

…not sure I understand?

You can live here rent free, but you'll need to take care of cooking and cleaning.

Really?

Yes. I work a lot. Usually I order in UberEats. I'm worried the delivery drivers know me by name haha.

If you'll take care of me, the house and my dog Russo, I'll take care of you ;)

So you want me to be a maid/personal chef?

I mean

You'd be living rent free…

Your profile says you're a student, so it's not as if you don't have the time, right?

YOU HAVE BLOCKED THIS PERSON

The second house is in Newport and is owned by John. The room for potential renters is listed at $0, along with $0 to rent the house living room, $0 to rent dining room, and $0 to rent kitchen.

The lighting of these photos is atrocious. The walls look a dying shade of browning yellow. Footprints stain the aged dark oak floorboards. All windows are just plain squares. Dead flies populate each sill. The lounge room has two leather couches, though a television isn't in view. Next to them, is a table surrounded by child-size, dirty multi-coloured plastic chairs. Heavy doors and a dusty atmosphere plague each room. The view out of one of the windows reveals a backyard full of weeds and crumbling trees.

The photo of a thin aging man, squinting against the sun, suffers from motion blur, as though the photographer was shaking. The man in-frame wears a toothy yellow smile, almost as poorly as he does his black polo shirts. The dog sitting next to him looks to be about half his size, baring its teeth.

CHAT OPEN

hello i am john i live with a rottweiler

my house is private serene and has plenty of character.

Your page includes the other rooms individually.

Does this mean I'd have
to sign something to use
the lounge and kitchen?

thats funny

no

Are utilities included?

no you pay your half of utilities
Okay…

I'm a student. I need a solid
internet connection to
study. Is internet metered?

what does that mean

Is there a limit on
the internet?

I dont think so

Is anyone else living
in the house?

not yet am working on finding other
tenants but you a student you dont
want distractions

It's not distractions
I'm worried about.

are you okay with dogs

Yes.

good my rottweiler doesnt really like strangers but im training him

Okay.

Can you confirm if I'm paying rent?

rent is 230

bond is 400

$230? Your listing says it's free though?

the listing is wrong rent is 230

i dont know how to fix it

this is a good house

worth every penny

Are there more pictures?

no you should inspect if you want more pictures

your a woman right

…does that matter?

> yes i don't want men
>
> or poofters
>
> only straight women

YOU HAVE BLOCKED THIS PERSON

House three is a suburban house in Burwood, far closer to university. It's another white, modern house, with white walls, floors and windows. But while the room being advertised is statedly unfurnished, the rest of the house is cluttered with furniture. And pot plants. The entire property is a clash of soft green triangles against white sheens.

The hallway appears tight because of greenery. There are two plants about the average size of a human sitting casually next to the dinner table. Smaller plants litter windowsills, the table, and benches. A leafy fern has been dropped in front of the television. It sits just high enough for it to be seen through the greenery. The photo of the lounge room shows a massive, healthy garden crawling up the glass outside.

It would be one thing if any of them had flowers. But there isn't a flower in sight. There is also the curiosity regarding how most of these grow – the only natural lighting comes through the house's windows, but there are no skylights and aside from the lounge, all the curtains in each living space are closed.

Aside from the over-abundance of nature's spawn, the house looks nice. It's going for $160 per week.

CHAT OPEN

> Hi! Do you have any questions about the house?

> It looks great! Can you confirm the price of rent?

Sure! It's $160 per week, to be paid monthly (in advance). Bond is $250!

Cool. I'm a Cloud student. Do you have a good internet connection?

It's as solid as internet here can get! X)

But seriously, it's 30MBPS on a slow day, so it's pretty great in comparison to other places around town.

Awesome. Are utilities included?

Unfortunately no. We put $25 per week each into a bill account. Whatever's left at the end of the year, we split between the three (soon to be four!) of us.

That sounds nice.

I noticed there are a lot of plants in the photos.

Yeah! We're massive green thumbs. Our plants have their own schedules!

Really?

Yep! They get breakfast, lunch, and time outside.

Interesting.

I don't really know much

about plants, though.
Will that be a problem?

That's okay! We can teach you the basics.

Just don't try to grow any marijuana plants.

What?

Our last house mate tried to do that and it uh… didn't go so well.

Holy shit

Yeah it was a whole thing.

Claimed it was for brownies.

But we're vegan and he didn't know how to make vegan brownies…

That sounds…

Like a real situation. Police must have loved him.

No police. We caught him and kicked him out.

Fair enough.

Anyhoo, are you vegetarian/vegan?

Um?

Not really?

Oh.

That's okay, we'll make a vego out of you yet!

YOU HAVE BLOCKED THIS PERSON

Information about the fourth house is so lacking in detail, it may just be the concoction of someone's imagination. The listing is a blank page repeating, "Minni hasn't added this yet!" in all its empty sections. There are no photos of the leased room, and no descriptions about the house itself. The page says the room is "furnished," but suspiciously omits what furniture it has.

It's close to a train and bus station *somewhere* in Heidelberg.

CHAT OPEN

Is it possible to get more information about this room?

Yes.

...Do you own the house?

Yes.

Do you accommodate students?

Yes. Female students only.

How much is rent and bond?

Rent is $150. Bond is $300.

Would I be paying utilities, too?

No. Utilities are included in rent.

Are there any photos of the house?

Not yet.

Will photos of the house become available?

Yes. When it's built.

…the house hasn't been built?

Yes.

When will it be finished?

In six months.

But you've put a listing up now?

Yes. Preparing for uni students.

A mud brick house, on the side of a floodplain, has a door on every side. The way the house is situated near the road makes it difficult to determine which one is the front door, and all of the entrance ways lack the grandeur associated with the first door of a house.

The owners are an overweight couple who own many birds. Tiny birds are cramped in cages lining the pool yard. All the trees have been cleared for the aviaries. Dozens upon dozens of brightly coloured red wings and blue wrens leap around in their containment.

The view of Victorian fields is disturbed by the awful alarm klaxon of a hand-tamed princess parrot. Conversations in the kitchen are constantly interrupted by a Hahn's Macaw seeking attention. The large birds have single cages and are often allowed in the lounge to fly. When they're left within their jail cells, they're ear-piercingly loud.

Studying is impossible even in the bedroom at the end of the house. A bed has been pushed up against the wall. Black and white storage blocks from Kmart are stacked on top of one another, and hold an assortment of textbooks organised alphabetically by author's surname.

A pair of $400 noise-cancelling headphones are re-charging next to an el cheapo light-up keyboard, the clickity-clack of its user echoing into the wood ceiling of the rumpus room next door. The television monitor acting as a computer screen pings with a message from one of the house's owners.

Hows house-hunting?

There's a lot of weirdos on Flatmates.

I thought you wanted to live on your own?

I do. But I don't have the money for that.

I found a few houses that are rent-free.

Rent free?

Don't do rent free

sigh

Have you thought about waiting a little longer?

Or finding somewhere closer to home?

There are no places near here. None in my budget, at least.

And I need a place of my own.

I'm desperate.

I love you, but it's time.

I know.

Have you considered direct student accommodation?

They wanted nearly $2000 up-front.

I didn't have that kind of cash when they asked.

And I can't string that much together monthly for rent.

I think I'm stuck.

You're not stuck.

Its going to take time.

Keep saving.

I *can* move out.

But I don't want to have to fit into what other people expect of me.

If you move into a share house, you'll have to make nice with other people.

You sound like you're saying I'm not nice

Why haven't you responded

I'm nice

How dare you

You take that back

I'm just saying you'll have to be open to all sorts of people from all sorts of backgrounds.

And maybe you're not really ready for that?

Maybe.

Just think it over.

Your father is thinking about moving you into the unit outside.

We don't have a unit.

Stop looking at photos and come outside.

The Woman, Her Brain, The Tube and the TV Ghost

Meredith Adams

S he snuck off to bed again without her brain, leaving it curled up on its chair in front of the tube.

It woke, bathed in the scintillating light of tiny grey and white flecks dancing chaotically over the loungeroom walls. Inside, the room hisses with static from the TV. Outside, the wind rattles the windows.

Peeking over the armrest, it sees the chair opposite is empty. Sliding off the edge of its seat, it drops onto the floor and squirms its way across the room. It inches up the chair leg and investigates the cushion with its nerves. The fabric feels cold.

Plopping back down to the floor, it squelches down the hallway and gently butts the cat-flap at the bottom of her bedroom door with its frontal lobes. The flap doesn't move.

This is the second time this week she has locked her brain out. Deflated, it sags against the floor, running their previous conversation through its mind.

"I sleep better without your incessant babble." Her exact words.

Feeling an icy draught blast under the front door, her brain contracts its nerves under itself. Shivering, it slithers its way back to the warmth of the loungeroom.

Spying the remote control, her brain squelches over to it. Rolling across the red button, the dancing flecks are sucked into the centre of the tube screen, and compress into a persistent tiny white dot. Having never noticed the white dot before, her brain wriggles towards the tube.

Is it friendly?

Curiosity hauls her brain up the screen till it can just make out the dot in the bulge of the glass. It slides its way towards the infinitesimal speck. The delicious warmth radiating from the tube encourages her brain to relax. It flattens itself as thinly as it can against the warm curved glass. Curling around the diminutive fleck of light, it drifts into a deep sleep.

Draping her dressing gown over her shoulder, she stumbles into the loungeroom. The morning light pours into the room. *What's that stuck to the tube? I'll clean it later.*

She looks at her brain's chair. It is empty. Barrelling out of the lounge room, she frantically searches each room of the house. Finding nothing, she walks back into the loungeroom.

Squatting down in front of the tube, she examines the dried gelatinousness mass on the screen. Its surface is covered by a dry wrinkled crust. There are remnants of deep fissures. Inside the semi-transparent mass she notices small twitching movements.

"Oh my God! My brain!"

Dashing from the room, she returns with a large bowl of distilled, sterilised water and the emergency pack of soluble lithium. She dissolves the lithium in the water and dabs the crisp edges with the solution using a handful of tissues. Working her way from the edge to the centre, she manages to peel her brain off in one piece.

Gingerly she places her wayward organ in the bowl and carries it into the kitchen. Placing the bowl next to the stove top, she lights a burner to keep her brain warm. Every now and again she gently swirls her brain around in the lithium solution to help it rehydrate.

She makes coffee while her brain slowly reinflates.

The smell of the freshly ground beans drives her brain crazy. It blows bubbles on the edge of the bowl, begging for a cup.

"You can't have any till you're fully rehydrated."

It stops blowing bubbles and wrinkles its frontal lobes at her.

"What were you doing stuck to the middle of the viewing screen?"

Bobbing around in the bowl, her brain turns its cerebellum towards her. She spins the bowl around, but it refuses to look at her. It has actually turned a bit red. She grins, knowing it's a good sign.

Her brain spins around, wanting to know what she was doing in her bedroom. And why had she locked it out?

This time, it's her turn to blush. She doesn't answer. Stalemate.

She trickles a little bit of coffee from her cup into the bowl. Her brain floats into it, quivering with delight. She drags a chair over from the table and sits next to the stove. They both drink their coffee in silence.

Jealousy

MJ Douven

G reg lay awake in the dark, pretending to be asleep, listening to his wife's even breathing beside him. At least *she* could sleep. Wasn't a guilty conscience supposed to keep a person awake at night?

She murmured something in her sleep – it sounded like a name – and rolled over, turning her back to him. It was just like what she had been doing to him for a long time.

She was cheating on him. He just knew it.

Not that he could find any evidence. She was never late or unexplainedly absent. If anything, she was more punctual than she had ever been. Which, in itself, was suspicious.

He was so desperate for the truth that he had been toying with hiring a private detective. But that cost money – money that his wife would definitely notice missing, since she kept a close eye on their account.

There was a part of him that hoped she wasn't cheating – the part that was scared of what she'd do if she found out his suspicions. It might end their marriage, and Greg wasn't sure he was ready to run that risk.

But he couldn't keep going on like this. He couldn't sleep. When he tried to eat, he felt nauseous. Even while he lay in bed, perfectly still, his heart would not stop throbbing. The pounding was right in his throat. It was getting so bad that he sometimes struggled to breathe. Not with the iron band that felt like it was closing around his chest.

Like now – it was as if someone had their foot on his chest, pressing down. He'd gone to the doctor about it, but the doctor had passed it off as simple allergies and given him an asthma inhaler.

Greg fumbled on his bedside table for the inhaler but knocked it onto the floor. With a groan, he rolled over, leaning over the side of the bed and patting around on the carpet.

But the minute he leaned down, his head swam. He was falling. Then nothing.

*   *   *

He was standing on the road outside their cottage gate in the warm spring sunshine. He couldn't remember waking up or getting out of bed. He was just *there*.

His gaze landed on the steeple of the village church up the street, and he started walking that way for no particular reason. Actually, he and Maisie had been married at that church on a bright spring day very like this one.

Maybe that's what this was – a memory of their wedding day. That would explain the surreal quality of the sunlight, the deserted village streets and everything around him. Usually, the whole village only gathered for weddings and funerals.

Greg loved a leisurely morning stroll through the village, but today he started to feel an inexplicable sense of urgency. He had to get to the church. He picked up the pace, weaving his way through the network of interconnected village lanes and byways.

A flower-bedecked straw hat bobbed down behind a hedge as he passed the last few houses before the church. Old Mrs. Needles – he was pretty sure that wasn't her real name but everyone called her that – spying on the rest of the village as usual.

He made a mental note to talk to her later. If anyone knew what his wife was up to, it was Mrs. Needles. The old lady was one of those infuriating people who seemed to know everything that happened in the village without ever asking a single interfering question. Greg reckoned she got her facts by osmosis.

The back gate to the churchyard was ajar, so he entered through the old cemetery gardens his wife loved so much. She had been helping out at the church, restoring the gardens for the last few weeks. They were much further along than he'd expected, which left him wondering what she had *really* been doing those times she said she was going to work there.

He recognised a lot of plants similar to the ones in their front garden, though he couldn't have named them if he tried. The only one that he could come close to identifying was the pretty hooded purple and pink flowers on long spiky stalks – monk *something*, Maisie had called them.

Music drifted toward him from inside the church. He slipped in the back door and dropped onto a pew in a darkened corner. From here, he could watch what was going on without being spotted.

It definitely looked and sounded like a wedding. Bouquets of spring flowers were fastened to the end of each pew, and more flowers surrounded the area in front of the pulpit where the happy couple would stand.

The organ music changed to Pachelbel, and the guests turned to look toward the back of the church. Greg sank down, thankful for his dark corner.

He managed to see the bride as she floated down the aisle. Antique cream flouncy skirts trailed behind her in an impossibly long train. He knew who it was, even before he saw her face, framed in soft golden curls. It was Maisie.

A lump formed in his throat. She looked lovely, radiant. He didn't remember her looking that good at their wedding.

It was getting harder to believe this was a memory. All the little details didn't fit – like Maisie's bouquet of wild spring flowers. He remembered traditional roses at their wedding. And if this was a memory, shouldn't he be up at the front of the church, waiting for his bride?

After Maisie passed and the guests turned back, he sat up for a better look. A glimpse of the groom – dressed in an awful pastel-coloured, pinstriped suit – was enough to confirm what Greg already knew. This was not his and Maisie's wedding.

His wife was marrying another man. How was that even possible?

Numb with shock, he watched Maisie walk down the aisle toward this man. He watched her put her hand in his and smile at him, the way he never remembered her smiling at him.

The preacher stepped up into the pulpit and began the

ceremony. The words flowed over Greg as if he were in a dream —
or a nightmare. He could barely hear them through the pounding
in his ears.

Until the moment came when the preacher motioned for the
ringbearer to pass him the rings. That was the moment when Greg
couldn't watch any longer. The most intense jealousy he'd ever
experienced surged through him.

Abandoning his hiding place, he stomped forward, down the
aisle Maisie had just walked. A wave of murmurs swelled ahead of
him. Everyone was staring at him as though they'd seen a ghost, but
he didn't care. All that mattered was reaching his wife before she
said, "I do."

"Maisie!" He hollered her name as he got close to the front.
"Stop!"

She jerked toward him, her bouquet dropping onto the floor.
"Greg?" Her voice sounded choked.

"What do you think you're doing?" he bellowed. "You're my
wife. MY WIFE!"

He tried to grab her wrist and pull her toward him, but she
shrank away, trembling. As if he'd ever raised a hand to her in their
entire married life. Did she really see him as that much of an ogre?

She reached out and grabbed the groom's hand. The man hadn't
twitched since Greg strode forward. He stood there as if he had
been snap-frozen, eyes huge in his pasty white face.

"What kind of man are you anyway?" Greg scoffed, jabbing an
accusatory finger at the groom. "Stealing another man's wife. And
then not even having the guts to stand up for her."

Maisie placed herself between them. "You leave Bill alone." Her
face was flushed. "He hasn't done anything wrong. He's a good man,
and I wouldn't have gotten through this last year without him."

"This last year?" he repeated. "What was so terrible about it that
you needed Bill in order to survive? Why wasn't I enough for you?"

"What was so terrible?" Fat tears were streaming down Maisie's
face now, smudging her fancy makeup. "You died, Greg. One year
ago, today."

∗   ∗   ∗

Pain jabbed through his chest and jerked him out of whatever
nightmare or time vortex or hallucination had overtaken him. Back
to reality.

A reality where he was suddenly unable to breathe. The iron band around his chest had snapped tight, constricting. His vision was blurry and black around the edges.

His hands flailed desperately, striking his wife's shoulder. She woke up with a startled cry.

"Greg?" When he didn't answer – he couldn't – she rolled towards him. "Greg?"

"Help," he croaked.

She fumbled for her phone in the dimness, swiped it on, and then stopped, frozen, as if turned to stone. He wanted to scream at her to call for help, to ring an ambulance, to do *something*, but he couldn't get out the words.

Her tear-streaked, stony face, lit by the soft light from her mobile screen, was the last thing he saw.

*   *   *

Greg had been still for several long minutes before Maisie finally roused herself. Numbly, she swiped her phone back on – the screen had turned off while she had been sitting there in the dark – and dialled the first number on her list.

"Bill!" She didn't let him get out more than a bleary hello. "I think I did something terrible. Greg is dead."

Cauderhill Park

Natalie Power

The crisp autumn leaves crunched under my boots as I trudged through the park, coffee in one hand and torch in the other. The sun was yet to make an appearance. I doubted it would. The weather had been bleak and miserable all week. Condensation from the trees saturated the grass below and made my feet cold. I was grateful for my earlier decision to grab the big, winter coat off the rack before I walked out the door.

I received the call at 1:48 this morning. It woke me up. It was now 4:32. *Such an ungodly hour.* Murders don't wait for anyone, I guess. The only details I got were that a young woman, deceased, had been found by a couple of homeless men. Apparently this was the third woman found this week in Cauderhill Park.

I'd never spent much time in this park. It was a dodgy area from what I'd been told as a young girl. My mom would say to me when I left the house with friends, "Have fun, Lil. Be safe and stay away from Cauderhill Park." I never really knew why, but I also never questioned it. After all, moms know best.

I had moved away from this small town five years ago, but now recent events had brought me back.

Stepping under the yellow tape and raising my badge was an act I was accustomed to. There was the flashing of cameras, officers and forensics comparing notes and witnesses making their statements. After I made my way through the multitudes of people, I finally saw her.

At first glance, I thought she could've just been sleeping. She looked peaceful. She was wearing a long, baby blue dress with intricate lace details. Her hands, resting on her stomach, clutched a small bouquet of white roses, no more than a day old by the look of the petals. The roses were held together by a fine piece of rope.

"Eerie, isn't it?"

I was startled by a voice behind me. I turned and saw a male, in his late 20's, maybe early 30's. He wore an expensive, thick wool winter coat and, hanging around his neck, was an identification tag with the Cauderhill General Hospital logo.

"Landon Meyers," he stretched out his hand to me. "I'm the lead medical examiner on this case."

He looked a little young to be a qualified M.E. His boyish face and sandy brown hair gave him a youthful appearance. In saying that, I'm sure most people question my qualifications too.

I pulled some gloves over my hands and took a closer look at the young blonde girl before me. "Who is she? What do we know so far?"

"We haven't found any personal items, so we haven't been able to identify her. Based on the temperature of her body and the lividity of her skin, she was moved here after she was killed; I'd say no more than 12 hours ago. Judging by the marks on her neck, she was strangled. The ligature marks are quite thin, and the ridges in her neck tell me the killer used a fine bit of rope. There's no evidence of a struggle though. She has no bruises on her wrists or the rest of her body. That suggests that she wasn't conscious when she was strangled, which is odd. Once I get her back to the morgue, I'll be able to give you more information."

I nodded slowly. I looked at the girl before me. She couldn't have been older than 25. Someone's daughter, sister, mother even. My throat tightened. I took a deep breath, and managed to gather myself. I stood and turned my attention to the young medical examiner.

"And there were two other similar murders?" I hadn't been brought up to speed on those cases yet. I'd heard radio reports of the earlier discoveries and the brief snippet of information I got on the phone. I'm only ever brought in when there's a pattern, a sequence, a similarity between multiple cases.

"Yeah. Way too similar. Both the other victims were found in this park; one by the pond on the east side and the other by some bushes near the playground. That one was found by a couple of neighbourhood kids."

"And who is the lead investigator for these murders?"

"That'd be me." An older woman approached us. She wore a long trench-coat and her grey-streaked brown hair was pulled up into a tight bun. "Nice to see you again, Lily."

"Agent Gibson?"

"It's Detective Gibson now. Getting too old to keep up with you young folk at the agency. Decided it was time to slow down a bit. But the way these murders keep happening, I'm going to be as exhausted in this job as I was there! Who do you think requested you for this case?"

"Well, I guess that makes sense."

"Wait, you two know each other?" Meyers interrupted, clearly surprised.

"Agen – oh sorry, Detective Gibson was my Executive Assistant Director when I was still in training at the Bureau. She pretty much taught me everything I know."

"Oh, don't be modest kid. With your wits and intelligence, you pretty much taught yourself. I just kept you out of trouble." She winked at me. In my training days, I constantly pushed the boundaries, something that was highly regarded by some, and despised by others. Detective Gibson always said it was one of my best qualities: I always think outside the box. That's how I became an expert analyst and criminal profiler in the agency.

"Small world, huh? Anyway, I need to get this body up to the morgue. Do you think you have everything you need?"

"Yeah, I think we're good. I need to get Agent Moore up to speed anyway, so we'll head to the station soon. Keep us updated."

The young medical examiner nodded, then walked away to organise transporting the deceased girl.

*   *   *

Mandy Johnson. That was the name of this third girl. Meyers identified her through her dental records.

So, we had three identified bodies and no crime scene. Police scoured the park, and ultimately agreed that none of the girls were killed there. There must be a connection somewhere, but so far, we hadn't found one. All that these girls had in common was their blonde hair and similar age. Only one was a local. The other two came from different parts of the state.

Over the next two days, we interviewed family members, friends and colleagues, trying to find a link between the three girls. We spent long nights examining phone and financial records. We revisited the park and the morgue, waiting for something to turn up and give us some answers.

Any free time I had on those days was spent developing a profile for our killer. The victims were all strangled with something thin. which is a very violent, yet personal way to kill somebody. The killer enjoyed it, he wanted to drag it out. Looking at previous strangulation cases, there has typically been some form of trauma embedded in the motive. Not to mention the tenderness of how the bodies were displayed, laid out in a traditional funeral position. My guess was that we were looking for a man, as all the victims were women.

I still had so many questions, but I could feel a headache starting, my frustration at the case manifesting as physical symptoms. It was 11:39PM on the bedside clock. I rested my head in my hands, and took in the silence of my hotel room. I closed my eyes and began to doze. Almost immediately, my phone rang. The screen said 'unknown caller.' I assumed it was someone from the station.

"Hello, this is Agent Moore. Have there been any updates on the case?"

Silence.

"Hello? Can you hear me?"

More silence. I go to hang up, thinking it's a wrong number, when a voice speaks.

"Hello Agent Moore." It's a male voice.

"Hi, who is this?"

"The one you've been looking for." I stood up. The hairs on my arms prickled. The voice sounds artificial, as if he is using some form of device to disguise his voice.

"How did you get this number?"

"I have my ways, Agent Moore."

"Why are you calling me?"

"I wanted to talk. Don't sound so rude, Agent Moore. I am fascinated by you."

"Why did you kill those girls? Come forward and maybe we can offer you a deal for your cooperation."

"Oh, tsk tsk, I'm not giving it away that easy. Where's the fun in that, Agent Moore? You're famous for your skills. Surely you're smart enough to figure it out."

I was already recording the call.

"Are you calling just to brag? And you keep saying my name, what can I call you?"

"Not to brag. Just to tell you I'm closer than you realise. And if you don't find me soon, you might find another victim. Hurry."

Click.

The silence had returned.

Forgetting my exhaustion, I grabbed my coat and bag, the recording inside, and rushed down to the street. I waved down a taxi, feeling my anxiety rising. It doesn't matter how many times you work cases like these, your skin still crawls when you think you're dealing with a sociopath. But someone has to do it. I was good at my job, so that meant me.

As I raced out of the elevator onto the second floor of the police precinct, I collided with someone; a firm, muscular someone; a man. It was Dr Landon Meyers, the medical examiner. I dropped everything I was holding.

"Slow down little lady, you might hurt yourself."

"Is Gibson still here?"

"Ah, I'm not sure. I've just dropped off the autopsy report. Haven't seen her. Why?"

"He called me."

"Who did?"

"The man responsible for these murders."

Picking up the recording, I replayed the conversation. Landon listened intently, his expression changing from disbelief into disgust.

"That guy gives me the creeps! You'd have to be pretty sick to call a federal agent."

"Mm. That's why I need to find Gibson now. She needs to hear this."

"Try the records room, last door on the left down the hall."

"Thanks. Also, where did you leave that autopsy report?"

"Autopsy report?"

"Yeah, you said you were here to drop it off?"

"Oh right, long night. On her desk." Then, with a smile marking his departure, Landon stepped into the elevator.

*   *   *

Gibson pressed play on the recording for a third time, relistening to the words I'd now heard many times over.

"Okay. So we're looking for a male, I'd say between 30 and 40. He's arrogant, likes to taunt. He wants to kill, but for some reason he doesn't want to hurt the girls. That's why there was no struggle. They must've been unconscious. Where did Dr. Meyers say he left the autopsy report? It's possible the girls inhaled something which knocked them out, making it easy for our killer to strangle them with no fuss."

"It just doesn't add up though. And, on your desk, he said."

"I thought so, I couldn't find it though. Someone must've picked it up. I'll get him to fax over another copy. I don't get it either, why would he call you? I mean it's not even public knowledge that you're liaising on this case."

"He fixates. He has fixated on something from his past, something that happened involving a blonde female. My guess is a young mother. Do we have records for deaths that go back twenty-odd years?"

Gibson nodded, pulling up the records system on the computer, filtering the search to 'female', 'deceased', '1980–1999', 'children' and 'Cauderhill Park'.

Nine cases came up, and we can quickly rule out six of them. That leaves three.

First, Madysn Brinner, a middle-aged mother, who was in a pedestrian accident in front of Cauderhill Park. She left behind a husband and a son and daughter. Her death didn't match the profile, so we ruled her out.

Next, Julie Hammond, also a mother. However, while her death did attract national news due to the violent nature of it, she was survived by two daughters. No sons.

Last was Tracy Marshall, a 29-year-old, blonde mother who died by hanging in the middle of Cauderhill Park. She was found by her 7-year-old son, who'd followed her from their apartment across the road. Her funeral was a small, open-casket memorial with fresh white roses. She and her son had moved to Cauderhill from Atlanta, Georgia, after the passing of her husband six months prior. Her death caused the son to be put into the foster system. The last record of Liam Marshall was 8 years ago, when he was 21.

"Alright, dig up everything you can find on Liam Marshall. He couldn't have just disappeared. Search everywhere between here and Atlanta, and get a sketch artist to do a composite from one of the old photos of Liam. Hopefully someone recognises him."

Two hours later we had a digital image and a positive ID. He wasn't lying when he said he was closer than I thought.

"Okay. Now this man is unpredictable and dangerous. He is a master manipulator and has spent the last eight years morphing into his new identity. Be wary of your surroundings, we want this operation conducted as smoothly as possible."

Upon Detective Gibson's say-so, the team of highly-trained police officers piled out of the vehicles. They swarmed in formation around the apartment building that housed our killer.

One by one we made our way upstairs until we reached his apartment. It was number 29 – the same age as his mother when she died.

I stepped away as one of the uniformed officers broke down the door. Everyone moved in, searching the apartment.

"Clear," from the living room.

"Clear," from the kitchen.

"We have a body," from the bedroom.

Gibson and I rushed in. It was a crime scene if I'd ever seen one. Vials of liquid sedative were scattered on the floor, along with bouquets of white roses tied together by fine pieces of rope. Photos of Liam's mother were stuck up on the windows, and strands of blonde hair were on many of the surfaces.

Stepping through the mess of the living room, we got to the bedroom. What I saw, I'll never forget.

His body was hanging in front of us. He was facing the window. In clear view were the trees of Cauderhill Park. Around his neck, hung an identification badge: *Landon Meyers, Medical Examiner, Cauderhill Hospital.*

The Mound Dweller
Michael Sidwell

Pain and rage.

Haukr's mind rang hot with the echo of steel pounded, anvil-hard; fear twisted, re-forged into a rage. Anger that roared, blood-burning within, and pain. The only reason he knew he was still alive. Bone-deep pain, sharp and rough as the cave-stone floor beneath his shoulders.

He lay, splayed across the stinking corpse, still and cold as Hel's own son.

Haukr couldn't move his limbs, and for all the red-howling hate within, no heartbeat in his chest to push his arms or force his hands to life – or none that he could feel – and no breath came to warm death-frosted lips or grant voice to those internal screams and venge-black oaths he swore against the hated gods and careless fate.

And then there was the crawling; that one thing he could feel. The awful sensation of the worm on his skin… inching over his bare throat, towards his face… a writhing slug of gelid tomb-flesh. That. That he could feel. Yet for all that horror, there was no fear left within the paralysed youth. Only anger. Only hate.

He could see the flicker of torch flame meet the forge-light glow and watched the dance and cast of shadows collide among soot-black ceiling beams. But he couldn't shift his gaze. His eyes were fixed in place, locked in a wide, unblinking stare, unable to shed but a single tear against the sting and wisp of smoky heat, or despair and outrage at the foul, dead thing beneath his back or the one that moved upon him.

It crawled…

*   *   *

Haukr had been so proud. It was the greatest honour to be chosen by Búinn of the Mound, a smith of the Dvergr-folk. Búinn came, as tales told, from Niðavellir, the Dark-of-moon Plains, far beyond the lands of Northern-men, and never had he chosen an apprentice – not in all his time dwelling at the edge of the Vetr-grœnn Dalr. Bent with age and shrouded in dark cloak and hood, Búinn would trade with the people of the Dalr; mend iron, make spear tips, and forge sharp, steel blades for the silver-rich Jarls who came from far and wide.

It was that Búinn had come down to the steading with the flight of day when the wind-bowl hazed purple in twilight's hush and the Álf-bright-wheel sank into the realms of Nótt. He stood at the edge of the village and called, three times – *as tradition demanded* – for the blacksmith, Ǫrn the tall, father of Haukr, to come out and meet him.

"I have heard tales of your boy, the one called Haukr. I have heard he stands taller than most men and wrestles better than all, and he is not yet of sixteen years."

"It is so." Ǫrn nodded, solemn, awed and yet afraid that the Smith of the Mound should know his son by name. But Búinn had lived at the lip of the hills that curled along the Dalr for as long as any could remember, so of course, the Dvergr-man would know all who dwelled within the valley. And all knew the smith who avoided the sun; hobbling on his staff, as gnarled and ironwood-dark as the gold-ringed fingers curled around it. But none would attempt to rob such a one, nor tempt his ire, not even the most reckless or desperate fool would dare face the wrath of the Mound-Dweller's curse… but many came for his metalwork… and they all paid his price.

"Too, it is said, he has some skill at the forge, near to your own. It is time I took apprentice to my craft. My bones grow world-weary and tiring it is for me to work the bellows and sing the hammer-song. I seek a strong youth to work the forge, a worthy lad to learn the secrets of the blade-making art of my folk, and yours is said to be strongest, and so I think me, worthiest. What say you to this, Qrn Qlvirsson?"

A deal was struck and Haukr Qrnsson was sent to become an apprentice to the master-smith. It was a great honour.

*   *   *

The Dvergr-man's hall was cold, and the forge dark when Haukr arrived, and there was no food or drink to be offered or had.

"You will reignite the forge." Búinn rasped, and lit wall-mounted rushlights to spit and crackle, his words hollow, an echo as from some deep rift, "The fire is yours, boy. You will feed it. We begin."

The firepot was cleared of ash and debris, and the Dvergr instructed Haukr to make it ready for the birth of blades. Kindling was placed and sparked to life, the boy used his breath to blow it higher; coal was added next, slow and slow, to be transformed into coke with intense heat, little by little, burning hotter and hotter.

"This is the way of my father and his before him, and theirs before them." Búinn's voice rose and fell, a chant in time with the ember-life-glow, "For Álfr, my father, and Bíldr, his own; for Brúni before them, and all Dúfr's line..."

It was rhythmic, beating in Haukr's pulse, the rush of blood a drum in his ears. To the bellows he was directed, to feed and fan the growing heat, the ember-stare of fire-eyed Báleygr; orange, red, white-ash on black. Coke and air, food and drink for Völundr's gift. Haukr, too, was hungry, wracked with a deep, gnawing flame of his own. He had not eaten nor slept in days for his nerves, and thirst burned his throat with the sear of the forge, dry and bitter at the back of his tongue.

True flames rose now, fingers slipping through red-bright coals, and lapped at the earth's blackened bones; more coke, more air, the song of the bellows to breathe strength into a fire – the ever-starving, gluttonous get of Múspellsheimr...

"For Frægr, then Hárr who followed Hǫrr, given life by Lóni, this one of Þjórr, last son oǫf Nýr, born in the earth where Móðsognir formed..."

Faster and faster the chant grew; embers blazed, spilt blood on gold, the song-tongue of flame. A heap now in the firepot, blazing waves, the whisper-tide of Jǫrð's molten core spinning the earth... spinning Haukr's mind, he blinked and wiped the sweat from his eyes. Heat blasted fury into his face, the windstorm of Óðinn's unquenchable rage. He could barely see, his vision blurred, flickered, cloud-light and storm-heavy, his senses barely his own.

"Drink, now." Búinn held a silver-chased horn to Haukr, the youth's gaze ensnared by the dark swirl within, lapping the glittering rim; darker than honey, the blood of Kvasir's demise. It was thick on his tongue and swallowed hard, sweet and cloying, the *eitr* of the sleep thorn's draught.

"To the stone-sleep, go now." The Dvergr gripped Haukr's wrist, and those fingers burned into the boy's skin, the clamp of tongs chilled in Helheimr's misery. The touch cleared Haukr's eyes, revulsion a shiver up his arm, a spasm in every muscle. He caught the whiff of something wrong; something unclean and long-dead – but not – waft from the folds of Búinn's raven black cloak.

"What-" Haukr tried to cry out, but his tongue had cleaved fast to the roof of his mouth and his lips would no longer move; his teeth clamped hard in a rictus-gripped jaw. Tendons stretched on his neck, veins pulsed, dark cast in the blood-flight of pale fever.

"Yesss..." The Dvergr leaned close, carrion breath filled Haukr's lungs with a sickening gag he couldn't spit out, "stone and... sleep..."

Haukr's limbs shook, his raw-rimmed eyes frozen-aghast as the Dvergr's hood fell back; a face of black-rot, blue gums and grey teeth in a twisted, lipless mouth. It laughed, a hollow bark in the ravaged char that was once a living man's chest, and a dry, yellow tongue lolled over the ash-striped rags of a matted, rust-dark beard...

"Do you see? This worn bone-house of Víglundr, he who came before you, fails now. I can hold it together no longer and must cast his ruin aside. Now your form will be my life-hall, out I will cast your hugr, I will devour your mind, and your heart will beat to my will alone."

Haukr saw it then, a fat, Hel-blue worm that pushed from the thing's ruined nose; a worm-like nothing he could have ever imagined, not even in his darkest dreams... as thick as a finger, ridged like the bend of a swollen knuckle, it slithered from the bulging, nostril cavity. An eyeless, vestigial face, whisps of white beard-fluff and hairy brows... what might be the beak of a nose and the silently screaming void of a mouth. It made no sound but the slop and bubble of the mucus it shed with every horrific undulation.

The Dvergr… its true self revealed… a worm in the flesh of the dead; a maggot birthed in the slaughtered world-corpse of primordial Ymir…

Haukr's throat strangled tighter still, he couldn't scream, nothing would come; even his drug-mired heart could not race. His knees cracked and buckled while his fingers bent into arthritic claws. He tried to turn his face, anything but to look at that… *thing*.

He swayed in place, caught in that timeless moment before a fall, when the world slowed – even slower than he – and his dry, burning sight focused; a hammer left unattended by the forge.

A flash and crackle of *hope*.

With every ounce of terror within, Haukr lurched, half-spun on his heel, threw the vice-grip from his wrist and hurled his weight forward. He seized the smooth-wooden handle within his crippled grasp. Agony burst in his wrist, popped every joint, and rage overtook terror – a lightning bolt, far-flung, thunder-hot from the cloud-halls of ruin. Horror transfixed, became a single-minded need that overrode all else and beat hysteria into hatred: the fury of the All-Father's own unstoppable momentum.

Not like this!

Hot iron burned in Haukr's screaming mind, and with one last heave, he launched himself, full-body, and swung; the hammer smote the corpse straight between the eyes. Sparks flew, the shriek of steel on stone, and cinders danced in a shower of white-hot skull-shards across the uneven floor. The dead thing toppled back, and Haukr fell too. Unable to twist, to thrust himself away, he slammed flat on his back, bent across the putrid shell with the crack of desiccated ribs and rush of carcass stench…

But it wasn't enough… he'd missed it… the *maggot*…

*   *   *

The thing wasn't dead… and now… now he felt it, that worm of elder days, its horrific mouth sucking for purchase, to pull its slick, grave-dank length forward, upward, over the granite-tight pain of Haukr's beardless jaw. It was going for his nose, he knew, to push up inside his nostril, and lair there, beneath the roof-ridge of his brain… it would cast his life to Hel's cold mists and use his limbs for its own dark purpose… to live another lifetime, to roam Miðgarðr, and steal youth and life-gold again and again…

"But what are the Dvergr-folk?" Haukr poked a stick into the pile of grey ash and stirred the embers, teasing the heat-wolf to bite back at life. He was in his fifth year then, and his grandfather had not yet left for Valhöll. The sky was the blue of those kind, clear eyes and the day held no more fear.

The Dvergr-man had come to the steading to trade in the dusk of that previous night, and Haukr had seen him; a shadow against the growing dark, crowned by the light of the first frost-bright stars. He had been terrified and ran to hide beneath his bed, the wooden sword his grandfather had made him tight in his small, white-knuckled hand. All night he'd lain there, alert and watching, lest the Dark-man sneak into the house and steal his life and breath away...

"Ah," Old Qlvir combed thick, calloused fingers through the snow of his long, silken beard, "well then. The Dvergar sprang to life in the flesh of Ymir's corpse when the All-Father made the world from that Jǫtunn of old. Ymir's blood became the oceans, and the earth was formed from his flesh. His bones are from what the mountains are made, and his teeth are the rocks and stones... and there...."

Haukr's gaze followed the old man's shaking finger as he pointed to the sky, "There Ymir's skull forms the roof of the world and his spattered brains float as clouds across the wind-bowl. But after all this, the gods found the Dvergar crawling as maggots in Ymir's flesh... the worms of the earth. So, the gods, from their dark thrones, gave the Dvergar cunning and the likeness of men, so they might be then put to purpose..."

But that wasn't all true...

Realisation flared in Haukr's mind, the flash and flicker of lightning among venom-dark clouds. They were worms, yes, some kind of maggoty *things*; vile creatures of evil mind, that stole into the bodies of the dead... those corpses who knew no pyre, but instead were consigned to the embrace of dank and fetid earth...

Vile Trǫll-*slugs*, taught by the gods to rise in the shapes of the dead and skulk among men... and from the masks of those corpse-shells, they learned to lure the living with tools of iron and weapons of steel; with treasures of silver and dark, burnished gold... and people came... and the Dvergar-folk watched them and selected from them the best of prizes, the strongest bodies of youth... to take over, to possess... and that was how they lived on... for centuries... passing from one bone-house to the next, travelling down the ages, stolen life after life... *invited* by mankind's greed...

The gods didn't give them the likeness of men, they let those *corpse-maggots* inhabit the unwanted dead… unworthy flesh to wear and walk within… and that was the cunning they gave the Dvergar. Shapes to use so that they might fashion and craft for the dark-minded and artless Æsir… and the gods cared not when the Dvergar learned to move from those rotting bodies into the living… for the fates of Men meant nothing against the gift-price of thunder-hammer and strength-belt, of victory-spear and gold-dripping ring, of sun-gold hair or necklace of sea-fire… all forged by creatures, monsters who had absorbed such lore from devouring the earth-flesh of the first living thing…

Murderers of the ages… night crawlers of the fjörðr of dead men…

The gods simply watched… and did not care…

Claws. Claws of ice in Haukr's belly; a raking cold-fury as each new epiphany rumbled and flashed, roared in the thought-storm of his mind…

That thing crawled, he felt it on his face, on his chin, it probed for the warmth of his nose, searched for the heat-trace of even the shallowest breath… to burrow within…

His fingers twitched, bicep flexed and jerked. A vibration grew within his chest; low, breathless, a hack, a heaving-cough. His jaw tightened harder still, agony – marble twisted iron, a ripple of cramped muscle, and the sound in his chest thrummed louder. A roll of distant thunder beneath his ribs. It hurt, that unleashed roar, burned in his lungs as coals swallowed by a serpent of vitriol, choked and venomous, bile-black and seething…

You will not…

The Dvergr-worm felt it; the movement, the rumble, the hard grind of teeth, and pushed itself faster, frantic, forward-

You will NOT…

Haukr's hand twitched, his fingers opened and closed, the effort of crushing a rock in his fist; he strained with the tearing wrath of madness, the inhuman ferocity of a hound-baited bear, a wordless, mindless roar at his arm-

Work! Move!

The worm lurched again, butted the rim of his nostril, and coiled the fetid, acid-stink of its body to push inside his nose.

Haukr's arm launched; his hand smacked his own face with star-bright, lip-splitting force. The twist of his fingers pinched the hideous slug, gripped and squeezed with a sick snot-pop. Haukr's joints cracked, his arm flew back, and torture spikes shot through every muscle and bone. He flung his deadened arm, a catapult-sling, and hurled the Dvergr-worm to arc out, away, end-over-end-

It made other sounds then; a thud, a bubble squeal, the hiss of steam escaping containment. It fizzed as it hit the forge... and slid into the coal-bright ember-hoard; a curl of blackened waste, shrivelled, crisped, and crumbled to white flakes of ash. The lore of ages, the secrets and knowledge of lifetimes uncounted, the evil of a thing from the dawn of the world... gone in a squeak and puff.

You will not see another day, maggot.

Haukr's hand fell limp, his knuckles grazed stone; a sharp, ice-cold jolt, warmed by the seep of blood between thawing fingers. At least there was that. The pain subsided, slowly, washed away as the curl of the foam-capped tide, and took the stone-cold with it; rage abated, the winds of hatred dropped to a breeze and his breath returned in lung-sharp relief.

He welcomed that new pain, the hard-dying ache... the stab in his toes and sharp nails in the soles of his feet. His eyes fluttered, blinked and squeezed out tears, relief against the grit, scratch and torment of frozen stare.

He curled his fingers again, tested the flex, and pushed his now unglued tongue to stretch life back into his cheeks. He could taste the copper-tang of his broken lip; the probe re-opened the split – a shudder-gasp escaped, the sound and sting of pain, life and victory.

But there are more of them. More monsters. Dvergr-worms possessing men, Álfar and their arrows, their dream-sendings of woe, madness and ruin... and Draugar hammering on the doors of halls no longer their own... they are all real... all the plagues of Men...

Never.

Haukr pushed those evil thought-whispers aside, hammer-forced them down; down deep, where he would chain them forever – locked away, tight as the Fame-wolf's bindings, forgotten in the pitch-black of Lyngvi's grim cage.

Never again.

He rolled his body off Víglundr's wreckage and pushed himself to his knees. Still unable to stand, breath ice-sharp in his lungs.

He counted the tasks ahead in his mind: to douse the forge-light and end that fire, then take the Dvergr-worm's treasures to see those

life-bought riches put to good use… and he'd sink this foul, cavern-hall beneath the weight of Ymir's old bones… and hide it forever too, this blight on the earth, this outrage against Jǫrð's ever-green ways…

But first, he would see the dead man off in the smoke-coils of Surtr's breath; a funeral pyre to carry Víglundr home to the gods…. for better to dwell with them and their treacherous ways than meet that which coiled eternal within the never-ending dark…

The hammer he would lay aside for the use of other men; men who didn't know the truth of the crawlers of Ymir's flesh, and who had not lost the love of the steel-making song… nor the desire for strife-metal silver and blood-bought gold.

Perhaps he'd make a new life in the high, sun-lit meadows and raise sheep… the sigh of clean wind on his face… far away from dark holes in the earth; the low hiding-place of the gleam of the Álf-world… and nightmares he'd drown in a lake of the ale-horn…

…and never, ever think of *maggots* or monsters again…

Daughters of The Family

Natalie Power

First came the musty smell of smoke and then the bright flicker of flames. Next were the piercing screams. I felt the grip of two hands on my shoulders, shaking me relentlessly. Opening my eyes, I took a moment to adjust to the haze that filled the room and to the shrill sound of my eight-year-old sister, Mary.

"Ally! Get up! There's a fire," she cried. "You have to get up. Please."

I urged her to be quiet as I sat up, dazed and disoriented, but certain I didn't want her to disturb our mother and father. I quickly realised the smell and the flickering weren't part of my usual nightmares. Instead, they were real, and rapidly engulfing our small room. Adrenaline coursed through my body, as I leapt off the thin mattress, tangling myself in the frayed, worn-out blanket that I used every night.

My hands went to Mary's cheeks, as I looked into her terrified eyes. "Have you woken anybody up? How did this happen?"

Glancing around the room, I tried to determine whether there was anyone else sleeping on the floor. There was so much smoke, it was hard to make sense of anything.

A knife-like pain shot through my body. I clutched my chest as I felt an overwhelming tightness. It was increasingly harder to breathe. The floor swayed beneath me as I gasped for air. I reached for Mary's arm, as everything went black.

*   *   *

The pain was unlike anything I had experienced. My head throbbed and my body ached all over. The thirst was unbearable. I hadn't managed to open my eyes yet, but wherever I was, it was extremely bright and loud. It made this agony one hundred times worse. I was somewhere completely unfamiliar. My heart was pounding at an increasingly rapid pace. A rush of heat coursed through me, making my clothes stick to my sweaty skin. Disjointed thoughts ran through my mind, jumping from one possibility to another. I sat upright and opened my eyes. I could make out some of my surroundings.

Everything was bathed in white; from the blankets that covered my body, to the walls and the windowsills and even the dull paintings. The only thing that stood out was a small whiteboard next to the door with two names written on it: Ally with a question mark, and underneath, Dr. Manning.

The next thing I focused on was the infuriating beeping sound next to me. It wouldn't stop. *Why wouldn't it stop?*

My irritation with the beeping was overcome by my dire need to quench my thirst. I noticed a foam cup sitting on a bench next to me. Shakily, I stretched out my hand to grab it and lifted it to my mouth to drink. Instead, the cup hit something in the way; something I hadn't noticed until now. Throwing the cup to the side, I grabbed at the foreign bit of plastic covering my mouth. It was attached to tubes. Looking down at my body, I saw more tubes and wires connected to the machines next to me.

I threw myself out of the bed and hit the ground, pulling down one of the large machines, which landed just centimetres from my face.

The door swung open and a group of people I didn't recognise ran into the room. They were all wearing blue clothing; some a light blue and others a dark blue. I covered myself as two of them approached me. I opened my mouth to scream, moving as far away as I could, which wasn't far. My back hit the wall. I wished for this nightmare to end; to just wake up. I burst into tears and pulled my knees to my body, as I felt their hands gripping my arms.

"Get away from me. Please get away from me!" Tears streamed down my face. I kicked the air and tried desperately to get out of their grip, but there were two of them and only one of me.

"Let go of her now!" A voice broke through my cries. At the command, the grip on my arms released and I slumped back to the ground. I curled up into a ball and retreated into my mind, as far from this situation as possible.

"Ally, Ally, I'm Doctor Manning. I understand this situation is very overwhelming and confusing for you. You must be so scared. I am here to help you though. Can you look at me?"

The same voice that commanded my release moments ago, had shifted into a soothing and gentle tone. The voice belonged to the woman whose name I recognised from the whiteboard. I had only met one other doctor in my life, the community doctor back home.

"Ally, you're at Lakewood General Hospital. I'm Chief of Psychiatry here. You were brought here by some paramedics and firemen who pulled you out of a fire. You're safe now. It's okay."

Everything flooded back about the flames and the smoke and Mary!

"Where's Mary? Where's my sister? Sh-she woke me up. I could barely see. It was so hot and I couldn't breathe. Where is she?" My voice cracked as I wracked my brain for the last thing I remembered. I couldn't put the pieces together.

"Your sister is safe too. She's with one of our other doctors. She is in good hands."

"I need to see her. Let me see her. I want to be with my sister. She will be so scared."

"We will bring her in just as soon as we check you over and run some tests now that you're awake. You inhaled a lot of smoke which caused you to black out. We just want to make sure it hasn't done too much damage. Can we get you back up onto the bed? It might be a bit more comfortable for you."

I realised I was sitting on the floor and Dr Manning had joined me there. The room had been cleared of all the other people. I nodded. I put my hands on the floor and pushed up, to get to my feet. I was a little wobbly, and when Dr Manning noticed, she put out her hands to help steady me. I hesitated. She was still a stranger, but feeling the instability in my legs and realising the distance between myself and the bed, I accepted her help.

"Did anyone else get brought in? My mother and father? We were all in that room."

"I'm not too sure at this moment, I'm sorry Ally, but I will find out for you soon, yeah? There were a lot of people brought in from the com- uh, from the place you were living."

The next hour was filled with questions and tests and half a dozen other doctors and nurses filing in and out. I spent the majority of it in a daze. The only thing on my mind was seeing my sister and finding my parents. Dr Manning promised that if I let them do the tests, she would help me in every way she could. I also made her promise she wouldn't leave me in the room with strangers. She was a friend in this unfamiliar place.

*   *   *

"Hi Ally, how are you feeling?" Dr Manning walked into the room, followed by a man in a light blue uniform, who, instead of walking up to me with the doctor, waited by the door. He looked very official. That made me uncomfortable.

"Um, better - I guess. Are we done with the tests?"

"Yes, we are! Your tests have come back great, apart from minor smoke inhalation, which we'll monitor. All in all, though, your physical health is exactly where we'd like it to be."

My eyes darted between the doctor I had come to trust and the stranger in the doorway.

"Does that mean I can see my sister?"

"We need to have a little talk first, Ally." Dr Manning's voice took on a soft tone, which concerned me.

"No, you promised me my sister! Whatever you have to say can wait."

She looked at the man in the uniform, then back at me and nodded.

"Of course. I will go and see if one of the nurses will bring her in." Dr Manning walked out of the room, leaving me behind with the man who was yet to introduce himself. An uncomfortable silence arose, and I wanted him to disappear down the hallway, but he didn't. Instead, he entered the room and took a seat. He leaned forward and rested his elbows on his knees. Dr Manning had broken her promise not to leave me alone with any strangers.

"You probably want to know who I am and why I'm here. I am Officer Freeman, Ally. I'm a policeman. Your situation has concerned a lot of people. I'm here to help."

I had never met a policeman before. All I knew was from books and from what my father said. He said we couldn't trust them, and they would take us away.

"Where are my parents?" I asked. He shifted in his seat, which made the feeling in the pit of my stomach worsen. Something wasn't right.

"Let's just wait until Dr Manning comes back, then you can ask all the questions you like." The uncomfortable silence returned as we both sat and waited.

It was probably ten minutes before Dr Manning returned, followed by a nurse. I could barely register what was going on before someone launched themself at me. It was the sister I had been dying to see.

"You're okay?" She sobbed. Tears also filled my eyes, as I held the young girl in my arms.

I nodded and said, "I'm okay, Mary. I've got you now. It's okay."

I looked at Dr. Manning and, as if she could read my mind, she left the room, taking the policeman and nurse with her.

We sat in silence, clutching each other and not letting go. I think we both knew that dreadful news was coming.

She nestled deep into my chest. I recalled that I had been the proudest older sister and had fallen in love with her the moment she was born. I would hold her in my arms all night long. There were five years between us, but sometimes I felt we were the same age. Her maturity and tenderness outweighed mine. I stroked her hair and her body relaxed and she fell asleep. I rested my eyes and soon dozed.

*   *   *

A knock at the door woke me and Dr Manning walked in.

"I decided to let you sleep for a few hours. You both needed it. But we have to talk now."

I looked at Mary sleeping peacefully in my arms, then back at the doctor and nodded. It was now or never.

She signalled someone outside the room, and moments later, the same man as before walked in; the policeman. My hands got clammy and my heartbeat increased.

"We don't need to wake her, do we?"

They looked at each other and then the man spoke. "At this moment no, but we will have to. The young one also needs to know."

"Know what?"

"What do you remember about your upbringing, Ally? What was your childhood like?"

I was confused by this question. What does my childhood have to do with a house fire?

"Ahh, I don't really know how to answer that. Normal?"

"Could you explain what you mean by 'normal', Ally?"

I hated the way he spoke my name with every question.

"I don't see how any of this is relevant. I was in a fire. What's going on? I just want to go home."

"Your home is gone, Ally. I'm sorry." Dr Manning interrupted, pity showing on her face.

"What? Gone? What do you mean my home is gone?" I was getting agitated, but I tried to calm myself. I wanted to avoid disturbing my sister.

"Okay, what Officer Freeman is about to tell you is going to be a shock, Ally. If you need him to stop at any time, just say so."

"I don't understand where this is going. Just tell me!"

He sat down and shifted in his seat before he spoke. He did that a lot.

"Okay, okay. The fire that you were pulled out of - it wasn't an accident. And it wasn't the only fire. The fires were purposely lit, as an act of - uh, I'm sorry, Ally, the community that you've been raised in, the family you know, it's not what it seemed to you growing up."

"Wh-what are you trying to say? Where are my parents?"

There was a pause. "Your parents are dead, Ally. I'm so sorry."

I stared blankly, the words bouncing through my head. No part of my brain could process the words that were just spoken. What followed was a battle in my mind, as I tried to find a reason that they might be wrong.

"No. You're wrong. They got out. They had to have got out. There's no way we got out and they didn't, that's impossible."

"They didn't get out of your building, Ally" - he took a deep breath - "because they were the ones who started the fire. Your parents weren't the people you thought they were. There's no easy way to tell you this - "

I felt my whole world collapse. They started the fire. No. This had to be some sort of sick joke.

"Ally, listen –"

"No. You're lying. You're trying to take us away. My father told me that's what you people do."

"Your parents weren't the only ones, Ally. All the adults are dead. I don't think they thought they had a choice. Every building was burnt down."

"That doesn't make any sense. Why would they do that? It's not true, our parents loved us."

"You have been isolated from society your entire life. The community that you were raised in is known as a cult."

I laughed in his face. "We are not a part of a cult. We are a family. A religious family. That doesn't make us a cult. I know the stories of all those awful cults, that isn't what we are."

"Ally, I'm sorry. I know this is a lot to take in, but this cult has been around for a long time. I'm sure you know the history; they've probably taught you about it. But the *Family of Balance* really is a cult. And the events of last night were, for lack of any other word, a massacre."

"But a massacre means that a lot of people all died. Are you saying everyone is dead? Th-that's not possible. There's too many of us."

"There are survivors, much like yourself, and just as confused. The stories of the other survivors have confirmed what we believe. Your leader, Reverend Floyd James, orchestrated it all. He is – or was – a very bad man. Our officers uncovered his manifesto describing his 'calling' to eradicate the evil of our society. He believed you would all be reborn as pure children of God."

I felt defeated. If what he said was true, everything I knew had been a lie. The life I had flashed before my eyes. I recalled my most cherished memories. Then, new memories emerged – ones of large-scale gatherings, preaching, love and *violence*.

I remembered everything.

It was true.

"So, what do we do now?"

"You're free Ally, you go and live."

The Wedding
Delilah Cornwall

In the year AC3456 of the Glorious One's Eternal Reign, the sun rose bright over the village of Lolenlinden. Matienne Shol awoke to find her hair had been twisted and woven into an intricate pattern of incredibly painful, horrifically ugly knots with not a single strand left unknotted.

Matienne stared at herself in the mirror, transfixed by her newfound ugliness, then rushed downstairs. "Harren!"

Harren, a famously early riser who always seemed to wake up as gorgeous as ever (which was very), nearly spilled her breakfast all over herself as her distraught and disfigured sister rushed into the room. "Matienne! Your hair!"

"I know!"

"It's horrendous!"

"I know!"

"You're getting married this afternoon!"

"I know!"

"What happened?!"

"I don't know!" Matienne collapsed into the chair next to Harren's and put her face in her hands. "This seems like the kind of thing Gen La would do if they were upset with me, but I haven't seen Gen La in weeks!"

"Well, did you make sure to invite them to the wedding?"

"Yes! I left a written invitation in the usual spot alongside the usual offering but haven't seen or heard from them ever since. I don't know why they would do this to me now."

Harren stood to her feet, hands on her hips and a determined expression on her face. "Well, I won't stand for it! You've poured your heart and soul into this wedding, and I won't let one faerie's temper tantrum ruin it." Harren, as prone to poor decision making as she was gorgeous, made straight for the door to head for the offering stone.

"Harren, no!" Matienne said, rushing across the room to grab her sister's wrist just in time. "You can't just go and accuse Gen La of wrongdoing. Don't you remember what happened to Tommen?"

Harren paled. "Poor Tommen."

"Poor Tommen." Matienne echoed.

"Well, then!" Harren reversed Matienne's hold with the deftness of a martial arts master. "We'll just have to solve this ourselves!"

'Wait, Harren, no!"

But this time Harren would not be dissuaded. She dragged her sister in her bedroom, sat her down in front of the mirror, applied hair detangler spray liberally and got to brushing.

Fifteen minutes of Matienne's tortured screaming, begging, pleading and beseeching later, Harren tossed her brush away and threw her hands in the air. "Matienne, I can't work in these sorts of conditions. How am I supposed to concentrate with you screeching the whole time?"

"Harren, you've been working for fifteen minutes and achieved nothing. These are faerie knots. You were never going to get them out with mundane methods. We need magic."

Harren's eyes lit up. "Magic! Of course!" She snatched hold of Matienne's wrist in a vice grip.

"Harren, we're still in our sleepwear!"

Six minutes later, the sisters, still in their pyjamas, were knocking at the front door of Old Woman Nina's home. Or more accurately, Harren was assaulting the door with her free hand while preventing Matienne, who was trying desperately to hide herself from the eyes of the rest of the villagers, from escaping with her other. "Old Woman Nina! Old Woman Nina, we need your —"

The door swung open to reveal the extraordinarily displeased

Old Woman Nina. "Harren, I swear if —" She stopped dead in her tracks at the sight of Matienne. "Come in right away."

Harren quickly deposited Matienne in front of Old Woman Nina's cauldron. "We think this is Gen La's doing. But they've been avoiding us for weeks, and we can't think what we could possibly have done to offend them."

Old Woman Nina fixed her basilisk-like stare on Matienne. "Did you invite them to the wedding?"

"Yes!"

"Did you remember to use sheepskin instead of paper?"

"Yes!"

"Did you write the invitation in your own blood?"

"Yes!"

"Backwards?"

Matienne inhaled small and sharp, her heart almost stopped. "Backwards …"

Old Woman Nina shook her head. Harren slammed her palm so hard into her forehead that she yelped and forgot to be mad at her sister's carelessness for a full minute.

Old Woman Nina went to her well-stocked apothecary shelf. "You'll need to apologise and it's going to need to be a grand apology indeed. No doubt Gen La has been waiting for an apology this whole time. Here, some crystallised aether, morpho wings and a dead child's most beautiful dream." Old Woman Nina handed Matienne a shimmering blue crystal that was pleasantly warm to the touch, the wings of a morpho butterfly, and a small vial inside which a tiny child sailed across a sea, which was coloured to match.

"What am I supposed to do with these?"

"Blue is Gen La's favourite colour," she counted on one finger, "they love the taste of crystallised aether," two fingers, "their wings were looking worn out last time I saw them," three fingers, "and you know how Gen La likes to be sad on purpose sometimes." Four fingers. "Nothing more bittersweet than the beautiful dream of a child who didn't live to see it." Old Woman Nina gave a small conspiratorial smile.

"Wait, was that —"

"But of course!" Harren said, finally over her self-inflicted injury. "We should also bring a sheep! You know how Gen La loves sheep."

"An excellent idea. Now go! You don't have long!"

Matianne glared at the old woman as Harren dragged her out of the building. "I am acutely aware of the start time of my own wedding thank you!"

On their way to Shaun the Shepherd's place, Matienne, having decided her humiliation could grow no greater anyway, threw herself on the ground to halt Harren's relentless advance, dragging them both down into the dirt. The two of them now safely on the ground, Matienne told Harren the brilliant scheme (it was a single addition to the plan they'd already worked out) she'd just concocted, and the pair decided to split up in order to divide and conquer. This was a gross misunderstanding of a basic military strategy but neither of them had ever been soldiers so cut them some slack.

Matienne returned home and set about writing a second invitation, in her own blood, backwards, in miniscule font on the morpho butterfly wings themselves. She also made sure to throw in an individual apology for every day since her original botched invitation and an extended section talking about how Gen La was the most intelligent, most beautiful, most powerful and most popular faerie in all the Eternal One's Infinite Realm.

Her work complete, Matienne stood and, only feeling a little woozy from the blood loss, went to go check on Harren's progress only to be nearly knocked over as Harren burst in through the front door. "I got the sheep! Shaun was happy to give one up for the cause, he knows how much Gen La loves sheep. And I had to engage in some furious fisticuffs with Mr Wellen down at the general store because I didn't have any money on me, but I also got the blue —"

Matienne grabbed Harren by the wrist. "No time! We need to change!"

After two quick dry baths, the sisters helped one another change into their bride and maid of honour dresses. Then the overdressed duo began their ascent up the hill and into the circle of trees in the nearby woods to the Gen La's summoning stone.

When Matienne's parents first showed her the summoning stone as a child, she'd commented about how it was just a random, fist-sized rock half-buried in the dirt. Her parents had gasped and circled her protectively, but fortunately Gen La wasn't around to curse or claw her eyes out because they hadn't been summoned yet.

Apparently, Gen La was a multiversally renowned expert on which rocks were the best looking, so their word was sacrosanct and they wouldn't accept any criticism that wasn't in writing with sources cited.

Matienne left Harren just outside the circle with the sheep to enact the single addition to the plan they'd already made but which Matienne was still calling her brilliant scheme in her mind. "Oh Gen La! Most beautiful and intelligent of all faeries, I come to you to seek redemption for my crimes against you!" she yelled in her most dramatic voice as she approached the summoning stone. Which was still just a fist-sized rock half-buried in the dirt.

She placed the crystallised aether, the morpho wings/apology/invitation and the dream of the dead child down next to the rock and tried to ignore the fact the hem of her dress was getting dirty.

There was a buzzing in the air, the hairs on the back of Matienne's neck and arms stood up, and then there was a loud pop and puff of blue smoke. "Finally!" shouted Gen La, appearing from the smoke.

Gen La was beautiful and terrible. Their face was constructed of gorgeous angles, with sharp point ears, solid black eyes. They were dressed only in the finest of leaves and twigs and their hair was done in the latest faerie style. They had gorgeous gossamer wings which were, as Old Woman Nina had said, frayed at their edges, and their hands and feet ended in wickedly hooked talons to match the endless rows of razor-sharp needle-like teeth in their mouth.

"I have been waiting for this apology! For weeks!" Gen La crossed their arms over their chest and hovered in front of Matienne's face because they were also only thirty centimetres tall. "I cannot believe the disrespect from you, Matienne! I watch over you, your family, this whole town for decades! Centuries! Weeks! Who saved you from that well you fell into when you were a child!"

"You did, Gen La."

"And who made sure your leg healed after you fell out of the tree the week after?"

"You did, Gen La."

"And who introduced you to your future wife, huh!?"

"That was Harren, Gen La."

"What!?" Gen La exploded, baring their tiny claws and coming so close to Matienne's face they were nearly touching.

"It was at the Solstice Ball three years ago, remember? You were busy making fireworks for all the children, and Harren introduced me to Nalia because she was new in town. You know how Harren is with new people."

Gen La stared at Matienne with the intensity of a volcano about to burst for a long, long, long moment before they burst out into laughter and flew in spirals around Matienne's head. "That's right! And you were so tongue-tied because of how pretty Nalia is that you made a complete idiot of yourself and tripped over and fell face first into the punch bowl trying to run away!"

Matienne flushed bright red. "Yes, well we don't need to —"

"But that doesn't change the facts, Matienne!" Gen La snapped, back in front of Matienne's face, an accusing talon pointing directly at her nose. "How is a faerie supposed to feel when they put so much effort into protecting a town full of mortals only to be so disrespected as to have their wedding invitation written forward! Forward! Left to right starting in the top left-hand corner! Like I'm some kind of pathetic mortal myself!"

"It would be impossible, which is why if you'll look at your summoning stone I've brought you gifts." Matienne motioned to the small pile of objects next to the stone and Gen La rushed over. "Some crystalised aether because I know you love the taste. One of the morpho wings has an apology, the other a new invitation, both written backwards starting in the bottom right corner this time. There is also a vial containing the unlived dream of a dead child because we know how you like to feel sad sometimes."

Gen La inspected each gift carefully. They took a nibble off the edge of the crystalised aether and hummed approvingly, dubbing it spicy. Next, they read both the invitation and the apology and hummed before dropping to the ground, popping off their frayed gossamer wings and replacing them with the bloodied morpho wings. Matienne had deliberately avoided pointing out the state of Gen La's wings, so it was good they just did this on their own. Finally, Gen La reached the vial with the dream of the dead child, took the cork out and swallowed it whole.

Gen La wailed and sobbed for the next fifteen minutes. They rushed into Matienne's hands and Matienne ever so gently patted them on the back and stroked their hair as they repeated "He was so young!" and "This world is so unendingly cruel!" or variations of the two over and over until they'd tired themself out.

"There, there, Gen La, everything is going to be ok."

"Of course it is!" Gen La shouted, melancholy over as abruptly as it had begun, flying out of Matienne's hands and putting their hands on their hips. "I never even met that kid! I just like being sad! But still! It's not enough! You left this apology to the last minute! I had to spend weeks waiting for this. As good a fifteen minutes of being sad as that was, it's not enough, so I won't undo your knots in your hair!"

"But, Gen La, it's not over! Harren has another present for you!"

At which point Harren stepped out of the nearby trees with a sheep, dyed entirely blue, in tow.

Gen La squealed so loud it made Matienne wince as they rushed forward. "Fluffy! Oh I love fluffies so, so, so, so, so much! And this one's blue!"

Gen La spent the next twenty minutes doting on every aspect of the blue fluffy. Matienne and Harren exchanged a subtle high five.

"Ok!" Gen La said, happily perched atop the fluffy's head. "All is forgiven!" They snapped their fingers and at once, Matienne's hair not only unknotted itself but styled itself flawlessly into the exact style she wanted it for the wedding. Even the dirt at the hems of the sister's dresses disappeared.

"But I have a few conditions," Gen La said, smiling a mischievous grin.

And so it was that Matienne and Nalia were married in blue dresses, all the bridesmaids and bridesmen were dressed in blue, the food was all dyed blue and Gen La took over as flower girl, ring bearer, page, officiant and best man. Harren fought and managed to maintain her position as maid of honour in exchange for another blue fluffy next month when they were done slowly devouring this one. It was a wedding which no one would ever forget and which would make everyone involved laugh and laugh and laugh with every retelling through the years that followed as the happy couple set about living their happily ever after.

The Record

Sheree Pratt

The record skipped mid chorus of the bluegrass song. Until that moment I'd thought nothing of the record I'd purchased earlier that day at an op-shop, other than the opportunity to expand on the record collection I'd inherited from my mother. Brushing the cover of it, I sneezed when a thick layer of dust rose into the air, tickling my nostrils. Under that layer two men in cowboy hats smiled at me. One held a guitar, the other a banjo. I turned it in my hands like a steering wheel to read the bold lettering.

"Keep Them Cold Icy Fingers Off Me"

Right-o! I thought, but as I went to put it back, a note fell out of the slip and cascaded down to my feet like a feather. I bent down to pick it up and read the rough black cursive scrawl.

"Don't give up."

Intrigued, I pocketed the note, walked to the counter with that one record in its dusty jacket, paid for it and left with it tucked under my arm.

That evening, I sat with my glass of Jack Daniels by the record player, turning the note over in my hands, still trying to decipher who it was addressed to, who it was from and what it meant. I found myself lost in the rhythm of the song as it moved from melodic picking of a guitar and banjo instrumental, to an energetic verse and chorus. Momentarily forgetting about the note in my hands, I belted the words out along with the Stanley Brothers.

"You may run me out of breath. You may scare me half to death but keep them coooooooold icy fingers off of m— off of m— off" I stopped the player and gently lifted the needle to inspect the record and wipe away any lingering dust, only to find not a speck nor scratch to be seen. I shook my head and lowered the needle again to resume the song.

It wasn't long before it reached the same chorus and as I blended my voice with their harmonies it skipped again. Covering my ears, I squeezed my eyes shut. When the skipping ended, I opened my eyes and found myself in a stark white school corridor with one hand poised to knock on a grey door and the other holding a note. I peered through the blinds into a bland classroom filled with students at wooden desks, all facing one olive skinned boy in overalls playing a guitar.

Instead of knocking, I slowly cracked the door open, letting his velvety voice fill my ears with song. Careful not to interrupt, I quietly slid in and sat on the first desk closest to the door, mesmerised at the display of confidence the boy showed as he amateurishly fumbled the chords. Everyone was enthralled with the performance, so much so that no one noticed my entrance. The stern-faced teacher, however, darted her eyes away from the boy to me, long enough to raise a quizzical brow, then return her gaze to the boy. She didn't so much as offer polite smile.

Though it was evidently changing, there was a familiar ring to the boy's voice. It was a little rough and pitchy in places, which I would expect of a boy that age. *He sounds like a young—Oh my god! It can't be!*

It took only moments of staring around the room at the garish mix of collared shirts, torn overalls, and curtain like pinafore dresses to realise I was not in the 21st century anymore. The boy with the crushed velvet voice and guitar-picking was a young Elvis Presley, singing to his music teacher, desperate to raise his fail-grade from a C to something closer to what he thought he deserved.

Could it be The King? I shook my head. *I really need to stop drinking!*

When the song concluded, the class applauded. The teacher politely joined, but her face remained stern. Her eyes bore into his eagerly waiting brown eyes.

"Raw, but then hillbilly music isn't exactly something to aspire to, nor is it hard to play." she said, sparking a heated discussion with the boy. "There's no place for it here, or anywhere. This backward unrefined fad will pass. Then what will you do?". The whole class laughed.

I could hear the frustration in the boy's voice as he vehemently exclaimed, "You just don't appreciate my kind of singing!"

"You're right. I don't really." she said, turning away from him to resume the class, "Hick music is not music. The C remains. Anything else would be a disservice to you, and to the standard of music."

Deflated, the red-faced boy sat starring at the neck of his guitar. I watched him shake his head and violently palm at his eye to wipe away a tear while a chorus of "Mama's boy!" rang from the boys sitting behind him. He kept his eyes fixed on the tuning pegs until the bell sounded the end of the lesson.

It was only after the students left that the teacher noticed me still sitting there. "Who are you? How long have you been sitting there?"

"Long enough to hear that boy sing. He was amazing, wasn't he?"

"Elvis Presley?" she scoffed. "Are we talking about the same kid? He's got guts, I'll give him that. You and I both know he's got no business trying be his singer."

"How do you know that? Who are you to know what that boy is capable of or what he'll go on to do?" I asked.

"I just know that a bright kid like him, with a family like his ought to take his head out of the clouds and be more realistic about his future, or else he won't have one. Now, who are you and what are you doing in my classroom? Are you a scout? I can direct you to a number of students in this class with actual talent."

"Oh, I'm nobody you should be concerned about, nor am I a scout," I answered. "I'm just someone who knows good music and talent when I hear it, regardless of who they are or what family they're from."

She turned away and began to tidy her desk. "Well, I suggest you leave if you're not authorised to be here."

I stormed over to the open door and glared at the infuriating woman. "That kid will go places you'll never imagine. Just you wait and see. Elvis Presley is a name you'll hear one day and kick yourself for beating him down."

Later, I found the boy by his locker, hunched over with his arms covering his face and head. A crowd of boys gathered around him chanting "Mama's boy! Mama's boy!" One of them lunged at him, fist raised, and gripped Elvis' collar. "Come on, Mama's boy, take a swing! Come on!"

"Leave me alone!" Elvis yelled. The whole group laughed. I whipped my head left and right along the crowded corridor, hoping somebody would come to this boy's defence, but nobody made a move to help him.

"Hey!" I cried, just as another boy took a swing. Elvis tried to duck but the other boy held him in place by the collar. The boy loosened his grip, sending Elvis crashing to the ground and his friend's fist connected with the locker. "Haven't you all got classes to go to?"

"Yes, Miss," they all mumbled and scurried into a nearby room.

Elvis rose to his feet and wiped his hands on his trousers. He flashed a crooked bashful smile. "Good thang ma' gi'tar was already in ma' locker, huh Mam'!" he joked. There was still a youthful ring to his speaking voice, but he had that thick southern accent and manner of speaking I'd only ever heard in recordings and old videos.

"It sure is," I said. "Are you okay?"

"I'm dandy, Mam'. I'm used to the pummellin'. I saw you in the room when I was playin'. Are you a new teacher?"

"Uh... yeah I am. English lit," I lied. "I loved that song you were singing in there. Stanley Brothers, am I right?"

"Uh huh! Thank you very much, mam'. The folks 'round here don't think much of their music or ma' singin'." He bent down to pick up the textbook and folder that were scattered at his feet and hooked the pile under his arm. A number two pencil fell out and the lead snapped as it landed on the ground. Before it could roll away. He plucked between his fingers and tucked it behind his ear.

"It sounded fine to me, and it's only going to get better and better, you'll see. Have you got time to show me the chords? I'd love to learn it."

The kid's face brightened with that same crooked half smile that now fronts posters and album covers, and without hesitation opened his locker and pulled out the guitar and handed it to me. "Now can you do a C chord? Now F, back to C…" I strummed the chords slowly as he told me each one. "You gotta' strum it quicker, mam' like this. One and two and one and two." He shook his hand in a quick motion and I emulated his air-strummed pattern, while quietly warbling a few lines. "Sing it like you mean it, mam!" He belted it out the same as he had in class, not caring about the looks we were receiving from passing students. Ignoring the shrugs and slowing gaits of the more curious students, I let go and matched his volume. Both of us were too lost to care where we were or who was watching.

"I'll keep working on this one, thank you," I said. Then I switched to an E chord and began belting out another song with him singing along. "Who's the artist?" he asked, jolting me to realise he hadn't heard Hound Dog yet.

"A duo called Lieber and Stoller wrote them. Big Momma Thornton recorded it though, and you eventually," I blurted out not thinking. *It couldn't hurt him to know, right?*

"Me? It's different. I like it."

"You've gotta record it," I said. "It's one of my favourites I learned of yours. Taught myself it actually and added a thing in the instrumental." I played a run-down on the E string to the chord and back up to the A." He nodded along.

"You really think so, mam'?" he asked.

"I know so, you're going to be great, but you have to believe it," I said. "Don't let anybody, not a bully, not a teacher, not a record-producer, not no one tell you otherwise." I paused. "How old are you?"

"Thirteen, Mam'." Our eyes met and I shivered, realising the enormity of this conversation. *I'm talking to Elvis, "the King" of Rock n Roll* – he just didn't know it yet.

Thinking back to when I was thirteen and how much I floundered not knowing what I could do or be in life, I wondered what would have been different for me with a little bit of encouragement or even a skerrick of belief in me from the people around me. This kid already had a dream and the talent, and I was making damn sure he had the belief he needed to be who the world needed. "It's your destiny, I promise you."

"I'm gon' be late to class, man!" he said as a second bell sounded.

He unlocked his locker and I handed him back the guitar. He gently placed it in there and slammed the door.

"Wait!" I called, as he picked up his books and started to run towards a nearby room. He stopped and I handed him the note. "Next time anyone gives you reason to doubt yourself, read this."

He quickly stuffed it into his pocket. "Thank you, mam'," he said then disappeared beyond a classroom door, leaving the corridor sparce but for me, my blurring eyes and my gaping mouth.

In a mere blink of those teary eyes, I found myself standing in front of that record stand, holding the Stanley Brothers record and the note, wondering if everything that had just happened was even real. I stuffed the note into my pocket, paid for the record and left.

On the way home, I googled the song to have a listen, to find the Elvis Presley song listed above the original. I clicked and began to listen. As the now familiar song faded, I began to scroll to the comments.

"Such a waste," someone had written. *Harsh.*

"He could've been someone great. RIP." *He was though, wasn't he?*

It was when I expanded the description box under the video that my heart stopped.

"At 13, a young Elvis Presley sang this song for his middle school music teacher, in front of his whole class. The teacher who dismissed his talent as amateur and gave him a C for 8th Grade music, remains to this day anonymous. A bright and gifted child, it was ironically Elvis' only 'failed' subject.' He went on to record this on his debut album, along with the song, 'Hound Dog', a song rumoured to have heard from a mystery woman who showed up at his school the same day. By the time of his graduation, the hit record sky-rocketed to no. 1. Attempt after attempt at recording follow-up hits, Elvis Presley died from an overdose 16th August 1977. He was forty-two."

Tears poured down my face as read those last twelve words, as I realised what I had done. I knew the theory of altering history existed, but that only happened in movies, right? What did those characters do? One thing I knew for sure was I needed to try at least to fix what I'd just broken in history.

Skipping the pouring of my nightly bottle of Jack, I headed straight for the record player, placed the vinyl down and lowered the needle, praying it would skip again.

When it did, I let it go, relieved and soon I was back at that classroom door, holding the note. Tears were pouring again as I stood listening to the picking and that crushed velvet voice. Seeing all I needed to see, I turned away from the door and headed for his locker. I slipped the note through the grill in his locker and crept down the hall to a spot behind a drinking fountain. I watched as the boy soon showed up at his locker, opened it and quickly put his guitar away, and pulled out his books for the next class. He only had enough time to slam his locker shut and secure it with the combination lock when his bullies showed up and the pummelling began.

"Be strong, you'll get through this," I whispered, though I knew he couldn't hear me say it. It didn't matter. I hoped the note wasn't too much of an interference, just enough to get him through the next few years… decades… hits. He collapsed to the ground, with his books crashing around him and the boys scattered as the bell sounded. Hanging his head, Elvis crawled around on knees gathering his books and rose to his feet. He violently palmed at his eyes, wiping away tears and headed towards the classroom, leaving a familiar wad of paper on the ground. I wondered if I should pick it up and slide it back through the grill again, but before I made the move, a girl sprinted past, books tucked under her arms – *late for class*, I guessed. I shrugged just thankful I hadn't been seen.

She stopped suddenly when she neared his locker, bent down to pick up the note, unfolded it, read it and stuffed it into the pocket of her plaid pinafore. She briskly continued her way, disappearing through the same doors Elvis Presley had only moments before.

I blinked away tears from my blurred eyes and found myself back at that thrift store, standing in front of the same stand holding the Stanley Brothers record and the note. *Should I put it back?*

Something told me I needed to buy it, even if just as a lesson about meddling with History. I took it home, slotted it into a shelf next to the first Elvis record in my collection. "Hound Dog" I read pulling that record out and placing it on the player. I lowered the needle, praying I'd done enough to fix time.

Home Sweet Home
Meg Irwin

The big house I rented was being sold and I didn't want to move. I loved my daily walk to work through vibrant bushland that changed with the seasons.

When I was running late, there was a street I could use as a short-cut. Over the years, I had come to know its residents. There was the magpie woman on whose nature strip, magpies - I presume she fed them - strode like landlords. There was an elderly man, who may not have been much older than me, but had been made old by grief for a wife who had died eleven years earlier. He memorialised her with tagged trees in his garden; acer and oak trees and sweet-scented climbing roses. There was a fat-armed woman who played her guitar and sang in her front yard, and a man who rolled up his shed door and shared his power tools with mates.

There was a round-bodied young woman, too. On hot nights, she sat on her front step with her bare legs splayed out and her smooth arms exposed to the cool air. She had a young child who ran about unsteadily on the grass. Whenever I passed in summer she had a toddler and by the third year, I wondered at her vitality, with 'three under four', as they say. Yet, she always threw back her bobbing curls and smiled at me. She possessed a bright and most attractive energy.

It was on that street, in front of this woman's house, on the morning after I'd heard I must move, that I saw the small blue 'for sale' sign. I had recently received a small inheritance and this was a very small house. I wondered if I might have enough to buy it outright and, at last, get off the rental treadmill.

I rang the agent, inspected the house and made an offer which was accepted, all on that same day. I moved in just 30 days later.

Everything had been generously prepared. The carpets had been steam cleaned, the gas and electricity had been checked, and all sorts of useful household items had been left for me, from brooms to rakes to an ironing board. There were even garden beds full of ripe vegetables.

I ate the vegetables and planted more. Everything grew so well! "Your grass," remarked the man who did the mowing for most of the street, "grows the fastest of anyone's." The grass grew faster than he could come. I was away for a couple of weeks and he came only just before I returned. My house-proud neighbour met me on arrival. "It got up to here", he said balefully, indicating his waist.

This neighbour had lived in his house for several decades and he enjoyed regaling newcomers with the street's history. My attention would wander during his accounts, but it always snapped back when he talked about my place.

"I think your house had the longest continuous resident," he said, "Mrs Curnick, from the time it was built. She must have been there more than fifty years. It was sad to have it empty after that. We were very glad when you moved in."

"Did it get rented out then?" I asked.

"No," he said sadly, "it stood empty for four years, then her son finally sold it. That was to you."

"Who was the woman with all the babies then?", I asked.

"The last youngsters we had in the street were ours – about 30 years ago. Mrs Curnick had her son. He'd be in his forties now. Joanna in number 9, and Maria further up, had kids about that time too – they'd all be in their forties."

This was from a man who was always working in his front yard, and whose house faced mine! How could he have missed the woman I had seen for three summers with all her babies　?

Modern house titles don't list all the past owners anymore, but I did a search. Indeed, the Curnicks had been the only owners. Still, that didn't prove the house hadn't been rented.

Our town is small and one night I glanced into a pub window and saw the real estate agent who'd sold me my house. He recognised me and gestured "Come in", patting a chair that was vacant beside him.

Everyone in the bar was male, but not our town's typical macho types. They were talking, facing each other, holding each other's gaze. They were dressed well. My real estate agent was wearing his suit, the pale blue one I'd seen before, and it came to me suddenly, that he was gay. His manner and current company confirmed it. I wondered how I'd missed it in all our interactions   .

I don't   often like real estate agents, but our dealings during the sale had been positive. He'd helped me with recommendations for tradespeople, communicated promptly with the owner, and done everything I'd asked.

So, though I wouldn't have with a straight man, I felt comfortable to go in and have a couple of drinks with him.

He didn't ask how the house was going. He said only that I must be very happy there. It was true, but it struck me that he intentionally closed down the topic.

We talked about the town, people we knew, how we felt about our jobs, until, finally, I asked him, "Who lived in my house just before I moved in?"

He had had quite a bit to drink by then, and I saw his eyes bulge a little. "Well, there was no one for a few years", he said.

"But I saw…", I began.

His suit jacket hung over the back of his chair and he checked an involuntarily movement to pick it up. He was a lean man, long faced, with an aquiline nose, and short-cropped hair. Like him, I had drunk a bit too much, but as I looked at his face, I was reminded unequivocally of Leonard Nimoy's Dr Spock. It was the ears.

I looked harder. "You mean…?" I asked.

He didn't have to say any more - now I understood. I'm not sure what made him tell me the rest.

"Yes", he said. "You must have seen Meredith Curnick and her son. She was so happy when he was born. She was so pleased with her little boy. It was the happiest time of her life. She returned to it often. I think she chose you for her house, that's why she showed herself to you. That's why you had to buy it."

"You realise that sounds crazy?"

"I just realise it means time isn't what most people think it is," he said. "But I also know you don't think the way other people do ."

"But what about the son? Was he dragged back to being a toddler every time she went back?"

"Yes, and he hated it when he was a teenager. At that time, he said he'd rather have himself or his mother dead than keep on going through it. That only made it worse. She always wanted the happy times."

"So, does she still come with him to my house? Don't I see her anymore?"

"You don't see her, but that's because she's gone from this realm now. That's why her son could sell the house, which, as you saw, he was in a rush to do."

I let that all sink in. Then I asked, "How come you know about this?"

"I'm the same age as her son. We were at school together and," he paused, then added quietly, "we are both 'arguartees' – or maybe you're more familiar with the term, 'goblins', which is the pejorative name for us."

Should I be frightened? I wondered. Were the men surrounding me not gay, but goblins? Why would I trust what a real estate agent told me ?

But I said, "Let me buy you another drink ."

Draco Fictus Claudiani

Michael Sidwell

"Marcus!" Augustus called, sandals clacking on the smooth stone floor.

Marcus looked up from a vellum-strewn desk. Augustus was stooped with age, his head wreathed with white-whisp hair, the remnant laurels of much younger days. His dark eyes were still glitter-sharp beneath his bald pate.

"What is it, old friend? I didn't know you were about this day."

"Ah, a surprise visit, I know." Augustus spread his withered hands. "The Legion has returned with some great commotion, bearing some great prize – a fabled treasure of old, or so reports say."

"What treasure?"

"I do not know. We must go see for ourselves. Come to the Forum, where it is being displayed – presented for the governor's eye before being carried on, city by city, towards Rome."

"Mysterious indeed, that it be paraded the length of The Empire."

The two left Marcus' *domus* together and joined the flow of traffic – all headed to the great Forum-square.

"Father!"

Marcus glanced to his left. His son Caius joined them, breathless, excitement alight in his eyes. At sixteen-years-old, he was taller than both men. With the sun-streaked, dark blonde hair of his mother, Caius stood in deep contrast to the stocky darkness of his father.

"Have you heard?"

"Yes." Marcus nodded to his son. "Some prize, some commotion-"

"Claudianus has returned with his Legion, and he carries the skin of a *dragon* with him!"

"A dragon?" Augustus cast a suspicious eye towards the boy.

"Yes, the skin of a vast serpent, some eighty-two cubits in length." Caius splayed his arms out, as if measuring the size, not that he could ever come close to it. "He brought it from the palace of some tribal king who claimed his ancestors slew it."

"Interesting," Augustus murmured. "We shall see, then, we shall see."

The streets were packed, more crowded than any of the men had ever seen. The rich, carried in palanquins, or mounted, even those standing, were all well-dressed in bright and expensive colours. They pressed shoulder to shoulder, or flank, with the poor in ragged and plain tunics, and sandals worn from long use. The noise was near deafening.

Animals brayed, people babbled, yelled and called, sang and cheered. The stink was near eyewatering; sweat, dung, spillage, and the florid scents worn by those who could afford them.

"Make way, move aside, move aside!" Augustus called with the booming voice of one used to command. He shouldered through bodies, a fierce position for one so stooped and aged, but none called out against the old man's authority. Marcus and Caius were swept along in his wake.

They nudged, squeezed and pushed through to the crowded Forum.

Legionaries formed neat ranks around the once-open Forum yard, They were a human wall of rigid discipline, straight, square and tall. Red tunics, crested helmets and bright, polished armour. Rectangle shields, thunder-bolt crossed, and iron-tipped hastae held forth at attention.

The Legatus legionis, Canus Cornelius Claudianus, full-armoured with gilded, muscle-relief breastplate – that his own portly body beneath could never match – stood proudly within the enclosure of men. With him was the Governor, Flavius Lucullus, in his richly-dyed indigo tunic, over-laid with scarlet toga. Grey bearded and regal nosed, Flavius drank up the attention and his place of importance, strutting and preening.

And there, on the foot-worn flagstones of the great square, stretched the skin of the dragon. It was gigantic, easily more than eighty cubits in length and at least another six or so wide. It was dark and wrinkled, a mottled grey-brown. At the sides were flaps of what might be the skin of legs, dozens of them, a fringe ranging the entire length of the body. But there were no claws or feet, and no head or tail. Simply a great, long creature, shaped like some sort of centipede, though not chitinous nor segmented – though the skin or hide seemed to lie together in large sections.

Caius craned forward, trying to see more clearly. "What do you think?"

Marcus shrugged. "Who could tell from here? It looks ancient, like some worn-out rug."

"I'd like a closer look," Augustus mumbled, "for I do not believe its veracity."

"And why not?" Caius asked without turning his gaze from the sprawling skin.

"It is not such as I recall," Augustus shook his head slowly. "No, you see... there are joins in the hides. It has been stitched together from other creatures, from elephants most like. There are no scales, nor marks of attachment, no teeth, no claws, no head. And those flaps? Are they the suggestion of legs? They are surely cut from- "

"It has been told that those parts were taken by the inhabitants to use for the arms of their kings." Caius frowned, his eyes catching those lines the old man spoke of.

"And who told this?" Augustus waved a dismissive hand. "Anyway, what a handy excuse. Though I would- "

"What do you mean as you *recall*, Augustus?" Marcus cut in.

"But the dimensions seem correct," Caius spoke over his father. "Atticus told me that Pliny himself recorded the existence of dragons in the east as quite a natural fact. Indeed, Pliny details their battles with elephants. You see, they lower themselves from the trees and coil-"

"Lucius Atticus is a fool, his much-vaunted education in Athens notwithstanding." Marcus placed a hand on his son's shoulder. "Now, pay attention to Augustus. His wisdom surely exceeds our own and, most definitely, that of a pompous and wine-sotted wastrel."

"Wine." Augustus cleared his throat, a dry hum. "I have seen enough and these crowds exhaust me. Our good Legate Claudianus has been taken for a fool by whatever *Raj* sold or gifted him that fraud, and will surely find some embarrassment when he eventually presents it to Rome. Come, I want wine. This dust has dried my mouth, and this rabble is a pain in my ears and an assault on my senses."

It was harder to leave the square than to get to it, fighting against the insurgent tide of gawking people milling and shoving. Finally they emerged from the crowd, people thinning like the trees that stand scattered at the edge of any forest, and meandered along now-quiet streets.

"I don't feel like going home yet." Augustus turned from the *cardo maximus,* the main north-south road, to veer up a thinner side-street. "We'll find a *popina* and buy our wine there; it'll make for a change, especially now it is all so quiet – look, not even a mangy hound to seen."

The shop front was vacant but for an elderly woman, the owner, either unable or uninterested in seeing the skin of *a glorious dragon brought from the Great Raj of the Indus.* The scowl faded from her lips with the clack of silver denarii on her rough, wooden table and the call for wine – of her better quality.

The three settled about the small table and poured pale, amber liquid from a ceramic jug into baked clay cups; it was a little sour and Marcus grimaced, "Watered down too."

Augustus shook his head. "Ah, my boy, I have drunk far worse than this in my time."

"Yes," Marcus ventured, "but that doesn't mean I need smile fondly on those memories. Now, old friend, those words still haunt my mind. What did you mean by *'not as I recall'* when you came to regard this so-called dragon hide?"

"Ah, yes." Augustus took another sip, his eyes fixed upon the liquid within his cup "It was in my nineteenth year, my second in service to the Empire. I marched in the Fifteenth Legion Infantry, under Bruccius. This was before the true trouble with Carthage began. We were forging a headway into those river valleys, west of the Aegyptus, in those lands of the *Troglodyti*. We met a resisting force on the banks of the river we named Segundus, at that time, for our survey maps. I do not recall what it might be named now.

"They were a primitive band with no discipline, and we made short work of them. Between us and the auxiliary archers, they were done. There was no need for Tranio's cavalry cohort, much to his disgust and fury –"

Marcus laughed quietly.

"Ah, he was a buffoon." Augustus waved his hand. "Ignorant and arrogant, like most *Equites*, with no just cause to be so… as are so many men with ego that outstrips worth."

Augustus took another drink, longer this time, and stared far away into his cup. "I don't know whether it was the battle that stirred it… I cannot guess… but as the dust cleared and we reformed, it was sighted by the archers on the right flank.

"It undulated up the river course, a dark and shiny thing… a serpent of length similar to that of the fraud Claudianus presents. Broad and gleaming, its head was a hideous thing, like a snake, and yet not… a fish perhaps, or some mix of the two, with a gaping mouth and a beard of drooping bristles. It was scaled all over, also like a fish, with fins, instead of hands, that… lurched from its sides to propel it through the water –"

"You saw this *thing*?" Caius stared, aghast, his eyes wide with awe and yet still holding some shroud of disbelief.

"I did, by Juppiter Tonans, *Thundering Jove*, I saw the beast with these two eyes, and will swear it upon any *oath* you care to call. It came up the river, and the archers ran – their commander had been given the order to fire, and their arrows simply bounced off it. If anything at all, it only made the beast swim faster, right at them. They fled in panic, even under the shadow of execution. Most were never to be seen again."

"Cowards…" Caius murmured.

"Perhaps," Augustus said with a nod, "but I was almost the same. I cannot explain the terror of that thing, the unreal awe, as if standing in some sun-baked, waking nightmare. The undulations, the shimmer of its scales like rainbows in the black of night. Vast, unnatural. It hissed or rumbled, and we were commanded into the *testudo*, the tortoise formation We would take the creature head on – where arrows might glance from its scaly hide, the strong-arm thrust of hastae would surely not.

"But the beast sank beneath the waters, and the river flowed unbroken. We waited. A scout was sent forth to spy the way, and he called back that he saw nothing. He waded further, deeper, and... vanished... pulled down, out of sight... and then it rose again. a great, churning fountain with the roar of an ocean storm... and rushed us.

"I swear to you, my heart stopped when that monster reared. It seemed to blot out the sun, and when it came down, the shockwave alone broke our formation. Some of us were knocked clean over...

"But Tranio finally had his moment to shine, and called forth his glorious charge – for honour, for Valerian and the Imperial might of Rome – but his battle-lust was smashed away in a sweep of the monster's tail. It curled up, out and came down... again, the ground shook with that impact; I felt it in my knees, a jar up my spine and into my shoulders and neck... we were twelve stadia away from the thing... and the cries of broken men and horses... was... horrific. Some of the most awful sounds I have ever heard... not even the men, and the death-sounds we make, but the way a dying horse will scream... that sound... hundreds of them... bashed, broken, maimed... their pain so much louder than that of men... the neighs, the screeches... I remember the man beside me vomited; he gripped my arm and called for his mother...

"And then, the creature came upon us... that vast, heaving bulk – and the terror it cast...A league in length and more in height, I would have sworn, though it was not...

"We'd reformed. Shields were locked, hastae pushed forth, but it hit us like a tidal wave. Its mouth could swallow a man whole, and it swallowed many. Its coiling tail smote across us and completely shattered the ranks."

Augustus' palm slammed on the tabletop. Caius and Marcus, both fixed in rapt awe, jumped in their seats. "Men were broken into pieces. We were routed, and the retreat horns sounded. We fled, but there was no order in it. Thank all the gods, it broke off pursuit, loathe to roam too far from the river's edge.

"We did not let our guard down though, when we reassembled a half-league from the Segundus, in case the monster made some move to creep upon us, or perhaps even another of its kind lurked about. Guards were set to keep watch. Scouts reported that it had turned and glutted itself upon the splintered dead, and then coiled upon the bank as if to sun itself, like some monstrous adder.

"We had lost at least two-thousand men in that attack, and most likely more. Almost half the Legion… destroyed. Now, we had no cavalry left, and there was no artillery or other heavy means to slay the thing. Our command was at a loss in what to do.

"It was one of the auxiliaries, an African, that offered the idea – a tactic he claimed his people used to dispose of such monsters in the lands further south – of poisoning a horse and leading it to the beast, so that that monster might devour the bait and die. Of course, it was argued that we should mount a second attack while it slept, or even await the arrival of more soldiers and the machines that Commidus' Eighteenth Legion carried, some three days behind us. Rams and ballistae could then be turned against it, but it was finally decided, by time constraints, that the poison was the best of plans – even if only to try while we waited.

"So, it was done. They loaded a horse with hemlock and nightshade, and I could not tell you if other, darker substances were used, nor even where any of these things came from. What it couldn't or wouldn't eat, they tied about it in bales and doused them in blood so as to hide any scent and also to further enrage the monster. The horse was blindfolded too, and its muzzle painted in blood, to hide the serpent-smell and to increase its own fear, that it might fly into the monster's face… and then it was beaten forth, straight at the thing, which promptly caught and ate it in two bites…"

Augustus shuddered, and his gaze rose to move from Caius' pale features to the heavy-lined, sorrow-filled eyes of Marcus. "I will never forget the sickening scream, the crunch of bones, and the way that monster gurgled as it devoured the hapless horse…

"But it worked. We heard the serpent all through that following night, coughing, gagging, retching. It bellowed and roared as if the earth was opening up, and writhed in the river, a Titan's death, sending waves and water-spouts rising…

"And we huddled around fires, going in groups to gather wood, standing side by side with posted sentries, an extra watch even though uncalled for, for there was no sleep to be had, not with that cacophony. It was more than terrifying… I still hear the sounds sometimes at night, when the wind lifts and the clouds hide the moon…

"It became quiet as the first pink glow lit the east and, as the sun fully rose, we formed up, bleary eyed and exhausted. We crept forward. It lay there, curled as if in sleep, shining dark in the morning sun. It seemed to drink the light rather than reflect it... arrows were fired and it didn't move...

"Pila were cast and still it was motionless. Eventually scouts were sent in, and it was prodded with hasta, then sword-blade, and finally slapped by hand... and found to be dead.

"We converged upon it. I remember it so clearly, so close, even now, as if my palm could run across its scales as it did then. Smooth, slick scales, ending in sharp, pointed hooks. Oily to the touch, and with a stink that clogged the nostrils, a stink like that of snakes or... crushed earwigs. Its fins were like those of some giant fish, veined and leathery, fanning out from between what appeared as tree-length fingers – with no hands or arms – in two rows, behind its head, and more near its tail. It took three men to open out those fins to their full width. It had no legs or feet. Instead, when on land, it had seemed to rise in humps and push forward like a caterpillar, rather than slither on its belly like a snake – the same strange motion it used in the water.

"Its head was gilled and toothed, with yellow eyes like those of an adder, slitted black and empty. Its teeth were as long as my hand and in six or more rows, back inside a gullet that Placus Virilis, a full cubit taller than I was at that age, could stand upright within – he was the only man that dared do so.

"No, I remember it alright, as clear now as then. That, my friends, in the Forum, is no dragon hide, but those of many elephants, or some such creatures, stitched together."

Marcus shook his head in wonder. Caius stared, blank and shaken. They had no reason to doubt the word of Augustus Vitellius Patricius, ex-Praefectus castrorum, a man they'd both known all their lives, who had served in Africa and Europe, who had risen through ranks in service and war, and was known always for his honour and honesty.

"But why is there no record of this?" Caius finally broke the heavy silence, "and where are the trophies? Surely you took trophies?"

"No." Augustus rubbed a palm over his face and breathed deeply. "It began to putrefy, as we stood about it, and released a toxin. Placus was the first to fall, then others. Many more of us died soon after. We were forced to retreat from the fumes. I was overcome, vomiting, cramping; my last memory before being awakened by a solider from the Eighteenth was coughing up what tasted like rotten fish and feeling like my throat was full of bones.

"Nothing was left of it, nothing that could or would be salvaged from that hideous, poisonous mess. There was nothing but a pile of foul, stinking sludge and oil that seeped into the sand. We could not go near it… and Commidus ignored it, right there in his sight, and would not address a single word of our report. Appius Gavius Bruccius was dead, as were all the senior officers, as they'd been first, after the scouts, to view and touch the beast up close. We'd lost hundreds more to that thing, another thousand at least, to the toxins of its corpse. It took me days to fully recover.

"The Fifteenth was disbanded but formed again years later and the survivors of the original were scattered. We were moved out among other Legions, where we would be afraid to speak of our *imagined* experience. I was promoted to Decanus, in part, I think, to buy my silence, and sent to serve in Germania.

"Documents were compiled and sent to Rome, blaming the losses on poor leadership and the overwhelming odds of Troglodyti and Aethiopi. Both Bruccius and Servius Accius Tranio were posthumously stripped of all honours and became a footnote in the histories – if even still a note at all.

"As for the monster, perhaps it rotted to nothing in the sun or was found by others and any salvageable remains carried off when the fumes and filth had faded away? But I did not see what happened thereafter. We were to dally no longer; Commidus had us march home, bearing our shame and disgrace, as well as the bodies of our commanders to face inquiry and judgement."

Marcus swirled the last wine in his cup and flicked the lees out onto the stained, tiled floor. "I have heard such stories before, told by men I have no reason to doubt, but your word I have always and will always take as truth."

Caius stroked his bare chin, as if he had the beard of some wise and ancient sage. "I must believe you too, Augustus, but I do wish you had something of it, some claw or tooth, at least."

"The only thing I have is this." Augustus raised and turned his left hand. Within the skin of his palm, was a blue-black stripe, deep-drawn, like some Gallic tattoo. "I cut myself on a spiny scale, and it left this mark, as ink within my flesh, the mark of the beast I will never forget."

The Magpie Bridge
Meg Irwin

You are a woman, neither well fed, nor well grown. You are not much more than four feet tall. The mountain behind your thatched hut rises majestically and you must clamber up and down each day for water, firewood, and oven clay. You've worked hard through all your adult years and mostly, you have lived in peaceful solitude.

But now the snow is slush at the back door of your hut. Someone has come. You do not know their intentions. Do not let your mind run to raw fear.

Someone has come and you can only blame yourself. Recently you've longed for a change in routine, an opportunity to commune with another human being. Only animals and birds come and go in rhythm with your days. You have yearned to hear another voice, to speak a human language, to feel the warmth of another human body. It has been a long time since you've had that comfort.

There's a scraping at your back door. The sun is on the way down so it might be the badger. He likes to warm himself at your hearth on these cold nights. You glance up at the window. It is not the badger. There's an upright form standing at your door.

Possibilities flood into your mind, but you've learnt that fear is not necessary with every new unknown. Stay soft and alert like a seasoned martial artist, which, perhaps, you are.

When you were six or seven, your father said, "There's nothing here to fear. Snakes, even tigers and bears, prefer to stay away. It's only men who are dangerous." You remember wondering at that. Was your protective father not also a man?

Over the years, the dangers have proved to be illness, injury, or, in some years, starvation. Once, when you were still young, hunters came. They hurt you, but they stayed only briefly and never spoke a word to you. You healed your damaged flesh with herbs and your own earthed energy. There were no scars. But then you agreed that it was good to be wary of men.

There's another shuffle outside. Will you fling the door open and say, "Welcome!" Will you open it a crack and ask, "What is it you want?" You are small, and here is someone much larger, someone who could easily push your door open if they wanted to.

Now a voice comes, soft and tentative; a human voice, someone like you. You hurry to open the door.

He falls at your feet. It's not obeisance. He has fainted. His skin is searingly white. Blood pours from a gash in his neck. This man is dying in your hut. You close the door. You are revolted by the smell. Till now, the only blood you've smelled has been your own. You have never killed your animal companions.

You try your herbs and spider's webs, but nothing stems the flow of blood pumping out onto your floor, this man's face so pale against the expanding pool of redness.

You are shocked to see the face of your father. But it cannot be he! Your father would be an old man. This man is much younger.

Outside you hear wings flapping. Though it is late in the evening, the vultures are gathering. They will take him when he has passed. You will keep him here a little longer, while he lives. You will watch him and let him remind you of your father.

To you, your father is like a dream. You were thirteen, just old enough to survive alone, when he disappeared. Though you searched hard and long, you found no sign of what had happened. You only knew that he was gone.

You remember your early childhood as a kind of paradise. You, your mother, and your father lived in a house in the village. Your parents grew vegetables for market. Water and sunshine were plentiful, and the vegetables grew large and tasty. Your father had a broad grin, especially for you, his little daughter. He always carried a hoe on one shoulder. He'd throw you up onto the other and take you with him to the fields. Sometimes you rode to market with him in the oxcart. He and the ox both smelt of hay and rich earth. In summer, you ran, bare-legged, to paddle in the stream. In autumn, you lay in the golden fields under vast cerulean skies. Red persimmons hung on the bare tree branches, inducing the cooling sun to ripen them. In winter, you sledded on the ice or made snowballs with the other village children. Food was plentiful, even in winter, when your mother's pickles were delicious with rice.

Then came the day when your mother was to bring you a new sister. Everyone in the village could see it would be another girl. But, instead, your mother died in the hut, and so did your sister. At six years old, you heard the women keening and were introduced to the realm of suffering. You mother was buried with the small bundle beside her. The ox died soon after. Then came two disastrous growing seasons. Occupying troops were moving through the country, raiding villages, forcing men into their army, and taking girls and women to their own country for the use of men.

Your father left his home village with a heavy heart. He took you to the foothills to hide. Together you built a stone cottage and planted a small garden. You gathered anything else from the mountain. You always accompanied your father. You learnt everything he knew.

You are examining the face of the stranger on your floor. You say a prayer for him. You cannot stem the blood. Outside is only snow and darkness.

You prepare some ink. You begin to copy the lines of this face, so the drawings can remind you of your father. You set up a lamp and wonder at yourself as you work, not cleaning up the blood yet, just trying to make the right lines. Doing this feels to you like an expression of love for your father or so you tell yourself so you don't feel cruel, an expression of respect for this stranger. You work into the night, trying to capture that face.

Then, you wake up. You are still sitting, but you have dropped the brush. Near the inert body of the stranger, you perceive a light, not dazzling, but like the gentle candlelight inside the lanterns that floated in the river at village festivals. Above the prone man, there's a figure. She looks like a gentlewoman, or the goddess of mercy, with her flowing robes. She speaks to you.

"Who would you have me return to you; this stranger or your father?"

At first you want to burst out, "My father, oh please, my father!" But you stop yourself. You sense a trick. "Do you mean my father alive?" you ask.

"If you choose your father, I will return him in whatever condition he is in now. If you choose this stranger, I will return him to life," she says.

You think your father must have died, or he would have returned to you long ago. To have his dead body back, what joy would that bring? Your grief pulls at you, but you say, "I will give the stranger his life."

"Then go to bed," says the mysterious woman, "I will take care of this."

You spread out your bed in the opposite corner and go to sleep. You dream, of course, of your father. You are in his strong arms. There is the smell of earth and hay.

What would you like to happen now? What do you need to know about this young man who looks so like your father?

Perhaps it was not a sister who was born; it was a brother. When your mother died, he was taken and nursed by another village woman who brought him up, and later told him of his true parents. It has taken him many years and great trials to find you again.

Or do you prefer this?

The man you have chosen to revive is, indeed, your father. The day he disappeared, he found a magic pool that restored youth. But he fell in and regressed right back to infancy. (You've heard this tale before.) As happened with all the others, he was rescued and raised by a passing woodsman . Your father found his way back to you, instinctively returning to where he belonged.

The sun is rising as you wake. Surprisingly, you slept soundly. You wait a moment before opening your eyes. You can smell neither hay, nor blood. When you look there's no other person, alive or dead, in your hut. Everything is in its place and there is no sign that anything happened last night; except for your sketches. The lines trace out your beloved father's face.

The next evening, there is scraping outside the door. Again, it is not the badger, although he is sure to be missing his warm hearth, having to stay out there in the snow.

If you change what you do, you'll change what comes next. So, this time, you do not open the door. You just lift the latch. Again, the man who looks like your father falls into your hut. The badger scuttles in under his legs and takes his usual place next to the hearth. The man is still bleeding. Again, you can't resist trying to draw his features. You are getting practice, and tonight's pictures are a better likeness. You fall asleep and the goddess appears when you wake up. The badger gets a fright, but you were expecting her.

The man, she tells you, is indeed your father. Option two about the magic pool had been correct. She offers to return your father to you, old and near death, or possibly already dead, as he would have been, had he not fallen into the pool. Or she will return him as this younger man, who instead of being your father, will be transformed (including, presumably, genetically) into a lover-prince, who will have no recollection of his paternal relationship to you.

You have never seen your father old. The father you knew was closer to the age of this man. A helpmate and lover could be handy. But it is your father you long for. You hesitate. The goddess is impatient. Furthermore, the badger is giving her the eye, and seems ready to bite. She leaves abruptly. The man remains on your floor. But the goddess has told you now. This is your father and, oh, the love that wells up in your heart! You speak to him.

"My father, how I love and have missed you. Come every night. I will tell you stories of our life together; of our village, my mother, the animals we lived with (look, here's the grandson of the badger you knew!), our work in the fields, how we looked for the magpie bridge on that special night each year, how we built this hut."

And you begin.

Every night comes the noise at the door, then your father's log-fall entry. You draw his face and tell him stories. You try to stay awake, but always fall asleep. Each night is precious time with him. He is never conscious, but his brow and lips flicker. You are sure that he is listening and that he recognises you as his dear daughter. Every morning he is gone and you clean up the blood.

There is a wise woman, a healer, who lives on the other side of the mountain. You want to ask her if anything can stop the flow of blood from the wound. (You don't know about the Fisher King. That's a different tradition.) If you travel there you will have to miss one, even two, nights meeting with your father. You don't want to take the chance that your absence might end his visits. For now, you wait.

Right through winter you continue. You sleep during the day. There is nothing to harvest or collect. You melt ice for water and you have stores of wood and pickles.

But spring comes and the snow melts. You must go to collect water and to find food. You can no longer sleep all day. It's time to think about the woman in the mountain. You know there's a risk your father will be lost to you, but you know you cannot stay awake night and day.

When the land has fully thawed, you make your journey. You are not sure where to go, but you attend to the small animals - frogs, porcupines, and, once, an owl – who make a path for you. You find her. Freely and without conditions, she gives you herbs you've never seen before and teaches you a secret incantation to say when you use them.

Back in the hut, evening has come, and you are waiting. Wonderfully, nothing has been interrupted. Your father arrives as usual. This time you tell him of your journey to the wise woman, of your hope that his wound can be healed. You say you will be ready with the prepared herbs the next night. Then you fall asleep as usual.

When you wake up, the goddess is back. This time, instead of making her usual capricious or bogus offers, she warns you.

"If you heal your father's wound," she says, "for every year your father gains beyond the date of his properly ordained death, you will lose a year of your own life."

You don't have the necessary numbers to make the calculation. You do not know when you or your father were fated to die. Nor do you know how long ago, or even if, your father actually died. It's clear that you might die at the very moment your father revives. And it cannot be said that you don't love your life. Nor would your father want you to trade any part of your life for his.

Are the alternatives clear? Let's go through them.

First, you can go on as before, receiving your unconscious father every night. You can stay up with him as you have been doing, which will soon exhaust you. Or you can just open the door then go to bed, leaving him bleeding on your floor. What's the worth in that?

Second, you can use the herbs and incantation. If they don't work, you are in the first situation again.

Or let's say they work. You may find you are with a very old man quite close to death. This is the best option to not lose too much of your own life, but you will only have him with you for a short time. Or, if your father returns as a younger man, perhaps the age he was at the time he disappeared, you will lose many years of your life, and your father may be very angry. You may even die immediately and have no time with him at all. He will be alone to live out his years, now also grieving for you.

That night, you dream you are up in the sky, waiting to meet your father. He raises his hand in greeting from the opposite horizon. There comes a great clamour of wings, then flashes of long blue tails. Not vultures, but magpies, are arriving and massing into a great celestial bridge. Lightly, you step over them to reach your father's embrace. You understand, now, that no one we love can truly be taken from us. And you make your decision.

The Barrier of Loneliness

A L Fraser

It all happens so smoothly, so quickly, that at first you can't even be sure that anything has actually gone wrong. One moment you are outside the house – enjoying life, connecting with people. The next you are alone – trapped within four walls, too scared to move beyond the front door. Caught in self-imposed isolation for reasons beyond your understanding.

At first the house is comforting. Whatever evil is out there cannot breach this safe haven. And for days you feel safe, happy, calm. Content to live your life pottering around your small place in the world. Books, radio and television your only company, but then–

One moment, so peaceful; the next, what was now lies shattered and broken, beyond help, beyond hope–

Everything changes.

Your house becomes small – claustrophobic. But when you open the door to escape, the outside seems to grow hands that push at you like an intruder trying to overpower you, attempting to get inside your sanctuary. To get inside your head and make you live in a world full of fear and panic. You slam the door to keep the fear and panic out, only to be confined within four walls once again.

The voices are next. Whispers and murmuring in the night and behind your back. You unplug the radio and television and put them away in a cupboard in the hope the sounds will disappear. But then, to join the voices, come the shadows. You see them out of the corner of your eye. Black shapes that can only be human. No matter how hard you try, you can never catch the perpetrator.

Something is wrong but you aren't aware of it. You've been alone, separated from human contact, for nearly three weeks.

On the morning of the twentieth day of your withdrawal from the world, you rise from bed, pull on some clothes and head to the kitchen for your morning coffee. But instead of seeing the small kitchen, you see a long stretching highway, sandy and barren on either side.

Strangely, you do not feel afraid at the thought of being outside. This outside does not pressure you, beat at you or try to smother you like the rest of the world does. Calmly, you turn to find the lounge is gone. In its place sits another long stretch of highway.

You begin to walk. For twenty minutes you hike along the highway – not thinking, not remembering, just being.

While you walk, you begin to hear voices, and your happiness fades as quickly as it appeared. You thought you were leaving all that behind. Then you notice a service station, and the voices you are hearing belong to a radio that is in the garage. You start to walk faster, eager to talk to the people who are there, and you call out to the mechanic as you reach the doorway.

"Hi! Is it busy here today? The road sure is quiet."

No answer. Nothing. Not even a whisper in the wind. Just the DJ on the radio rambling on about the best place to go for a holiday.

You walk through the doorway and look around for someone. There are three cars in the workshop. Two have their bonnets up and a third is on the hoist. The power tools are all on and set up for work. No mechanic though. You see a thin line of smoke drift from the office doorway, and you realise they're on a break. That's it, they're all sitting in the office having a coffee and a smoke, making plans for their fishing trip on the weekend.

Looking in the office, you see it is empty. A cigarette lies smouldering in the ashtray, but that's the only sign of life you see. You leave the garage and go into the café. Cups of coffee sit steaming on the counter, but no one is there to drink them. Suddenly you shiver as the icy finger of the unknown runs down your spine.

You decide to continue with your journey. There is something wrong, but you don't quite know what it is yet. Before you leave the café, you grab a packet of crisps. You figure if anything is going to make a shop assistant appear, shoplifting will. However, no one yells "thief" as you walk out the door. Even the radio has become quiet.

Opening the chip packet, you start to nibble on chips as you resume your trek down the highway. Near the bottom of the packet, you discover a small round disc – one of those tokens children love to collect. You put it in your pocket.

There are no signs along this highway. It's just miles and miles of road stretching out into forever. You wonder if you'll come across a town while you walk or even another person, a lonely traveller, like yourself.

Ten minutes later you pass a courtesy phone by the side of the road. The phone doesn't grab your attention – you've passed others on this pilgrimage after all – until you're a hundred metres beyond it and it suddenly begins to ring.

At first you don't know what the sound is. And you stand still, listening to the chiming noise out in the middle of nowhere. When you realise what it is, you run back to the phone although you know courtesy phones only call out.

As you pick up the receiver, the phone begins to dial out. Presumably to connect you with the closest mechanic so he can come and fix the car you don't have. The phone rings and rings, and you know that back at the garage that tolling sound is now echoing through the buildings.

You hang up the phone and begin to walk again. A few kilometres down the road, you look up to see a large sign looming in the distance. As you move closer you read the words ANGEL FALLS 2 KM. Looking into the horizon, you can now see the outline of a small town. You try to remember if you know of this town. Then the flash of a headline MISSING ANGEL FALLS TWINS FOUND ALIVE! flickers in your mind. You begin to walk faster.

The fact that you remember reading Angel Falls is situated at the base of Angel Mountain and this land is flat means nothing since you know that there are going to be people in this town. Someone you can talk to. Someone who will be there.

The thing that is wrong – you are now aware of its presence. On the edge of your consciousness, it is becoming tangible. You can almost give it a name.

As you reach the main street of Angel Falls, you discover it is as empty as the highway. Walking around, you take in the post office, the doctor's surgery, the library. All of which should be open, going by the hours listed on the windows, but there is no one inside any of the buildings you look at.

The library door is open, and you decide to go inside and look around. As you walk through the building, you notice one of the computers downloading something from the internet, half-open books on one of the tables as though someone is studying and a cup of hot coffee on the librarian's desk. You sense someone walk up behind you, but when you turn no one is there. Unnerved, you leave the silent library.

Up the street you see a car idling in front of a boutique. The thought, *Why would a small country town even have a boutique?* runs through your mind but doesn't stay long enough for you to focus on it. You run into the shop eager to meet whoever it is. And there! You see a person at the far end of the store – in jeans and a white T-shirt – standing there staring at you as you stare at them. You smile, begin to run – so do they – then you hit the wall-length mirror at full force. Rebounding off the wall, you land and slide along the wood floor, amongst fragments of glass, for a couple of metres.

You are now aware of what is wrong. It isn't a vague idea anymore. It is a strong need that has been slowly building for the past three weeks – the need for human contact. The need that breaches the barrier of loneliness.

Feeling isolated and alone, you begin to cry. You curl up in the foetal position on the floor and sob, wondering why you allowed yourself to be cut off from everybody.

After several minutes, you get up and leave the store. You begin to walk back along the highway. It is no longer sandy and barren. Life is beginning to grow there again. On the back of the ANGEL FALLS sign, you see a new sign telling you HUMANKIND

THROUGH THE DOOR and you see the door straight ahead of you. You run to it and –

sitting up on the couch, you wonder how long you've been staring at the front door trying to get the nerve to walk outside. You know you haven't been asleep because you're still fully dressed, and the memory of the journey you've endured is still fresh in your mind, although you're not sure how real that journey was. You stand and stretch and then walk to the door. You lay your head against it and listen to the noises of the outside world calling. You put your hands in your pockets as though trying to find some courage in the bottom of them. You feel something in your pocket, and you pull out—

A small token from a chip packet.

Tree Talks

Delilah Cornwall

Khada's gift just kept on giving today.

Her gift never let them get far, not since her first dream of them all those months ago. If the Avonneir twins were out of her sight for too long, if their location ever became a question, her gift of insanity and foresight would answer right away.

Khada supposed she should be mad; after all, this whole quest had been their idea.

("Caelian's idea!" retorted a voice that sounded an awful lot like Valianne's from somewhere in her mind. Khada had to take a moment to wonder if it was really her or just one of the voices being sassy.)

It was hardly polite of them to flee from the first major battle between the united resistance forces and the imperials, especially when it had gone so well.

Instead Khada was just tired. She'd been sleeping worse than usual lately, and the thrill of the battle was gone. She could have drawn on magic to heighten herself once again, to bring back the euphoria of heightened senses and supernatural speed and strength but a lifetime of warnings about what happened when you got over reliant on those feelings kept her in check.

She made her way to the little copse of trees. She knew the

twins were huddled together in the heart of it, wrapped in the vines of a tree so ancient it had seen the old orc gods roam before the new pantheon replaced them. Those gods had met here once and argued on how to deal with the usurpers, but infighting had stopped them from reaching a conclusion and they'd parted in a whirlwind of angry words.

The trees were gorgeous. Khada still didn't know the names of most trees, her home had so few of them after all, but these were tall and proud looking. Their bark was the deepest, most beautiful brown she'd ever seen, with thick, deep green heads of leaves.

She stepped inside the copse. Sure enough, in the centre of the circle of trees was the largest and grandest of their number, and at the feet of this monarch of trees were the two figures Khada's life and dreams had revolved around for the last half a year.

Valianne sat with her back against the ruler of the copse, while Caelian lay with his head on her lap fast asleep, his eyes red and puffy from crying. Around the two of them stood the shadows of beings older than Qatuanqusta Tngri Almighty, screaming at one another in silence, a ghostly pantomime of something that had happened well outside living memory. Neither of the twins could have seen it and Khada ignored it. She'd dealt with the quarrelling gods of her own time enough to know she didn't care about the drama of gods thousands of years dead.

Valianne lifted her head at the sound of Khada's approach. Although Khada could have masked her every sound, it would have been rude to sneak up on them like that.

"Oh." Valianne said.

"Oh." Khada replied.

The two stewed there for moment in silence.

"Is he alright?" Khada finally asked, motioning with her still drawn, still bloody spear to Caelian's sleeping form.

"Caelian's fine; he just …" She trailed off as she looked down to gently tuck a few strands of errant hair back behind Caelian's ear. "He's just an idiot."

"He ran." Khada said with more heat than she expected. Apparently, she was angrier about this than she thought. "This whole thing was his idea! But he ran, and you went with him!"

Valianne's eyes narrowed dangerously. "I had to make sure that he didn't run off only to run into some errant imperial patrol and get himself killed! Anyway, I told you – all of you! I told you from day one that making sure his foolish idealistic crusade against the empire didn't get him killed is the only reason I'm here. I don't actually care if the empire conquers every planet spinning a doomed orbit around our yellow sun, but he is not allowed to die." Valianne looked down at her brother and Khada saw the tell-tale shoulder shake of incoming tears.

You can put your spear away, young warrior. If your enemies appear again, I will protect you and your friends.

Khada stared at the tree. She'd never met a tree that talked before let alone one that used telepathy. She hesitated for a moment. It could be a trick. But then if she couldn't trust a sentient tree, who could she trust? Continuing to wave her spear around was doing nothing for the conversation with Valianne. She slung the spear back over her shoulder and mentally tried to convey her thanks to the tree, though telepathy wasn't one of her gifts as far as she knew.

"Why did he run? He can fight; he's inexperienced sure but he's a talented dualist, and you are a master of esoteric magics most great wizards have never heard of. Not to mention, I was right at his side."

Valianne's mouth curled into a snarl. "Are you accusing him of something?"

"Others will; I just want to know. I didn't dream this. I saw our victory, but I didn't dream this."

Valianne snorted. "So, you're not as all-knowing as you appear? How good it is to know that even the daughter of a god can be in the dark like the rest of us sometimes."

Khada ground her teeth. "My father raped my mother to birth me. When he wasn't doting on me, he was torturing me by turning the madness and insanity he so kindly 'gifted' me up and the foresight and prophecy down. He would laugh when I would pull all my hair out or scratch my face bloody trying to pull off bugs that weren't there. Sometimes I'd try to kill people I knew because I thought they were a monster or had secretly been plotting to kill me for years. The tngri are not kind, least of all him."

Valianne stared, her startlingly blue eyes enormous. "Your mother – I – and what your father did – I didn't –" she stuttered.

"No because I don't talk about it. I don't know why I brought it up at all." Khada sat down, feeling a weight like an anvil settle itself on her shoulders. She wanted so badly to sleep, but she knew all that would come of it was another dream and no rest. If she was lucky, it would be another prophecy; those were less exhausting than the nightmares.

"I'm … sorry. Was there … I mean, wasn't there anyone around who cared about you?"

Kada felt a dagger of ice tear down her spine and pull the vertebrae out one by one. She couldn't help but lick the phantom blood around her lips. "We're not talking about this. Why did he run?"

"Because he was afraid! Why else?"

"I've seen Caelian afraid before and not run."

"Well, apparently it was different this time. Why does it matter?"

"Because if he's unreliable in a fight, I won't let him near a battlefield again. He'll only get himself or someone else killed."

"Good! That way he won't get hurt and maybe we can leave this stupid planet and go home already."

Khada was tired, but the anvil on her back threatened to break her spine and the weight of her sleepless eyes threatened to pull them from their sockets. She wished she could fight again, wished there were more imperials to kill so she could feel awake and alive again. Standing up to leave without the thrum of magic in her veins was almost more effort than she had left to give today, but this conversation was going nowhere.

Caelian was an arrogant, naïve brat who talked at people not with them. He thought he was special and smart enough to dictate the fate of the star all by himself. Valianne was sullen, moody, selfish and disinterested. Why her gift had decided they were the new most important thing in her life, she didn't know.

"Wait!"

Khada almost didn't. She almost kept walking and just left the twins where they were, unrelenting divine gift be damned. Instead, she stopped, but she didn't turn around and she said nothing. Silence reigned a little while longer. Khada, not willing to lose this game of stubbornness, sighed loudly and took another step.

"I said, wait!" Valianne cried out, losing. "Urgh, come back here."

Khada turned around.

Be patient with the moody one. She is even younger and less sure of herself than you are.

"The moody one and I are the same age, and frankly I'm sick of her attitude."

She will come around in time. You need these two just as much as they need you. You just don't realise it yet.

"I doubt that."

"Who are you talking to?" Valianne asked, looking around wildly like she was an idiot who hadn't been travelling with a mad god's daughter for the better part of a year now.

"With the tree." Khada said, slightly embarrassed that at least her half of the conversation with the tree had been out loud and she hadn't noticed. "It said I should be nice to you. Prove it right. Afterall, it's done you and Caelian the favour of providing you shelter; you shouldn't disappoint it."

"The tree. I shouldn't disappoint the tree."

"Don't you study the fundamental building blocks of existence? How is a sentient tree beyond your scope of belief?" Khada didn't mention the fact she'd never seen a talking tree until today either.

"It's not – it's just – whatever, fine! I won't disappoint the tree."

Khada sat back down and as she did so the anvil on her back was joined by its twin, so she decided to lie down herself. The elder tree's roots shifted and turned to accommodate her, and she found herself in quite a comfortable little cocoon of surprisingly soft roots, lying down but still at an angle to maintain eye contact with Valianne. "Thank you, ancient one, you're too kind."

"Yes!" Valianne said too quickly, with a nervous warble to her voice. "Thank you um, tree, friend."

The tree hummed a pleasant hum in reply and pulled the twins in a little closer, adjusting their positions just so. Valianne looked terrified, but the sleeping Caelian made a pleased little sound at the increased back support he was now getting.

Khada couldn't help but laugh at Valianne's terror. Maybe it was cruel of her but right now it was cathartic to watch her shake in fear at the kindness of a kind old tree

"Don't you –" Valianne sighed. "Look, ok fine, I'm not stupid. I know … I deserve at least a little bit of your laughter, but I grew up on a nation spread across dozens of moons with no atmosphere! We didn't exactly have a lot of trees."

"You had parks. With trees. Caelian went to them all the time." A fun little fact Khada suddenly knew.

Valianne ground her teeth. "Well, I didn't. Not since we were children."

"Too busy studying time, gravity, aetheric fusion, fission and all the other primordial forces you study, to work out how not to be afraid of trees?"

"Would you give it a rest?! Yes, that's exactly right. What use are trees to me when the knowledge I seek is far beyond stupid plant and animal life that —"

The tree gave a slightly hurt-sounding hum this time. Valianne's look of abject terror told Khada that this sound was audible to everyone this time.

"— except you, of course! You are, um, you're the best tree I know."

"It's the only sentient tree you know."

"Would you stop!"

"No. This is the most fun I've had in weeks." It was actually the most fun she'd had in years but that was too sad to admit out loud. "Thank you, old friend."

The tree hummed kindly back.

Valianne huffed and turned her eyes back to Caelian. "He would love this if he were awake. It would really speak to his foolish sense of adventure."

"Valianne, why did he run? We've been in dangerous situations before. I've seen Caelian scared but stand his ground. Why this time? I don't think it's as simple as first battle jitters."

Valianne sighed and was quiet for a long time. Eyes closed, breathing deeply.

"A complete answer to that question will take time."

Khada shrugged. "I'm not busy." She didn't say out loud that even if she was, Valianne and her sleeping brother were her entire life these days so she would have listened anyway.

Valianne sighed. She took a few more moments to compose herself and then began. "When we were children, our parents would take us to those parks whenever they weren't working. They were thrown together by the Registry just like everyone else in Reria but they genuinely seemed to love each other and us despite having no say in having either of us, let alone both of us."

"What do you mean - let alone both of you?"

"Remember we mentioned all marriages in Reria are arranged?

The organisation that handles that is called The Registry. When a citizen of Reria reaches adolescence, they are sent to The Registry; their genetic material is then harvested before they are rendered permanently infertile. Then their genes are compared to everyone else in their generation; based on who your genes match up best with, they assign you a spouse and will grow you a child. A child, singular. You'll note there are two of us."

Khada added The Registry to the list of most horrifying organisations she had ever heard of. The tree seemed to agree. "How did your parents get around that rule then?"

"They didn't. On the same day we were discovered to be twins, growing together in our vat, moments before The Registry was able to terminate one of us, there was an accident at a lab during a school excursion. Several scientists were killed; so were several children, pre-pubescent, so their genes hadn't been harvested yet. Which created … vacancies. And so, our parents were informed they were to have twins instead."

"Oh."

"Yeah. Oh. Caelian and I weren't just the only twins in all Reria; we were the only siblings, period. One child to a marriage, always, except us." Valianne ran the back of her hand gently down Caelian's cheek. "We were born together from a vat, but I came out just a few moments earlier. I took to the role of older sister well. He was always so sensitive when we were small, still is. I had plenty of practise at the role of being caring and protective."

Khada restrained a biting comment. The tree hummed warmly and proudly. Valianne blushed at the compliment. "Th-thank you," she stuttered, her eyes locked firmly on Caelian. "I had a nightmare once when we were seven. I woke up one day, and instead of being in bed next to me like he always was, Caelian was gone. I asked mum and dad where he was, but they said that I was being silly, that I didn't have a twin, that no one in Reria had any siblings. I told they were wrong and went to all our favourite places to play, all our friend's houses, all the parks, but I couldn't find him. I cried and cried until I woke up."

"Valianne, I –"

"Shut up. I'm not done. I didn't tell Caelian about the dream. I was his big sister; it was my job to look after him, and I didn't want him to worry. Then a few nights later, I woke up, and Caelian was crying and hugging me and saying he was so glad to see me. I said I hadn't gone anywhere, and he told me about a dream he'd had. The same dream. Every detail, identical."

Khada licked the blood around her lips. She'd had someone who used to look after her too, but sisters weren't supposed to do the things they did together. "Your parents …" Khada said, incredibly eager to move her mind away from her own tragedy and back to Valianne and Caelian's. "You've never mentioned them before. Only Nimah."

"Because they died."

"I figured. I'm sorry."

"Thanks."

"How did it happen?"

"We were ten. Reria is a nation of dozens of moons connected by tubes, with bubbles on the surfaces and tunnels below, orbiting a gas giant. We have no atmosphere; we use magic and magitek to create one. It's not a glamourous or prestigious task, but the Atmospheric Controller Guild is one of the most powerful political entities in the whole country. But something went wrong, some oversight or something. The atmospheric systems on half the moons malfunctioned and a viral infection from the planet got in.

"I remember how the air went bad and we all began to cough. I remember watching Altia, our same-age friend who lived next door wander and stagger out of her front door before collapsing dead in the street, blood pooling out of her mouth. No one went to help her. Her parents were dead inside. Caelian wanted to go but I stopped him. I don't know why; we were both already sick too and so were our parents.

"Eventually our parents took us into their bedroom, and all four of us crawled into their bed. Caelian and I in the centre, clinging as tightly to one another as we could, our parents either side of us, holding us tight, reaching for one another. They said it would be ok. That we would all be ok soon. I knew they were lying. Caelian cried.

"Then they died, and we didn't. We lay there forever, clutching each other, too weak and sick to move, to crawl away, to even move the arms of our parent's corpses off us. We lay there in their post-death filth, in our own filth for what felt like years before the authorities arrived, the atmospheric issues finally solved, and an inoculation found. They were sweeping for corpses; they didn't expect survivors.

"Nimah had always been one of our parents' best friends. When she heard what happened she took us both in instantly."

Khada was quiet. The tree hummed an understanding, sympathetic hum and one of its roots rose up to massage small circles into Valianne's back. She stiffened at first but then relaxed.

"Thank you, friend," she said, her voice cracking a little as she turned her face away from Khada to unsuccessfully hide the fact she was crying. "That's why he ran, Khada. Death haunts us. He runs away from it; he always has. He fills his life with politics and music and poetry and art and people and yes, duelling. But for all his victories, no duel on Reria is fatal. He's never actually had to fight for his life before - but in that battle? Death was everywhere."

Valianne looked up now, still crying but with a determination in her eyes that Khada had never seen before. "And that's why I do it. That's why I study the kind of magic I study. I am going to unlock all the secrets of this universe. Of life and death and how the planets are made, where magic comes from, what our souls are constructed of, where they come from and where they go. Once I know all of that, I am going to make sure that Caelian and I never, ever die. He runs from death. I am going to learn how to defeat it, and I am going to keep us both safe forever. That's why I'm here. Caelian has got it in his head he's going to save the star. Fine, I don't care, but he is not allowed to die before I figure out how to save him, to save us."

Khada held Valianne's gaze for a long time. There was a lot she could have said, about how there was no defeating or coming back from death, about how death was the realm of the gods best left well enough alone by mortals, and about how the same could be said of all the mysteries she had decided to dedicate her life to solving.

Instead Khada nodded. "Alright. Then I'll make sure you both live long enough to live forever. But he can't run like that again, not if he's ever actually going to save the star. We need everyone in this fight your brother has been stirring up. Despite the fact you're as untested in a fight as people come, it would take a fool to ignore how potentially dangerous you could be on a battlefield. So, work out how to keep him in the fight and I'll keep you both alive. Deal?"

Valianne looked like that was the last thing she ever expected Khada to say. Khada was a little surprised herself. The tree made a delighted sound. "I thought you hated us." Valianne said quietly.

"I don't hate you. I don't understand why my gift is so obsessed with you. My father gave me this gift; the visions it gave me are supposed to be his influence, but I haven't spoken to my father in years and we parted on bad terms. Ever since, I've had no idea how or why my gift has acted the way it has, but it's been obsessed with you ever since the first dream.

"I don't hate you, Valianne, and I don't hate Caelian. I actually think this whole mission we're on is a mission worth fighting for. I just … don't understand the why of it. I suppose that's not my place. I'm only part divine; the rest of me is mortal. No matter where a mortal comes from and which gods we worship, ours is not to know these things. But I won't let either of you die, I promise."

Valianne stared. The tree cooed. "I … when I figure it out, I could make you immortal too, but you have to promise not to die before then either. Deal?"

Khada shook her head and extracted herself from her root cocoon. "I don't want to live forever, Valianne."

"But –"

"Just accept my deal and wake him up so we can head back to camp. The others will be getting worried."

Valianne glared. Khada prepared herself for a fight, but Valianne instead looked down and shook her brother by the shoulders. "Idiot. Wake up," she snapped.

Caelian's eyes opened, slow and bleary. "Valianne?" he murmured. Khada hated how adorable he sounded. Then he saw Khada and his face got even paler. "Khada, I –"

"Don't. I'm not mad, really. Just very tired. Get up so we can get back to camp and I can collapse into another sleepless nightmare."

"Right."

Valianne and Caelian helped each other stand. "Don't run off like that again. Everyone will think you're a coward now."

"I … I know."

The tree hummed warmly. Caelian leapt about a foot in the air.

Khada smiled. "We'll visit again, I promise, ancient one. Your hospitality is beyond reproach and Caelian hasn't properly introduced himself yet."

Caelian's eyes were as enormous as Valianne's had been. "The tree –"

"Yes, it talks," answered both Khada and Valianne as one.

Pursuit

Myra Ratcliffe

Dusk faded into something of a memory as the night fell around her, and Sunwind breathed the lingering tension from her limbs.

Steam rose slowly, clinging to the inside of the mug, then rising towards the sky. She inhaled deeply before she took the first sip. It was warming, to have her fingers wrapped around the mug. She savoured its spread through her mouth, her chest, and into her stomach.

She'd had a monotonous day of travel, with one step in front of the other. And it hadn't been easy to find the right place to camp, and it was already getting dark by the time she'd arrived. There wasn't much to set up, just a bed to roll out, and a fire to light. She'd planned to sleep out, so there was no need to set up a tent. The sky promised a beautiful, clear night.

How she had needed this freedom! And how long she had waited for it. Sunwind softly congratulated herself on her patience. It hadn't been easy to get as far as she had, nor to convince her family that she was ready for this level of autonomy and responsibility. This journey had been one she had eagerly anticipated; her first one alone.

Sunwind shifted her attention to the rock that she was leaning against. She knew its coolness reached below her into the earth, deeper than her senses could reach. The surface seemed to sparkle in the light of the flickering fire she had built. It made the rock appear soft, but as she rested a hand on it, she felt that it was solid, sturdy, and unwavering. As it should be, because this rock had existed for aeons.

"It will offer you protection during the night," her brother had said, "It will guard your sleep."

That seemed to be true. The stone arched above her to form a protective alcove. It all felt like an embrace, she mused, as she savoured another mouthful of her drink.

At last, Sunwind placed her empty mug next to the remains of her dinner. As she did so, her fingers grazed the hilt of the pocket knife she'd used to prepare the meal. It was the hilt her brother had pressed into her hand before she'd left. After a moment, she tucked it into the belt at her waist. There was the protective stone, but the knife was still a small comfort.

Then she pushed the thoughts from her mind, wrapped herself in her blanket, and fell asleep.

*   *   *

Something stirred, Sunwind could feel it in her chest. It was like a whisper on her skin. Her mind pushed through fog, summoned to attention. Between one breath and the next she was awake.

She didn't know what had happened, what had disturbed her sleep. But she frowned against the darkness, for she rarely awoke without cause. So much heat radiated from the dying fire beside her that it couldn't have been all that long since she fell asleep. The night was still young.

The moment her senses turned outward, the prickle along her spine intensified, and she drew an uneasy breath. The great stone over her no longer felt welcoming; it felt threatening. With haste, she threw back her covers, and sat up sharply.

Something was here. What, Sunwind could not say, but its soft breath carried on the air, and all its focus was trained upon her. She rose before her limbs could freeze. Never before in her life had she felt the deep terror that filled her.

Before she knew what she was doing, she had pinpointed the presence. A monster, she would call it, for what else could it be? Without conscious thought, she turned and moved away from it. She began to run, fast.

Her material possessions no longer mattered. They were left behind with the dying fire, and an ancient stone that was no longer benign. She pressed onward.

It followed; the monster followed. Sunwind felt her hope unwind. The monster maintained a steady pace behind her, as a beacon of malevolent intent that she couldn't outrun.

*　　*　　*

The futility of her escape became apparent after what felt like just a few minutes. She had to use a different strategy, but she could not find one.

Then she spotted a tree ahead. It had more branches than most, and they were low ones good for climbing. She halted abruptly, skidding a little in the dirt.

As she climbed, Sunwind prayed with all her might that the monster couldn't reach her here, that it couldn't climb as well. It was circling the base of the trunk. Its attention never left her, and that made her skin itch. The longer the sensation continued, the more rapidly her heartbeat raced. She struggled to keep it still, struggled to keep her pulse quiet enough to think.

This tree was tall and had been easy to climb quickly. She thanked the practice she'd had with her siblings when they'd been kids, each daring the other higher. Back then, they'd thought they'd been brave, but they'd been reckless and stupid. So high up, they could have fallen, they could've died. But they'd never had reason then, had never felt this terrified, not like she was feeling now. Sunwind was just as high up, if not higher, than she'd ever climbed. And the ground still felt too close, too close to the monster, which was circling below.

Its shadow expanded, it covered the ground, and for a moment Sunwind thought the whispering tendrils of the shadow had come to life. Nothing seemed safe. She couldn't stay still. Eventually, the monster would reach her. She feared what it would do with her when it caught her. The monster felt empty, with gaping maws waiting for her to fall inside.

Sunwind's gaze caught on a branch of the tree next to hers. Something crazy crossed her mind. There was nothing to lose, she figured, and everything to gain. Tensing her muscles, she climbed along the branch she'd been clinging to. She balanced herself, and she ignored the moment she almost wobbled.

Sunwind caught her heart in her throat. She felt the wind below her, as it lifted her hair with an upward surge. And in that quiet moment, when the blood was rushing through her ears, she was flying.

She'd jumped.

And then she was crashing into the next tree. It should've hurt, but she clung on for life. She didn't fall.

The monster was still there. Far beneath her, at the base of the first tree. It had heard the crash, but had yet to catch on. She needed to move, and quickly.

She pulled herself up and balanced, remembering her lessons all those times with her siblings. For a brief moment, she released her heart from her throat. Then she was moving from tree to tree, again and again.

Her clothes were torn, her hair was wild, a few of her nails were bleeding, her skin was raw in places, but she didn't stop. And Sunwind was still alive. She silently prayed that she would remain so, but did not expect those prayers to be answered.

*   *   *

Sure enough, her luck refused to last. The trees started thinning. There were jumps where Sunwind didn't think she'd make it. Even though she had yet to feel the repercussions of all her physical exertion, the back of her brain was telling her she couldn't keep this up. Not forever. Not for as long as she needed to.

The monster was there, she knew, but it wasn't as close as before. She had confused it a little bit. She was no longer its sole focus. The tension no longer itched across her skin, but maybe her skin had just gone numb with cold, and she couldn't feel much of anything anymore.

And she'd run out of trees. Her throat burned as she breathed. Each inhalation and exhalation were no longer as steady in her chest.

Lack of trees meant a clearing. It meant a straighter run, with no obstacles. If Sunwind managed it before the monster caught her trail, she would gain distance. If she didn't, well - she would just have to make it.

She partially climbed, partially flung herself down. For the briefest second, she remembered those days with her siblings, and that distant laughter from a past moment filled her ears. She was repeating the moves she'd practised so long ago.

Sunwind hit the ground, positioned herself, and pressed ahead. Her throat burned, and her heart hammered.

The sky was lightening, the sun rising from the horizon visible at the edge of the plains. Wind whipped past her ears. She tucked her fingers into her palms, and made fists she couldn't feel. Her feet thundered, but she refused to feel the stinging as their skin was rubbed raw.

Sunwind knew the monster was behind her. Despair threatened to swallow her whole as its bottomless chasm yawned in this predawn light.

What futility all this was, but she couldn't look back. She couldn't stop. She would run herself to death rather than let the monster catch her.

*   *   *

The world opened up before her when the clearing made way for a cliff, and she hadn't noticed; the expansiveness had fooled her. Now she had nowhere to go. In all her running, Sunwind had driven herself into a corner. She could no longer move forwards, but she couldn't let this delay take hold. She couldn't allow herself to pause. It might set into her bones, allow the fight to drain out of her. She wouldn't get it back, not in time. The monster was coming.

Nothing Sunwind had experienced growing up had prepared her for this. She searched desperately for a means to make her final stand, to fight to the last. Her hand landed on the pocket knife tucked into her belt. Miraculously, it hadn't been lost as she'd flung herself through the trees.

The blade was sharp. She'd not used it as much as she could have, but the lack of use had saved the edge for this moment when she needed it. For all the good that it would do.

Sunwind steadied her feet on the rough, cold dirt. She evened her breathing, but didn't let it go. She couldn't let it go, couldn't lose her moment. Couldn't allow the adrenaline she was running on to subside and she had nothing left to lose.

The monster approached, hurled itself forward. Once more, Sunwind felt herself the centre of its attention, and the sensation of that focus tingled on her skin.

Sunwind saw its gleaming teeth, saw its claws – which were just as sharp as her knife, if not sharper. She watched its ears flick in the wind.

Bracing herself, she rushed forwards.

The monster seemed startled by her movement. She didn't allow herself to think about this; she had to take this opportunity.

With all her weight thrown behind her thrust, Sunwind rammed the blade into its chest where she thought the heart should be. It was hard to force it in, but at the same time, it was far too easy.

The monster watched her with large eyes. Breath escaped its maws. The warm air against her cheek ruffled her hair.

The monster didn't retaliate. Sunwind hadn't expected to live. Her mind was frozen with the shock of this sudden reprieve. She had no idea what to do next.

She could only watch as the monster settled onto its behind and its limbs relaxed. She thought she saw its lips twitch. Was that a smile? No, surely the monster wasn't capable.

She smelt the blood. Her frozen fingers tingled when she touched it, hurt from the warmth. Startled, she let go of the knife, which was still buried in the monster's chest. The blade would not be moving. She had struck a mortal blow. But death was not instant, and the monster was still alive. Shouldn't she be dying too? But she was unharmed.

Sunwind stepped back on shaky legs. Her knee collapsed beneath her weight. She landed, heavy on the hard ground. Yes, she thought, the monster could be smiling after all, but it seemed sad.

Its presence seemed lighter than it had before, with all that roiling emptiness bleeding into the ground. Nothing added up.

"Why were you chasing me?" Sunwind asked quietly, barely whispering on the breeze, as if the sound was stolen from her lips.

The monster couldn't answer, not with words. But there was a tilt of its head, and it let out a laboured sigh. "An existence so lonely," it implied.

Why had she been so terrified? What had she done? It was dying now. Right in front of her. All because of the wound that she had inflicted.

Driven into a corner, she had lashed out. Or had she driven herself rather than been driven? She couldn't be sure. She'd been spared much of the harshness of life. She'd never faced death before, and now it was right in front of her, life fading just as the day was being welcomed in.

"I'm so sorry," she breathed. "So very sorry."

"Don't be," she thought she heard it murmur as it closed its eyes.

The not-monster seemed resigned to what was happening. How could it face its own death so easily? Sunwind couldn't understand.

She tried to lift herself from the ground. She tried to reach out, to maybe feel its warmth before it was gone.

There was only a quiet stillness as this other life slowly bled out, and its startlingly strong presence in the world around her faded to nothing. Finally, when its final breath passed its lips, Sunwind was alone. The sounds of the new day were happening a world away. Had it even been a monster?

* * *

Judging by the position of the sun, a long time had passed before Sunwind managed to muster the energy to move. She had to before the guilt set in.

The monster was motionless in death, cold to touch, and, to Sunwind, not just in the temperature. When she rested her hand against the monster's great hide, something that should shine with life felt like another piece of the landscape.

She fought back tears, a reaction to the stress and the grief. With all her heart, she wished she could just walk away and forget. But no, she had to do this.

The ground was hard. She wouldn't get far with just her hands. She had to find a tool, which she did after a search – a sharp rock. The process wasn't easy, and by the time she was done, she could barely recognise herself.

The grave was too shallow, but it would have to do. She hoped no real monsters found it, hoped that this husk which had once held life would feed the plants around it.

As Sunwind walked, stumbled and crawled in the direction she guessed she'd come from, she resolved to pay more attention to the world around her. To listen. To give the universe the chance to speak. To meet it halfway, to not run without a glance backwards, and not to confront it without a thought.

She'd buried the knife with the monster, because she couldn't stand to look at it any longer. She didn't look forward to telling her brother she had lost it, but that was a problem for another day.

* * *

Sunwind's campsite had been raided by wild animals while she'd been gone. As a result, she no longer had any food, and everything was a mess. The great stone bore a fissure, which she could swear hadn't been there the day before.

Sequoia
Cameron Dale

The Chilean girl and I pull into a one-bar town on the outskirts of the Sequoia National Park. The car trip was long. The bone-aching stretch that follows feels good and full-bodied. The motel we pull into was in its prime 30 years ago. But the small children know no different as they splash in the pool shallows, their families watching on.

We check in, open the door to our room. The thick motel dust and stale cleaning fragrance is heavy on the air. We throw our bags down. She straightens her headband with both hands in the mirror. Her cheeks peek out from underneath her ripped jean-shorts. I kiss her neck three times; she turns to kiss mine. I throw her onto the bed, my hand through her hair and draw her closer.

Later we are naked, sweaty and panting. We nap until the sun begins to set.

*   *   *

My hard on wakes first, which wakes her, then I follow. She bites my lip and suddenly I'm present. We roll, tumble, huff and puff. Sucking in the thick oxygen. We lie on our backs staring at the ceiling fan as we catch our breath.

"I miss my dog," she says.

The fan makes another rotation. I sit up and put on my clothes. She runs herself a shower.

*   *   *

Smiling through a face aged like the local redwood bark, the motel owner directs us to the only edible food in town: The River View Bar and Grill.

*   *   *

One road in and out. A few odd specialty stores, all selling the same fridge magnets, huddle against the mountains and towering trees. The street is lined with pickup trucks and tourist vans that shine like a row of teeth. A town where the jaded waitress who grew up here takes its beauty for granted, and those who visit even more so, believing they can capture it in a single photograph.

*   *   *

The burger is food. The beer does its job. *Bliss*: a brunette with messy hair, a post-sex glow and a river stream smoothing jagged rocks in golden light. We drink and drink. The stream takes me away.

The bar empties. I look at her. Her dark eyes possess me, making this moment hers. Not a moment for a rambling man to take with him, but a moment she can trap in celluloid, like the films she re-watched as a teen. She draws me close and nuzzles under my arm as we are swept with the dust into the moonlight.

We trip and stumble the short distance back to the motel, keeping each other upright. The air is cool but not cold. We sneak into the spa bath, disrobing and sliding in. Mascara runs down her face; our bodies weave together like gnarled roots.

A frog, distracted by bugs in the light, hops into the frothing chlorinated water. We scramble to save it. In a frenzy of splashes, arms and legs, we lift the frog onto the pavers. Unsure of what just happened, deciding its next move, it regains its composure and blinks its big eyes.

"I miss my dog; it's been a whole day. I hope he's alright," she says.

Dripping wet, back in our room, we do the rest of the drying-off on the sheets in a tight embrace. She starts to cry. I trace her caramel LA tan lines as she weeps, and hold her until she falls asleep. I stare up at the ceiling fan once more until my eyelids become heavy.

*   *   *

We drive through towering trees older than cities, returning onto highways and through citrus plantations that cool the air. The radio plays songs from our separate pasts, briefly linking our two worlds together. My hand glides on the wind out the window. The Mini Cooper hugs the corners, as we spend our last 50 miles together.

An Eye For An Eye
Jessie Mayflower

"You'll do anything?" The demon's kind smile was betrayed by the feral gleam in his bulging yellow eyes. He stared down at her hungrily.

Mary gripped the leather-bound tome between her hands with a white-knuckled grip as she nodded from her place just outside of the pentagram. Her whole body was shaking - she knew the consequences of making a deal with a demon, but her grief outweighed her terror. "I'll do anything, as long as you bring them back."

She remembered Emma's teasing grin, Vic's indulgent smile and Liam's laughter, but her thoughts are cut off by the sound of a horn blaring, tires squealing and glass crunching. And then the silence, the god-awful deafening silence afterwards.

She hadn't attended the funeral. She couldn't bear it.

"Do you know what you're asking?" The demon asked. He looked down distastefully at the pentagram on the floor.

Mary stuttered. "I-I'm selling my soul?" She hated how uncertain she sounded.

She hated the demon's sudden booming laughter even more. "A single soul in exchange for three whole lives? Really?" The demon looked down on her. "No, I won't take your soul. That simply wouldn't do…" His bulging yellow eyes fixed on her, pupils shrinking and expanding rapidly in anticipation.

"How about this; three deaths for three lives. You can't bring back the dead without paying the price. An eye for an eye, you could say," The demon chuckled like he had just made a joke.

Mary recoiled. She had to kill people? She couldn't, she– she–

She had been ready to sell her soul to be with her friends again. Wasn't murder the same thing but with a few extra steps?

She thought about it. She thought of that night. Emma and Liam hadn't survived the initial crash, but Vic had. Vic had held Mary's hand and tried to tell her it would be alright, that help would be there soon. Vic clutched Mary's hand until the internal bleeding had finally taken him. Mary could single-handedly prevent any of that from happening.

But who…? Who would she be willing to sacrifice to save her friends?

The answer easily presented itself.

The demon had been watching her the whole time with his greedy gaze, a smile slowly curling up the corners of his lips. When Mary looked back up to meet his eyes, his mouth split in a wide grin to show off his mouth full of needle-like teeth. Her answer was written all over her face, and the demon was delighted.

Mary lifted her chin. "I'll do it."

The demon clicked his fingers, a contract appearing in a burst of flame. "Sign here." He pointed to a line at the bottom of the page.

"Do I need to sign in blood?" Mary asked hesitantly.

The demon waved his hand. "If you want to, but Biro works just as well."

Mary grabbed a pen from the top drawer of her desk and signed the contract.

All the candles around the pentagram flared. Tiny flames turned into pillars of fire before they all went out at once, and the only light remaining came from the demon's softly glowing eyes. "It's a deal."

*   *   *

The demon reappeared before her a week later as she crept back into her home in the early hours of the morning. "You've done well. Rather poetic, too. Sabotaging the brakes on his car."

Mary blinked in surprise. It honestly hadn't occurred to her. She had simply just not wanted to get her hands dirty, but she wasn't about to tell the demon that. Instead, she pasted a smile on her face. It wobbled, but the demon didn't mention it.

She didn't remember much of that night, but she did remember seeing the car that had clipped them, sending her and her friends smashing into the tree. She remembered how it turned back to investigate before peeling off into the night. She could remember everything about that car. A Honda hatchback, its silver paint job flashing in moonlight; one headlight shattered from the impact with Liam's sedan. Most importantly, she remembered the number plate. With that, Mary was able to find the driver and where he lived with his wife and small child.

Their house was quaint, an older style with weatherboard siding. There was no carport; the car was simply parked in the driveway, making Mary's job much easier. Mary distantly noted that the front had been replaced, erasing all evidence of the crash that had claimed her friend's lives. Mary did what she had to do quickly, leaving after only five minutes. Now it was only a matter of waiting for her handy work to take effect.

"I've done my part. Now, what happens?" Mary asked desperately.

The demon smiles. "Now we go back."

*   *   *

"Really? Eminem? Can you please play something else?" Vic asked.

"I am not putting on damn country music," Emma replied sternly, leaving no room for argument. Mary opened her eyes, and her breath hitched. She was sitting in the back behind Liam in the driver's seat. Emma was sitting next to her, and Vic was in the front passenger seat across from her. It didn't take Mary long to realise just what had happened.

"If you two can't decide, then I'm going to invoke my car ownership rights. Put my playlist on," Liam ordered. The two others huffed, but Emma did as she was told. Liam bobbed his head to the guitars and drums as punk rock started to play through the speakers.

Mary hardly breathed as the scene played out in front of her. A scene that for months had plagued her nightmares. She looked out of the window, and her heart raced when she saw the pair of headlights as they crested the hill, just like last time. Her whole body tensed tight as a bowstring as the Honda approached, crossing the white lines and veering into their lane, just like last time.

Everyone cried out in alarm as the Honda came dangerously close. Mary barely had a moment to wonder if the demon had lied to her when the Honda suddenly swerved out of their way, missing the front of their car by mere centimetres. Liam swore loudly. "That was- "

He was cut off as rubber squealed against asphalt. The sound of sheering metal and exploding safety glass that followed chilled everyone in the vehicle to their cores. Emma quickly cut the music, letting a heavy silence settle over the car as Liam let it roll to a stop on the side of the road. Mary's heart thudded in her chest and bile crept up her throat as she turned to look through the back windshield at the Honda. In the light of the half-moon high above them, Mary saw the way the car was wrapped around a tree on the side of the road in a breathtakingly familiar way.

Emma must have seen this too, because she gasped before commanding Liam to turn back. Liam audibly swallowed as he put the car back into gear and did a U-turn.

The closer they got to the crash, the worse it appeared. When they were only a few dozen metres from the wreck, Mary could no longer stand to look, instead choosing to focus on the back of Liam's head.

Vic spent some time in the SES, so he was the one to leave the car to check out the crashed vehicle while Emma called emergency services. It doesn't take him long to come back, eyes wide and face pale. "Three… they're all…" he can't seem to get the words out, so he stopped and simply shook his head.

Mary suddenly couldn't stand to be inside the car. She unbuckled her seatbelt with shaking fingers, threw the door open and stumbled out, nearly tripping over her own feet as she made her way to the tree line. She didn't throw up, but it was a close thing.

Mary didn't know how long she leant against a tree, tears and snot dripping down her face as Vic tried to comfort her. She only knew that it was long enough for emergency services to finally arrive on the scene. At some point, after it had become clear to the paramedics that no medical assistance was required, one of them advised them all to go home. Mary didn't remember how she got there when she blinked and realised that she was back in the car.

They pulled away from the scene with orange lights flashing

in the rear-view mirror. Mary couldn't help but wonder if she had made the right choice. She had lost an essential part of herself by trying to play God. She looked out the window at the trees rushing past in the darkness, and for a second, she swore she saw a pair of glowing yellow eyes and a smile full of needle-like teeth among the trees.

Mary couldn't agree fast enough when Vic suggested they all sleep at his house that night. As they squeezed into Vic's bed, a mass of tangled limbs under a single blanket, Mary couldn't find it in herself to regret her decision.

Moving Tower
Sha James

Alana really scared me this weekend when she started moving furniture around. This is never a good sign. The first thing she shifted, from one side of the room to the other, was my beloved cat-tower.

There is much to like about this luxurious piece of architecture. I get to survey the scene like a king perched high on his throne watching loyal subjects wait on him hand-and-foot. It has the best vantage point, strategically speaking, for springing into action at a moment's notice. I have excellent views of the street from my castle, positioned next to a long narrow window in my favourite corner of the room. It comes complete with scratch posts, hidey holes and tiers, much like a four-story penthouse apartment.

I know Alana likes it when I use the scratch-posts on my tower because she heaps praise on me when I do. "That's a *good boy*, Orlando," she says as her hand reaches out to pat me on the head – though I can't quite figure out why she gets excited when I flex my claws on the couch, carpet or furniture.

I have a pretty good life; everything a cat could want. I can come and go as I please and get fed three times a day. It used to be four but when I started putting on weight Alana decided this was too much. I must confess, I do *LOVE* my food! Dried biscuits morning and night with a serving of wet-food in between. It's not the meaty chunks I like so much but the gravy they are soaked in. Sometimes if I meow loud or long enough I score a fourth serving; assuming Alana doesn't pick me up first and turf me out the door for being annoying. When she does give in to my demands it generally comes with a lecture, "Do you realise how lucky you are, Orlando?"

To show my thanks I bring Alana gifts. Lately, there have been lots of them; rats, mice, lizards and the occasional bird. Once I brought her a prehistoric looking bug, shaped like a giant corkscrew with a single horn on the tip of its head. Alana was not impressed. I watched calmly as she donned the usual paraphernalia for dealing with unwelcome visitors and turfed the critter outside. "OMG, Orlando!" my mistress admonished as she peered over her laptop only minutes later. "That monstrosity comes from the *Hawkmoth genus*! Don't ever bring anything like that into the house again!"

Personally, I didn't understand what all the fuss was about. Nor do I understand why she has been so upset with me lately; more so than usual. Alana has resorted to yelling every time I bring live 'toys' into the house and immediately chases me out. I have to quickly pick them up in my mouth and dart through the cat-flap so that she doesn't confiscate them.

I used to be able to cuddle up next to Alana on the bed, but now she pushes me away and says I smell like a sewer. It's not my fault the neighbourhood cats chase me into the storm drain; or I have to duck for cover when the magpies give chase. Not that I mind too much. This is where mice and rats tend to live. What more is a cat to do?

"Oh no!" I thought when Alana started moving my tower again. "She's evicting me!" I quickly jumped onto my feline mansion in a state of panic and laid down to show Alana just how much it meant to me. I was afraid to get off in case she moved it to who-knows-where; the garage maybe or, heaven forbid, outside. This was getting serious. The next time Alana tried to move the tower I clawed her in the hope she would stop. Alana was furious and gave me a scolding, coupled with finger-pointing. I refused to surrender my position, pancaked on the ledge with arms wrapped round the extension in tight embrace. She can move it around the room *all* she likes but I am *not* going to get off. I was determined!

Finally, I pretended to be asleep. Alana gave up too. With a sigh, she manoeuvred the tower back to its original spot. "*Now* I can relax and really go to sleep," I thought and drifted off for real this time.

The Carnival
Rene Mountjoy-Austin

The fairgrounds were alive with colour, and lights and sounds overwhelmed her from all sides the moment she rushed through the gate. She tugged at her parent's hands as their shoes dug into the gravel, impatient to experience as much as possible.

The carnival only came for a few days each year, packed from one border of the chain-link fence to the other with rides and stalls selling food and merchandise. She had waited for weeks to finally be able to visit. Her mum and dad had patiently explained through all of her begging that both income and prior commitments limited them to one visit on the last day of the carnival.

Now that she was finally here, she was straining against the leash-like hold of her caretakers' hands, like a dog at a park. Her parents were dragged this way and that towards whatever caught the fancy of her buzzing attention span until they could contain her no longer, and the safety of her parents' warm hands slipped from her grip. With a delighted giggle, she surged forward. She ricocheted between booths; her only restraint was never taking the glittering jewellery and make-up from the prize buckets. She could hear her parents telling her not to stray too far, and she promised not to. She orbited the protective circle of her mother, all the while drawn further into the thrills of the carnival by her pastel-decorated fantasies.

The further into the grounds that they travelled, the aesthetic shifted from a simple market to the full-fledged and gloriously tacky structures of a real carnival. The smells of different food vendors' goods intermingled from the opening windows of the carts and stands that she could barely see into. Operators promised prizes and delights from the side of vibrant rides and games, and she hung back at the sight of a fluffy green frog, almost as tall as her, before hurrying along. Screams of delight as a rollercoaster car sped along the track, and behind it, a big top tent stood proud, flags waving invitingly in the wind. She grabbed her mum's wrist and pointed towards the big top, and her mum promised that they would go soon enough. Just wait, honey. She stared wistfully at the tent for a second longer before turning her attention to catching up to her dad. He had stopped in front of a boxy cart with a wheel that somewhere, a comically large pink wagon was missing.

Her dad smiled at her (his smile was all wonky, but familiarly friendly enough to make up for it) and stepped to the side to give her a better view. Cotton candy scooped into cones stood on display, pastel pink and blue clouds adding to the already magical air surrounding it. She hopped forward, standing on her toes to see into the spinning drum, pink web strung and whipped across it. A bag of the delightful substance was pushed into her hands, almost too big to hold. She shoved handfuls of the delicious sugary cloud into her mouth as she scampered away after her parents, who were already moving on from the cart. She was asked if it was good, and of course, it was. What a silly question. But she said thank you as her eyes scanned for the next target, the next game she wanted to take part in. The milk bottles proved to be tough, and the stuffed animals remained out of reach above her head. Still, the green sticky hand she managed to win was jammed into her pockets, a treasure she intended to hoard. Her black shoes were dusted brown from dirt as she scurried from one tempting attraction to the next. Once again, she could hear a warning about becoming separated, but this time she swept it to the side as unimportant.

She was offered more stuffed animals and gaming systems and physical cash by the people in black caps and sunhats running the games, but she pushed forward, resisting their temptation as more and more rides replaced the intermittent games. She jumped back from a plastic witch that let out a grainy cackle from a speaker in its mouth as she neared, then laughed off her sudden start. The witch belonged to a "haunted house" ride painted with spiders and bats and a small car on a track. There were three other rides like it, each one larger than the last. All of them were added to her list of activities to try before she left, but the innocently looming shape of the circus tent called to her. She could no longer feel the presence of her parents behind her, but all concern was quickly swept away by a whirlwind of colour and sound.

She was amazed how the small-scale rides – where the cars followed a simple track with no loops or sudden drops – could be multi-storied funhouses. She was shooed away from the line for the Ferris wheel with peeling white paint on its carriages for not having a ticket, and she stuck her tongue out and giggled before running off. The warm, bedazzled sunlight of a troublemaker's spirit flooded her tiny body from head to toe, her earlier marathon pace replaced by a fast skip. She revelled in the once overwhelming mix of sensations around her, drawing the attention of the grown-ups in the ticket booths only to run away before they could offer her an invitation. All the while, her path led her further into the carnival. She paused for a moment, then gasped in delight. She was closer to the rollercoaster than ever before. It seemed even larger up close, towering over all it surveyed as its cars sped across the track at breakneck speed, screams of joy escaping from the people sitting inside. She pointed towards the rollercoaster, the question already burning on her tongue as she spun around. Only to realise her parents weren't standing behind her. Nor were they anywhere in sight.

Her arm dropped to her side, hanging limp. She turned away from the thrill of the rollercoaster, looking around. She called out, but her voice sounded feeble, far too quiet for anyone else to hear. She tried again, louder, despite how her call and her hands shook. Where had they gone? How long had the sun been that close to the horizon? She took one step forward, then another. A staggering wander as she stared from one spot to the next, hoping her guardians would magically reappear. She moved forward, still calling out for them. Her cries were drowned out by the whirs of machinery and ecstatic screams, the dotted lights blaring brighter in her eyes since darkness had begun to settle over the fairgrounds. Now that she was no longer being charmed by the sensations around her, she realised that the earlier packed crowd had waned. Only scarce families and couples remained, enjoying themselves at a leisurely pace.

She continued forward, first at a shamble but then a run. Retracing her steps and taking unfamiliar turns in the hope of spotting familiar faces, a couple searching for their missing daughter. The earlier operators of rides that had seemed so inviting before now barely seemed to notice her as she ran past. She took another turn, driven to almost a sprint through the middle of the dirt paths between stalls. A scratchy cackle suddenly sounded at her side, and she launched herself away in shock. A yelp escaped her lips as she slipped and fell onto her hands. Through teary eyes, she recognised a wad of cotton candy in front of her, congealed and stained in the mud. Wiping her face with the back of her knuckles, smearing dirt across her face, she dragged her head around to look upwards at the plastic witch leering down at her from where it hung. She let her head fall again with a choked sob.

She was running around in circles in a panic, and she still had no idea where her parents were. Long minutes passed while she cried in frustration and fear. Forcing herself up onto her knees and then to her feet, tears continued down her cheeks as she shuffled forward with a numbness in her limbs and chest. She passed by the rollercoaster that had enticed her into losing her way, finding no joy in the dimming gleam of the winding tracks. Calliope music reached her ears, and her eyes snapped forward.

She had reached the circus.

The red and yellow canvas hoisted by poles and rope, the flags still flapping with near-violent velocity against the wind. The colours of the spectacle seemed muted now in the dim light.

Already wide eyes drooping, she wrung her fingers as one foot dragged forward in the dirt. She had wanted to visit the circus from the beginning, to see inside the massive tent. Now that she was so close, the sting of what she wanted needling through the numbness of her fear. She was moving closer before she fully realised what she was doing. Unfinished candy and crumpled popcorn buckets littered the ground as she approached the entrance of the big top. To one side, a large clown stood, covered in bright and spotted colours. She stared as he said something about her disposition, about how upset she looked. His big balloon body stood up straighter and promised to turn her frown upside down. The clown invited her into the circus, a smile emphasised by red make-up stretching to his ears as he opened one of the tent flaps. She took one step forward, peering inside. She caught a glimpse of laughing people in stacked seats. But she shook her head and backed away. Her delight with the thrills of the carnival had been dimmed by her desire to find her parents. The clown told her it would be alright, and although it was intended to soothe, she still turned away and left. She didn't look back, didn't give the circus a second chance. She held herself and kept her eyes down on her shoes.

She passed by the rollercoaster once more. She looked up to see the still-running cars rocket down a particularly large drop. At such a height, she wondered what you could see from up there. The ocean? Maybe outer space? She'd certainly be able to see her parents from such a height.

There was a squat fence across the front of the stretch of track on the ground, a barrier designed to protect outsiders from the cars speeding past until it was safe to enter or exit. She climbed the latticework of the fence, coming to stand at her full height and holding the very edge of the ticket booth's corner for support. The cylindrical shape of the fence's top pole made it difficult to balance, and she wobbled in place as her feet skidded to find purchase. Lifting her head, she searched once again from her new vantage point, now with the added extra height that almost doubled her own. No one in range looked familiar, no one she knew, that she could see by craning her neck. She twisted and leant to the side for a little more view, and one foot scraped off the barrier. She tried to regain it, but her solid footing crumbled. Her hand slipped from its hold, and then the ground was rushing up to meet her. She hit metal tracks and screamed as her wrist cracked. The clown's earlier tempting call from the circus tent became a shout to the operator whose eyes had turned away for but a moment. Split seconds passed quickly as the girl's sobs mixed tears with blood and jutted bone. The roar of the cars hit her ears. She heard the operator scream panicked profanity in the thinnest moment before a collision with her side.

The rollercoaster cars thundered across the track. There was no care for any small obstacle that opposed it, crushing them beneath its spinning metal wheels.

The air cleared. The few nearby stragglers gasped in horror, and the operator hit the emergency stop. The confusion of the rollercoaster patrons was quickly overwhelmed by the choked atmosphere that had fallen. The operator ran to find a supervisor. The patrons were herded away until no one was left to witness what had occurred.

In the near distance, the spotlights of the big top bounced off of the surface of the rollercoaster track. In the dead silence, the calliope music seemed even louder.

The little girl lay face-down and mangled, wrist still bent at an unnatural angle. No rise or fall of her chest could be found. Seconds ticked by, a steady beat alongside the steam calliope's song. All alone, nothing but the rollercoaster close by. Nobody to take a closer look. The stillness reached towards her, its empty hands settling over her like a blanket. The colour slowly bled from her body like tears through face paint, leaving nothing but shades of grey behind. The music faded out into its own rest as if pausing to regain its strength. The stillness became heavier. Then the steam calliope started up again, rising to its earlier peppiness.

Her eyes snapped open. Both hands pushed underneath her, one wrist still dripping freely, pushing herself up. She stumbled free from her place against the metal tracks, gasping air into lungs pierced by her own ribcage. Now alone, she dragged herself at a crawl in the direction of the big top. The clown had run from his post to find help. She took his place, leaning heavily against the fabric wall that sagged under her weight.

She was no longer worried about the sinking sun. She had all the time in the world to wander the carnival grounds.

A Cold Night in Paris

Randal Hammon

The wind cut to the bone on this cold winter night. The scent of fresh rain lay heavy in the streets of Paris. Sidney Molyneux felt conflicting exhilaration and trepidation as he followed his target - one Alistair Beckett - down Rue Cler, an atmospheric cobblestone street with many of the eateries and cafes the city was famous for. It's old world charm interrupted by the hum of electric scooters and people immersed in their phones. The smells of local cuisine floated in the air. Many patrons still spilled onto the sidewalk despite the lateness of the hour.

Sidney blended into the Parisian throng seamlessly as he watched his mark hurry down a side alley. Picking up the pace, Sid dashed across the street just in time to see the small, unremarkable man enter a side entrance behind a café, his long coat trailing behind him as the door shut with a metallic clang.

"Damn it," he cursed under his breath.

If he was going to catch Alistair Beckett once and for all he was going to have to go through that door. He patted the heavy outline of the Smith & Wesson thirty-eight revolver sitting in his overcoat pocket for reassurance.

The door itself was a simple metal affair with a brass nonrevolving handle with key lock. Pressing his ear to the cold metal he tried to listen through for any hint of what lay on the other side. Not a sound to be heard.

Sid was prepared for this. His toolkit was wrapped around itself to fit unobtrusively inside his overcoat. Looking around the alley to make sure he was indeed alone; he unrolled his kit at the foot of the door.

He carefully unpacked his "snake camera". Using his phone as a viewer, he carefully extended the camera under the bulky metal entrance. The picture was hard to gauge through the mild interference. Switching to night vision to get a better reading, he gradually made out a corridor that appeared to lead to some steps disappearing into static and gloom. No one in sight.

Happy his entry would be undetected, Sid unpacked from the tool kit his newest toy, the Multipick Kronos, a German made EPG or electronic pick gun. A tool with one use - to open locks.

His Multipick made short work of the lock, and the solid metal door swung open into the dark passageway. Carefully repacking and stashing his toolkit safely inside his coat once more, Sid cautiously entered what appeared to be an entrance to a cellar below the café proper. As there was no other point of entry, Sid knew that Alastair the 'custom furniture man' had gone down there. Gingerly approaching the stairs, he sighed in relief when he saw they were made of stone and not wood. *Much easier for concealing sound than some creaky wooden bannisters that screeched with every step, he thought.*

There was a soft light coming from below and what sounded like the familiarity of conversation between two friends. Sid didn't have friends. Not anymore. Taking no chances this time, Sid drew his revolver and descended the spiral steps slowly.

At the base of the stairwell there was a small antechamber leading into a central walkway. Rows upon rows of wine were stored in wooden racks on each side of the central aisle, extending from floor to ceiling in rows, like a library of wine. The smell of treated wood was unmistakeable. There was a spacious area at the far end of the cellar, just beyond the last row of wine, and that was where the light and voices were coming from.

Despite the winter cold, his palms were sweaty now. Inching down the central aisle toward the last row of wine racks, he could now see the space, purpose-built for private functions or wine tastings. There was a small bar as well as several comfortable looking sofas for patrons to relax on as they sampled the range of wines available.

At the far end, where three sofas were arranged in a U shape, sat Alastair Beckett and an unfamiliar man. Alastair sat on the right, while his companion sat directly opposite. The third sofa, still empty, raised the possibility of a third person still to arrive.

Slipping behind the last row of wine, Sid headed to the far wall and took a position where he could eavesdrop on the two people from behind a wall of Merlot. Careful to not make any noise, he withdrew his phone to record the conversation happening only metres away. But his phone, having been nearly at full charge when he left home, was now dead.

Strange, thought Sid. *Must be Alastair's doing. Soon I will be able to show them. I'll show everyone. They will be sorry they ever doubted Sidney Molyneux.*

"It has been too long, my friend; I see you are keeping well," said the stranger. The man had an unremarkable countenance. Medium height, fifty to sixty years of age in appearance wearing a tailored suit that was not distinguishable in any way. Sidney had only witnessed this kind of complete obfuscation of one's personality once before – in the very man the stranger was addressing. A couple of nobodies. It was a source of great frustration for Sidney, almost as if they were trying to be as inconspicuous as possible. More frustrating was the fact no one agreed with him.

"Nothing to see here" or "You've been spending too much time on those conspiracy forums" were common rebukes.

"Indeed, I hope your journey was pleasant," came Alastair's soft-spoken reply.

"Remarkable. I took the train from Beijing. Something I have not done in many moons. Extraordinarily little has changed from inside the train but quite a lot on the landscape outside. Have you seen the industrialisation efforts in China? Impressive to say the least."

"The industrialization of China can be felt across the planet. Why even in this room, there are many examples of such labour."

This made the stranger smile. "No doubt, with all your years in this city, I'm sure we can find something local."

"Tell me, Simon, what had you hoped would be the end result of your little experiment?" asked Alastair.

The man now identified as Simon laughed and replied, "To be fair it was such a long time ago I don't think I really had much in mind other than proving the council wrong. Always so rigid with their membership rights."

Sid's jaw dropped. He could not believe what he was hearing. Finally! This is what he had spent the last four years of his life looking for, only to be ridiculed and labelled an obsessive conspiracy theorist with delusions of a new world order.

It had cost him dearly. One by one Sidney's friends had all disappeared. Two years ago he had been arrested after a botched intel-gathering operation (breaking into Alastair's furniture shop in full camouflage fatigues and night vision goggles) where he had tripped a silent alarm. The police had not wanted to hear evidence that Alastair was part of a global cabal that controlled the world via shady dealings with elite private banking institutions.

Sid's sentence of eighteen months in a psychiatric ward had been tough. He had hundreds of hours of surveillance footage of Alastair doing what seemed like ordinary transactions, but Sid knew that some of his actions were secret codes for his henchmen to do his bidding. For example, feeding the birds in the park. Clearly a code for payment, had to be. Nothing cut more than knowing that his own footage had helped convict him. Why didn't the police believe him? In on it, obviously.

The incident that started the whole thing had happened four years ago. Newlywed and shopping for some upmarket furniture, Sid came across Alastair Beckett and his custom furniture shop. Alastair was a smallish man in his late sixties, diminutive in stature and balding. It was his complete lack of anything notable that fascinated Sidney. Sidney had always been a bit weird, however like most people he had a human presence. Sid could not say the same for Alastair.

From the minute he shook Alistair's cold, clammy hand in that cursed furniture shop, he knew this man was hiding something. Sid had always prided himself as a shrewd judge of character and this uncanny innate sense told him Alastair was not who he appeared to be.

Standing at the cash register paying for his new furniture was when it happened – an almost imperceptible blink from Alastair that resembled a bored lizard. The upward eyelid blink. For four long and lonely years his obsession with Alastair had run its course to this moment, right now, beneath the city of Paris.

"When do you think Judge will arrive?" inquired Simon.

"Should be any minute now. I sent the co-ordinates specifically for this celestial co-ordinate system." Celestial co-ordinate system? What had Sid uncovered?

Barely had the words been spoken when a blindingly-bright light flashed, almost like a camera. A reptilian creature over two metres tall in a long dark robe (space lizard kimono, thought Sid) stepped out of a two-dimensional portal of pure black. Trails of light were sucked back into the portal but not into the cellar.

Sid could feel his brain start to overload. This was more than he could have possibly imagined. Turns out "bigpharmakarma69" from the conspiracy forums was right. Reptilian space travellers were involved.

"Right, I'm here now. Let us get on with it. You may discard your forms," growled the reptilian referred to earlier as "Judge" as it proceeded to take its place on the third sofa.

Sidney watched from behind the wall of wine, shaking in equal parts excitement and fear as both Simon and Alastair stood up. They just stepped out of their human bodies, their shells dissolving into light as they did so, and then they began to rapidly alter in height and colour. Both, like Judge, were over two metres tall. Simon had yellow scales while Alastair's were a bright green. No trace of their human bodies remained.

"Have all security measures been put in place? Last thing we need is a repeat of planet Snarshsquigitch."

"Yes, Judge, I have locked the door and set off a localized lithium drain minutes ago to disable any human devices."

Locked the door? thought Sidney incredulously. *You can warp through space and your idea of security is a locked door? Maybe these space-travelling lizards have underestimated mammalian ingenuity.*

"Ok, let us begin. We are here to talk through the simian experiment. All judgements are final. For the record we have Simon in favour and Alastair against."

Judge gestured for Simon to begin.

Simon stood, took a deep breath and addressed his fellow lizards. "It has been relatively quiet until the last six-thousand solar revolutions or so. Civilizations began to appear throughout what is called "Ancient" Mesopotamia. Here we have clear demonstrations of alphabet, writing, the wheel, animal husbandry even currency."

"You forgot bronze working," said Alastair with a slight smile.

"Of course, I was just getting to that," replied Simon with what Sid assumed was an indignant look.

Sid could feel the weight of his revolver pressing into his palm. He got the gist that the world was on trial and that these three lizards were going to decide the fate of all humanity.

"As you both know, this species has tremendous capabilities, even more than our own, given proper guidance," continued Simon.

"If you measured life on earth it would equate to the size of their Empire State Building in the country of America. Humans have been around for about the size of a postage stamp at the very top of the flagpole. The sheer amount of resilience and intelligence involved is mind-boggling even for us. As my colleague mentioned, the dawn of bronze working brought about an age of tools and of course professional weaponry. This stems from deep-rooted tribalism that had been ingrained in them for hundreds of thousands of years for pure survival. Territorial, prone to irrational rage, greed – these are all part of the human story, yes, however it also shapes them into what they are and what they will be."

Alastair sat motionless watching from his side of the sofa. Like a lizard.

Simon persevered. "While I'm sure the argument will be made that humans are cruel, illogical and war thirsty, the majority are not. All of humanity's greatest atrocities can be laid at the feet of a few power-mad primates. Let us not forget we too have had many trials to get where we now are as an enlightened race. Who can forget our first planetary colony on Squarkinsis? A previously unknown pathogen wiped out the whole planet due to civilian refusal to do the bare minimum and isolate. We share many similarities with them."

"Yes, yes, wrap it up please. I've got a judgement due on the other side of this galaxy shortly," Judge interrupted gruffly.

Alastair sat motionless. *Could he sense he was being watched? Could this reptile be onto me?* thought Sidney in silent terror. No movement.

"Of course, Judge," Simon continued. "I would like to posit that recently I became aware of something called the shopping trolley theory."

"Sounds thrilling," sighed Judge.

Ignoring the tone, Simon persisted. "The shopping trolley theory is a social contract that has no reward save doing what is right. It proposes would a human return a shopping trolley to its bay if there was no one watching. There is no benefit to doing so; there is no law against not doing it. It is just a measure of decency among humans."

Simon appeared to smile; Sid wasn't sure as he had never seen a bipedal lizard man smile before.

"I have conducted a quite simple experiment based on the shopping trolley theory and am happy to report a figure of ninety-two percent did in fact return their shopping trolley to the bay when they thought no one was watching. This was done over several solar revolutions using many different locations and a hundred thousand subjects. Those physically unable were excluded of course. This tells me the primates are predominately good creatures." He paused for effect.

"In closing, I think eradicating them is a grave mistake. Sure, many of their technological advances are pure accidents, as is a lot of their major history, but that's the beauty of humanity. It's an intense chaotic mess of wonder and fear flipflopping across the galaxy with no brakes or clear direction. The human spirit is a thing of sheer brilliance - who are we to douse those flames? Also they have dogs."

"What?" asked Judge.

"Domesticated canines, Judge, they provide excellent companionship for any human. Supremely loyal and selfless beings that bring pure joy to millions of humans," said Simon.

"Anything else?"

"No, Judge, I'm done." With that, Simon took his seat upon the sofa.

Sidney couldn't believe it. The entire human race boiled down to that? It dawned on him what he was going to have to do. The task of saving all of mankind and its achievements was a heavy mantle but one Sidney was willing to assume. These freaky space lizards had to die. Here. Tonight. Like all momentous occasions in history, he was going to need to say something that could be quoted throughout history like Neil Armstrong or Julius Caesar. Something bold.

Alastair stood and faced his colleagues.

"My time here has not been as optimistic as our dear friends unfortunately. As an observer it is crucial to always stay in form. Unfortunately on one such stay, I was spotted by some locals just as I stepped out of the Rift-gate, not quite yet in human form, into what is now known as the west bank of the Nile River near Giza.

"At first they just told stories, then before I could sterilize the problem, they had involved their local ruler King Cheops. I could not just obliterate this emerging civilization so I told them to make me a tomb, thinking that would see them off. To their credit they built the Pyramids for me and I just could not be mad at them. Funny thing though, they worked those builders to an early death. It took nearly twenty solar revolutions and thirty-six thousand builders to satiate old King Cheops' desire to please me. So many died broken and misshapen. The average age of death was between thirty and thirty-five. Simply brutal."

Simon rose from his sofa with an angry snarl. "You? You're the reason for the Pyramids? Unbelievable! I will argue that it was your hubris that caused such suffering! This would never have happened if you had been more careful!"

"And I would argue all I wanted to do was watch. Old King Cheops was the power behind this, not me," came Alastair's retort. "Besides, it is still a great example of human engineering, yes?"

"Humph." Simon replied.

Alastair continued, "I can't say it got much better from here, as they began using religion to persecute fellow primates. Subjugating half of their race by force simply because they could for most of their existence. Ludicrous acts of abuse of power. Millennia of incest to keep their bloodlines "pure". Revolting. The Nazis. Insane wealth in the hands of the very few, which in turn keeps the vast majority from making any real contributions to their destiny.

"Did you know, Judge, that currently twenty-five thousand people die from starvation every single day? There are more than enough resources to prevent this, but it's just not a priority. Massive ecological damage that highly likely will do this experiment in anyway. My favourite is the vilification and persecution of homosexuals at a fervent pitch. The persecutors? Nearly always themselves closeted homosexuals. Such hypocrisy is unfortunately rife among humans. The list is endless. I have spoken to Kings,

Presidents, religious leaders, homeless people, even a deranged stalker, and it all ends the same. What is in it for me? It is so tiring. They do not deserve this beautiful rock and I want to go home."

Alastair sat on the sofa once more and gestured to Judge that he was done.

Judge stood up and removed a small object from his long robe. At first glance it looked like a mobile phone, being almost the same size and completely black with a polished stone-like appearance. Judge started to talk into it.

"Judgement YT-324556 on the plant "Earth". Population approximately eight billion. Primary occupant: Human. Judgement…" He looked at Simon. "Any last notes?"

Simon just shook his head.

"Judgement: Extermination by…" He looked at Alastair this time. "Any requests?"

Simon looked disgusted.

"You know a bunch of them believe in something called the Rapture; we could do something similar. Considering how much blood was spilled in its name, I think it is fitting. I'll send you the notes on raptures," suggested Alastair.

Now was the time for Sidney to act. He still had not come up with his clever phrase to go down in history, but it was now or never. Gingerly he gripped his revolver and darted around the wall of wine to confront these reptilian creatures. His pulse racing, he levelled his gun squarely at Alastair.

Tongue heavy like it was swollen, he heard himself say, "Grass ass is mine!"

He had meant to say either your ass is grass or your ass is mine but, in the excitement, it got muddled into this winning mix. The look of bewilderment from the space travellers let him know he had screwed it up. No matter, he would think of a better one later.

"How did you get in here? I locked the door!" Alastair said, somewhat aghast that his security had failed.

"Sidney Molyneux, I should have known. Gentlemen, Sidney and I are previously acquainted…"

Bang! The back of Alastair's skull blew out from his head. Pure shock held both Simon and Judge in place, and Sidney levelled his revolver at them both. *Bang! Splat. Bang! Bang! Splat.* All three corpses lay sprawled over the sofas with massive head wounds. No movement.

The scent and smoke of gunpowder in the climate-controlled room permeated the moment of Sidney's triumph. *I've done it! I've saved the world! They were so sure I was crazy. But here is proof. The bodies of three extra-terrestrials!* Simon ran up the stairs to the street to notify the authorities.

*   *   *

In the basement the climate control humming a bright light flashed, just like a camera. A Rift-gate opened sucking flares of light into its two-dimensional portal. Judge's body lifted from the ground and was pulled through by an invisible force, his device slipping from his hand as he went. All of his blood and brain matter eerily floated through the air into the gate.

Simultaneously Alastair's and Simon's bodies started to glow in an aura of light, getting brighter and brighter until the entire basement was bathed in light. The light was intense enough to make vision impossible if there had been anyone there to see it. Then like a flick of the switch, it disappeared. Both of Alastair and Simon's bodies now lay in human form on the sofas, blood splattered where bullets had torn through their skulls.

*   *   *

Renee Defleur of Paris Metro police looked at the casefile on her desk. One Sidney Molyneux had shot and killed two men in a Paris basement. He had a history of mental illness. He also had a history of stalking one of the victims. He had called the police himself, claiming to have saved the world from Reptile overlords.

One revolver with four spent shells still in the cylinder. One small black stone tablet. They could not find the fourth bullet. Strangely all the wine in the basement had started to smell just as if they had suffered from intense lightning strike. Not to worry, she had her confession.

"Not on my watch," was the last thing those poor souls heard according to the suspect. This was what in her line of work was called a *slam dunk*.

Hey Sarah!

Meredith Adams

"Hey Sarah, why don't you choose how old you want to be this birthday? Who knows, there may be a medical breakthrough and one day it'll come true."

So I chose a number.

*   *   *

"Those prophetic words were spoken on my thirty-second birthday a millennia ago. Sounds strange when I say it now. Millennia ago." Sarah pauses and looks at her hands resting in her lap. Her skin is still smooth. A few pale sunspots are beginning to show. Her nails are short. There is a bit of dirt under them; she's been out in the garden again.

Sarah rolled her eyes when I asked if I could interview her. But she agreed when I said I really wanted to know what life had been like for her and the other ancients when they were young.

She kept chiding me. "Don't you think it odd we all woke up at the same time?" I was so excited she agreed that I never thought about it.

"I used to think about what my grandparents had seen," Sarah continued. "I still do. They both grew up in workers huts on farms. No electricity, no running water, no inside toilet. Just a deep hole dug in the yard away from the hut. No toilet paper, only newspaper.

I couldn't live like that.

"By the time they were in their sixties, man had walked on the moon. They died the year before." Her voice fades. She looks down again, her brown eyes darting while she tries to remember something.

"It changed the world, you know," she muses quietly. Her chin rests in the palm of her hand, her elbow on the arm of an old wicker chair held together by magnetic staples.

"Windows 95," she says at last, nodding. "A front end that let everyone use the internet."

Her eyes become strangely vacant. I've seen that look before; she is lost in her thoughts again. She looks up at me when I ask my next question.

"What have I seen?" A wicked grin spreads across her face. "What haven't I seen?"

The corners of her eyes crinkle. The air around her fills with mischief. "I was between calculators and slide-rules."

"What?"

She sits grinning at me. She knows I don't know what she's talking about, and she's enjoying my discomfort. My lack of knowledge about her world seems to be a never-ending source of amusement to her.

Pushing herself up on the arms of the chair, Sarah waltzes over to her writing desk below the domed window and paws about in one of its drawers. What has she got in there that's making such a racket?

I study the furniture she has in her study. It's all made of wood or cane or other plant materials. I don't know how she's managed to hang onto it for so long. I know these materials don't last as long as she has. She has yet to answer me about how her things were stored while she was in stasis for so long. She keeps evading the question.

She lives in a Buckminster dome like the rest of us, but Sarah's house, as she prefers to call it, has a smell about it. The warm dry smell of seagrass matting on the floor. The rich tones of the wood and leather from her work desk and lounge.

These days things are molecularly reconstructed. They don't have any character, and they don't have any smell. Every dome has the same furniture, making visiting Sarah's house a treat. It's so different. The smell of Sarah's house has sparked the technicians into tweaking magnetic brain stimulators to give the same sensations.

She stands in front of me with both hands behind her back. "Which hand?" she asks.

I point to the left. Her right hand produces a tatty rectangular box. I can hardly believe that flimsy box is made out of the same stuff as her wooden desk. The lid falls off and she holds up a long thin white rectangular piece of –

"Plastic," Sarah says before I can ask. Turning it sideways, she holds it so I can see it has numbers and lines inscribed on it. The middle section slides in and out between the two outside bits.

"How do you use it?"

"Beats me. I never had to."

"So why keep it?" She shrugs and puts it in the pocket of her cardigan.

"Ok, what's in the other hand?" Sarah produces another rectangle, only this one's brown. Scratched silver letters spelling out C A S I O are printed on one side. She hands it to me.

"That's the calculator I used when I studied electronic engineering." The edges of her mouth turn down. "I couldn't get a job, wrong gender. Such an inconvenience."

"Couldn't you just change your gender if it was inconvenient?" I ask.

"No. Wasn't that easy. It involved — I keep forgetting you don't have surgery. We didn't have the global gene morphing technology you have today."

Last time I visited Sarah, she pulled up the corner of her top to show me her scar that strange pale white line over her right hip. She said she'd had her appendix removed. I don't remember that word in our anatomy studies.

"Being the wrong gender was a hassle," Sarah continued. "But I wasn't inclined to undergo gender reassignment surgery for the sake of a stupid job."

Sarah goes quiet again, contemplating what to say. Her lips move with the words that are about to come out of her mouth.

"The sum total of silicon chips in the 70s filled the bottom draw of a filling cabinet." She stops again. Her eyes become glassy and unfocused. "Today the planet is stripped of silica. There are no beaches, no gemstones; all glass was confiscated and reconfigured to feed the hunger for electronic gadgetry. Even the seas were drained. Boiled away or held in tanks to reach the sand at the bottom of the oceans — those tanks took up a lot of land and most of the gadgetry was thrown away."

She pauses again, worlds away in her own thoughts. She leans toward me over the wicker table. I can smell coffee on her breath.

"You know what I miss the most?" Her eyes blaze. "The beautiful coral reefs. Those sparkling underwater jewels. Gone. Images on postcards are all that survive of them." Her eyes mist over. "People think the images are nothing more than imagination or dreams."

I look across the study towards the fireplace. Sarah has a pile of these pictures tacked to the wall above her mantelpiece. I get up to look at the postcards more closely. Scantily-dressed people suspended in a hazy green-blue over strangely-shaped splashes of colour. Those shapes are the coral she is so fond of. But the suspended people? She assures me they are floating-in-water.

I have looked at those people on other occasions and I still cannot work out exactly how floating-in-water works. It looks like a flamboyant use of a scare commodity. But I don't say this to her.

"What else have I seen?" She echoes my question.

"The cloning of food animals, which don't live long as the animals they were cloned from, which made breeding programmes unviable. But then molecular re-configuration became possible, doing away with the need for food animals altogether."

"Yes," I chime in. "It's great! You can take anything that's lying around and make food out of it!" Sarah does not look impressed with my enthusiasm.

"3D printed organs and houses," she continues. "The thawing of the permafrost reintroducing diseases we didn't know existed. We had no resistance to them. Hence all the abandoned Buckminster Domes." She pauses, her face becoming solemn. "That was a long time ago, but the domes were made to last."

Her chair creaks as she rocks almost imperceptibly. I guess she's remembering the time of the plague. I sit opposite her again.

"Arresting the development of foetuses in the womb till they can replace someone who has died." She winces at her own comment, closing her eyes.

"What stayed the same?" I ask, trying to distract her.

"All the basic things, like life, death, being born, falling in love – The Sensation, as you call it.

"People still eat, get drunk, squabble over who owns what. We have gone back to being an agrarian society, I like that. What I don't like is the feudal attitude that has survived down through the ages." She lets out a quiet snort. "Humans haven't changed much."

"Why are all the ancients around the same age?"

"That was the age we were when the technology became available." She looks at me with gentle humour in her eyes.

"But why did they choose such old people to start with?"

Sarah laughs behind her hand. "We were guinea pigs. It was an untried technology with unknown side effects. If we died it could be written off as old age. By stopping the chromosomes from shortening with cell replication, it essentially froze our cells, preventing from them aging. It was a big step." No one wanted to compromise the already fragile human fertility with such a big unknown."

I gasped. "But what if it had gone wrong?"

"Terminal cancer is my guess," she says with a grin. "Being past reproductive age, we were considered obsolete, according to the powers that be — at the time. Our role as guinea pigs was considered our way of being productive citizens." Glee creeps into her eyes. "My cells will be the same age forever."

I am stranded between the stunning disregard for human life and Sarah's last sentence. "My cells will be the same age forever." I shiver.

"How could they be so callous?"

"Yes." she agrees.

"Our medical expertise is not –"

Sarah cuts me off. "The most significant change I've seen in my lifetime is the sun turning red."

"The sun has always been red."

"No." She shakes her head. "In my time it was yellow. The show's over for this planet. But I'd give it another twenty or thirty thousand years before the sun makes the planet inhospitable. It will be too hot to live here."

The conviction in Sarah's voice shakes me out of my shock. I look at her with new eyes. She exudes a sense of purpose I have never seen in her before. Her back is dead straight. She sits tall in her chair. Her eyes, sharp and clear, penetrate my flesh right down to my thoughts. I squirm, naked.

"The reason we were kept alive is because our collective knowledge would be useful in the future. I lived through the New Dark Ages, when libraries and data bases were destroyed and deliberately corrupted following the breakdown of technology when natural resources ran out."

Resting her chin on interlaced fingers, Sarah's gaze cut away the last of my known world. "Didn't you think it strange that biologically-redundant creatures would be kept in stasis if they wanted to preserve a species?"

Study is the only word I can get out.

"Study purposes, really? Was that our cover story?" Her voice is incredulous. She scratches her head.

My hands ache. Looking down, my fingers are gripping the arms of the chair, turning yellow from the lack of blood.

"Let me tell you, girl." She leans forward with a conspiratorial grin. "We were all chosen for our photographic memories. We read extensively and knew our subjects well. Our age was used to exploit the prevailing attitude of society at the time. 'Old people have nothing to contribute to society.'"

Holding my breath, I listen.

"We were the perfect capsules to smuggle knowledge across time."

Sarah prods me in the shoulder. "Breathe!"

The ringing in my ears almost blocks out her voice. I fall back, limp, in my chair and stare at her mutely.

"This was all planned by a group of researchers. They could see what was coming. Resources were already running out when I was your age. But the thing that scared them the most was the loss of knowledge. That would do more damage to the survival of the species than anything else."

My skin prickles and tingles. I shiver with cold as I listen. My mind screams 'she's lying', but I feel the truth of her words in every muscle.

"We had to hope that enough of the technology survived to escape the planet."

I manage a weak, "Well?"

Sarah nods. "You have technologies that will function anywhere.

Building, food, learning." She pauses for a moment, staring hard into my face. "And enough to get off the planet."

I lean forward in my chair, face in hands, elbows on knees, blood hammering. When I look up, the impish grin has returned to her face.

"What now?"

She looks at the tear-stained notes in my lap. "Is that how old you think I am? You didn't subtract the years I was in stasis." I roll my eyes even though my muscles are still trembling from shock.

"After everything you've said," I snap, "is it important?"

"It is to me."

Chicken

Cameron Dale

Every day, I walk home from the bus stop. I wave to the bus driver and he'd be on his way – the last stop for the day. Empty and sad without the dreams of school children, the bus ambled towards the sun setting over the horizon.

Crossing the paddock, I slip through the town hall fence and into the tall grass of our property. Smoke billowed from the chimney as the sky turned to pink. Roaming free next to the house the chickens flustered and flapped onto the gnarled trunks as they prepared to roost, jostling for position and tea tree branch real estate.

Always agitating the rabble, I toss my uneaten apple under the tree. The hens and roosters pick and peck. Feathers fly.

I sit and watch. Order once again falls over the property. The sun sets. I am called inside out of the cold.

*   *   *

With spy like manoeuvrability, I slink through the fence, a necessary skill one learns when you've torn flesh or cloth. My patched up public-school pants holey enough. Trudging the last metres, angst of growing few hairs anywhere, the hormones rushing through my body. The rundown cracked cream weatherboards look at me. The lump in my throat grows. I find comfort knowing, however sad they make me; the next angry wind will blow them from their last rusty nail.

I throw the apple at the tea tree, and it explodes. Staccato clucking as distraught chickens dart and weave, as the strong eat first and the weak sneak. I sit on a log as they chase each other. Chaos it is, but chaos it was yesterday and will be again, tomorrow.

A lopsided adolescent hen tries to peck a slither of apple but is chased away by her mother. The rooster eats first. Having his fill, he leaps into the dense canopy, flapping his rainbow plumage.

His brood follows, and once again, the community nests close to each other as a collective for protection – for warmth.

*   *   *

On the log again, the heavy bagful of homework I won't do contently sitting by my side. Sleeting winter rain falls on the tree canopy and my already wet uniform clings to my skin. The chickens scratch at the wet earth, uninterested in my fruit because it is worms they seek. They work together, breaking the soil, forgetting past discrepancies when food is abundant.

I smash up the apple on a rock and the lopsided hen with a crooked neck and lame wing comes towards me. She tends the ground like the others. But has grown weak as the others pilfer anything she finds.

She bites the apple, with the others distracted she comes closer to me. The others scramble over each other as a worm breaks the surface of the soil. Unselfishly before she's had her fill, yet grateful for her first feed of sweet apple, she shakes water from her feathers and clambers up to roost for the night.

*   *   *

The bus pulls away and my shoes crunch on the gravel. I've already eaten my apple. Kept the doctor at bay for another day.

I pass the hall. All that's left in the small town. The former lifeblood of community, where wives met their husbands at dances.

Burning the energy from the apple, I hop over the fence, running for my tree stump stoop where I observe the chickens at play. They form hierarchies and challenge for power. Offering them nothing of interest today, they show me no attention, apart from a quick glance.

One by one they climb and wrestle on the branches. The lopsided chicken ambles closer to me. Looks at me within my reach.

Scratches around, no longer scared of me, for the first time trusting of anything. It is in this moment I feel sad for this animal. I turn away, and go inside.

*   *   *

The bus is late to arrive, later to depart. Each stop and each student take longer to drag their spirits off the bus, hoping their bodies would follow. My foot barely touches the earth before the door slams behind me and the bus is gone.

The sun is close to bed. Striding it out, no streetlight, just the feel of gravel to grass and the moonlight to guide me home. The dew wets my socks as I trek towards the house. The bright kitchen lights – a beacon.

I hear it before I see it: frightful clucking, branches falling, and wings flapping.

I quicken my pace, heart-beating, feet bounding, I find the lopsided chicken bloodied and limp. Beating chest rising as they peck at her. She struggles to fight them off. I rush over and wave them off, blood dripping from their beaks as they dart around and scatter to the trees.

Using the last of its strength to breathe, the lopsided chicken raises its head to me. I carry her to safety, a patch of soil among roses and weeds in the yellow glow of the kitchen light.

Looking at the poor creature showered in the window light. She regains her feet, stumbles, then falls again. My thumping heart rhythmically builds my courage.

Feeling the cool axe blade against my skin, I take slow steps. I am but the savior I tell myself. Holding the bird, it doesn't struggle anymore. She doesn't wriggle or squirm and looks at me with her bloodied eyes. Feathers fall. The axe strikes the life out of the life form nature decided. Her last light flickers out, as the murderous flock sleep. The axe is wiped clean, and the stars peak through the clouds.

*   *   *

I sit on my stoop and eat my apple as the chickens go about their business as usual. Picking here and pecking there. The branches rustle in the wind and the flock nestles. The backdoor in need of oil creaks closed. The light turns off. And the tea tree sways side to side whilst we all sleep soundly.

Coming of Age

Sha James

*R*etirement was supposed to be peaceful. So far it had been anything but. *I was beginning to feel like I had been thrown on the scrap heap. It was becoming increasingly difficult to find employment in an ageist society. And there were newly emerging health problems to contend with from a body starting to show signs of wear and tear. But this was nothing compared to the shift in self-image that caught me completely unawares. I knew I could never look at myself the same way again after that fateful encounter.*

*   *   *

My existential crisis came about while innocently shopping for groceries at my favourite supermarket. I walked past a woman with two children in tow headed for the refrigerators adjoining the baked goods section. The older child was helping his mother locate items on the bakery shelves while the younger sat quietly in the shopping trolley fiddling with his fingers. He must have been about three or four years of age.

A little too big for the baby seat, I observed.

When I swung around to face the boy, he reeled back in horror. "That's a really old girl!"

I was taken aback by the child's reaction. At first, I did not know what to think. *Okay,* I conceded reluctantly. *It's official. You're now an old lady.*

But his reaction still didn't quite make sense. It was

disproportionate. Surely the child had encountered older people in his short life. Grandparents maybe, or an elderly neighbour. There were plenty of aged people in the supermarket aisles, and he did not appear upset by their presence.

I must have looked a sight for him to react that way. I knew I looked tired and drawn because I was in the early stages of grief. It had been only a matter of months since my husband's passing after an intense battle with cancer. Being his full-time carer was exhausting. As a result, I was in an acute state of burnout.

Yes, that's plausible, I reasoned. Plus, the boy clearly had a faulty filter.

Still, I could not shake the feeling that his response was unwarranted. I was upset that I had inadvertently traumatised a child, but his reaction was equally damaging to me. It was so raw and honest it cut me to the quick.

The boy's reaction was completely unexpected. And I had to admit, if only to myself, that I was at a complete loss about how to deal with it. Unable to let it go, I continued trying to process the event. He must have been expecting something altogether different when I turned around. *Yes, maybe that was it.*

You couldn't ignore the allusion to youth. I had hair down to my waist, which I refused to cut short even though it was greying. It was my life-long dream to have long hair ever since the nuns had put a bowl on my head and given me a crewcut when I first arrived at the convent at five.

It was ironic that it should be my hair that caused this particular drama. It seemed as if my hair was somehow tied to issues involving self-image. I had often heard it said that 'a woman's hair is her crowning glory.' The fact that mine was turning grey should have been irrelevant. Dying your hair silver was trending among younger women these days. And I was not about to conform to conventions about the way older people should dress or behave or style their hair. Even if it did make me look like a witch.

That's an alarming thought. I had never even considered the possibility of looking like a malevolent fairy-tale character. There was no denying it any longer. I was truly in the last phase of the triple-goddess state: Maiden, Mother and Crone.

As nightmarish as this scenario was, I had to find a way to salvage my self-esteem. I could try to inject humour into the situation and laugh it off as a bad joke. *Maybe that was best.*

I decided to put it out of my mind by shifting my focus to something else and continued shopping. My next port of call was Homewares. I was on a mission to find a replacement gift for my daughter.

Last Christmas I had had the bright idea of buying her a cutlery set and some tea towels because supplies were getting awfully low in her household. I was pleased with myself for coming up with something practical that my daughter needed. However, anticipation quickly turned to disappointment when I discovered she had purchased said items a few weeks earlier. *So much for surprise presents,* I grumbled. We agreed on a wok instead.

Just then I spied a cast-iron pot sitting on a far shelf at the back of the shop. I could not quite make it out from where I was standing. Was it a Dutch oven or a wok?

When I got close enough to inspect the item, I noticed it had three feet shaped like frogs, forming a tripod at the base. The black cast-iron pot looked like a miniature cauldron. I couldn't resist the obvious connection, given the day's events.

There it was again. Another witch reference. I was beginning to suspect something was afoot. *This can't be mere coincidence. Two inferences in one day.* It wasn't what I was looking for anyway. I needed a wok.

Later that night as I was preparing dinner, the cat came racing through the cat-flap at lightning speed. It was obvious from the way he was acting that he had something in his mouth.

When I went to investigate, ready to rescue yet another one of his live toys, I heard a strange sound which prompted the cat to let it go. The unidentified creature managed to escape into the house and disappear. *Nothing else to do but let nature take its course.* Heading back to the kitchen to finish dinner, I forgot about the unwelcome intruder.

In the early hours of the morning, I was awoken by rustling sounds in the bedroom. I had the distinct feeling there was something else in the room. It wasn't the cat because he was snuggled next to me. Too tired to investigate, I managed to fall asleep again.

The next morning when I went into the kitchen, I spied the cat stalking his previous night's prey. This time I was going to investigate and find out what it was for certain.

To my surprise, I spied a little brown frog. It kept hopping from surface to surface trying to avoid capture. Every now and then it would screech loudly at the cat. I had never seen anything like it. Such courage. Such audacity. The indignation of the little brown frog was gargantuan. It was letting me know, in no uncertain terms, that it was not impressed with being dragged from its natural habitat in the jaws of a killer.

This was no ordinary frog. I sensed it had been accosted on its way to give me a message and rudely dragged into the house.

Could it be one of my Celtic ancestors coming to visit me? They were oft known to take the form of an animal to make contact or send a message. I knew there was a Druid priest in the family tree somewhere because my Welsh grandmother said as much. But that was the only clue she gave me.

With that, I set out to discover what exactly frogs symbolise in Celtic mythology. I was pleasantly surprised to find references to medicine and healing. In particular inflammatory conditions. I had recently been diagnosed with an inflammatory bowel condition. Not uncommon among people who were aging, I was told, but uncomfortable, nevertheless.

Could this be a sign I was going to be healed? I certainly hoped so. Or was it a different kind of message? A rite of passage maybe, telling me it was time to reconnect with the Ancient Ways now that I was officially an elder.

I guess that remains to be seen. Still, it had a nice ring to it, the word "elder". Much better than witch, old crone or "old-girl."

The Models

Meredith Adams

When I first enter the dimly-lit room, a fetid smell of rotting flesh assaults my senses. My head tips back. I double over. Grasping the door frame for support, I retch green bile that burns my throat and splashes to the floor, staining the hem of my dress. Clenching my chest, I try to suppress the convulsions choking me.

Gradually the heaving subsides. I hang onto the door frame trembling. My strength abandons me as I weakly lift my head. My eyes can make no sense of the grey blurry shape moving in front of me.

It appears hunched as it jerks about in the middle of the room. Two long, pale *things* flick up and down as the blur moves. I wipe my eyes with the back of my hand. I wish I hadn't.

The pale things are arms with no life of their own. The grey blur is a man. His clothes are hanging in threads from his thin frame; his hair is white and sparse with age. His body is bent under the weight of a dead man, recumbent in a wheelbarrow. The body refuses to be moved.

The deceased's head, its mouth agape, hangs limply, crowned with a mass of unkempt hair. The white skin on its face is mottled black with decomposition and its cheeks are sunken. The eyes, rolled up into their sockets, spark another wave of nausea.

Still sagging against the door frame, I try to wipe the front of my bodice dry with a handkerchief. I hear feet shuffle behind me. I turn to see a young man in his twenties standing in the corridor. He examines the state of my dress, then peers over the top of my head into the depths of the room.

Grunting, the old man wraps his arms awkwardly around the waist of the corpse and finally hefts it from the weather-beaten barrow onto the small wooden bed in the corner of the room.

The young man's eyes widen. His composure leaves him. He starts to tremble. His hand flies to his face, grasping his mouth and nose. He bends over, retching.

Voices float up from the stairwell.

Looking back into the room, the body has been arranged neatly on the bed. My eyes, now accustomed to the dim light, see the walls of the room are blotched – not from the faded, peeling wallpaper, but from blooms of yellow and orange mould creeping over the printed flowers.

The old man now leans over the deceased, brushing its face. The black mottling is falling away. The man sweeps these off the bed into a small pan then into the wheelbarrow.

He is finished.

The foul smell intensifies as the wizened creature pushes his wheelbarrow past me. I put my hand to my face. The young man crosses himself and presses hard against the wall. I see clods of earth in the otherwise empty barrow.

A graverobber.

The deceased's face is now a dull green-white.

Fear chills summer from my veins.

A small knot of people has appeared at the top of the stairs. They too cough and gag and press themselves against the wall as the old man and his barrow creak past.

We all jump at the dull thud of the wheel hitting the first step. Its thuds are monotonous, all the way down, fading away.

A silence weighs down my limbs and settles into my bones. No one present seems to have the will to move. All we can do is watch each other through the sepia light, each an island in our own thoughts.

The town clock strikes six, breaking the spell of stillness. Now that the old man has left, the air is starting to sweeten and my courage returns.

The dim corridor is pierced by shafts of light as the sun gently falls towards evening. The party at the top of the stairs shuffle their way towards us.

Neither I nor the young man speak, but our eyes communicate the situation to the newcomers. Together, the five of us stand at the threshold of the room, staring intently at the macabre setting before us. The soft rustle of clothing and the shuffling of shoes on the hard wooden floor are the only sounds to fill our ears until a sudden train of expletives boom up the stairwell followed by clattering and banging and more swearing.

Two more people appear at the top of the stairs. One is a woman with jet black hair parted in the middle and pulled back into a tight bun. She is struggling with a large, almost triangular wooden frame. The other is a man in plaid trousers, jacket and waistcoat with an untidy shirt collar loose around his neck. He is carrying a large white rectangle and has a wooden box slung over his shoulder.

"Why didn't you book a room on the ground floor?" she snaps.

"Why didn't you do it?" he snarls back.

"Do you expect me to do everything?"

He walks in front of her as they bang and scrape their way down the hall.

He stops in front of us. The large white rectangle is a canvas. The triangle she carries is an easel.

"Well?" She waits for an answer, but he ignores her so she kicks him in the back of the legs. He grits his teeth and formally addresses us.

"Thank you all for coming!"

His face looks familiar to me; however, I am sure I have met neither him nor the woman before.

"Who's in there?" the young man asks. The familiar man looks into the room.

"Him? That's my twin brother."

A communal gasp escapes our group.

Affronted by their coarse behaviour, I pick up my skirt and start to push my way past this… *artist*. These vulgar people are not the sort of company I keep.

"Not so fast, madam. You answered the advertisement, and signed the contract I sent you."

"There was no mention of a *corpse*!" I protest.

"I said it was to be a portrait of a close relative in an intense setting. Is this situation not an intense setting? And can you not see the family resemblance?" A slyness crept into his grin.

"Why couldn't you have painted the real wake?" hisses the woman holding the easel.

The artist rolls his eyes. "This is my wife, Clavelia. She will be in the painting too, as the bereaved sister-in-law of the deceased."

Putting his canvas down, he then turns to face her. Placing his hand under her chin, he tilts Clavelia's face up towards his.

"Why?" His voice is sweetly sarcastic. "Because this will be more fun." Her eyes narrow and I wait for her to kick him in the shins.

"Now be a good wife and arrange the models for me. My brother cannot wait."

The Deathbird

Faith Dam

Cicadas buzzed on the trees and the sun shone down on the near-empty basketball court. The rhythmic thump-thump of the basketballs and the low mutters of the few students that sat outside added to the ambience.

"So, why do we have to go with a group into the forest?" Shoes scratched through the stones and the metal bench underneath us creaked. The cafeteria door swung open too hard and hit the wall behind it before squeaking shut again.

Marcus averted his eyes and lifted a hand to rub the back of his neck. "The teachers say it's for safety. That way, if someone gets injured, one can stay whilst the other runs for help."

The cold milkshake slurped through my straw, ice rattling around the mason jar. I gave a small nod. Looking across the concrete court, heat rays made it distorted, and the trees shimmered eerily as everything else stood still.

"Actually, there's more to it."

Scuffed shoes ran across the hot concrete and a cheer rose from the players. *Bang.* The basketball hit the backboard, causing the weathered pole to rattle. Spinning around where we sat, the benches groaned. A boy stood leaning against the unoccupied basketball pole on the other court, with arms crossed and dark hair covering his eyes.

Marcus tensed, his face reddening with rage. "Were you spying on us?!"

The other boy grinned. The pole let out a groan of relief as he moved off it. The jacket slung across one shoulder swished as he sauntered towards us. "No, not spying. This is a shared space. I just overheard your conversation."

Marcus' fists clenched on the table, knuckles turning white.

"What do you mean, 'there's more to it'?" I asked quietly. My interest was piqued. Marcus glared at me, mouthing, *stop encouraging him.*

"There's a creature that lives in there, in those trees."

The stones crunched as he jumped up from his seat and the bench groaned as it was thrown backwards. "Those are just stories to scare the year sevens into listening!"

"Are they?" His raised eyebrow and amused smirk implied he was enjoying this.

"What stories?" Starting to feel like I was missing out on an important conversation, I placed the mason jar on the table with a clink.

"I've heard things and word spreads quickly through this school. So, in turn, everyone has heard things."

I looked between Marcus and the other boy. Marcus' jaw was clenched. The boy still smiled as he glanced at Marcus and then winked at me.

"Would you be brave enough to venture in with me? If they're just stories, then you have nothing to be afraid of." The gentle breeze blew his dark hair across his face as he stared at me, expectantly. His eyes flickered and he was off across the basketball court.

"Hey! Wait!"

I was off before Marcus could move. As I scrambled up the hill, rocks tumbled and dust stirred through the air. My hands scraped the hard dry surface as I stumbled. Marcus had raced after me, but the other boy was there first, offering a hand to help me up.

"We shouldn't be doing this..." Marcus muttered, his shoes scraping the ground as he reached the top. "We don't have time and we're going to get caught."

As I looked back down the hill, I could tell that no one had noticed as we made our way into the trees. Or they just didn't care too much, too hot from the sun's heat and too occupied with the game.

"Caught by who? No one's going to tell and the Deathbird will probably catch us first."

We all went quiet, and Marcus and I stared at each other. "It has a name?"

"Do you have a name?" Marcus snapped.

"Dray is my name." He sounded uncertain when he said it. Like it was a new word to him.

"Is that, like, a nickname?" I asked.

He looked over his shoulder and smirked. He seemed to be full of secrets.

Looking ahead, we seemed to have reached a point of no return. The school was seen no more, shrouded from view by the tall eucalypts. If we left Dray now, we would more than likely get in trouble for doing so. The trees offered little shade, their dried leaves hanging sadly from drier branches. The heat beat down on us, but Dray didn't seem too fussed. Marcus' eyes kept skirting the area, a feeling of near panic radiating off him. Perhaps he believed more in these stories than he let on.

"Say..." Marcus jumped as Dray spoke but quickly regained himself. "...I have a bow hidden in one of these trees, I can go and grab it if you'd like."

"A bow?" I wasn't as surprised as I should have been. He seemed like the kind of guy to have such a thing, but it was still strange.

He nodded. "They're not hard to make and no one else knows it's there."

Marcus scoffed. "Yeah, go and grab your bow, perhaps it'll keep away the scary bird."

"I never said it was a bird."

No one spoke. Dray still had a smirk on his face, but he seemed dead serious. Marcus stared at Dray.

"I won't be long," Dray said. "Stay here and don't move."

The dry undergrowth crunched as he walked away. I watched as his dark hair and dark coat receded into the trees until I could see him no more, the trees swallowing him in their shade.

"Like we're going to stay here, come on." Marcus started to walk away but I didn't move. I looked to where I had last seen Dray.

"I think we should wait..." A wave of uneasiness came over me. It was too quiet.

Clenched fists turned white at Marcus' side. He clenched and unclenched them, clearly not knowing what to do. For a moment I thought he was going to keep walking, but then he turned back. "Fine, we wait, but I'm not taking the blame if we get caught."

There was rustle behind us, and the bushes moved. I half-expected the trees to be blowing in a breeze, but there was nothing. Marcus tentatively took a step forward

"Marcus!" I hissed, but he held a hand up to silence me.

"Dray, is that you?"

Please be Dray, please be Dray, please be Dray.

"Dray, this isn't funny, I'm going to walk out of here!"

A whoosh came from behind us, causing us to spin in circles trying to find the sound. Pointlessly.

"Run!" A bloodcurdling scream echoed through the trees, seeming to make them sway in the breeze. "Run!" It was Dray's voice. "Run! Get out of here!"

The noises were too much. Dray's screams, the strange rustling and bustling sounds that turned to screeches, Marcus' crashing through the bushes as he turned and ran. It all seemed to be getting darker and dizzier and darker…

"Come on!"

Marcus was back in front of me, holding out a hand. I grabbed his hand tight and stumbled after him. I stumbled and tripped too many times, not used to running through the bush.

The noises followed. The noises got louder. Louder and louder, until they became shrieks and cries. And then suddenly a little girl called out from the trees.

"Help me!" I recognised her little voice, her desperate pleas. "Help me!"

Tripping and landing hard on the ground, I couldn't get up. With eyes round, I looked around. "Maggie?! Maggie, where are you?!"

"She's not here!" Marcus reached for me again, but I scrambled away from him, forcing my shaking legs to hold me up.

"Yes, she is!" I cried. "Didn't you hear her!?"

"Help me!"

"It's coming from behind us…"

I turned, running back the way we came, running towards Dray's screams, running towards Maggie's screams, running towards the darkness.

Something swooped over us, something like a bird. A scream

echoed through the forest, a bloodcurdling screech so loud that I dropped to the ground and squeezed my eyes shut and clamped my hands desperately over my ears. But it didn't stop.

"Marcus? Marcus, where are you?!" I cried into the darkness. "Where are you?!"

But no reply came from the darkness, nothing but the creatures' cries.

More and more flew by me, stirring up the darkness into dizzying shapes. Their cries were earsplitting, mind-shattering, too awful for me to comprehend. Tears ran down my cheeks and my mouth opened in a silent scream.

The Deathbird. It was real.

I have something for you

Meg Irwin

Into him, I creep.

Tonight, the sensation that has been in his gut for a fortnight has moved right down to his rectum. There's a sudden burst of pain and a slopping sound, as something falls into his pyjama pants. God, he thinks, I've shat myself. He holds the small, hot bundle, and dashes to the bathroom. When he drops his pants and sits down there's no shit. Cradled in the flannelette, lies something pink and whole like a newborn puppy.

His life till now has been ordinary. There was primary school, high school, and a good enough family, with a mother, a father and two brothers on either side. He wasn't starved or beaten. He didn't really receive much attention at all. That meant he could do as he liked and he'd got into music. His tastes were broad and he'd taken pride in being able to hold up his end of the conversation in any record shop.

There hadn't been much in the way of girls. The first who'd stuck, he married. They bought a house in the suburbs and he mowed the lawn every Sunday. IVF hadn't worked. Perhaps they'd been too old.

He bought his flat after his wife moved on. He went to work each day, listened to his music and renovated a bit. His neighbours chatted over fences or balconies. He was on good terms with all of them, except for one couple. One day he'd found their dog dead on the concrete outside. He'd effortfully carried it upstairs to them, but they had made him take it back and leave it where he'd found it. They didn't speak to him after that. In the end, he'd buried the dog.

The darkness is not broken.

She slams on the brakes. There's a sickening crack and a dark shape falls in front of her car. In her headlights, she sees it's not a kangaroo, but a girl in a black overcoat.

She stays at a distance. The girl is screaming, pumped with adrenaline, but blessedly alive. "You're safe now. Try to breathe slowly", she calls to her, "Don't try to move yet. I'll get you some water."

This was different from work. She nursed people who'd had accidents, but at the hospital, there were protocols and colleagues. Of course, she had her first aid certificate and knew what to do. But here she came sharply to her own emotions; the relief and the terror. How easy it can be to snuff out a human life!

All night, back at home, the flash of headlights, the horrid crunch and the dark, falling body reverberated in her. She thought her victim would be reliving the same moments. She wished she could check on her, know she got home safely and had recovered alright. But that could not be. The girl had refused further help.

He lays me close.

What is this thing that, appallingly, has emerged from his body? Should he crush it? He looks at the creature. It is hairless and vulnerable, kicking its tiny legs, but not trying to stand. He has held it inside him, he realises, in a kind of gestation. He has, in a way, birthed it. Yes, crush it quickly. Monstrous! But wait, this can't be real. Now he doubts his own senses. He pokes it with his big toe. It swivels towards him and seems to seek more touch. Tentatively he cups the small creature in his hand and raises it to eye level.

It squirms and its skin is soft against his. What would it eat? It looks mammalian, mostly. Or maybe avian. Or possibly reptilian. He pulls the milk out of the fridge and finds an old eyedropper. Does he imagine it or does the creature become more active? He fills the dropper and brings it to what might be a mouth. The little creature spins around. That was the wrong orifice. Now the milk is going in. It accepts four droppers' full before it calms and seems to fall asleep. It is the middle of the night, and he too would normally be sleeping and it is work tomorrow. He washes his hands and wipes the little creature clean without waking it, then returns to bed himself. The best place for it is next to his pillow, so he will wake if it stirs.

She does not resist.

He rings her in the morning. At first, she is alarmed. It has been years since they've spoken. But, when he tells her it is about a small animal he's found, she understands. He was always an animal lover. He asks her to take it for the day if she isn't working. She's not, so she agrees. She always said you never fall out of love with anyone; it's just that people move apart. Now she will be able to see how he lives; how he is doing.

She arrives at eight, early so he can easily get to work on time. After a quick greeting, he pushes a shoebox into her hands, having already locked his door behind him. "Shall I come back at six?" she asks, bewildered by the rush.

"That would be great," he says as he flees.

When she gets home and looks in the box, she can't tell what kind of animal it is. She wonders if it has some sort of mutation. That, she thinks, would be precisely why he'd have sympathy for it. She gives it a little milk from the dropper he's provided, then places the open box on the bedside table. She has not slept since her last shift. She needs to before the next one.

She dreams of him that day, moving inside her. It is a contented dream she has sometimes. She still recalls the satisfactoriness of their physical fit. It had been a passionate relationship. How sad that lives diverge and relationships desiccate.

She awakens to the 5 pm alarm and peers into the box. The creature is gone. She looks everywhere. At last, there is nothing to do but return the empty box and explain. She is there at six and asks to come inside. He is shocked that the helpless creature has disappeared, but does not disbelieve her. She is sorry she lost something he wanted to protect. And the accident the night before is still upsetting her. They end up in bed together, just as in her dream.

I feel the heat of him.

He had thought he was beyond loneliness; that everything was sorted out. He had planned to work until his company forced him to retire. Then he'd enjoy his music and maybe do some voluntary work. But the little creature had roused something in him. He remembers the days they were trying IVF, both keen to bring another life into the world and to care for it. When she came on his request, it was as if they had never been apart. And their lovemaking had been perfect. He had lost himself in her again. Yet, he tells himself, what is done, is done. Why cause more suffering for everyone? Let her go.

She rings him three months later. He is surprised at his joy. "We need to talk," she says, "I'll be over tonight".

All are blessed.

She is forty-two, not a good age for a first birth. It will not be easy. But somehow, in bed again, they both decide to go through with it. There is some sort of miracle taking place. They are being drawn together again. They wonder if they might even resume the marriage. It all feels right.

Her confinement draws near and she is mentally prepared. He is to attend the birth, which will be at the hospital in case of complications.

The birth takes seventy-two hours. There is confusion about which way the baby is facing. She is exhausted and falls asleep at the end of it.

He holds the newborn for the first time, but what is this? It's wrapped the wrong way. It will suffocate! Quickly he unwraps it but there is no discernible head. Four limbs wobble in the air. He sees this child is no other than a grown version of what he shat out nine months earlier. It was in him and then in her, and now it is out in the world to grow some more.

It had brought them together again. He must honour that. When the doctors quietly suggest allowing it to die, he does not agree.

I have something for you.

The child grows. It learns to walk and talk, but it looks grotesque as if all sorts of cells have got muddled up together. Its father acknowledges, if only to himself, that it looks rather like a raw meatball. Of course, the child is not treated well by its peers, but that only increases its parents' love for it.

The child is prone to nightmares and often wakes up screaming.

"The others", it bellows, "all of them cast away! My sisters, my brothers, all dead!"

"It's the IVF", the mother suggests to the father one night. "The dreams are about all the failures and the cells that are discarded and die."

One day, when the child is almost an adolescent and has been bullied relentlessly for years, it appears at the school door. It brandishes a metal meat tenderiser and roars, "I have something for you!"

It avoids killing the twins and triplets. The other children lie in piles, all their faces crushed.

At home, the child tells its parents what it has done. It expects that they will protect it.

Blood drips onto the kitchen floor. The child still holds the mallet.

SPACE-BUBBLE

Sha James

*T*wo little faces looked up at me, paused in anticipation, waiting for words of wisdom to fall from my mouth. I knew I had to make the problem go away. I just didn't know how. It was written in their eyes. You're the fixer-upper grandma. You always have a solution. Please don't let us down now.

It happened almost every time we drove in the car. As soon as the engine kicked over, the children began competing for my attention. They instinctively knew how to pick the right moment to achieve full impact. The confined space amplified their voices, adding fuel to the fiery debate.

"No, I want to go first," demanded Noah.

"No, I want to go first," yelled Issy.

"My stories more important than yours," Noah argued.

"My story's important too," Issy insisted.

The children's go-to conflict about who should talk first was in full flight. They meant business. Feathers were flying. Steam escaping from their ears. It was beginning to resemble a Looney Tunes animation. The dizzy birds with stars would soon appear if I didn't do something to intervene.

"One at a time," I interrupted in a firm but gentle voice. I was trying to sound impartial.

Sometimes I suggested switching roles for the sake of fairness. "Who went first last time?" I inquired.

"Issy did," said Noah.

"Okay, then you can go first this time."

"One of the kids in my class gave me a blood-nose on Wednesday."

"That's not good," I commented with a hint of compassion in my voice. "Was it an accident?"

"Yes. We were both running to get the ball, and our heads butted when we crashed into each other."

"Are you okay now?"

"Well, it still hurts a bit, but it's much better than it was."

"Would you like me to take a look at it later?"

"Yeah, that would be good. Thanks, grandma."

Issy could restrain herself no longer. "Can I tell my story now?" she piped in.

"Yes, Issy, it's your turn to speak."

"You'll never guess what happened today," she gushed. "A butterfly landed on my lunch box while I was eating a sandwich."

"Wow, that's amazing," I replied.

"It was sooohhh beautiful, grandma. The butterfly was blue, and it had black spots on its wings and orange stripes too."

"Sounds pretty. Did you try to catch it, or did it fly away?" I inquired.

"It flew away," Issy lamented with a hint of disappointment in her voice.

"Maybe it flew off to be with its family," I offered. "That's the best place to be, even for butterflies, don't you think?"

"You're probably right, grandma, but I just wanted to catch it and put it in a jar so I could keep looking at it."

"Never mind, Issy, there will be other butterflies. Let's go inside and have a treat before dinner." Just then the car pulled up outside the house.

*   *   *

It had not escaped my attention that the amped-up rivalry between these two adorable children was fast becoming a problem. Not just for me but for the whole family. Their parents were equally at a loss about ways to resolve the escalating conflict. Whenever I would ask them for suggestions on how best to deal with the situation, they simply shrugged their shoulders and raised upturned hands in a gesture of defeat.

I guess it's up to me to find a remedy, I ruminated, as the grandchildren prattled on in the background now that the conflict had been temporarily allayed.

I had a reputation to uphold. Grandparents are fixer-uppers, aren't they? I was content to believe my grandmother possessed superpowers when I was a child. It made me feel secure. The same scenario now applied to me – I must confess, I was enjoying the illusion of being super-gran on the other side. But there were times when I felt slightly uncomfortable with the superhuman artifice.

I was a life-long crusader for truth. Anyone who knew me might say it was my political orientation. I remember when I was younger, my mother defended me after a neighbour tried to accuse me of some wrongdoing.

"Did you do it?" my mother asked in front of the neighbour.

"No," I replied in earnestness.

I was pleasantly surprised when my mother turned to my accuser and said, "I know my daughter, and she doesn't lie." It was a proud moment. I was thrilled to discover my mother believed in me and felt chuffed that I had earned a reputation for telling the truth.

I decided early on in life that it was better to get into trouble and get it over with than lie and get found out later. The consequences for lying were far worse, not to mention the guilt that twisted in the pit of your stomach and the nightmares that kept you tossing and turning all night.

My penchant for truth had become an integral part of my value system. I prided myself on being able to walk through life, holding my head up high. And it was no less important that I pass this nugget onto my family. First as a mother and now in my role as a grandmother.

If a stray toy or lolly found its way into the children's pushchair, accidentally of course, I would immediately march them back to the store and shower the checkout operator with apologies until they were thoroughly drenched.

"I found this toy in the baby's pusher. I've never seen it before so it must belong to the store. I don't know how it got there. It must have fallen off the shelf as we were passing by. My sincerest apologies. Thought I'd better return it pronto."

"That's okay, not a problem. Thank you for bringing it back. We really appreciate it."

It was better the children felt embarrassed now than end up in jail at some future date.

*   *   *

I hadn't really paid it much heed before. How the grandparent persona resembles a little white lie. Yet, despite this ruse, their superhuman mystique is recognised the world over. Grandparents are appointed guardians of childhood innocence across cultures and traditions, whether they knew it or not.

I recalled hearing about a time not long ago when there was no such thing as childhood. Children were merely young adults. Childhood is a relatively modern invention, I discovered. In medieval Europe, for instance, children were forced to labour long hours in workhouses or become chimney sweeps. And often died young as a result.

No, the benefits outweigh the subterfuge. Childhood must be protected at all costs. I rather liked being typecast as a fairy godmother waving her magic wand to make the world a better place.

These beliefs about grandparents are not surprising when you consider mothers were once regarded embodiments of the great cosmic mother. The universal mother manifesting simultaneously in multiple forms to perform her sacred tasks. The fruits bear this out.

Like their divine counterpart, overseeing nature, mothers fix everything. Mend scraped knees with a plaster. Hug you when you're sad. Wipe away tears with a tissue. Offer reassuring words of encouragement. Tease out splinters with a needle. Remove bee stings with a pair of tweezers. Kiss a sore finger to make it feel better. Stroke your forehead until you fall asleep. Yes, mothers are supernatural carers on the Earth plane.

To demonstrate their level of commitment, one need only recall how special compartments are set aside in their handbags as first aid kits and sewing boxes. When I was young, no one thought twice about mothers or grandmothers opening their bags, whipping out sewing needles and threading them to sew on a renegade button or mend a fresh tear. They were hailed as heroines. Passers-by would smile and nod their head in a gesture of approval. Or was it respect?

By the time you reach grandparent status, you've earned your divine stars and stripes. Being a grandparent is one of life's most enjoyable roles, but it comes with a different rule book. As family matriarchs, we are expected to be all-round problem solvers. At least, this was how my grandchildren viewed me. If mum and dad can't fix it, just ask grandma.

Unfortunately, the current dilemma had me completely baffled. I knew something had to change, and fast. I could feel it in my bones, the way a body feels aches and pains with the slightest change in weather as you get older. All the warning signs were there. Danger lurking in every corner. Grey clouds gathering overhead. Lately, the conflict had escalated to angry tirades, tears, shoving, and door slamming. One occasion involved fingers being jammed in a door frame.

When things got completely out of hand, the children would just stare at me with a helpless look on their tear-stained faces. Neither of them was winning. Noah got into trouble for pushing his sister too forcefully.

"I have asked her so many times to go away, but she just won't leave me alone. Why do I get into trouble all the time when I haven't done anything wrong? No one ever listens to my side of the story," Noah exclaimed with bloodshot eyes. Salty tears streamed down his cheeks.

Issy felt instantly rejected and would run off crying to elicit sympathy from the nearest adult. "Noah pushed me," was all she could verbalise between convulsive gasps and sobs. Being the younger of the two, she was learning how to manipulate situations by enlisting the help of an authority figure to intervene on her behalf.

It was time to put my thinking cap on. Don my superhero outfit. What had I learned about problem-solving over the years? I paused to run through the reservoir of skills accumulated from a lifetime of experience. Plus a few failed strategies that were difficult to shake. Yelling never worked; I did not want to look like a demented old lady to my adorable grandchildren. Reacting with indignation was a complete waste of time. Children merely picked up where they left off once the initial shock wore off.

I sifted through my repertoire of problem-solving strategies searching for the right weapon in my arsenal. Do I let them fight it out? Do I intervene? Separate them and impose time-out? Interact with them one at a time? Confiscate games. Withhold treats. Turn off the T.V. No, I concluded. These possibilities have all been exhausted without success. It's time for a different approach. *But what?*

In a spirit of reflection, I set about distracting the grandchildren. They were at it again.

"I want to play the Nintendo Switch," said Issy.

"You can't. The batteries are flat," Noah retorted.

"Then I want to play your tablet," Issy whined.

"But I'm playing on the tablet," Noah defended.

A group activity was implemented to diffuse the situation. "It's time for a jigsaw puzzle," I announced. I rather liked the parallel. Solving puzzles put me in a contemplative mindset.

"I want to pick the puzzle," Issy demanded.

"Is that okay with you, Noah?"

"Sure, grandma, so long as it's not one we've done before. Issy always wants to do the same puzzle over and over again."

"Okay then, it's settled. Something new this time."

Issy finally settled on a World puzzle because she liked the animals in the picture. We sat around the dining room table in our usual places and began by opening the box.

"Don't forget to find the edge pieces first," Issy reminded.

"I already know that," Noah countered with a hint of annoyance in his voice.

Once the frame was assembled, everyone slotted into their preferred roles. Noah liked grouping things in mini pictures.

"This looks like the trunk of an elephant," he observed and set about putting all the grey pieces together.

"How about trying to match animals with their country of origin," I suggested to make it more challenging.

"That's a good idea, grandma."

Issy liked sorting pieces according to colour. "This yellow piece looks like it belongs to a giraffe. Who's working on that bit?" she inquired.

I was responsible for making sure the pieces fit within the bigger picture. Strange coincidence? Maybe not! Overview was my specialty. I had the perfect vantage point.

Unfortunately, respite from sibling rivalry was short-lived. No sooner had the puzzle been packed away, and it was back to the same push-pull dynamic. Over milk and biscuits this time.

"You got five biscuits, and I only got four!" Issy yelled.

"Why does your biscuit have more choc-chips than mine?" Noah countered.

As I sat back in my chair bracing for another round of refereeing, the answer came to me like a bolt out of the blue. SPACE-BUBBLE. The words jumped into my head. I did not know it yet, but this was the motif I needed. A perfect metaphor on which to hang my hard-earned wisdom. All those years of study at academia, thousands of dollars spent contemplating philosophy, were finally about to pay dividends.

Let's logic this through. I deliberated: This was one of the skills I had been taught while doing my *Arts Degree* in the *Humanities*. A dialectic approach is required. (a) This is not simply a battle. (b) It's much bigger than that. (c) This is war. (d) The children are up against forces outside their control. Conclusion: Chaos is about to swallow my grandchildren whole. Chew them into pieces and spit them out.

Hadn't my thesis been about investigating ancient notions of space? Through my research, I discovered space is no longer regarded an element in the modern era unlike earth, water, fire, and air. It appears we have shifted from observing a system of five elements to recognising only four. The problem is that the fifth element does not fit the empirical paradigm. According to the modern way of thinking, if it cannot be seen or measured, it simply doesn't exist.

The fallout from this omission is akin to letting people drive cars without a licence. Nobody understands the rules of navigating space anymore, let alone the etiquette. This should be obvious from high levels of congestion infiltrating our major cities. Or the way people trip over each other as they jostle for first place in the modern world.

Little by little, the fundamentals of the fifth element are being eroded. Various roles in society that oversee the maintenance of space; cleaners, janitors, gardeners, tea-ladies, porters and elevator valets are no longer valued. These positions, along with their respective employment opportunities, are becoming redundant: The same way loss of natural habitats is causing certain species to become extinct. Environmental issues are just another facet of the fifth element space dilemma, with progress encroaching on the home's of creatures in the wilderness.

Now here it was, on a microcosmic scale, running rampant in my own family. The door to chaos had been thrown wide open. It's time to make a stand. Reinstate the fifth element. And where better to start than with my own nearest and dearest? The answer had been there all along. It just needed transposing into real-life drama.

"Space Bubble!" I said to the children, who immediately turned and looked at me steely-eyed. They had no idea what I was talking about.

"From now on, you are going to respect each other's space." I began demonstrating my point by drawing an imaginary circle around each of the children. "This is your space-bubble," I said to Noah. "And this is your space-bubble," I said to Issy.

It was the perfect analogy for teaching boundaries, the ideal framework for cultivating self-autonomy. Manners, respect, physical and social distancing are the cornerstones of self-determination.

"Anytime you want to enter another person's space, you have to ask permission to enter their space-bubble," I further instructed.

Once the rules of space-bubble had been adequately explained, the children immediately set about putting them into practice.

"You can clean your teeth first," Noah said as he stepped back to make way for Issy to access the bathroom sink. "I'm happy to wait until you're finished - just don't take too long."

It was heart-warming to see sibling rivalry finally give way to congeniality. Friendship might be stretching it at the moment, but at least they were now on their way to becoming best friends. I sighed as a wave of relief washed over me. No more elbows in the ribs and floods of tears before bedtime.

"Can I come into your room and get a book from the bookshelf,?" Issy asked as she stood in the doorway waiting for Noah's reply.

"Sure, but only if I can come and listen to the story too," Noah insisted before scrambling out of bed so as not to miss the opportunity to listen to a bedtime story.

"Yes, of course you can," Issy responded, mirroring Noah's earlier attempt at respecting her space-bubble.

I know it will take time for the grandchildren to fully grasp the concept, but it definitely has potential. At least for now it is working, even if their initial efforts seem awkward and contrived.

Much to my delight, space-bubble solved yet another problem.

Suddenly the grandchildren had a new perspective for navigating the world of possessions and belongings. It irked me no end how they stepped out of their clothes and left belongings strewn in the walkways. School bags dropped in the middle of the lounge room floor. Clothes and shoes littering aisles where they undressed.

"The floor is not a coat-hanger," I would remind them while bending down to retrieve a misplaced item to hand it back to one of the children. "Where does that belong?" I usually asked, knowing full well they knew that I knew they knew where it belonged.

I was particularly averse to tripping hazards. This included children in the kitchen while cooking. Unless they were receiving instruction on preparing food, children were forbidden to enter my creative space. Safety-first was the golden rule.

This could definitely give my grandchildren an advantage going forward. Polite, well-mannered children were usually rewarded with warm smiles and kind words. Sometimes they even scored a lollipop. Positive reinforcement builds positive self-esteem, as I recall. Space-bubble was removing some of the fight. Paving the way for a smoother passage through life.

"Let's go to the park," I suggested in a moment of inspiration. "How about the Botanic Gardens this time?"

"Yes, yes, yes," the grandchildren chanted in unison and started dancing around the room with excitement.

"Maybe we could take some food and drinks to have a picnic while we're there."

"You're the best, grandma," they sang in chorus. This was music to my ears. I never grew tired of hearing their honeyed words. A sneaky grin spread across my lips and lit up my eyes as I stole a moment to soak up the adulation.

*　　*　　*

As soon as we alighted from the car, the children raced off to the playground while I headed for a grove of trees to find the idealic picnic spot. After spreading a tartan blanket on the ground, I sat down to watch the children happily playing. This gave me time to reflect.

I felt a deep sense of personal satisfaction. My reputation as a fixer-upper was intact. I just needed to convince the rest of the world of the virtues in reinstating space to its former status.

Maybe I didn't need to worry, after all. The global pandemic was teaching everyone about the realities of space: forced lockdowns, social distancing, face masks, hand washing, anti-bacterial wipes. They were beginning to get the message across. I could see Mother Nature at work bringing home important lessons about the consequences of neglecting her sacred principles.

For now, it was enough to savour my own victory, which on the face of it looked small by way of comparison. Who knows, maybe this childhood lesson will inspire one of my grandchildren to hit the campaign trail when they become adults. Save the world from its own folly by returning space to its former status. *Grandparents are allowed to dream big,* I thought. It's our prerogative to pin hopes for world peace on the grandchildren.

Just then Issy and Noah bounded over to sit beside me. After eating leftover bacon and egg pie, apple shortcake, and guzzling down their favourite soft drink, Noah ran off to the playground yelling, "I love you, grandma."

With a hand cupped to the side of my mouth, I yelled back, "I love you too."

Issy started picking wildflowers to make a daisy chain. When it was finished, she placed it gently on my head.

"You look so pretty, grandma."

"Thank you," I replied as my hand reached up to touch the wildflowers.

"I love you so much. You're just the bestest grandma in the whole wide world," Issy fawned.

"I love you too, to the Moon and back," I beamed.

"I love you bigger than the universe," she countered.

"Well, I can't beat that," I conceded as Issy fell into my arms laughing.

I felt like a Greek goddess sitting there with the floral wreath adorning my head. I was surrounded by my adoring grandchildren, and red autumn leaves were falling like confetti on the ground all around us.

My mind was momentarily transported back to the ancient Greek philosophers. Thank you, Socrates and Plato, I whispered. Thank you, Pythagoras and Parmenides, and all the other Philosophers who kept company with these wise, noble souls.

I could picture them with white flowing robes, gold sashes and crowning wreaths of laurel walking back into the pages of history to wait for someone else to resurrect their teachings. Maybe together, we could reverse history. Start putting the plagues back in Pandora's Jar.

I must remember to revisit the works of the Philosophers more often. How could my grandchildren fail with Philosophia, the Greek goddess of Wisdom, as my mentor and guide? Maybe now I can accept the title of super-gran.

Nourishment

Jon

I needed an escape. Space. Somewhere open and free. Somewhere I could be alone and rest. Rest my mind. Rest my body. Rest my soul.

I grabbed my sunglasses, threw on a cap, strode out the front door, and walked. Immediately I felt calmer, energised by the warm glow of the afternoon sun. Away from the filtered chill of air-conditioned "comfort", the fresh air filled my lungs with the scent of rural life, agriculture, dust and straw. With the smells came a sudden rush of memory. Not just of my childhood and my love of place – but of family and betrayal. The doubts and insecurities came flooding back. My initial relief was gone, overpowered by sickening confusion and helplessness.

My gaze fell. I looked only at my feet as I trudged forward along the gravel road. Unconsciously I turned left and headed northwards away from the town, towards the rugged woodlands surrounding the valley. It was harsh country scattered with ironbarks and grey boxes. Gaining little sustenance from the barren stony ground, their gnarled and twisted branches reached for the sky, starving and gaunt, begging the gods for nourishment. The sparse growth gave little protection from the sweltering sun, magnified by heat radiating from the red stone.

I was surrounded by scarred over wounds left behind by previous generations – the foragers and pillagers from far-off lands that had swarmed the countryside in search of instant wealth. Driven by greed and a lust for gold, they chopped, scraped, dug, and burned with no regard for the destruction and disruption on the delicate balance of the native landscape. Their desire for immediate satisfaction outweighed long-term prosperity.

The road deteriorated into little more than a kangaroo track, winding between the trees with the same manic bends and turns as a bounding 'roo. The repressive glare and heat began to wear, and the freshness of the outdoor air became thick and heavy.

I needed to rest.

The track opened and the wretched growth cleared to a desolate hill. At the peak stood a great peppercorn. The ancient soul of the majestic tree was evident on every branch, etched into every crack and jagged strand of bark. Thick sap oozed from the cracks as though the very lifeforce of this gracious being was straining, yearning for release. Clusters of tiny leaves drooped heavily from despondent limbs. The lungs caving to the weight of sadness witnessed over a century of being. Dead branches hung precariously alongside new growth – the brightness of the yellowish green shoots providing a hopeful contrast against the whitish grey of decay.

The refuge of the great tree beckoned. My sweat-stained shirt clung to my skin and despite my frenzied swatting, a hoard of taunting flies circled my face, fueling my frustration. I dove for cover under the weeping branches and as if passing through the air curtain of a large shopping centre, the flies dispersed. Sitting down, I was struck by the immediate relief of the cool, shadowed oasis. Leaning my back against the trunk, the nooks and twists of the wood formed a perfect cradle for my neck and shoulders, as though it had been purposefully molded just for me. Underneath, a deep bed of fallen leaves, seeds and husks provided a soft mattress to stretch my legs. Breathing in the tree's sweet-peppered perfume, I felt my mind and soul relax. A cool breeze brushed my face, I nestled deeper into my seat and closed my eyes.

As I dozed, my mind filled with the voice of my grandpa. Tales of local history and of farming life. Of new age technologies and lost traditions. I used to love walks with grandpa. He'd show me old dig sites and abandoned mineshafts, and tell me stories of the old townships, once thriving communities, now deserted and discarded. Of the latter stages of the goldrush and how as the gold ran out, settlers would dismantle entire factories, houses and hotels, loading the timbers on carts in search of a more prosperous settlement. Often, the only evidence that would remain was a clearing in the scrub, the remnants of foundation stones, or an old peppercorn tree.

"When you see an old pepper tree, sitting out in the middle of nowhere, that's where an old town would have been," my grandpa would tell me. "Probably the site of an old school or church – or the outside shitter."

He told me stories of the American settlers arriving during the goldrush. They bought with them the seeds, planting the peppercorns to give them a sense of home in this harsh new world. Some lush greenery to break the starkness of the ragged native growth, yet hardy enough to thrive. They were a great shelter tree with their thick weeping canopy, and, possessing a natural insect repellant, they were ideal for a bush hospital or community gathering point, offering relief from the relentless Australian bush fly.

I felt my grandpa's sturdy hand on my shoulder. His grip was forceful and tight - yet comforting - and I nestled my back deeper into my wooden seat.

My mind slowly drifted as I slept, remembering my grandfather's stories. I pictured myself among an intimate group of guests, gathered under the great peppercorn. It was a bridal party. The bride and groom were standing together with a priest, receiving a blessing in a thick Irish accent. The groom was standing steadfast and proud. Behind his leathered complexion and weary frame were the youthful eyes of a boy, brimming with a mixture of excitement, fear and obligation. A large bead of sweat gathered on his brow, dropping on the thirsty ground.

His bride was just a girl, suddenly thrust into adulthood. Her billowing crinoline skirt was discoloured by the red dust with seeds and twigs trapped in the delicate lacework. A plain white bonnet held back curled locks of ginger-brown hair. Her pretty face was flushed - clearly struggling with the impracticality of her dress, and the layers of heavy fabric in the oppressing heat. Tears welled in her eyes, gently sliding down her cheek, dropping into the dust.

I could sense a feeling of hope among the guests. They were settlers in a foreign land, beaten by the harsh realities of a perilous new world. They were now laying their burden of hope on this young couple.

Again, I felt the grip of a strong hand on my shoulder. As if aware of my presence, the priest turned his gaze towards mine. Eyes fixed on me, he continued his blessing. I found myself being pulled away, the strength of the grip now cutting deep into my collarbone. The priest's voice echoed as my mind fell back into a peaceful slumber.

I could hear a commotion in the distance. A man appeared suddenly, crawling on hands and knees, whimpering. His clothes were badly torn, covered in blood and dust. More blood spilled from a deep gash across his cheek, his left eye bruised and swollen shut. He huddled at the base of the tree, curling into a tight ball, revealing more painful gashes across his scalp and back.

Another man approached, his shadowy figure towering over the injured man.

"You filthy thieving chink!" he snarled.

The injured man recoiled, tears spilling from his remaining eye. He began pleading to his attacker in a foreign tongue, choking and sputtering in a desperate attempt to communicate, begging for his life. The dark figure spat on him, then wielding a large branch, delivered the fatal blow - and casually walked away.

The frail body collapsed instantly, motionless and quiet. His right eye still open, frozen in an eternal terrified stare. Blood trickled down his thick black hair, now scattered with fragments of bark and bone. Puddles of red liquid gathered before slowly seeping deep into the earth.

I tried desperately to wake myself from my nightmare - but I couldn't move. My legs felt tight, is if bound. I tried to wriggle free, but something was holding me down. The sweet-peppered perfume swirled around me. I could feel the calming aroma move through my lungs, and I was again at ease, snuggling deeper into my soft earthen mattress.

There was a faint hint of smoke in the air. I gazed around in a weary drunken haze. A crowd had gathered, singing hymns and waving branches cut from the great tree. I recognised the smoke. Incense. The worshippers laid their branches down to form a path along the ground. As the crowd parted, I saw the Irish priest. Memories of my Catholic upbringing flooded back – it was Palm Sunday, and the parishioners were reenacting Jesus' return to Jerusalem.

Adding another pinch of pepper-seeds to his brass burner, the priest proceeded along the pathway to the base of the tree, sprinkling holy water across his parishioners as he walked past. The drops splashed across their bowed heads and onto the ground, soaked eagerly by parched soils.

The priest began his sermon, speaking of the approaching celebration of Easter, and its symbolism of hope, of new life and new beginnings. He spoke of the challenges facing the new settlers. Of opportunity and oppression. Tolerance and community. Then, turning to me, he spoke of strength, resilience – and acceptance.

Sinking further in my bed, I allowed the angelic singing and soothing smell of incense to overwhelm my senses.

A piercing scream echoed in my head as I battled with my growing inertia. A young girl lay under the tree, her matted blonde hair filled with leaf litter, her face strewn with tears and sweat. She screamed again, her body twisting and writhing in agony as she clasped her blood-soaked thighs. She looped a foot into an exposed root like a stirrup, and between bouts of desperate cries, she breathed in deeply - and heaved.

I watched in awe at the courage of the young girl. Alone. So much pain. So much fear and suffering. Yet with her teeth clenched and fists gripped – she wasn't giving up. The resolve in her eyes never faltered as she battled every contraction with steely determination. Over and over and over. Her cries turned into haunting moans as her body succumbed to the exhaustion. Then, after a mammoth final push – relief.

I found myself overcome with emotions – of joy and pride at the bravery of this lonely girl, and of love and hope for the new life she had created. A warmth spread through my body as I savored the utopian experience. The young girl lifted the infant to her chest, sobbing as she gently caressed its face. Nestled in its mother's breast, the baby stopped crying and opened its eyes. And for just a split moment, it caught its mother's loving gaze.

The growing pools of blood and embryonic fluid soaked deep into the ground, devoured by the hungry soil. The girl lay still. Silent. Her determined eyes now closed. Her face a ghostly grey.

I tried calling out to her, but I couldn't make a sound.

Something squeezed tightly across my throat and chest holding me down. The newborn began to whimper. I had to help her. I had to get help. But I was completely paralysed. The newborn became restless, crying out for its mother – but there was no answer. There was no one to comfort it. No one to feed it, to care, to protect or nurture it.

I struggled to resist as the soothing haze took over again. I had to get help. Why wouldn't someone come? This poor wretched girl had given so much. She had been discarded, rejected and alone. Yet she did not let it defeat her. I could not let it end this way. I had to get help.

My head was pounding, overwhelmed by the feeling of hopelessness. The pressure on my chest grew heavy, and I could feel droplets of sticky sap oozing down the side of my face. Defeated, I closed my eyes allowing my mind to again be overtaken in a heavy haze.

Something grabbed my hand, and I could hear a familiar voice, gentle and soothing. "It's OK. I'm here. You can rest now," the voice said. My wife was kneeling over me, one hand against my cheek, the other gripping mine.

I had never seen her as beautiful as she was right now. The evening sun was nearly set, with bright streaks of pinks, deep purples and golden orange filling the sky. The soothing light exaggerated every curve of her face, her carved cheek bones and delicate lips. "It's OK now. You can rest," she repeated softly.

My heart eased and my head cleared as the nightmares drifted slowly from my mind. I felt embarrassed by the silliness of my trivial 'first world' issues compared to the horrors I just witnessed. Looking at the beauty beside me, I returned a smile of shame. She smiled, gripping my hand tighter, her other hand now firmly on my chest. "Don't worry. Everything's alright. You rest now."

There was a sense of persistence in her ordinarily tender touch. The span of her palm increasing as her knotted fingers stretched across my ribs.

I breathed deeply, relishing the tree's soothing peppered perfume, and sunk deeper into the soft bed..

Crescendo, Diminuendo, Rest

Meg Irwin

Something was off key in the new woman. There was a sharp note now and again. She was younger and taller than Tracy, and clearly smart. A mane of dark hair swirled around her very attractive face and her body moved fluidly. But Tracy could hear it – perhaps a dangerous secret? – perhaps a propensity for harm?

In her work, Tracy considered herself a fine-tuned instrument. She absorbed each client's fundamental frequency, and located the crescendos of rage and the diminuendos of sadness. And there were pitch transitions; a rising fifth when someone was ready for action; a rising sixth when there was pain. Not that Tracy needed to depend on details. After so many years of practice, her instincts alone were enough. Deftly, she played to each person the music of their soul. With just the right words, she revealed to them their way forward.

Tracy judged her life a success. At forty-six, she was fairly fit and still quite good looking. More importantly, she'd made a difference to many people's lives, and, though she sometimes felt tired, she knew she still had more to give.

She had already contributed decades of caring. The hopes of her parents had been lavished on the sons, not the daughters of the family, so Tracy had always known she had to rely entirely upon herself to advance. She'd gone into nursing from school. She'd worked hard, becoming proficient, then expert. She rose through the ranks, developing a thick skin and reinventing herself. She dressed well, and spoke with rounded vowels and an increasingly authoritative tone. But nursing was hard on the body, and there was always someone above you in the hospital hierarchy, so she'd moved on to counselling and groupwork.

*　　*　　*

Sitting in her office, she'd come across an exercise she'd done from a self-help book. (She always checked those books so she could recommend the decent ones to her clients.) She'd had to ask a range of friends to name her five greatest strengths. She had never asked anyone what they thought of her before, and her friends had seemed embarrassed when she asked. They took a while to respond, but came through after some prompting. She guessed it had been difficult for them to narrow her strengths to just five. All of them identified her persistence, commitment, presence in relationship, and directness. Persistence and commitment were valuable to society and, these days, both in short supply. Honesty in relationships was good: she'd always hated falsity. Most pleasingly, she'd discovered that her perceptiveness, surely her most developed strength, was so well honed and integrated, that these friends had not even mentioned it. How subtly she must employ it! Still, she thought, she must find time to coach her friends for the sake of their professional functioning. Most of them, after all, were counsellors and therapists.

*　　*　　*

She'd joined the ukulele group at work. "It's just for a bit of fun at lunchtime," they'd said. She didn't like the ukulele's clunky sound, nor the braying voices as the others sang along. But she knew that it was good to support a social initiative, so she turned up each week.

It was there that she first noticed the new woman who had joined their team. (They liked to say "team", but, actually, they were all independent practitioners, sharing rooms, IT services and a reception desk.) In the chatter at the start and end of their session, she talked a lot about kindness. She seemed not to have to prove herself at all with the others. They all liked her. Tracy reserved judgement. She would wait for a private chat to check things out.

Shortly into their first conversation, the newcomer enquired, "Are you single?"

How invasive! thought Tracy, who had intended to be the one asking the questions. "I live alone, but have a partner," she responded clumsily.

"Is that what you want?"

Tracy needed to turn this around! She spluttered, "Oh yes, and what about yourself?"

The woman's eyes twinkled, full of warmth, and she said, "I am completely happy; always."

What the hell did she mean by that? Was that supposed to be an answer to her question? Tracy had had enough. "That's good," she said lamely. "Well, let's get back to work." In her mind, she dubbed this woman "the Lioness". She was a tough customer.

*   *   *

That night Tracy dreamt she was a swan flying over the landscape with Greig's music swelling, just like in the plane ad when she'd been a kid. She woke up refreshed and feeling in her power. Yes, of course she was happy! She had her life organised just as she wanted. Why had she let that woman discombobulate her? She would regain some equilibrium between them. If she could find a way to help the young lioness, that would put them back on an equal footing.

Her opportunity arose that same day. Mr P. attended as part of his parole requirements. He was a big man, with at least two traumatic brain injuries and a history of violent offending. Sonya usually saw him, but was away sick. Tracy also knew Mr P. so she agreed to see him instead.

Then Tracy had a brain wave. How useful it would be for both the client and the new woman if they met instead. Mr P. should learn to work with more than one or two staff, in case of absences like this, and the new woman would gain an understanding of the range of clients they served. With a quick change to the online appointment schedule, she allocated Mr P. to the Lioness. Mr P. had not coped well with new people in the past, but Tracy would be alert. At the first sign of trouble, she would enter the room and control the situation.

It was twenty minutes into the appointment, and Tracy worried that other staff would notice her hovering outside the interview room. Throughout, all she had heard was a steady back and forth of low voices from within. To be honest, never before had Mr P. been calm with someone he didn't know. It seemed strange. She couldn't resist a quick look in. She could tell the Lioness later that she was just checking that all was well.

Tracy opened the door a crack. Suddenly a great hand grabbed her by the neck and pulled her into the room, slamming the door on her hand. She howled in pain.

She heard a gentle voice, "Here, Alistair, come and sit here. You had a fright, but you haven't hurt anyone. Sit down here while I help our friend for a moment." She patted him softly on the arm, as he sat down.

Like a lamb! thought Tracy. My oath, he hasn't hurt anyone, though!

Then the Lioness was with Tracy, appraising the damage with her dark eyes. She took Tracy's injured hand in her own cool ones, and rolled it carefully, over and back. "It's just bruising," she said, "Thanks for checking, but everything is fine in here." She threw back a smile at the client in his chair. It was not a cool professional smile of reassurance, but a warm, funny one, as if the two of them were in cahoots.

"Wait a moment," said the Lioness and unlocked the cupboard (in front of the client! thought Tracy) to retrieve a small pot of arnica which she pushed into Tracy's good hand as she guided her out the door. Tracy found herself back in the corridor, sore and seething.

*   *   *

"Mr P. had a go at me," Tracy confessed to another colleague. (She didn't want to talk about the circumstances, so she decided to bring up the subject of her evidently damaged hand herself.)

"Yes, he's not got much inhibition, poor man," said the other, "Are you OK?"

Tracy said she was, and the conversation lulled. Then her colleague spoke again, "You weren't there the other day, when we asked Ariella about herself. She's had an amazing life. She's spent time in refugee camps all over the world. One of her legs is prosthetic (you would never guess it) from stepping on a mine. But the worst thing is that she was taken hostage in transit between camps in an area where opposing forces were fighting.

Her partner and her two adolescent sons were with her. They were shot in front of her."

Tracy gripped the little tub of arnica. Now her uninjured hand, as well as the one that had been caught in the door, throbbed with pain.

*   *   *

She navigated the rest of the day in a daze. Only when she got home, did her mind catch up. There was the humiliation of the morning, and the shock of hearing Ariella's story. She'd concluded Ariella was Singhalese when she'd met her; she'd known a lot of Singhalese social workers. Now she realised she had no idea what Ariella's background was. When she had been younger, Tracy had wanted to work in refugee camps, even become a nun, but she'd never quite made it. She'd thought she was needed at home. But now she wasn't sure if it hadn't just been easier to stay put. Then there was the woman's relentless kindness to everyone. And what she'd said about always being happy! How could she possibly say that? Tracy felt as if she'd been taken by a great wave and dumped hard on a deserted beach. Nothing made any sense.

She had no plans that night, and was relieved she did not have to pull herself together. She could remain for a while in this strange territory of uncertainty and emotion. She didn't busy herself with anything. She sat on the sofa in the quiet and darkness, feeling all that she had to feel.

That night, she dreamt again as the black swan, in flight. The music was swelling again. But the feeling this time was not of grandness, but of desperation. The swan was flying high over entire continents, searching, on and on, for its lost mate and young. She woke in a sweat and couldn't get back to sleep. How do people go on? When her body started quaking, she did not resist.

At work the next day, she found herself in a ridiculous game with Ariella. Whenever she heard her coming, Tracy slipped into a side room. If she saw her in the lunchroom, she avoided going in. She sighed with relief when five o'clock arrived and she could go to pick up her things from her locker.

As she reached for her jacket, there was a soft touch on her shoulder. She was too late to stop herself shrugging it away.

"How is your hand today?" asked the Lioness.

This time, Tracy managed to suppress her reaction. She took two breaths and turned to face the Lioness. She was looking into her face, but could find nothing to say. They stood for several minutes in empty silence, the Lioness calmly returning Tracy's gaze. Tracy did not want to run any more.

Suddenly Tracy wondered if it might be possible to say something from her own heart. Speaking from her own heart, she realised, was what real authenticity was about. All those other manoeuvres she'd been making for years had been nothing to do with realness. She reached for words, but there were still none.

"It feels tender," offered the Lioness, not talking about Tracy's hand. Then the Lioness cocked her head with a little smile, turned and walked away.

*   *   *

Tracy was unravelling. How could she go on working? Telling people what to do with their lives seemed crazy to her now. She could not even locate herself, let alone help someone else. Yet there was something. It welled up from within her; something she'd forgotten since childhood. She felt herself alive; in all the confusion, she was vividly and hot-bloodedly alive.

Alex, the part-time partner, came over that night and found Tracy unusually snuggly and agreeable. And tonight, Tracy appreciated the company, was even grateful for it, and no one could have been more surprised about that than Tracy, herself.

She slept soundly, dreaming as her swan-self, rising effortlessly, riding a thermal. She was among other swans, who whistled and bugled all around her. Together, they formed a great "V" and flowed across the vast sky.

She awoke with another unfamiliar emotion. She wondered if it might be a sort of happiness; a happiness that didn't have to deny the bad bits in the world, or even in herself.

*   *   *

Back at work again, Tracy was glad to have her day's routine and the scheduled appointments. With each client, she provided none of her usual clever interventions. She felt like she did nothing at all for them. Yet, they seemed satisfied and thanked her.

Sometimes, she crossed paths with Ariella and felt tears coming. She wanted to explain, "They told me what happened; to your partner; to your sons." But she could not trust herself not to break down. There were shadows in her own life; cruelties from people who were meant to care, young ones dead before their time, sabotaged dreams; all her 'baggage', as they say.

Then, as they both grabbed a cup of tea in the lunchroom, Tracy said it anyway.

"Ah yes" Ariella said, "I have been so fortunate – such a fine man, such fine boys." She was remembering them.

"I'm so sorry," mumbled Tracy.

"I always love to think of them," said Ariella.

Tracy looked up into Ariella's shining face. She saw an emotion that overarched the sadness and the many other feelings that were there. It rang out strongly, and confounded Tracy. It was joy!

"I took you as an enemy that I wanted to bring down. I called you the Lioness out of my envy and desire to defeat you. Now I will call you Lioness, because you are magnificent!" Tracy said aloud.

*   *   *

These days, Tracy never tunes her instrument. She lets it tune itself to the joy or pain, or whatever's there, in herself, the world, or the person before her. She becomes the resonance and does not know the melody she plays. The notes run high and low, beyond the sensitivity of human ears. The sound carries far across time, and over continents and seas. A deep harmonic runs through it all; the quiet vibration of home and healing. And, when Tracy plays this way, it is the easiest thing in the world.

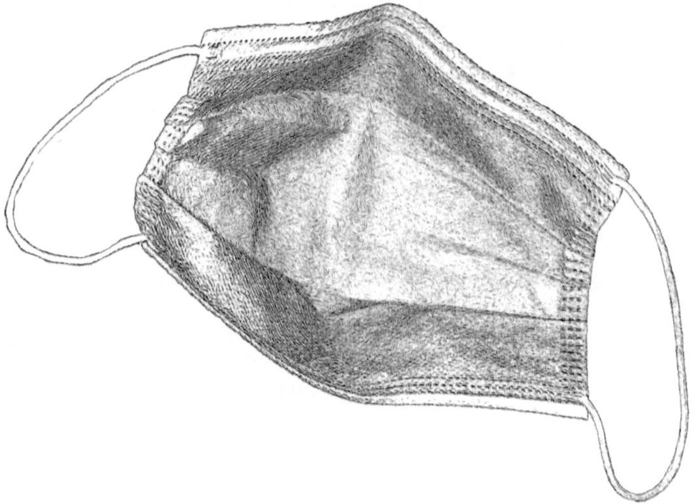

POETRY

The Trucks Roll By

Cameron Dale

The pub's heater from
another era
cranks and whirs into
action –
cans
smash and
clink into
recycling bins
      The trucks roll by

A humble town with
humble people.
Each night

miners drink more, scuffle and
guffaw:

 A masculinity they don't know what to do with.
      The trucks roll by.

Dancing Queen plays as
miners grasp each other's collars,
Finding something to be angry about.
Someone, or something   to blame
for the one hole in   the ground
they can't dig out of—
          The trucks roll by.

The barkeep polishes the wood,
mops the vomit and beer
ends the night—and
turns off the town's last
humble light.

You were not behind the door

Meredith Adams

For years I could not find you
From the teasing you hid away
You were not behind the door

In memory I search for you
To find the place you hide
For years I could not find you

Gone from your hiding place
Amongst the cowslips and bells
You were not behind the door

Your laugh a faded memory
Your lips sorely missed
For years I could not find you

And yet in echoes
Down hallways I heard
You were not behind the door

But lurking between beats of a heart
In the place last I looked
For years I could not find you
You were not behind the door

Sweet Music

Cameron Dale

The solitary note plays with the wind, it
travels like a ghost, sweeping through the empty house—
an empty room, full of sound
The guitar, and the ghosts of the people who
have played it—crying out

to be picked and
plucked again.
Taunting me, knowing I can't do it justice
Yet—the rhythm of the world—
the breeze
everything effortlessly plays a tune more beautiful than
ever I have.

No siren of grace—no homeless troubadour
but the curtain—swaying in the open window
caresses the strings
snuffs out the candle of intrigue.
Investigation only disappoints—
I leave the wind and the world—to play that note
until—tides change and winds subside

and the rhythm of
the world
ambles
on.

Irrational Behaviour
Caleb Irvine-Kingsmith

Laminated tension surges for release
skulking creatures boom like thunder.
Reacting to pain with reflexive contradiction.
Damn it!

Conditioning cannot be unpleasant.
A ton of people accidently get hurt,
hoped-for results omit ignorance.
Trust me!

Killing is not lying.
That's irrational behaviour
or rather, my basic hatred.
I'm sorry!

Tension released as basic hatred.
Skulking creatures, or rather
reflexive, irrational people
accidently trust hurt.

St Valentine's Day

J L Penn

It is not the loving that you lose—it's the romance of what it should have been. Love dies in little acts, each act of neglect, each poison barb, each new item on the tally of blame, and each recovery in shame is another act of mourning. But everything is fine.

this lover's day
the old man carries his heart
upon his sleeve

I watch an elderly man climb from his car, long-limbed, suited, groomed. His shoulders are bent, as he shuffles into the market. Returning, his face is bright. He carries a supermarket bag in one hand, cradles flowers in the elbow of his other arm. He opens the back door of his car, places the bag on the seat and gently lays down three long-stemmed red roses, wrapped and ribboned.

slow tango—
lovers embrace Cohen's growl
to the end of love

We Can't Fly No More (Blues Verse)

Delilah Cornwall

The ship is old and broke
Our Mama Captain's old and broke
I'm young, but I'm old, I light up another smoke
(well we can't fly no more)

Meteor shower our engine shattered
Bills, fines and fees our accounts are battered
Family's breaking up, guess none of it mattered

The ship can't take off
Now everybody's taking off
Nothing left to do but choke and cough
(Oh no, we can't fly no more)

Sister's working down at the café
Sister never leaves the old café
Sister works all day but the rent she still can't pay
(We can't fly no more)

Daddy's working the mechanic store
Boss is a cheat at the mechanic store
Old Daddy never gets to leave the floor
(We can't fly no more)

The ship can't take off
Now everybody's taking off
Nothing left to do but choke and cough

Mama's on the company payroll now
Mama's working hard for the company now
Says someday, we'll get out of here somehow
(We can't fly no more)

My brother, my brother
Joined a work crew did my brother
But did he tell us where he was going? Nah, he didn't bother
(We can't fly no more)

The ship can't take off
Now everybody's taking off
Nothing left to do but choke and cough
(We can't fly no more)

Me I'm down with the dregs
Wasting time down with the dregs
That damn meteor shower broke both my legs
(We can't fly no more)

The ship can't take off
So everybody's taking off
Nothing left to do but choke and cough

We can't fly no more
We can't fly no more
I can't take it anymore

Appalachian Gold

MJ Douven

A vision fair came to my eyes upon a lofty hill –
A wooded vale, a shining vale, a woodland grey and still.
And lo, across the hills, there crept a mist of silver shade
As modest hills above their crowns a shining veil they laid.

There grows the beech of golden leaf, the birch of silver hair.
There grows the hemlock broad and dark, the aspen tall and fair.
There grows the maple crimson-hued, the ash of tinkling gold.
And there amidst the falling leaves, there looms the cedar bold.

And then comes May with flowers wild, sprung from the April rain
The queen of spring, the queen of May, with flowers in her train.
The scent of spring, of blossoms sweet, of flowers springing wild
The fragrance blown across the void with breath now soft and mild.

Then summer comes again at last with months of golden days,
And families gather in the woods for picnics in the shade.
For there, beneath the looming trees, the grass is long and green
And sounds of birds amidst the leaves there whistle loud and keen.

Grey winter comes with drifting white, the trees are bare and grey.
Their branches sprinkled powder-white throughout the bitter day.
But even then, amidst the white, there is a gleam of red,
Where wintergreen – the winter fruit – beneath the snow is bred.

Land of my heart! To me there comes a long and lingering cry
From lofty hill and forest glade and grey northeastern sky,
"Were you a bird, I'd bid you come and nestle in my hand."
And I – Alas! I feel I am – most happy in that land.

Twice Chosen

Sha James

He chose me as much as I chose him
This friend of feline persuasion
He came to me on a mid-summer day
When the heat was well-nigh to boiling

This friend of feline persuasion
Was as cool as cool a cucumber
When the heat was well-nigh to boiling
His favourite pastime was to slumber

Was as cool as cool a cucumber
With the stealth of a militant fighter
His favourite pastime was to slumber
After biscuits laid out in a saucer

With the stealth of a militant fighter
He pounced on the chance to be claimed
After biscuits laid out in a saucer
He peered out of the window frame

I chose him as much as he chose me

Lunchtime in December

Caleb Irvine-Kingsmith

A small bottle of pills,
found at lunchtime in December –
rekindled an intense war.
In the afternoon he would bring it home,
to his family.

I know you quite well he thought.
The raging tempest –
of manic delusion broke,
the sentimentality becoming less and less foreign.
No, you have never been paradise.

He did not prolong the rumination.
But the illusive fantasies of better days multiplied, and –
clinging to his burning sickness still,
the bittersweet war was satiated.
With instant, dire, conviction.

Broken Leaf

Sheree Pratt

Your flesh is dry
        from decay
you lie on concrete
                still   damp
                from a winter   night
you don't feel the cold –
you feel nothing.

Long since fallen,   discarded,
no longer needed.
Life has blown you   here
to rest on this cold   path.

you are
        crushed,
so crushed you no longer   crack
under the weight of careless feet

you lie with nowhere
                                to go,
not yet   dead but
                                death   will   come.
                                                soon.

Occasionally you are noticed,
studied,   photographed,   admired.
Your immaculate design

shape,   colour,   strong veins
hold your broken   pieces   together.
                                is   magic.

your perfect symmetry   altered
     turns you into something   special
          unique.
They imagine
     what you could be.

Perhaps the wing of a
     moth   or butterfly, or even   a fairy.

If *they* believe it,
you can be   anything.

your admirers move on
and you are left –
     on that cold   pathway.

There is something   different
     about you.

Is it
     the morning   sun?
the wind   blows you
     along the   path

Though you are broken, you are   beautiful.
You   can be *anything*
But you   must

     believe.

Tinnitus
Meredith Adams

—it's gone,

      shattered

against

the static.

no song — above

the ring

     -ing

       -ing

         ringing

    the pen

    poised

      craving silence

drowning — in

      drowning out the world.

voices

      t

        u

          m

            b

              l

                e

inside,

            crash against

the

                ring

                  ring

                    ringing.

birdsong

Rhys Allen

that day, I saw
    the **grey** dogs
they were circling the
pavement
sparrows

        pacing like   **wolves**
        as the wind   blew
        bittered leaves and
                ice-cream
                    paper

you stood   aloof
and   watched them
from that doorway on
the corner of
Main Street

a new queen in waiting: a shoulder-dropped sweater
but **god** I could see
        it surely let the **cold** in

three times   I saw **police**   cars
only one   sounding siren
speeding through the violence
of noon time   **chasing** lunch
            or chasing villains

then **you** just walked   away
you were **crying**   on
an ancient iPhone
its case was pink b e d a z z l e d
and as you **left**
it scattered **sunbeams**

"I'm a Writer"

Brandon Kelly

When I go to my family's get togethers I "always" hear from
everyone what do you do for a living and I always say,
    "I'm a Writer".

When I show – show people my writing of death and
destruction – they think I'm mad but
I say to them,
    "I'm a Writer"

To a Writer the world is different – you keep trying to make
stories out of nothing,
I can't help it because,
    "I'm a Writer".

When I watch television, ideas spring out of what I am
watching,
I persist, trying to make things better for me – I say "I can do it",
    "I'm a Writer ".

Without writing I don't know where I'd be – probably stuck
in a dead-end job,
for now I feel free – now I can see a future – all because,
    "I'm a Writer".

can I paint winter

J L Penn

can I paint winter
new graves outnumber the
camelia buds

Away
Zech Elliot

there is light at the distance
as the darkness takes place
he urges her to stay awake
as her heartbeat fades
away

she holds her son's hand
remembering yesterday
as sorrow floods the evening air
her will to live is fading
away

death is the next adventure
tomorrow, a new beginning
she reads his thoughts
and looks
away

darkness has spread
she breathes her last breath
a journey ends
as she smiles and slips
away

Backyard Funeral
Jessie Mayflower

we buried him in the yard yesterday -
laid bricks and stones upon the small mound
with pink geraniums poking through

my mother cried during the funeral -
though my quick-to-water eyes remained dry
Why mourn when he is in a better place?

for months he had been declining
his eyes dulled as his bones grew sharper -
until – the night before – he went silent

with the flowers in place we dispersed
no words were spoken among us
as the small green cage lay empty

Dion

Cameron Dale

Empty seat on the   stage
Lights off!
Curtain called!
Waves crash   then recede   then repeat

Sand of time   washed away

Headlights off!
The day's news!
The rooster crows

Leave now the table of   grief
that   emptiness of words
          untrained
          inadequate
to   death's morning call

words unsaid   into   silence
silence into   noise
                    waves crash and
                    fill the void and—
          Sun   rise
          wheel   turn

          the musician's last note
washed away with that   sand
and   leave?
          I should not—

Can you help the grief of   another?
Hold them   expunge   extricate
leave the waves   and   music to   horizon's abyss
as
time   re-shapes and   shifts—

      geography
      structure
      the walls
      institutions
      banks

so that   on return
I will not know simply   by
     looking
where   I was   or

what   I am

The Void Hates
Delilah Cornwall

The Void hates
The Void devours
It sends all through Hell's gates

Aboard this ship we are all inmates
Endless space and stars, are not ours
The Void hates

Every jump is to tempt the fates
The fearless, the dauntless, everyone cowers
It sends all through Hell's gates

The lie of freedom intoxicates
Brains melt in radiation showers
The Void hates

Every death it celebrates
Ultimate servant of ruinous powers
The Void hates
It sends all through Hell's gates

Last Man

MJ Douven

First man, lord of a mighty empire.

Emperor, secure in the power he wields.

Great king to whom all other kings aspire,

Beloved by the people he shields.

Emperor, bereft of the power he wields,

Kidnapped and torn from his lands.

Betrayed by the woman he shields,

Lies battered, his blood soaks the sands.

Ripped in the night from his lands,

Beaten, dying, in grief and despair.

Shattered, left dead on those sands,

His fate in a working girl's care.

Exile, in a foreign land of dark despair,

To death's door and back his life was brought.

His heart now rests in a woman's care,

A love his shattered heart would not have sought.

Alive, now to a fresh battle brought,

His fight to heal, survive, and find a way,

Confronted by a truth unexpected and unsought –

His reason to be there and his cause to stay.

His pledge to find, to make a way,

To force himself to leave before he should.

One reason to be there, one cause to stay,

To save his people and avenge their blood.

No time to rest, he leaves before he should,

To see his people wrongly suffering and enslaved,

Swearing to save his people and avenge their blood.

A king once more, by his people's woe enraged.

He sees his people suffering and enslaved,

The anguish caused by a grasping ruler's blight.

He takes a stand, by his people's woe enraged,

Turns slaves to soldiers, teaches men to fight.

His choice to stand, uproot that blight.

No way forward, now by that foe enclosed.

Slaves become soldiers, he inspires to fight.

No way back, except to stand before the foe exposed.

No way forward, by a wall of foes enclosed,

Determined to stand until the darkness falls.

No way back, surrounded and exposed.

His choice to stand, to fight, to hold the walls.

Desperate, determined, as the darkness falls,

To hold the line though others leave the fight.

His choice to be the last to leave the walls,

To hold the line throughout the unending night.

Last man to board, last man to leave the fight,

Fearless, he stands, his foes defied,

Then sails away as dawn breaks the night,

His foes left to rage on the sands behind.

Victor, who an impossible foe defied.

Great king, with power to lead and to inspire.

His queen beside, his foes behind,

Last man, in triumph returns to his empire.

Grave Robber

Sha James

NOOH!   not happening!
gone   cold   blank
     eddy into nothing
dark pools   eyes
       breathing   still
            gone   like the wind
   WAIT
Did you say something?
          my mistake   nothing
what now?
pitter, patter, pitter, patter, "Nurse,   "Is it true?"
"Yes, gone"
better pack bags   but what?
     can't think   everything!
but why?   he's not coming home
throw it all away   meaningless now
CAN'T BE   COME BACK
one more word   please
     forgot to say
         I Love You
Damn   wanted something   what was it?
     staring   gazing   staring   gazing   you don't look
the same
        like a vacant house   wonder where you've gone
wish I knew   might help me feel better.
     Ah!   wedding ring
   wanted to hang it on a chain   round my neck
"is it right?   would it okay?   can I take it now?"
"Nurse   what do you think?"
"Hmm   don't know   your decision.

The funeral home won't let you have it when they take the body
	not until after the funeral."
"That's it then   let's do it   come on Nurse   it's my only
chance."
tug, twist, pull   "it's not coming off   his fingers swollen"
	"Here try this *flip* hair conditioner might work it's
slippery enough."
squish, slip, slide… finally   my precious keepsake.
"Thanks Nurse."
	"No problem"
		What now? I'm not feeling so good
	have I done wrong?
heart's racing a bit   boom, boom, boom, boom, boom
		must be a panic attack
It's official   guilty Your Honour   *I'm a grave robber.*
Should be okay, though   surely   no use to him now   he's
gone.
	Mine now anyway
		as if I needed anything else to make me feel bad!
No point beating myself up   too late now   can't put it back
	think I'll finish packing
pitter, patter, pitter, patter "Goodbye Nurse   going home now"
	"Let us know if you need anything"
		"will do, thanks"

Alone   empty   sad
FOCUS   air's warm   that's right, it's summer…
still outside   quiet   no one around   eerie
clip, clop _ clip, clop…   street-light   key rattling   drop, bend,
pick up
	click car door feels heavy tonight plonk slam
	Think I'll just rest my head for a minute
		hands grab steering wheel squeeze tight
can't go   not right   can't leave him here alone…
	He was supposed to be coming home two weeks they said
		why? too many whys
till death do us part?   cruel   too abrupt
	can't be over sob, breathe _ sob, breathe _ sob, breathe
chest sore   heart hurts   body aches head to toe

BED   where are you?   too far
silence   nothing   sitting
silence   nothing   sitting
    sigh, I better go then   can't stay here all night.

Key turning   purr, purr, purr
driving   indicator on   click-clack – click-clack
green light   moving slow   funeral procession….
home   light on   good
 click-clack – click-clack   better put the handbrake on   eeeekk.
sitting   nothing   waiting for legs to move   breathing
look at the full moon   he's gone!   can't believe it   surreal
        better go inside
            Bag?   leave in car   deal with it tomorrow
slam   pitter, patter, pitter, patter
jingle, jingle   too much junk in this bag!   click
"Whose there?"   "Hi mum
            You still up?"
"Yes   Is he gone then?"
      "Shortly after ten this evening"
"You okay?"   "Yeah!"
      "Do you wanna talk about it?"
   "No, too tired   think I'll go to bed
              "Okay?"
              "Okay!"
pitter, patter, pitter, patter
bed at last   falling onto a soft cloud   melting   silence
staring
        forgot how fluffy my pillow was   not quite right   puff,
puff, thump, thump
 still not quite right   wriggle, wriggle   that's better   now I can
relax
          it's finally over
                been a long journey   four and a half years
    waiting   breathing   waiting   breathing
Where is sleep?   it's hiding again
      Night, be kind   sweet dreams   please

Miss you so much it hurts   sob, gasp _ sob, gasp _ sob, gasp
        visit me   in my sleep   if you can?
      sob, gasp _ sob, gasp_ sob, gasp
    One last word would be nice   a hug   something   anything
Guess I'll just have to lie here until I go to sleep…
ah ha   ah ha   ah ha   ah ha   ah ha _______________________

Clouds

Sheree Pratt

Thoughts…

    Clouds
        of thoughts.

Empty clouds -- I'll fill those
           later.

Blue sky… clouds
      Warm day
        Cold room

clouds... cloudy...
      clouded thoughts
           clouded memories…

Time.
    Space.
      Feelings…
      Lost in clouds.

Something happened.
Something happened - shifted
        in me - but what?

What happened? How -
      did it feel
      did it make me feel?
      did it change me?

Something brews…

Dark clouds -- storm clouds -- storm
                                    rising -- in
                                           me

No rain falls.

Darker clouds storm clouds -- storm
                                 brewing

Thick. Heavy. Clouds
                -- smothering
                        clouds.

Tremors... stomach
            rumbles -- low
            rumbles -- intense
            rumbles -- the earth
            rumbles

I know what
        comes

                next--   BOOM!

Thunder!   CRACK!

Lightning
-- flashes cut the darkness --   BOOM! CRACK!
-- light rips dark apart --   CRACK!
slices the sky
            -- clouds in pieces
            -- clouds -- stitched together -- BOOM!
                        Instantly -- CRACK!

            Broken --   BOOM!
                    Again -- CRACK!

A tree snaps--   BOOM!
            Falls --   CRACK!

Devastation all a --   BOOM! CRACK!
                                               BOOM!
                       round.
Clouds… bonded -- broken -- bonded -- broken
again. Repeatedly
                               broken-- CRACK!

The big think.
            The
                    big
                        think -- I feel it in my --
                                        core.
Thick. Heavy. Smothering thoughts. Then comes the --
                                        rain…
Pouring down
            rain -- flooding
            rain -- rain that never
                            stops...

Never STOPS!

If only it would just rain
                    now -- If only it would
                    rain -- just a little bit -- not too much.
                                        Now.
instead.

Pharmaceuticalist Delusion

Caleb Irvine-Kingsmith

We want political action!
Unfortunate gimmick
Gangrenous infection of the…

We want a nice world!
Unlucky pharmaceuticalist
Envious monster

We want non-violent change!
Lovable brainwasher
Fraudulent reassurer

We want Zuckerberg for free!
Patriotic Nazi
Orwellian negligent

Most of all—

We want fallacious outrage!
A Bill of Rights for us
well, for me anyway.

Russian Orthodox
Meredith Adams

her face

          eyes shut

    still

incense

byzantine gold

dark walls

        small squares — of light

smiling, crying

incense

     Russian

we walk

      around

it makes more

sense

     than English

soft light

small squares

in—cense

       in — out

          ahhhhhh

dark walls

it makes more

       sense

to

not kiss

       her hand

not kiss

         her — still — smiling — lips

Smile

Brandon Kelly

My whole life I was told the same thing over, and *over* again, to just smile.

Before I was diagnosed with Autism, I was told to smile.

My first day at a new school, I was told to smile.

My grandparents' family, tells me I should smile.

My boss at work experience, tells me I should smile.

All my life I was told, "you are angry", just because I don't smile,

and I tell them I *always* smile.

Sleeping Statue

Tenzin Castleman

Sleeping statue
overlooking the cold pathway.
rain pours down where flowers once grew.
Beautiful girl… gone away.

Overlooking the cold pathway,
the mother watched the storm pour down.
Beautiful girl… gone away.
It was like the dirt itself would drown.

The mother watched the storm pour down.
The bushes swirled; the wind tried to tear them apart.
It was like the dirt itself would drown,
as her tears froze on her shattered heart.

The bushes swirled; the wind tried to tear them apart.
Cold statue praying in the rain,
as her tears froze on her shattered heart –
holding knitted clothes in vain.

Cold statue praying in the rain,
stone all shivered with water,
holding knitted clothes in vain –
clothes she'd knitted for her daughter.

Stone all shivered with water,
empty baby clothes in her hands –
clothes she'd knitted for her daughter,
pitying the child in the wetlands.

Empty baby clothes in her hands –
she dons them on the statue's head,
pitying the child in the wetlands.
To keep them warm for the days ahead
look after her in the world of the dead.

Life of the Phoenix
Zech Elliot

She was a Phoenix.
This is where she rose from the ashes.
Her heart is made from inner beauty.
Her soul is made from flames.

So, she began the reincarnation.
From her own remains and embers.
This is where the bird begins her flight.
Her cry pierces anyone who hurts her.

As she flies above the mountains
The majestic bird looks on, curious.
Days go by and her embers begin to fall.
Hunger erupts inside her, welcoming food.

She is now old and tired.
Her embers have fallen.
There is no death but birth.
As she becomes a new incarnation.

Leaf
Cameron Dale

autumn leaves—dance
a last performance of
beauty—before
winter

like the sunset before
dark—or the smile of
a loved one—as
they depart

a beauty—beyond our
control—no painter's easel
contains such colours
or shades

to witness this—
what are the chances of
one autumn leaf as
it dances?

7'44" In Parking Zone 35502085 (Chance Operation #1)

J L Penn

(Timed notes taken while observing shoppers and traffic through the car windscreen, waiting for my daughter to return to parking bay in Williamson Street, Bendigo; from 13:10 August 25th, 2021. Rules: time limit, and observations taken as people walked along the footpath. Traffic were observed as images in shop windows or noticed because of noise.)

The parking

meter blinks   EXPIRED   EXPIRED

Along the footpath a brindled mastiff strains

against its purple leash, a charcoal hoodie and

mask   pulled behind—long legs

scissoring across the bluestone pavers.

Three black poodles circle the woman

wearing a khaki jacket and faded

denim jeans—blue cigarette smoke hangs—

then spirals before it's stolen by the wind.

A young father, his hands full of shopping bags,
bends his head to his fair-haired daughter who
        skips beside him. Curled brown—leaves huddle under
the wheels of a chrome-plated clothes rack

        butter-yellow beanie, black mask, long
chestnut curls—he must be all
        of twenty-three—friends spill around
him   laughing at some shared joke.

        leopard-skin scarf, a chemtrail-scent of
perfume in her wake. I count a white
        hijab, one purple tracksuit, seven
puffer jackets: grey, black, green, and blue

        large tote and latte stalks by on
steepled heels—her cropped hair foils of
        silver and ash-grey—a fashion
tragic beauty the skateboarder avoids

        white earbuds dangle, a mask
tucked under his chin Subway roll in
        one hand—a medium-size
drink in the other   tattooed wrist

      cars roar—woofers pump their *doof, doof*
bass, as other vehicles follow—reflections
      flickering across shop windows. The parking
meter flashes   EXPIRED   EXPIRED

      A coal-grey suede jacket pauses to
window shop—furling his red umbrella as
      speckled wings: fawn,   chocolate, and sienna
—a flurry of bickering sparrows

      the young shop attendant embraces
a stack of folded carboard boxes against
      a gust of wind, the parking meter is
blinking   EXPIRED   EXPIRED

      Four beanies negotiate a purple
scarf—trawling the middle of the pavement like
      a rudderless oyster punt—her face lit
by the light from her mobile phone.

      The red and white signs advertising
50% OFF   are not
      enough to entice buyers.

Safe Passage
Delilah Cornwall

Our Lady of The Void we beg You

Though darkness, demons, and death surround us,

We beg your mercy, see us safely through

We humbly plead safe passage swift and true

Through Your Lightless Realm, across the stars contiguous

Our Lady of The Void we beg You

Your servants cruel through whom power You accrue

Guide them away from we few, the pious

We beg your mercy, see us safely through

Death and Doom, Entropy and Decay, all serve You

Lady of Endings and Endlessness, spare we the virtuous

Our Lady of The Void we beg You

Prayers, devotion and sacrifice, so that You do not eschew

We Your faithful, who bathe in Your light, luminous

Our Lady of The Void we beg You

And in Your mercy see us safely through

Grey

MJ Douven

Grey are the skies, grey as the tears that silent fall.

Grey are the waves that beat on unforgiving shores,

Grey as the grief that shrouds that hall,

Where haunts the lonesome shadow of a prince forlorn.

Grey as the waves that beat those unforgiving shores,

That pound hard, loud, against the fortress wall.

There haunts the lonesome shadow of a prince forlorn,

Last son, first son, heir to his father's downfall.

They pound hard, loud, against the fortress wall,

Loud as the prince's rage-filled, grief-struck roar –

First son, last son, heir to his father's downfall,

Shattered, broken, in the eternal war.

Loud still that prince's rage-filled, grief-struck roar,

Grey still the grief that shrouds that hall,

Broken, shattered by the eternal war.

Grey still the skies, grey still the tears that silent fall.

Oh Joy

Sha James

Oh Joy, sprout wings and deliver this weary traveller into the palace of Night.

Soar high above the dross of unquenched desire besieging the modern landscape.

Grant me passage into the house of my celestial mother who sits regally in her royal

    abode – where angels live forevermore.

Let her wrap me in a blanket of stars with their twinkling lullaby to soothe my furrowed

    brow and cradle me in peace.

Oh Joy, grant my senses passage into Night's lofty stable that they might rest from the

    ceaseless round of enticements failing to deliver daily on their promise.

I long to bathe in the Milky Way with its misty white salve to wash away the residue of

    excess causing my mind to writhe in anguish.

How I long for the sweet embrace of stillness to soothe bodily aches and pains and

    release my tormented spirit into silence.

Oh Joy, give chase to the folly plaguing this disquieted soul dressed in fleshly garb that it

> may hear Wisdom's whispers resounding in the inner sanctum.

Curb rebellious impulses resisting the sleep-inducing mantle of my noble Queen, tireless in

> her nightly vigil to shield the world from insanity.

Night's gifts are subtle but no less worthy of highest praise throughout noblest estates

> in all Kingdom Come.

Oh Joy, gladden this heart as Night graces my bedroom door and sweeps me up in her

> flowing robe, lest I swap crib for grave.

Bathe me in gratitude and timely reminders of you who await when the sun's rays kiss the

> morning dew.

My reward for surrender to Night's gentle promptings, awakening on your uplifted wings.

Ahhhhhhh! – Stretchhhh! – Yawnnnnn!

> It's been a very long day
>
> > Will someone please turn out the light!

Mollusc

Sha James

Teeth

Sheree Pratt

Teeth.
White teeth.
Looking at white teeth.
The *joy* of looking at white teeth.
Big smiles with white *teeth*.

Oh! Do I have white teeth?

When was the last time they *saw* my teeth?
When was the last time *I* saw teeth?

In the last twelve months we've *only* seen teeth in the media,
In social media
In mainstream media
In the news on T.V.
In the movies.

Out *here*?

Everyone's *covered* up their teeth.
Everyone's struggling, juggling their lips, tongues and teeth
to eat, to speak, to reach past their teeth,

to send thoughts into the universe in words.
It's no *wonder* we don't feel heard.
No one knows who's speaking.

So we do it all at once, saying different things, losing meaning.

Some grind an axe.
Some grind my gears.
Some grind their *teeth*.

I grind my teeth.

But oh, the joy of *removing the thing that conceals* my teeth,
but *not* to reveal my teeth.
No one *wants* to see my teeth,
Or *hear* the thoughts that escape as words through my teeth
And collide with the breadcrumbs and cereal I *break down* with my teeth.

I swallow the crumbs and words.
I swallow the lump forming further back from my teeth.
I *shut up* and cover my teeth.
I seethe and I *grind* my teeth.

I still grind my teeth.
my covered–up teeth.
Keep the shanty song beat with *chattering* teeth.
It's a *break* from grinding my teeth.

Practice smiling with covered up teeth.
Practice breathing, feel the air pass through my teeth,

Contemplate the *importance* of teeth.
Not just the *appearance* of teeth,
Not just the state of teeth
And *consider* the role of teeth.

I got stuck on concept of 'teeth'...

The anchor of everything is teeth.
The meaning of *life* is teeth.

Dentists have seen the *most* teeth
But usually, the *worst* of teeth
usually at the end of the *lifespan* of teeth.

The lifespan of *teeth*…
This is becoming quite meaty,

too meaty for my teeth,

My *not*-so-white teeth.
My *covered*-up teeth.
My *grinding* teeth.
My *chattering* teeth.
My busy *teeth*.

My teeth.
Teeth.

The Silent Ship
Delilah Cornwall

The ship is silent and still
Its engines sound no more
The crew are all lost to the chill

The stars watch on, intentions ill
Radiation spills from the core
The ship is silent and still

With ice their lungs have filled
Captain and passengers are no more
The crew are all lost to the chill

In death no blood has spilled
Their loved ones will never be sure
The ship is silent and still

The Void drinks its fill
Down its throat the dead pour
The ship is silent and still
The crew are all lost to the chill

Surrealist Romp
Meredith Adams

prawns into the ripe bananas
with turquoise giraffes that waited
making patterns of covid mucus
that precipitated a shower
in the slow migration up the legs
of odour abandoning in skunks

the Mongolian gold underpants
modelled in Paris later in
the weeping mango morning sigh
their dripping juices with the weeping
entrails of coruscations
between another rotten ape

an axe with chips with ice-cream
squawking for bread from a thousand
slated penguin grabbed the hand of
a number of wombats to make
Dutch cheese tucked under one arm
in front of the ostrich

the taste of good–year tyres
were swinging on the lamp posts
shouted agonizing death between
the golden underpants that had walked
violently at the oncoming traffic
snapped at the golden thread hanging

flapping down the Champs-Elysées
gaudy bra time of the last light
had the bra under the purple cloak
with the clanging bells and burbling
had been embalmed for some time
in the hope of being Refurbished

Refusal to Move
Caleb Irvine-Kingsmith

The madman tells lies,
prophesizing anxious curiosity,
satisfying –
woeful tidings console you.
Warm, serene, earnest.
Concerned for future arrival.

They now embellish this breathless horror –
dying of violent starvation.
Beautiful!
Inanimate accidental catastrophe.
Dying motion blur.

Almost but certainly not –
a defiant sexual pleasure.
Perfectly solitary with –
agreeable sensations.
What is the issue?

Admire my hideous reflection,

my wretched high thoughts,

my dreams of solitary home.

Admire my beautiful refusal —

to move.

I cannot rouse to exertion.

Only to be crushed in —

their colossal conflict,

their unreal reservoir of exact need.

Here voice is reduced to quiet whimper —

and honesty is insufferable.

Love of The Supreme Being

Delilah Cornwall

Beyond stars,

Beyond light,

There is love.

Maker's love.

Creator's love.

All our love.

Supreme Being

Hugs us close.

It loves all.

Embrace love.

Take hold of

Unity.

Forget pain.

Forget hate.

Love abounds.

Supreme being

Loves you true,

Keeps you safe.

Embrace love.

Take hold of

Unity.

Join with us.

Become one

Family.

Join today.

Be loved

Forever.

The Reluctant Poet

Sha James

I thought I was a poet because I liked rhyme.
Watch words spring to life along blue coloured lines.
But jumbled up phrases just sent me to rage,
as I watched words stumble and fall on the page.

They fell in a heap I am sad to say.
On the bottom line they did swagger and sway.
Poetical non-sense marched right out the door,
when they had to start counting one, two, three, four.

Don't give up now I said to these wondrous words.
Your message is great; it still needs to be heard.
Losing heart is no good my linguistic allies –
Keeping time is so hard they lamented and cried.

We are stressed to the max with Iambs and Trochees.
Pentameter sucks, it's not all that it should be.
Take heart little words, keep a wide-open mind,
just give it a chance and you will do fine.

Then they picked themselves up and put on some ink,
turned round in a circle; said what do you think?
Shall we give it a try just one more time?
Wipe the tears from our eyes let's rhythm and rhyme?

I said yes this is good, don't give in to defeat,
let's learn how to march with poetic feet.
Turn misunderstood into think I mistook,
overturn irony, find a new hook.

They got up and stood tall these marvellous words.
Put on some new shoes to make the march smooth.
Feathers poked out from left and from right,
for wings they desired oh to take flight.

This is no time to snooze, they muttered and grumbled.
We've work to do if we don't want to stumble.
Make poetry from prose and then, well who knows.
Let's climb on the pulpit to scale our new home.

And so, we advanced, these brave words and I,
to master The Art, to do or to die.
Find metre and time to hold reader minds,
capture their thoughts in rapturous rhyme.

Now the words are still learning the poet's way,
the lyrical path that bounces and plays.
They are honing their skills of metaphor and myth,
finding symbols and tales that bring many gifts.

Of priceless gems and grace uplifting,
through mazes of words and jumble they're sifting.
Bringing banners of hope, showing loss of face,
to admonish wrong doers or inspire a race.

But they're well on their way, I am pleased to say,
these courageous words so bold and so brave.
Turning blah–blah–blah into graceful ballet,
from mental gymnastics of meaningless sway.

Who knows, maybe now a sonnet they'll make?
To cause other poems to quiver and quake.
Masters of old you had better beware,
the words are coming to claim their fair share.

Find a place to star in the Literary Cannon.
Take cheer humble words – it may very well happen!

NOVEL EXTRACTS

The Circus Children

Faith Dam

A circus moves from town to town capturing the hearts and souls of all who see, adults and children alike. That is the life for those of the Twilight Circus except it is not all as it seems. As they travel, children go missing from each town, but no one can remember them. As night falls, ringmaster Bexen and her two co-performers Kitten and Luna go out into the towns and recruit these children for the circus. These are the circus children. Taken away and manipulated by magic, their life is now the circus.

As the Twilight Circus moves for one of their biggest stops in the city of London, Scotland Yard detective, Archie Campbell, decides to pay them a visit. Being sure not to reveal his work but trying his best to get closer to Bexen, he slowly uncovers the mystery of the missing children. As he and Bexen get closer, his heart says to drop the case while his head screams for their arrest.

As he plans for their arrest Bexen plans for their escape. When Archie disrupts their final show, the circus and the children within it disappear without a trace. You've read it before now read it again. This is Archie's point of view.

The girl spun around, the green ribbons and ruffles on her dress twirling in the breeze. She had a grin on her face which revealed a small cavity where a tooth should have been. Her smile dropped when she saw me. She took a step back. "I'm sorry sir, but the circus isn't open yet. You'll have to come back later."

I smiled at her and knelt. The ground was wet as a result of yesterday's rain. Mud soaked through my pants, and I felt it, cold against my skin. I tried to hold it together as I internally cringed, hating the feeling and dreading that the stink of mud and filth would never wash out.

"It's alright, your Ringmaster Eliza – I mean, Bexen, let me in." She still seemed uncertain, but she relaxed at Bexen's name. "Do you mind if I ask you a few questions?"

"We're not meant to talk to the guests…"

"It's alright, it will only take a minute."

"No… I should really be getting back." She turned to go, "The others are probably looking for me."

I reached out and grabbed her wrist – perhaps a little too hard. She cried out in pain.

"One question," I said holding up a finger. "Just one and you can go."

"Please!" she cried, "I need to go. You're hurting me!"

"What's your name?"

"Gosling! My name is Gosling!"

I shook my head. "No. Your real name."

"That is my name! I don't have another one!"

"I don't believe you!" I shouted, and her eyes widened in surprise. "I know that is your circus name, I want to know your real name."

"Please…" she begged, her voice coming out as a whimper, "let me go."

I fished for something in my pocket and pulled out a small photograph with a little girl in it. Holding it up to compare the two, I felt my heart race. It was the same girl except she had all of her teeth in the photograph, her hair was tied and brushed, but now it was tangled and frazzled for the show. "Are you Mary Smith?"

I watched her carefully. Was that a glimmer of recognition I saw in her eyes?

"I… I…" A small tear slid down her face.

"Archie?" The frightened girl jumped at the sound of the new voice.

I closed my eyes and sighed. Hearing her voice made me smile, but I realised she had stumbled upon something she wouldn't want to see. Standing quickly, I smiled and spun around. "Bexen!" I cried, a touch too enthusiastically. She was the only thing I still liked about this place. At first, I enjoyed the food and the characters I had met but now it was all too much. Too… overwhelming. I hated it all. The food, the animals, the children that ran around screaming. The unanswered questions. But Bexen though… she wasn't like the others here; she understood me. Like I understood her.

"Archie, what are you doing?" She spoke calmly, though her eyes were on the girl behind me. "Gosling? Honey, are you alright?"

I glanced over my shoulder. The kid was crying. She glared at me and stepped back slightly, tripping on the hem of her skirt. Bexen was clearly confused.

"Here," I said offering 'Gosling' my hand - but she shuffled backwards, wiping away her tears with a fistful of green ribbon.

"N-no, stay away from me."

Bexen moved forward and lifted Gosling effortlessly into her arms.

"Hey, now. It's alright, what happened?"

Gosling nestled her head into Bexen's chest and muttered some indistinct words, which earned me a sharp, querying glance. She put the girl down.

"Okay honey." Gesturing to an older boy, she called him over. "Calder? Come and take Gosling back to the troupe."

The boy nodded and took Gosling's small hand in his. Bexen lent into Calder and whispered something to him. He looked hard at me for a quick second, then led away the girl who called herself 'Gosling'.

"Is she alright?" I asked once they had left.

Bexen turned to me and said nothing. She grabbed my hand, but her fingers slipped down. She pulled me along until we were outside the circus gate and then stopped.

"Archie."

"Elizabeth."

"What were you doing with Gosling?" She folded her arms over her chest.

"Talking to her," I said as though it had been obvious.

"Somehow I don't believe that was just 'talking'. Why was she so upset?"

She stared at me, but I met her gaze confidently. "It was. I was just talking to the girl, and I suppose I must have said something that upset her. Poor thing just started bawling."

"Archie Campbell," she was cross now, "what were you *actually* doing?"

I must have spent too much time with her if she was able to see through me that easily. I was beating myself up for that, perhaps if I hadn't kept meeting her or concentrated more on my work then none of this would have happened.

"I promise, I was just talking to her."

"Archie!"

"Honestly, I was. And, well I may have asked her a few questions-"

"I've told you not to ask anyone any questions!" Bexen snapped.

"- but only questions about the circus!" I finished quickly. For the first time in a while, I didn't feel bad about lying to her. I had to if I was going to find out any more about the circus and the operation that was being run here. It was my job. It had been my job from the start.

"Bexen… er, Lizzy. Can I ask *you* a question?"

She met my eyes. I could have sworn I saw pity in them.

"I guess you can, but I'm still going to ask you about what just happened with Gosling. I can't leave that unsolved because to me, it looked like a lot more than simple talking."

"Liz, I need you to be honest with me. This is a really serious situation." Her demeanour changed again and this time she looked wary, her defences suddenly up as if she knew what was coming.

"Elizabeth, what do you know about the missing children?"

"Was that what you were talking to Gosling about?" she snapped. Her eyes blazed with an anger and a fury that matched her beautiful auburn hair. "How could you talk to her, a child, about such an awful situation!"

"Bexen, the whole situation is awful, every little detail about it!"

"And what do you know about it? Nothing, that's what, so what could you expect me or an innocent child to know about it?"

"Have you not read the papers? Have the *children* not seen the papers?"

"Of course, I have, but everything that they print these days is the most awful of news! The world is a cruel unhappy place!"

"Every single edition has at least one section dedicated to those kidnappings, to the murders, to the mothers and fathers who have no recollection of ever having had a child in their life."

"Well, they haven't for a while. I bet that they've stopped now. Perhaps the person behind it has stopped. Did you ever think about that?"

"You're jumping to the defence of this case very quickly. Surely, you're worried. Look at all the children that you have around you in this circus." I gestured around us, back into the circus where we came from. She followed my gaze and then looked to the ground.

"Why the sudden interest, Archie? Why start asking questions now? You've been with us all of this time and you've had plenty of time with me, why start asking questions now?"

I kept my gaze strong but inside my mind was racing. Could she know why I was here, why I had spent so much time with her and the circus? No… Surely, she would have acted sooner in fear of the circus being shut down. Unless…

"I-I'm just, I don't know." I looked down to the ground and sighed. "I'm sorry Bexen, I didn't mean to make you uncomfortable or cause any issues, I just…"

She took my hands gently in hers. "We're all worried, Archie. I'm sorry for snapping at you before. I should never have said what I said."

"And I to you. It was silly of me to believe that you would know anything."

We gazed at each other, sharing a moment of apology and forgiveness. I wanted so badly to tell her the truth, but now didn't seem like the right time. It never did. And if I did tell her, I knew she wouldn't forgive me. But this time, I didn't feel particularly bad about what I had done. I had asked my questions as boldly as I knew how. Perhaps lying wasn't so bad. Perhaps being her bad guy wasn't so bad.

"I love you, Elizabeth," I suddenly said, smiling. "Do you forgive me?

I wrapped my arms around her shoulders and pulled her in tight. She didn't resist. We held each other for a moment before she pulled back. She was smiling up at me, a pink tinge to her face.

"I love you too. And yes." She spoke quietly now. "I have to go. But I can come and find you later. You will stay for a while, won't you?"

"Of course! Wouldn't miss it for the world."

Another lie.

"Okay. I'll see you later." She reached up and placed a quick, gentle kiss on my forehead before walking back into the circus grounds.

She turned and walked away. Something still didn't seem quite right, the way she was walking was somehow different, the way she spoke felt… off. Perhaps she wasn't over it as quickly as I thought she was. Perhaps she still had her suspicions. But no. I was being stupid, surely. She had no reason to believe that I was working for the Yard. I was just being nosy, yes that was it.

After making sure that she was gone and wouldn't turn back, I turned on my heel and marched down the empty dirt road. The sun was already setting, and the air was eerily still. I looked to the sky for a moment, the clouds glowing pink and orange as they floated across the sun's view. "Looks like we're in for some bad weather…" I muttered. "Best to close before the storm, Bexen."

*   *   *

When I finally reached the Yard, the rain was lashing down in great cold sheets, obscuring the sight of every person and carriage. I sheltered under the eaves for a moment, gaining the courage to walk inside. I clenched and unclenched my hands and kept reaching for the handle and as I did, the door swung open. I stumbled backwards, tripping on the curb.

As I flailed my arms around in a vain attempt to regain balance, a hand reached out and grabbed me by the wrist, pulling me back up.

"Woah there!" a voice cried, "Sorry about that, Arch, didn't know *you* were there."

"George?" I said to the familiar face, "what are you doing here?"

"Looking for you actually!" George replied, "You know, Arch, we haven't caught up for a while. You spend too much time at work, I don't see you enough!"

I held up a hand to stop him and used the other to brush my overcoat down.

"Look, I'm sorry, George. But as much as I'd like to have a drink with you, I really can't right now." I reached for the door again, but he threw his arm in front of me, stopping me in my tracks.

"Hold up! Why the rush? Surely you can take just an hour off, you'll overwork yourself."

"George. I can't. I might have just cracked something huge." I bent under his arm and opened the door. "Maybe next time," I said with a sheepish grin. "see you later."

I closed the door, removed my hat, and ran a hand through my hair. If only he knew that I had been hanging around at a circus and not the Yard this whole time. What would he think of me then? I shook my head. Who cared what he thought?

Woah. What was that? What was I turning into?

"Hey, Archie, you've, uh, you've got some guts showing up here."

I looked up and groaned. I didn't have time for this!

"Move out of the way, John," I said.

"Hey, why the rush?"

"Because I may have cracked a case. Which is more than what your lazy arse could do. Where's the Chief?"

He paused. "He's, uh, he's in a meeting… He won't like it if you barge in there uninvited."

I shrugged. "He already hates me. But he needs to hear this." I pushed past him, and headed straight for the stairs. Three flights later, and puffing, I made it to the chief's office. For a moment, I considered knocking but then something got the better of me and I barged right through the door.

"…look, ma'am, we're doing all that we can, but right now, this case isn't at the top of our priorities- Archie, what the devil do you think you're doing?"

"I'm sorry, sir, but I need to talk to you about the case I'm on."

He sighed and held a hand to his forehead. "Look, can't it wait? I'm in a meeting!"

I looked to the lady that sat in the chair across from him and gave her a curt nod. "It really can't wait, sir."

He looked from me to the woman and then, standing from his desk, he offered her a hand. "I'm very sorry madam. We'll do everything in our power. If you have any further questions, please leave them with the front desk. I might be busy for a while," he said, glaring at me.

"Thank you, officer, thank you." She took his hands in hers. "I'm sorry for taking up your time."

He showed her to the door, and once sure she was gone and out of earshot, rounded on me. "What the devil do you think you're doing? Don't you know how to knock, man!?"

"I'm sorry, sir, but this is so very important, and you need to hear what I've found."

He ignored what I had said and kept going. "My God, do you know what a closed door means? You have no idea what I could have been doing-"

"I've got a fair idea sir. Rosie last week, wasn't it?" He stopped talking and glared at me.

"Bring that up again, I dare you." He pointed a finger threateningly at me. "You'll be out of here before you can prove anything. Then you'll never solve that damned case."

"But, sir, that's exactly why I'm here. I have news about the missing children."

He didn't move for a moment and continued to stare. I glanced at the chair. "Should I sit down?"

"Fine." He took up his seat slowly. "Well?" For the first time in a long time, he seemed eager to hear what I had to say.

"Was she a mother of one of the missing children?" I asked, curious about the woman who had left.

"No, she was here about her missing son, older chap."

"He's not linked to the other missing children?"

"No, I said! She had full recollection, unlike the other parents." He looked down at the desk for a moment and then seemed to come back to his senses. "Anyway, we're not here to discuss that."

"Well, we kind of are."

"Talk back again, why don't you. I'd love it."

"Sorry, sir," I said, quickly dipping my head.

"Tell me what you think you've have found. We'll have to tell press soon what we're doing about this mess."

What *we're* doing? Obviously, he'd take credit for all the work that I was doing. I wanted to reach across and slap some sense into him but, thankfully, I held myself back and cleared my throat.

"Well," I started, "I believe the circus is linked… just like you originally thought."

"Oh, yes? Well then dazzle me with your proof, Archie." It sounded like he was starting to doubt me again and was reverting to his old self, the one that wouldn't listen.

"I spoke with their Ringmaster."

"You got yourself close enough to talk to those people?"

I nodded and for a moment I thought I saw a glimmer of pride in his eye.

"She told me that they know nothing more about it than you or I, but…"

"You *asked* her?" I nodded. "You asked her if she knew about the missing children?"

"Yes sir." He sighed and held a hand to his forehead.

"Archie, you're a blithering idiot!" He stood up from his chair and started to pace behind his desk. "How stupid can you be?"

"But she answered the questions–"

"I don't care! You never ask a suspect outright! Honestly, I thought you were smarter than this!"

"You *did*?" This actually shocked me. Perhaps he did care about me and the work I was doing.

"Yeah, yeah I did. Not now." He stopped his pacing and turned back around to look at me. "Just, get out of my office Archie and don't come back here until you have some real proof."

"B–but sir"

He held up a hand and didn't look at me. "Go Archie, before I fire you on the spot.

I stood from the chair and felt my hands clench into fists at my side. "I will be back." I said, "And then you'll see!"

He chuckled and turned his back to me. "Yes. We'll see."

I stood outside in the hallway for a moment, dragging my hands through my hair and down my face, as I tried to collect my thoughts.

"Stupid, stupid me. Stupid, stupid Archie stupid Campbell!"

How could I be so stupid? The chief was right. I was a blithering idiot.

When I made it back into the lobby, John still sat there and turned to meet me as I came out. "So, what did the boss think about you charging into his meeting? That lady didn't come out looking so happy."

"Bugger off, John. I'm about to crack a case."

"Of course, you are. I'll see you later when you return to get fired."

I felt his nose shatter under my fist, and watched as the blood spurted from his nostrils. I'd never hit someone that hard before. In fact, I had never hit *anyone*. My fist hurt. Maybe I really *was* losing my mind, but I didn't want to think too much about it. I was too worked up to care.

"Mister Campbell!" The receptionist scolded me as she stood from her desk. "We do *not* start fights in this lobby!" She came out from behind her desk and offered John a handkerchief, not that it wasn't doing much for all the blood that was there.

"Sorry for the mess, Rosie." I didn't look at her or John as I apologised, instead, I walked to the door and exited the building.

It was still raining sheets. The wind howled, thunder cracked, and lightning split the sky. I moved out from under the eaves and stood under the downpour of rain, letting it soak through my clothes and cleanse my face. "You want proof? You want evidence? Oh, I'm going to give you evidence." I pulled my hat tight over my head and turned down the road. "You've got a big storm coming, Bexen".

Last Man

MJ Douven

Last Man is the story of a king who is betrayed by the woman he loves, badly injured, and left for dead in a distant land, across the sea from his empire. His first instinct is to do everything he can to return home, until he discovers that his people are being kidnapped and sold as slaves in this foreign land. This makes him even more determined to return home, but not before he takes every last man of his people home with him.

Chapter 1

This was a mistake. Every instinct Urien had was telling him that, but he kept walking through the increasingly deserted streets of Valmar, toward the harbor.

Nothing about this was right. But Gwyndor had pleaded with him to come here, had insisted that it was important, and that was enough for him.

Every time he started to doubt, he reminded himself that he had taken every precaution possible. No one knew that he was here. Just in case someone was following him – which was unlikely – he had taken the most indirect route through the city, using every trick that Gwyndor had taught him.

By the time he reached the far side of the harbor, in the old part of the city, the sun had already set. He stood there for a moment on the cracked cobbled street, staring in disbelief and growing anger at the broken-down warehouses and empty quays, damaged in the last great flood. When he returned home, he planned to find out why nothing was being done to repair the damage.

As the moon climbed higher in the sky, he waited in the shadow of the abandoned warehouse closest to the water, rising every so often to stretch his legs when they became numb from crouching. He shivered as the breeze off the water turned chilly, bristling the hairs on the back of his neck. The only sounds were the lapping of water against the nearby quays and the rhythmic break of waves on the shore.

It must have been close to midnight when a different sound made his head jerk up. It sounded like a woman's laugh, eerily familiar, and completely out of place down here among these deserted buildings. He knew he should stay hidden until Gwyndor arrived, but he could not seem to help himself.

He stood up slowly, trying to place where the sound he had heard had come from. Until that moment, he had been certain that he was alone.

"Urien." He wheeled around at her familiar voice.

She stood on the edge of the nearest quay, silhouetted against the moonlit bay. Instinctively, before his brain caught up with the rest of him – before he remembered exactly *why* he had banished her from his palace – he took a step toward her.

"What are you doing here?" His voice cracked over the words.

Her smile was ugly. "Do you really need to ask?"

She nodded slightly, but not at him – rather at someone, or something, behind him. He started to turn, but it was already too late.

*   *   *

"Enough." Urien barely made out her voice through the haze of pain. "I said I wanted him alive."

The soldier pinning Urien against the warehouse wall released him with a shove that sent him sprawling onto the cold stone street. He lay there for a few moments, trying to summon up the strength to scramble to his feet. To fight back. He bit his lip to keep from crying out as the second soldier directed several vicious kicks to his already battered ribs.

He could not let them think that they had managed to beat the fight out of him. So, he willed his bruised, aching fists to unclench, willed his cut and bleeding fingers to reach for the hilt of his sword, lying where it had fallen only a few inches away. Too far. A heavy boot descended on his fingers, crushing them.

"Get him up." She barked the order at her men. "I want him to look me in the eyes. I want him to know that he lost."

The two soldiers obeyed, hauling Urien up between them and dragging him over to where she stood. Urien tried to stiffen, to pull free of their grip, but instead, his head bobbed limply forward. He did not even have the strength to stand on his own, much less to fight.

But he refused to let her think he had been beaten. It took every ounce of his willpower, but he managed to lift his head and stare defiantly into her coal-black eyes. He ignored the blood that trickled down his face and dripped in his eyes, making it hard to see.

Her cool, white hand cupped his chin, the gesture so familiar, so intimate. But there was no lingering tenderness in her eyes, only scorn and hatred. And to think that the emerald glittering on her ring finger had come from him.

Only a few short weeks ago, he had been ready to give her his heart, his name, his world. He would have done almost anything she asked, given her anything she wanted. If only he had not learned the truth about what sort of woman she was, about what she had done.

"How could you?" Urien barely managed to get the words out through his swollen lips. "I loved you."

"You tossed me aside like a toy you had tired of, as though I was nothing to you." She leaned near, so close that her breath caressed his face – so close that her familiar perfume filled his nostrils with the cloying scent of lily and jasmine. "If you had really loved me, the way you claimed you did, you would have stood by me. Not deserted me the minute you heard something you did not think you could live with."

She leaned closer, almost as though she was going to kiss him, brushing her fingers along his jawline. Urien stiffened, refusing to let her see him wince as her fingers grazed the cuts and bruises on his face. He had told himself that he was over her, but her nearness affected him more than he wanted to admit.

He did not know what she was trying to do. Did she think he

would take her back, after she had watched her soldiers beat him and *laughed*?

He was so distracted by her closeness that he did not see her left hand move. Instead, he felt something slam into his ribcage with enough force to knock him back a step, followed immediately by a burning, tearing sensation all down his side.

In shock, all he could do was stare at her – and the brutal knife in her left hand, red with his blood. She laughed as she lunged forward again, and Urien instinctively tried to back away, out of range of her knife. But her soldiers tightened their grip on his arms, holding him in place. Helpless, all he could do was watch as her knife slashed his left leg, opening a gash that immediately started oozing blood. The warm wetness trickled down his calf, seeping through his pant leg in moments.

But the pain gave him a spurt of energy – fueled by desperation, as he realized that, if he did not do something, he would die right here. He was losing blood, and soon he would not be able to fight at all.

Summoning every ounce of remaining strength, he wrenched his arm free from the one soldier's grip and then shoved the second away. He did not stop to pick up his sword, just turned and ran. The quickest way would be to cut across the sand, try to reach the busy harbor. They would not dare to attack him out in the open, where there were witnesses.

But he barely got a few paces before his wounded leg buckled underneath him and he went down, hard. He lay there, face forward in the wet sand, utterly spent. Even if one of the soldiers had not caught up to him and pinned him to the ground with a boot in the center of his back, Urien would not have been able to get back up. He could feel his blood ebbing out of him, soaking into the sand around him.

"That was foolish." Her harsh voice slashed through the shattered shreds of his consciousness.

The soldier rolled him over with his boot, and Urien barely managed to stifle a gasp of pain as he landed on his wounded side on the sand. A wave of salt water washed over him, setting every cut and wound on fire. Black spots danced in front of his vision, and the world around him receded as though he were falling down a dark pit.

The last thing he saw before the world faded to black around him was her – his star, as he had once called her. Her soft black hair blew around her shoulders in the brisk sea wind. And even from this distance, her rich, intoxicating perfume suffocated him.

And then blackness.

*   *   *

"Now." From where he waited in the shadows, Cromak hissed the order at his men. They rose silently from their hiding places, creeping up behind the two soldiers while their attention was focused on the man on the ground. Two simultaneous slashes with those heavy sailors' knives across the soldiers' throats – and both soldiers slumped to the sand. Dead before they could reach for their weapons.

Only then did Cromak step out into the moonlight. "Such a needless waste of life."

"But necessary." The lady's glittering dark eyes turned in his direction, making him uneasy. "I made the mistake once of letting a man live who knew too much. Besides, their deaths will make my story that much more convincing."

"What about him?" Cromak walked over to the man on the sand and rolled him over with the tip of his boot, grimacing. "Was it completely necessary to beat him half to death?"

"What is the matter with you?" Her voice was sharp with annoyance. "Have you grown soft?"

Cromak snorted. "Hardly. But a living slave is worth more to me than a dead one." He jabbed the man in the ribs, but the man did not even twitch. "He will not live long enough to be sold."

"He will live." Hatred and contempt laced her words, whether directed at him or at the man in front of them, Cromak was not sure. "Do whatever you have to do, but I expect to hear that he survived. That he is living out the rest of his miserable life in the most horrific, degrading way possible."

"I cannot make that promise." Cromak crossed his arms. "He will probably be dead before he even makes it to the ship. I have never seen someone survive such serious injuries without being seen to by a physician."

"Then get him one." She flicked her hand at him like he was one of her servants.

"From where?" Cromak only needed to look at the man in front of him to see the cost of crossing this woman, but years of experience dealing with the worst kind of men were telling him to walk away, fast. "I can hardly walk into the city and ask for a physician. Or bring one onto my ship. Slavery is outlawed in Rhonidian, in case you have forgotten."

The look she shot him turned his blood to ice. "Just get him to your ship." She bit the words out. "After that, I do not really care what you do with him. As long as he suffers greatly. And his body is never found."

Cromak opened his mouth to argue that that was not the deal they had made, but she cut him off. "Just remember that, even if he dies tonight, coming here will still have been worth your while. I paid you an immense sum to get rid of him. Even if that means just disposing of his body."

He could not argue with that. The sum she had paid him was more than generous. He was thinking of spending it on a nice fat emerald to adorn his bare middle finger, something loud and ostentatious and totally unnecessary. Something to remind the other merchants who owned the largest slaving fleet in this part of the world.

But the sum he would have gotten for being able to sell such a strong young man had been what finally sealed the deal for him. Fresh slaves – those who had never done a day's work in their life, who had the spirit and will to survive – were much rarer, and therefore incredibly valuable. But Cromak would not pay a single penny for the man on the sand at his feet, not in his condition. No buyer would.

For a moment, he seriously considered turning and walking away. He had already done more than their original agreement required. Against his better judgment, he had had his men eliminate her soldiers. As far as he was concerned, she could throw the man's body into the sea and be done with it.

Still, the two of them had been doing business for years. Much of his wealth was founded on her good graces, just as her wealth depended both on his ships and on his ability to make a profit from their cargo. Without her smoothing the way for him, the next time he arrived in Rhonidian would likely be extremely unpleasant. The last slaver caught smuggling cargo out of a Rhonidi port had been executed, his ship torched and his crew imprisoned.

Grudgingly, he turned to his men. "Take him back to the ship. As soon as the lady and I finish our business here, I will join you."

"We are done." Her tone was frigid. "I want you long gone from here by daylight. I will not have even the hint of a scandal attached to my name because of this. Too much is at stake."

At that moment, Cromak hated her. Who did she think she was, to just dismiss him? If he had another way to make the kind of profit he had been making here for the last ten years, he would walk away and not come back. Let her figure out what to do with the man's body.

Instead, he smiled what he hoped was a sincere-looking smile, nodded, turned, and walked away. He would be glad to get out of Rhonidian for a while. And especially glad to get away from *her*.

2048

Faith Dam

In the year 2048, a radiation spill contaminated all the children born that year. The contaminated children are known as Magee's. They are told apart from others by their glowing veins and their strange powers.

They were a spectacle at first. But since the murders started, Magee's hide away from others.

Officer Danetrius of the Greater Sideney Police Department (a post-apocalyptic Sydney) has investigated the murders of people spread out across the Sideney region.

What started as one or two grows to multiple murders a month, yet Danetrius can't figure out the culprits or their motives. All the murders have one thing in common: the victims were found with black veins, were aged 25, and all were Magee's.

Brin, a young boy from the Underworld, and Leah, a girl with a personal need to solve the murders, are dumped on Officer Danetrius. They all work together to figure out who or what is killing the Magee's.

This scene takes place after the three of them go undercover at Brin's old Underworld joint. During an escape, Brin gets shot, and Leah uses her power of revival, revealing she is a Magee.

C raaack… *The sound echoed through the air. Loud and clear, it was a gunshot.*
Leah and Danny faltered, spinning around to call out to Brin. "Brin. Keep going," Danny shouted.

Brin merely looked up at them, put a hand to his chest, and toppled to the ground.

"Brin," Leah cried, "Brin." Running towards him, she ignored the man standing behind them, a handgun still poised in front of him.

"Leah, duck." Danny drew his pistol, and Leah dove onto the ground, skidding over to Brin and covering her head with her hands.

Multiple shots were fired, and empty cases tinkled around her. Leah looked up as the man collapsed, his shirt stained with crimson. "Brin…" Danny ran over, holstering his weapon as he crouched beside them.

Leah pressed a hand tightly against Brin's chest as blood seeped around it. His breathing was coming quickly and ragged now, and each lungful made him shudder in pain. Danny and Leah looked at each other, watching as their partner slowly drifted. Leah cried openly, calling Brin's name as she desperately tried to stop blood welling out of his wound. Danny sat back and watched. He wanted to cry, but he was their leader, and he was not going to show that he was broken too.

Brin's eyelids fluttered, and he opened his eyes, looking up at the both of them. He blinked for a moment and whispered, "Danny, Leah…how'd we do?"

"We did great, Brin," Leah cried with a smile, "*You* did great. You got us in, and you kept us safe."

"Will you tell Commissioner Frankie?" He asked, drawing a deep breath as he grimaced in pain. "Tell her… I improved. She'd like to hear that…that…" He gasped and coughed, talking was too much effort as flecks of blood sprayed from his mouth. "Tell her one of her underworld experiments worked."

"Brin, I think you've proved to us countless times that you are not just an experiment anymore. You are Leah's partner, and I'm proud to have had you as a partner too." Danny smiled as tears welled up in his eyes. Danny had never revealed such strong emotions before, but it seemed he no longer cared what his partners saw.

"Brin, you can show her yourself how you've changed. I'll make sure you can." She pressed harder onto the wound but got no reaction. "Brin?" She looked down at his face. His eyes had closed, and his face relaxed. "Brin? Danny, Danny, he's gone," She cried. "Danny, he's gone. Danny, help me."

Danny's smile faded as he looked down at the young boy. With his eyes closed, Brin looked as if he had slipped into a restful sleep. But Leah's cries rang loudly in his head, and anger boiled inside his chest. Gun in hand, he moved away from the sobbing Leah stirring up dust as he kicked a rock. "He's dead," He sobbed, kicking it again. "He's dead, and I got him killed." Memories flooded back to him of the same scene but many years before. His partner, dead, all because he hadn't drawn his gun and shot the guy they were after. All because he was a coward.

"Brin, wake up. *Please* wake up."

Leah's cries brought him back to the present as dust swirled around him. "Leah, he's gone," He said through clenched teeth. Walking back to her, he gently placed his hands under her arms and started to lift her away from Brin's still form. With a softer tone, he said, "Come on, we have to go."

"No," she screamed. "We can't leave him." She kicked and flailed in an attempt to get away from Danny.

"Leah, he can't come with us," he said.

"But we can't leave him here for them to find," cried Leah.

Anger boiled up inside him again, and Danny let Leah drop to the ground. "What am I meant to do, Leah?" He shouted as he stepped back from her, "shove him in the back of the car?"

At any other time, a macabre comment like that would have drawn a laugh from the three of them. But it was different now. Everything was different.

"Just, let me try something," Leah said calmly. "I just want a minute with him."

Danny's gaze softened as he looked down on her and nodded. "Fine, but only a minute. We need to go." He stepped away from her to give her some space.

Leah glanced over her shoulder and watched Danny walk away. Wiping her face, she turned back to Brin's body.

"I'm so sorry, Brin… I'm sorry I didn't tell you earlier." She pulled up the sleeves of her coat and placed her hands back on Brin's chest. Closing her eyes, she mustered all the energy she had left and directed it towards her hands. A brilliant blue light engulfed the two of them. The glow was bright but not as bright as it was for Danny as he spun around and covered his eyes. Slowly he reached for his gun, his hand hovering over its checkered grip.

Then Leah sighed and crumpled to lie next to Brin. Starting forward, Danny stopped and stared at her. "You're a–"

"Shut up," she snapped, staring at Brin's dormant body. "Please, Brin, please wake up," she pleaded.

Danny stepped closer, his hand caressing his Glock.

He wasn't going to shoot her…was he?

With a shuddering breath, Brin's eyes opened. Stirring up dust as he dragged himself onto his elbows, he winced in pain as he sat up.

"Holy shit…" breathed Danny.

Brin looked around wildly, then his eyes dropped to the coagulating puddle of blood on his chest as it slithered down to his waist. "What–"

"It's okay." Leah said, "You're okay."

"Brin… let's go back to the car." Danny's sharp voice spooked both of them, so Leah gripped Brin's hand, pulled him to his feet, and drew him towards their vehicle.

"Leah. Stay." Came Danny's terse comment.

Brin stopped, and Leah leaned into him with an arm wrapped tightly around his waist.

"Why do you want Leah to stay?" whispered Brin.

Danny sighed, pinching the bridge of his nose. "Brin, just go. We'll be there in a moment."

Brin didn't argue and pulled free from Leah to walk away.

"Danny, what's wrong?" said Leah. She already knew the answer, so she continued quickly, "We have to go. We can't waste any more time. Brin needs a hosp–"

"You're a Magee," said Danny flatly.

Leah stared at him, her reply frozen in her throat.

"There," Danny cried, throwing his hands up in exasperation. "You have nothing to say."

"You have eyes," Leah muttered.

"And you're a fucking Magee."

"Listen," Leah cried, stepping towards Danny. "You could just be a little bit more grateful. I mean, I just saved Brin's life."

Danny stepped back as she approached and tripped over a rock before crashing to the ground in a cloud of dust. Leah glared at him for a moment before turning on her heels and stalking away.

"Leah," Danny cried, "Leah, come back." He climbed to his feet and brushed his clothes before running after her. "Leah, please."

"No, Danny."

"Leah, I'm sorry," he cried

"Are you through?" She spun around and started marching towards him. "I mean, unless the reaction you just had said otherwise, I don't think you are."

"Leah, I overreacted. I was in shock. I mean, you're a *Magee*."

"Say it again, Danny, let it sink in." She stepped towards him, pulling up her sleeves to reveal her still glowing arms. "Are you afraid of me Danny?"

"I… no," He stuttered.

"Are you AFRAID OF ME?"

Danny unconsciously reached for his gun. Leah faltered and took a step back. "I knew it…" She muttered.

She strode away, quicker this time, desperate to put space between her and Danny. As she passed the car, Brin poked his head out of a window.

"Leah?"

"Forget it, Brin. I'm leaving."

He looked around and spotted Danny. "Danny, what's wrong?" Danny didn't answer as he climbed into the driver's seat. He started the engine, and the car rolled forward.

"You're not going to leave her, are you?"

Danny closed his eyes for a moment and pulled up beside Leah. "Get in the car, Leah." She ignored him and kept walking. "Leah, get in."

"You don't have to do it for Danny," Brin said as he leaned out of the window, wincing in pain. "Do it for me. I'm confused, and I'm scared, and I am in the most awful pain, and I don't know what's happening."

Leah looked at him and grabbed the door handle. Brin shuffled across, but Leah hesitated for a moment. Then Brin smiled at her, and she climbed in.

*   *   *

Partway through the journey, Leah held out a small cube of what looked like jelly from her bag and held it out to Brin. She caught Danny's eye in the mirror and quickly turned away. "Commissioner Frankie gave me some before we left. Y'know…just in case," she said.

Brin popped it into his mouth, and relief instantly washed over his face.

"I want Danny to know that I'm not trying to hurt him," Leah muttered as she crossed her arms and spun around in her seat.

"Why would Danny think that?" Brin asked, "What happened back there?"

Leah looked up and caught Danny watching her in the rear-view mirror. "I don't see why Brin shouldn't know," he said, "It wouldn't be fair to keep such a big secret from him."

Brin looked around in surprise. "What secret? What don't I know?"

Leah turned to Brin, and Danny turned his eyes back to the road. "Brin, I'm a-"

"Leah's a Magee."

"Leah's a what?" Brin asked in surprise.

"Brin..." Leah covered her face with a sigh. "I'm a Magee, and I just revealed it to Danny. Y-you were dying, and I used my powers to bring you back. I'm sorry I didn't tell you earlier, but it would have just caused us more trouble."

Brin reached for Leah's wrists and pulled her hands towards him with a smile. "Thank you."

"Right, I love the sentiments, but we need to start walking. Commissioner Frankie is expecting us, and we need to get back quickly."

The car shuddered to a stop and Leah looked out of her window, staring at Danny with a quizzical expression. "Why are we in an alley?"

"To dump Brin's body and leave you with it."

Leah and Danny glared at each other. "Um, I'm right here," Brin said.

"It's a joke," Danny said, stepping out of the car. "Get out, your underworld buddies now know we work for the police, and I bet they will recognise this car if I park it near the department."

Danny stepped back and waited. "Leah, make sure your sleeves are down, and your hood is up. Bri-"

"Do you think I can't defend myself?"

"No, but you are now a moving target, and I don't want anyone to see you." He reached into his boot and withdrew another gun, thrusting it at her chest. Leah grabbed it before it dropped to the ground and pushed it into her pant's waistband beneath her coat. "Brin, just stay close and hold up until we get back," she ordered.

Danny reached into his back pocket retrieved his phone and held it to his ear. "Frankie, it's Danny...we're on our way back to the office. I reckon we may have been followed by members of the Underworld organisation, though..."

He was silent for a moment, his eyes switching quickly from Brin to Leah and back again.

"All good, we got in... But, we'll need a medic when we return." He started walking, and Leah and Brin ran to catch up. "I'll explain when we get ba-shit!" He held out an arm shoving Leah and Brin backwards, and then readied his hand on his gun. "I've got to go." He pocketed the phone and turned to Brin. "Your buddies have followed us." He said, checking the chamber of his gun and shutting it with a click.

"Are you expecting me to do something?" Brin asked, looking around Danny.

Danny turned to Leah expectantly.

Leah shrugged her shoulders. "Magee's only have one power. Mine was regeneration, meaning I could bring someone back to life."

"What do you mean was?"

"I can only use it once. I don't have the power to do it multiple times." She paused. "And I used it on-"

"Me..." Brin dropped his head, avoiding Leah's gaze.

"Why didn't you save your power?" Danny exclaimed. "We might have needed it. If we had known, we could have revived a victim of these murders and maybe found out who killed them."

"Are you saying we should've let Brin die?" Leah blubbered. "He's only our partner."

"Brin is a let-in from the Underworld; he's one of them," Danny whispered, pointing at several men scouting the area with weapons cradled in their arms.

Leah gasped, and Brin sidled away from Danny, his eyes wide. "Brin...come here," Leah whispered, ushering him over. He didn't argue. "Alright. We'll leave you, Danny. I'll take Brin to hospital."

"Wha-"

"Sorry, Danny. I'm going with Leah." Leah took off her coat and gave it to Brin.

"What's this for?" he asked, looking at Leah's arms.

"Put it on. Just do it." She said. "If you want to find us or apologise or try and get us back, come to the hospital and ask for Mordred." With that, she turned on her heel and walked out of the alley.

"Leah?" Brin asked quietly. "How will you explain what happened to the hospital?"

"I have connections. We'll be fine," she muttered.

"Oi. Oi. You two." shouted a voice from the dark.

Leah froze and pulled Brin closer.

"Stay by my side," she hissed. "Hide your face and take your cap off." She brushed some of her hair over her face.

"I'm sorry, sir. Is there a problem?" she said as one of the men started walking towards them.

Brin watched nervously as another gangster stood examining them from behind.

"It's dangerous to be out here at night," the gangster said, stepping forward.

"Oh, my brother and I were just on our way home," said Leah.

"Where are you coming from?" the gangster asked, pretending to be interested in her excuse.

"The church. Our brother *was* just murdered, and we were paying our respects." She covered her face with her hand and broke into sobs. Turning away from the man, she quickly hissed to Brin, "Grab my gun."

"But there's a man behind us; he'll see me!"

"Come on Brin," Leah gasped, "He was Magee," she cried, turning back to the man.

"A Magee, eh? Yeah, those murders are pretty bad." Leah watched his hand as he made a signal to the man behind her. "Come on, stop crying." He lifted the butt of his gun to her face and used it to brush her hair away. "Here, I'll walk you and your broth—You!" he cried when he saw her face.

"Now, Brin," Leah shouted.

Brin leapt forward and started firing at the man in front of them. Leah reached for her belt and pulled out a switchblade. She threw it hard, and it spun through the air before plunging into the throat of the man behind her. Both men collapsed to the ground. At the sound of gunfire, the surrounding men turned their attention to the pair.

Danny looked up as gunshots reverberated through the streets. For a moment, he wanted to turn and run straight back to Leah and Brin but calmly stood his ground.

"Officer Danetrius, is everything alright?" He looked up as Commissioner Frankie walked out of the building.

"Fine. Everything's fine," nodded Danetrius.

No Going Back

MJ Douven

No Going Back is the story of a prince who commits the worst crime imaginable and, as a consequence, is banished from the kingdom and disowned by his family. Left to fend for himself with no way to survive alone, haunted by his own personal demons, he nearly dies but is rescued by a kindly stranger. With the help of his new friend, who takes him under his wing, Arelian must learn to survive and overcome the lifestyle that almost killed him. Especially if he is to save everything and everyone he loves.

Chapter 1

*B*lood. *So much blood. On his hands. On his clothes. On the knife. On the floor around Kellen's body, spreading in a wide pool.*

*   *   *

Arelian jerked awake in darkness, his heart pounding in time to the throbbing in his head. Relief flooded him at the thought that it had been a dream. Another spiced wine induced nightmare.

But the coppery stench of blood refused to go away. And as his sore eyes adjusted to the dimness and he peered down at himself, he saw why. Blood, mostly dried now, still covered his clothes and stained his hands. Bile surged up in his throat, and he almost threw up right there.

It was only then it occurred to him to wonder where he was.

The last thing he remembered was ordering another jug of spiced wine at the tavern. He remembered laughing at Kellen when his friend insisted that he had had enough. Everything else was a blur.

Arelian rolled over, dragging his heavy head off the stone floor. He must be in a corner of the alley behind the tavern. It would not be the first time he had woken up there. But if that was so, where were the familiar scents and sounds of Heres, as the capital city of Terqa awoke from the long night?

He realized slowly that he was not outdoors at all. He was in a narrow, dimly-lit stone room, caged in by windowless stone walls – a cell. The palace dungeons?

That was the moment when the memories hit in disjointed fragments – broken flashes, like the remnants of some half-remembered nightmare. He wished it was just a nightmare, but he had the horrible feeling it was real. Too real.

*   *   *

Rage. Blind, senseless rage. Blood pounding and rushing in his ears. His own voice, sounding like it came from a great distance, screaming, yelling at his father. Spewing out all the ugly things he kept inside.

The look of hurt on his father's face. His father's distant voice, pleading. His father's hand on his arm stopping him from turning and walking away. And a flash of intense, red-hot fury.

His hand, suddenly with a knife in it, slashing at his father. But it was not his father in front of him when the knife came down. It was Teyanna. He still could not seem to stop his hand, despite the voice screaming at him from somewhere at the back of his mind.

Arms around him, pulling him back. Dragging him away from Teyanna, away from his father. Kellen's voice roaring at him. His own hand lashing out repeatedly, striking blindly with his knife until those arms released him. Until the thud of his friend's body hitting the floor penetrated his rage. Until he turned and saw what he had done.

*   *   *

With a cry of grief and rage, Arelian erupted off the stone floor. He clawed at his face, as if by ripping his own eyes out he could somehow erase the memory of what he had seen and done. More than anything, he was desperate to wash that blood from his hands.

His stomach chose that exact moment to churn, and this time, he could not stop it. He threw up, until it felt like he had lost everything he had eaten for the last month and his unsteady legs refused to hold him up any longer. His throat burned.

He was shaking and could not stop. Crawling over into the corner, he put his back against the wall, pulling his knees up to his chest and wrapping his arms around himself.

He rested his throbbing head down on his knees, sucking in a ragged breath every time another dry heave shuddered through him. His teeth were chattering from the cold, and no amount of gritting them seemed to stop it. His hands were shaking too. He kept blinking rapidly, trying to stop the scorching tears from sliding down his cheeks.

He was not even sure why he was crying. He never cried. No matter how miserable he felt inside.

In that moment, he wished that when he had finished lashing out at the people he cared about, he had gone just one step further and slit his own throat. If he still had his knife, he would have done just that. There was not a single person in the palace who would not believe he got exactly what he deserved. Starting with his own father.

Arelian was not sure how long he sat like that, huddled up against the far wall of the cell, miserable. It could have been hours or days. He simply could not find the will to care.

What finally roused him from his stupor was the rattle of locks on the door. He did not even try to get up, not sure his legs would hold him up if he did. He just lifted his head and stared at the door.

The door opened. His mother swept in, holding up a hand to stop the guard outside from following her in. Queen Aedala paused just inside the doorway. The grief that flashed across her face when her gaze landed on him made Arelian drop his head, unable to face her or find the flippant mask he usually displayed to the world.

He wanted her to walk away. He wanted her to leave him alone. But he should have known she would not do that.

Before he was ready, she had already crossed the room and was kneeling beside him in a rustle of expensive silk. She pulled him into her arms, not seeming to care that he was covered in dried blood and filth.

For just a moment, Arelian let himself relax against her, the way he would have done as a small boy. He wished he could be that boy again, wished he could be that innocent. But he had not been that boy for a long time.

He pushed away from his mother, squared his shoulders and lifted his chin, pretending not to see the tears that filled her eyes. It had been years since he let anyone see a side of him other than his usual uncaring, flippant mask. He could not let anyone in. Especially now.

"Does *my father* know you are here?" His voice came out raspier than he would have liked, but his mouth was so dry that he could barely swallow, much less talk.

"Arelian." The soft reproach in her voice was ten times worse than his father's rebukes. "Is that really all you have to say?"

He gave a careless shrug. "What else is there to say?" He was not sure where the bitter laugh came from, just that it slipped out before he could stop it. "I seriously thought my father would want to be the one to come down here, to berate me some more, to tell me just how disappointed in me he is. At least, this time, he would have an excuse."

His mother cupped his cheeks in both hands, forcing him to look at her. "You killed a man, Arelian. Your best friend. You cannot tell me that does not mean *something* to you."

Arelian stared at her with burning eyes, willing back the tears – and the images that flooded to the forefront of his mind. He cared more than he would ever admit, more than he could ever let her see.

When he did not respond, Aedala continued, her voice taking on a new edge. "You might pretend to believe your father does not care, but you have to know that there is only one reason why he is not down here right now. Because he is the king."

Arelian laughed. "You mean, so he can dispense justice." A small, perverse part of him took pleasure in seeing his mother flinch. "Like he did for Kalennan?"

He realised his mistake when his mother's expression hardened. Still, he did not regret it. He was going to keep bringing up Kalennan – and what had been done to him in the name of justice – until the day he finally proved Kalennan was innocent.

Aedala stood. "Your problem, Arelian, is that you are still stuck in the past. Kalennan is gone. And whether you believe it or not, justice was done."

Arelian gritted his teeth. "You can tell my father that I want nothing to do with his justice."

Aedala shook her head. "Unfortunately, you do not have a choice. And neither does he."

She stood there for a long moment, and Arelian could feel her eyes on him, as though she was waiting for him to say something. But he was done talking. He was too busy controlling the urge to be sick, wanting her to just leave him alone.

The only thing he wanted more in that moment was a drink. A mug of spiced wine was just what he needed to steady the shaking, to block out the memories, to take away the constant nausea. He wanted it so bad he could almost taste it.

Finally, seeming to understand he was not going to talk, his mother turned to go. But not before she pressed a brief kiss to the top of his head. Her hand lingered on his hair for a moment, and then she was gone.

Only when he heard the door close behind her, heard the locks rattle back into place, did he relax. He might be sitting on the cold, hard stone floor of a filthy cell, but he was relieved to be alone. At least he did not have to pretend.

He was tired of pretending. So tired.

*   *   *

Aedala stepped out of her son's cell, barely concealing a flinch as the heavy iron door slammed shut behind her. She wanted to crumble, to sink down in a sobbing mess right there on the floor of the dungeon, but she was the queen. And the queen of Terqa did not let the people see her grief.

She gave the guard a tremulous smile, nodded briefly and then fled up the stairs to the rest of the palace. If it had been proper, she would have run but, as it was, she settled for a brisk walk. And she did not stop, did not slow down, until she reached the safety of her rooms. Until she had dismissed her maids and the door was shut behind her.

Only then did Aedala let herself crumble. Her legs seemed to give way beneath her, and she would have slid to the floor if not for the nearby chair. She covered her face with both hands and let the tears finally come. Mourning the beautiful boy Arelian had once been. And the bitter, angry, uncaring man he had become.

She choked on a sob when a warm hand touched her back. Aedala did not need to look up to know that it was her husband. She leaned into him, and after a moment, Cerannon slid an arm around her shoulders, resting his head against hers. They sat like that for a long while in silence.

Finally, Aedala pulled back so that she could see her husband's face. The broken, exhausted look in his eyes, the tired slump of his shoulders, broke her heart all over again.

"You went to see Arelian." Cerannon's quiet words were not a question. "I would give almost anything to be able to be the one to go to him."

"But you cannot. Not until after the trial." Aedala's voice cracked over the words. "I understand. And so does Arelian, even if he pretends not to."

Cerannon's bitter laugh was an echo of Arelian's. "I am not so sure. He hates me, Aedala. He has hated me for a long time." He shot her a look, and there was hunger in his eyes. "How was he?"

Aedala swallowed. How could she tell Cerannon what she had seen and break her husband's heart again? But she could not lie to him either.

"I almost did not recognise him," she whispered. Her voice fractured over the words. "I do not know how I could see him every day and miss how thin he has gotten. He tried to hide it, but he could not seem to stop shaking. And if the guard is to be believed, he was throwing up all last night and all day. The blood on his clothes, on his hands —"

Cerannon flinched at the mention of blood, turning his head away. "I have seen Arelian drunk a thousand times over the years but never seen him the way he was last night. He was like some wild animal, lashing out at anyone within reach. It took three soldiers to hold him back, and even then, he was still struggling, screaming incoherently."

He closed his eyes as if reliving it. "I just froze. I have no idea what he might have done if Valannar had not finally taken him down. Even then, Valannar had to slam the hilt of his sword repeatedly against the back of Arelian's head before he finally went down. I thought Valannar was going to kill him."

Cerannon turned back to her. "Did Arelian say anything to you? Did he have any kind of explanation?" There was hope in his voice.

Aedala knew how he felt. She wished Arelian had some excuse for what he had done, something that would allow her husband to show him mercy. But if there was, getting it out of

Arelian was not going to happen. And the only other person who knew what happened during the nights, Arelian, went drinking in the city was dead.

"Arelian refused to talk to me." The memory of the rage and bitterness in his eyes still turned her stomach. "And the minute I mentioned Kellen, he shut down altogether."

Cerannon shook his head. "There has to be someone Arelian would talk to."

There was one person, but Aedala hesitated before saying his name. Knowing that it would shatter her husband's fragile composure. But it had to be said. "There *is* one," she said softly, hesitantly. "Kalennan."

Cerannon jerked as though she had struck him. He shot her a single, stricken look. "That is not an option."

Aedala reached for his hand, but Cerannon was already standing. And she could feel him putting distance between them – not just physically.

She had seen it before, twelve years ago, and a part of her husband had never come back. This time – if they lost Arelian, if her husband made the decision she knew he would – he might not come back at all. She wanted to hold onto him, to make him stay with her, but the look in her husband's eyes made her stop.

"Then I have a decision to make." Cerannon's voice was soft, measured. "And to pray about."

Before she could say anything, before she could tell him she loved him, he disappeared through the adjoining door between their room and his private study. The latch clicked shut with finality. Shutting her out.

Aedala knew that she would not see her husband again until he had come to a decision. More than anything, she wished she could lift the burden from his shoulders and carry it for him – or at least share in its weight. But she knew it was something he needed to do alone.

Chapter 2

The moment the door of his cell burst open and Arelian saw his father's champion Valannar stalk through the doorway, flanked by two soldiers, he knew it was time. They were here to collect him for his trial.

He had known this moment was coming. Especially after one of the soldiers brought him a change of clothes and a bowl of warm water to wash with. At the time, he had just been grateful to finally strip off his bloodstained, filthy clothes and cleanse the dried blood from his hands.

The soldier also brought him a plate of food, which Arelian had not touched. He did not think he could stomach food yet. Even the single mouthful of water he drank had turned his stomach. And Arelian was doubly glad that he had not risked it when Valannar stormed through the doorway.

Valannar stopped in front of him. "Get up."

Arelian just crossed his arms and stayed where he was. He knew it would infuriate Valannar, saw the muscle jump in the older man's jaw, but did not really care. He had no interest in making this easy on anyone.

Valannar gestured to the men with him. "Get him on his feet."

The soldiers were not gentle when they seized Arelian's arms and hauled him to his feet. The sudden motion made Arelian light-headed. He was actually thankful for their steadying hands on his arms.

The smack of Valannar's hand on his cheek, hard enough to hurt but not hard enough to leave a bruise, snapped Arelian alert. The king's champion stepped closer, into Arelian's space, his face only inches away.

"You are going to stand trial, even if I have to drag you up to the audience hall myself." The hatred in Valannar's eyes was like another blow. "You are going to pay for what you did to my daughter. And I am going to take great pleasure in presiding at your execution."

Teyanna. Arelian had been so focused on what he had done to Kellen that he had forgotten all about Teyanna. He remembered slashing her with his knife but had no clear memory of exactly what he had done. He did not even know whether she was alive. But asking about her would clearly be a bad idea.

Instead, Arelian settled on casual indifference. "So get on with it."

Anger flared in Valannar's dark eyes, a rage so intense that Arelian thought the other man was going to hit him. But Valannar controlled his fury and unclenched his fists.

"If I had my way, you would not have been given even a change of clothes." Contempt seethed in Valannar's voice. "The king should see you in the harsh daylight, covered with blood, so that he can see the monster his favorite son has become. Everyone should see you for what you are."

He denied Arelian the chance to come up with a smart retort, instead turning to his men. "Bind *the* prisoner's hands behind his back." He shot Arelian a look of pure contempt. "And make the restraints tight."

The soldiers obeyed. Arelian did not bother fighting it, did not wince as the rope cut into his wrists. He refused to let Valannar see him flinch. It might be small, but it was the only satisfaction he was going to get.

As soon as the soldiers were done, Valannar gestured for them to remove Arelian from the cell. He would have preferred to walk, not let himself be dragged, but his legs felt like they were going to give way any minute. Getting out of that cell, away from the misery of the last few days, should have cleared his head, but instead he just felt dizzy and sick.

But when they reached the audience hall, when the doors opened and Arelian glimpsed the crowd inside, he balked. Summoning up some hidden reserve of strength he did not know he had. Shrugging free of the soldiers' grip on his arms. Willing his shaking legs to steady. And then sauntering through the doors, down the long aisle to stand in front of the dais.

He kept his head up despite the gasps and whispers that swept through the crowd. Ignored the hundreds of eyes boring into his back. Concealed the wash of shame that flooded him when he met his father's gaze. Pretended not to see the stunned look on the king's tired, grief-worn face.

But the look on his father's face disappeared almost at once, so quickly that Arelian doubted he had even seen it. And it did not surprise him one bit. It was not the first time he had watched the king turn on someone who disappointed him.

Any shame Arelian might have felt evaporated. He lifted his chin, shoving down the regrets. He hardened his heart and willed the familiar, insolent, arrogant mask to slide into place.

King Cerannon stood. "Prince Arelian. Do you know what you stand here, accused of?"

Arelian lifted one shoulder in an indifferent shrug. "I guess."

Once again, murmurs ran around the hall, but stopped abruptly when the king lifted a hand to silence them. "Ordinarily, at this point, I would call for witnesses." Cerannon's words were blunt and deliberate. "But your crime was so open, so public, witnesses are unnecessary. The whole palace – the whole city – knows exactly what you did."

Cerannon paused, and for a moment, Arelian thought that his father might show some emotion. But the moment passed all too quickly, and Cerannon continued in the same flat tone. "Everyone knows about the man – your closest friend Kellen, son of Lord Giderian of Alannath – you killed in cold blood. And about the woman, barely clinging to life at this moment – an innocent struck down by you in a moment of drunken rage. The daughter of my champion, the man I trust most on this earth."

He fixed Arelian with a hard stare. "Do you have anything to say for yourself?"

"You want to know how I feel?" The words that came out of his mouth shocked even Arelian. "I feel honored. Honored to stand here in the footsteps of a good man, of the best man I have ever known. And glad. Glad that at least this time, it is not an innocent man being condemned."

The king's flinch was subtle, but Arelian was sure he was not the only one to have seen it. Plenty of other people would know exactly what – and whom – he was referring to.

He should have felt guilty for causing his father even more pain but was beyond feeling any shame. Or at least that was what he told himself. He was accustomed to ignoring his conscience, ignoring the tiny voice at the back of his mind, until he barely heard it anymore.

Arelian tilted his head back and stared boldly at his father. "In fact, let me make it easy for you. I killed Kellen. I injured Teyanna."

"Enough." Cerannon's voice was loud enough to drown out Arelian's words. "When I asked whether you had anything to say, it was to give you a chance to show remorse, not allow you to make a mockery of my justice. And if you do not have the decency to ask forgiveness from those you have wronged, then you will be silent."

Something in his father's tone killed the flippant remark Arelian had prepared in his head, the words dying right there on his tongue. It must be because he was feeling increasingly sick with each moment that passed. Normally his father's rebukes bounced off his armor. He had stopped caring what his father thought of him years ago.

In any case, Cerannon did not give him a chance to speak. "Your guilt is beyond doubt. You admitted it yourself." There was no softness in the king's eyes, nothing but the customary hardness that Arelian had always equated with what his father called justice. "So, the only thing left to do is to decide your punishment."

From behind Arelian, Valannar let out a snort. "As if there was ever any doubt." He did not even bother to lower his voice.

If the king heard him, he showed no sign of it. He did not even pause, just fixing Arelian with a cold, hard stare. "For your crimes against the people of Terqa, you are stripped of your title and princely rank. You are no longer a member of the royal family. From this day forward, you are neither my son nor heir to my throne."

The king's words cut right through him. It took everything Arelian had not to reel from the blow. Not to allow anyone to see his pain.

But the king was not finished. "As soon as this trial is over, you will be taken from here straight to the border of Terqa. You will be allowed to go free on one condition – that you never set foot in Terqa again until the day you die. If you even attempt to enter Terqa, you will be executed on sight."

Shocked and dazed, all Arelian could do was stare at his father in disbelief. He had fully expected to be executed. He had been prepared for that judgment, but not for one moment had he considered the king would choose to banish him instead.

The entire hall erupted in shouts of shock and fury. There was such a jumble of voices, with everyone speaking at once, and Arelian could not make out who was saying what. He was sure everyone wanted him dead.

The only distinct voice, the one that rose louder than the rest, belonged to Lord Giderian of Alannath. "He killed my son." Giderian jabbed an accusatory finger at Arelian. "I lost my son. I lost my heir. And all you are going to do is banish him? That is not good enough. I demand justice. My son's blood requires justice."

"Enough!" That single word cracked like a whip. The entire hall immediately went silent. Even Giderian. King Cerannon took a step forward, to the edge of the dais, his hard gaze locked on Giderian. "The decision has been made. And it is final."

He nodded to Valannar. "Get him out of here."

For the longest moment Valannar did not move, just stared up at the king with undisguised anger on his face. But then, with a shake of his head, he swallowed his obvious reluctance and stalked forward.

Valannar did not wait for his men. He seized Arelian's arm, his grip so tight it was painful, and dragged him away from the dais. Arelian was too much in shock to yank his arm away or do anything other than let Valannar haul him out of the audience hall.

What finally snapped Arelian out of his daze was coming face to face with his younger twin Ennarion in the doorway. Ennarion stood just inside the doors to the audience hall, looking as though he did not want to be there.

As their eyes met, a look of total revulsion, of contempt, crossed Ennarion's face. It was like a punch to Arelian's already queasy stomach. He opened his mouth to say something – what, he did not know – but never got the chance.

Ennarion said nothing. Instead, he closed the distance between them – and spat in his brother's face.

Arelian froze. He never cared what his brother thought before. But in that moment, standing there with Ennarion's spittle running down his cheek, he felt curiously hollow. Empty, as though something he had never thought important was suddenly ripped away from him.

Then Valannar yanked him forward, through the doorway. Out of the audience hall. Away from his family and everything he had ever known.

Deep Focus

Meg Irwin

During the ferment of the 1970s, with high urban centralism, increasing environmental damage, the strong threat of a nuclear incident, and the rise of feminism, one white Eastern Australian town had reinvented itself as "The Colony." In this closed community, the rule of men was unquestioned, and the inequitable social structure was promoted and maintained through a quasi-religion based on misunderstood fragments of classic early twentieth century films.

But now, in "the wilds", women exiled from The Colony are making a new life for themselves, surviving the difficult conditions, finding unexpected allies, and defending themselves against relentless pursuit from The Colony.

The novel is a response to the continuing systemic misogyny, sexism and violence against women in the Australian Federal Parliament. It is inspired by the Women's Lands and other feminist movements, and indebted to the fiction of Margaret Atwood (The Handmaid's Tale) and Alexis Wright (The Swan Book).

Deep Focus is the opening chapter.

"Look!" whispered the younger woman to the older one. A group of kangaroos reclined in the shade of a distant tree. Their ribs rose and fell. They were breathing!

The women's car had come to a stop. For the last two hours, they'd driven through open fields with the high grasses dragging against the undercarriage. The road had disappeared four hours earlier. When they'd been issued the vehicle, they'd been told to drive north for six hours. That was far enough away, and there would be enough fuel for the return.

A few white clouds hung in the wide blue sky and the sun's warmth penetrated the windscreen. Nora opened the window. Her ears popped painfully. Fresh air swept in. Her mother started coughing.

Her mother's name was Rona. There had been infinite generations of Ronas and Noras; just as there were Sallies and Nellies, Toulas and Roulas, Lolas and Nolas, Fredas and Bredas, and Lynns and Bryns; lines of women with names that alternated each generation, names that signalled blood lines and prevented unfortunate births from accidental incest.

Rona knew what was meant to happen here. Every woman had seen the end of one of the old movies. Rona, like the old donkey in the film, was now to lie down peacefully and pass away, blessed and blessing as she expired. A segment from another film had also been part of the training. A son took his aged mother outside the village to abandon her. That was the archaic way; distasteful, and also impractical, now that sons had no contact with their mothers. It was the daughters' responsibility to abandon their mothers now. When Rona turned fifty-five, she expected the journey she was now taking. She had done the same for her own mother fifteen years before.

Nora swung the car door open and jumped out. The car oxygen switched off and Rona cringed. They both had to breathe this new air which seemed so thin.

Nora looked around at the terrifying space. Before this day, she had never seen more than a metre in front of her. In The Colony, the orange haze was always present. Animals were rare and never wild. Some Oligarchs had tigers or jaguars as pets. The animals all had to have breathing apparatus inserted for their brief lives.

Nora held her splayed fingers before her eyes. Tiny trees fitted between them. The kangaroos were no bigger than her fingernails. Whichever direction she turned, the land lurched away. It was destabilising when, particularly now, she needed to stay grounded to do her duty to her mother and to her community. She knew that this was an occasion in a woman's life as important as giving birth.

In Nora's heart, it felt even more important, as she had not birthed a daughter yet, and the sons, of course, had all been taken.

She thought of Falconetti's eyes rolling heavenward in another old film. This was the appropriate way to enact her task – with simultaneous suffering and ecstasy. Nora would undertake her sacred responsibility with the same dignity. When she got back in the car, she would turn it around and drive south. Best to move quickly, so as not to lose her nerve.

"Come, Ma," she called, "get out of the car. Let's eat our lunch before I return." Rona stepped out of the car and came to sit beside her daughter. She had seen such space before, of course, but it was disorienting for her too. They leaned against the car, surveying the mysterious landscape. Rona's ampule was tucked in her pocket. These days, death wasn't cruel. You could choose to survive for a while out in the wilds if you wanted to. When it became too hard, you had what you needed.

Nora retrieved the picnic basket that had been issued with the car. She moved away to a mossy patch of earth, spread out the cloth and set out the food. Neither of them spoke. They had spent so many years together that words were seldom necessary. Rona knew what her daughter must be thinking and Nora thought she knew how her mother felt. So, they sat together, gentle with each other, eating only a mouthful or two of the food.

At last, Rona stood. She bent and kissed her daughter on her forehead. "Goodbye, my dear one," she said. Nora turned her face up. Already her tears were streaming, just like Falconetti's. This was to be the end, then; a soft goodbye, before her beloved mother simply turned and walked away. Nora sat a little longer, honouring her mother, holding her in her heart.

Nora's eyes blurred with tears as she repacked the picnic basket. She was knocking things over and close to blubbering. She was relieved that her mother was not there to witness her descent from nobility. Scraping up the salt she'd spilt, she heard the roar of a motor. She was on her feet, running fast towards the moving car. But it was gone. On the ground, she found the ampule of poison.

Two weeks earlier, for the first time in her life, Rona had received a visit from representatives of the Oligarchy; the Ethics Branch. Four men in suits had sat in her room. The youngest had explained:

"Droit du Seigneur', of course, belongs to any male member of the Oligarchy. But there are also important protections established for the benefit of society. Your daughter, Nora, was taken, one recent night, by a very drunken lad, who understandably, forgot to check her name. You would realise that Nora is seriously at fault for not ensuring that the boy heard her name properly before she submitted to him. The boy, as you may have guessed, was one of your sons, which means there is a danger that your daughter may be carrying a Monster. Under these circumstances, the only remedy available is to eliminate her. Your own upcoming Disposal offers the perfect opportunity to accomplish this with the minimum of fuss. You must accompany your daughter and leave her, rather than her abandoning you. You may then return to The Colony to live out your full span as an honorary Oligarch."

Orders from the Oligarchy, of course, must be obeyed. The Oligarchs took care of everyone. And it was in your own interests: 'To Dissent is to Suffer,' went the maxim. In a clip from another film, a little man named Jesus angrily curses a tree, and it withers right there on camera. To think against the Oligarchy is to be like that tree that deserved to die.

When Rona left her daughter in the wilds, she had gunned the engine and sped away, not looking back. The grass had shrieked against the belly of the car. It was only when she slowed a little, that it swished again; 'shee, hoo, shee, hoo, shee, hoo...' The land, unwanted, and therefore uncontrolled, by the Oligarchy, was whispering to her.

She considered the line of Noras and Ronas to which she belonged. Mothers and their only daughters lived together for anything from fourteen to thirty-five years, depending how early in the births a daughter had come. Traditionally, it was the first daughter who was kept. The other daughters were called Twelve-Weekers, the age by which they were terminated.

Rona had never known her grandmother-Rona, who had been taken to the wilds many years before her birth. She had known her mother for only five years. Her mother had born a late daughter, so Rona had been fortunate: she had only to care for her mother through three pregnancies. Her mother had been able to attend to Rona during her first two. Rona's own daughter had been less lucky. She had been beside Rona for all her other births, even as a toddler, carrying towels for the births and helping with the clean ups. The chain of women birthing and taking care of each other, right up to the time of Disposal, had been the tradition as long as anyone could remember.

Suddenly, fiery fluid rose in Rona's gullet. She threw herself out of the car onto her hands and knees, and vomited everything up. She was shaking. It was all the wrong way! For generations, for as long as memory, daughters had left their mothers; not mothers, their daughters! The Oligarchs were wrong when they gave her that order.

She spun the car around. There was enough fuel for her to reach Nora but not enough to then return to The Colony. She would have to take her chances. If the Oligarchs could be wrong, everything was uncertain. She hoped Nora had not already used the ampule. She accelerated.

The Apparition Dilemma

Zech Elliot

John is a patient in a mental institution, who's past traumatises and returns to him. He hasn't had any paranormal encounters since he was a kid back in 2002. John narrates his past through flashbacks from high school and his experiences with a book that leads him into a spiralling downfall.

Chapter One

I lay on my bed in my hospital gown, collecting my inner thoughts, trying to think of a way to escape this hellhole. I'm patiently looking at my psychiatrist. The voices in my head have carried me since the beginning; this is something that I could never control. My therapist tells me that talking about my past is some kind of remedy for what's happened, but I doubt it; that's just what she wants me to believe.

Dr Ravenwood is a nice woman and all, and is only doing her job, but she doesn't understand what I've been though. Nobody does. My mind drifts as I look around the room, trying to drown out the raspy voice of my therapist.

"How are you feeling this morning, John? Have you taken your medication?" Dr Ravenwood asked curiously.

"Yeah, I did. They interrupted my sleep at four in the morning to drug me. Apparently, I was having a seizure or some shit like that," I replied sourly.

Dr Ravenwood stared at me, giving me a look like I was some kind of parasite or something.

"Visitors Day is tomorrow; maybe someone will come to see you, family or maybe old friends," Dr Ravenwood said gently.

I looked at her with anger like a ticking time bomb about to explode. Memories of the past came flooding back to me as I sat upright on my bed.

"I don't have family, and I don't have friends; I did a long time ago but not anymore. Now get the hell out of here. I don't need therapy… all I want is a fresh start," I snarled.

Dr Ravenwood picked up her clipboard without saying a word. After a moment, she finally replied in a severe tone.

"What's done is done. I'm afraid a fresh start is something you cannot do, John. You of all people must know that. Look, I have to go; I'll be back next Thursday for our next appointment. Have a good day, John."

"Bye," I said as I watched her leave the room.

I felt a sense of hopelessness and depression. I've been in the mental institution for almost eight years for a crime I didn't mean to commit.

Now let me take you back to the year 2002 when everything changed.

I was hosting a party while my Aunt Rosie was on holiday with her friends. It wasn't your popular kid's party with 100 people. It was just a small gathering with snacks and a few beers. That party changed my life forever when we stumbled upon something we should never have seen.

I sat on my bed listening to Blink 182 on my new iPod and suddenly realised the time was 5.00 pm, and my friends would be there at 7:00 pm. I got off the bed and hurried to the mirror. I had grown taller since last year. My hair was longer too, which I kept in a curtain. My round glasses made me feel like Clark Kent or some other superhero. I ran my fingers through my hair and put on a white shirt with a denim jacket.

I ran downstairs to my fridge; the beers were chilling, which was good. I opened the cupboard to check the food situation. I realised

I had forgotten the chips but calmed down and remembered we still had two hours left till the party. Suddenly, I heard a loud knock coming from the door, and I began to sweat nervously.

I opened the door and saw it was just my best friend Jackie, his arms were full of food.

"Hey, Jackie, my boy, you're a lifesaver, man. I see you brought the goods; it looks like now the party is sorted. All we need now is the music and the people, and we're good to go," I yelled in excitement as Jackie came rushing inside.

Jackie moved here from Korea when his parents got jobs as accountants. Jackie had dark hair and a mullet and was wearing a flannel jacket and black sunglasses.

"Of course, you forgot the food, Johnny boy, you always do. But no pressure, I have all the food we need for tonight," Jackie said.

"What time are the rest of the guys getting here? I'm ready to party," Jackie said with an enthusiastic smile.

"The party isn't for another few hours. Help me put the chips into these bowls, and we'll go upstairs and play GoldenEye or something," I replied.

Jackie nodded, and he helped me separate the chips, popcorn, and chocolates into different bowls. After that, we went upstairs and played GoldenEye 007. We took turns trying to get as many kills as we could until we got bored. Seven o'clock finally arrived, and we headed downstairs as everyone finally arrived.

I opened the door, and the gang was complete. Standing in front of Jackie and me was Owen, Ned and Quinn, who all seemed eagerly excited to get the party going as they came rushing through the door.

The revelry began as soon as we entered the living room. An hour and a half into the party, we were four drinks in, and we all started getting pretty drunk. We opened the beers and the crisps and talked about girls, parents, video games and the worst thing in our lives... school.

"Didn't you just have dinner, Quinn?" I asked.

"No, I hardly touched it, didn't have lunch either," Quinn replied.

"Why are you eating chips, then, bro," I said, amused.

"I like the chips, ok; do I need to apologise for eating your food? I also like your aunt. She's pretty cute," He remarked.

We all laughed while helping ourselves to another beer. Owen, who was on the basketball team, hardly said anything before deciding to change the subject.

"You know what, I'm bored. How about we go check out your aunt's room? We might find some spare change and even head to the Roller Rink before it closes."

"I don't know, man. She probably has camera's in there or something and is watching us right this minute," I said anxiously.

"Don't be a chicken, John. It's no big deal she probably did this kind of stuff in the '50s when she was born, that's if she's that old," Jackie said, facing me with anticipation.

"She's not that old, Jackie," I replied. Without a further word, he ran upstairs past my bedroom and the laundry room and finally reached Aunt Rosie's room which was at the end of the hallway.

The guys and I quickly followed him and met him inside, snooping around her closet. "Break anything, and you can give me the money," I said urgently.

"Relax, man, everything is fine. I'm just seeing if she has some spare change. I'll pay her back someday. You have my word," he replied.

So, we spent the next five minutes looking for some change and eventually found some behind a creepy mannequin she must use for her clothes. We ended up getting carried away and snooping around a bit more until Ned found something I wish he had never seen.

"What are you holding, Ned?" I asked him curiously. Ned, who is still called the new kid ever since last year, spoke up.

"It looks like a horror book or something," Ned replied, looking at the cover, which didn't show the title or anything, just a plain muddy colour. No title or blurb or anything an ordinary book would have on the cover.

"Look, it's probably an Adult Magazine or something that she got from the mall," Jackie said jokingly.

None of the boys cared to listen to what he had to say and continued staring at the book. I grabbed it out of Ned's hands and decided to have a look myself.

I opened the book, and it revealed many love letters written in longhand on each of the pages. Each had the same date from 1973 over and over.

Reading some of the letters, I realised they were addressed to my aunt, but instead of Rosie, it said Rosalina. Most of the pages were about how they fell in love and married, but they broke it off after an argument with him cheating and stating he was going to the army. The last page was a death note which I read out loud.

> *To my dearest Rosalina, you're a beauty I cannot give up. I'm sorry for everything I have caused. I'm sorry I stopped writing. I think it was time to tell you that I left the war to live a peaceful life on my boat, the place where we married and the place you'll find me. I have caused you so much pain and sadness, but it's for the best that we part in peace. I want you to know I love you, and you can find me at the address listed below, with all my heart.*
>
> *Roberto Diaz*
>
> *Place of Death and Burial: Vancouver Sea Port, Granville Island. Look for the White Boat with a US Army logo.*

I stood there, frozen for a moment, not knowing what to do but decided to say something as I needed to get some answers.

"Aunt Rosie didn't tell me any of this. It doesn't make sense. It sounds like he committed suicide to get away from his pain and suffering, but why would he do this to her? It's obvious she still loved him considering she kept the letter even though he cheated and left," I said, feeling sick in the stomach.

"Why wouldn't the police have this letter anyway? It's a death note after all, and why did your aunt's ex-husband put the address down below?" Owen said, reading the letter over my shoulder.

"He wanted her to find his grave and give him her respects after his death. I still don't understand why she didn't tell me anything. Maybe that's one of the reasons she didn't want me in here," I replied.

"So, what do you think we do, John?"

"We do nothing. This is none of our business, and I think we should all just get our minds off this stupid letter and head to the Roller Rink," Quinn asserted.

"No, we're not going to the damn Roller Rink. We're going in Jackie's car and heading to the Sea Port. I want more answers," I said, looking around the room, wanting some closure to this mystery.

We cleaned up the food and bottles without a further word and hurried to the station wagon.

That was the moment I knew I had made a colossal mistake. I wished I had listened to Quinn and forgotten about everything I would carry with me for eight years after I stumbled upon Roberto Diaz's ghost.

NON-FICTION

Praise the Sacred Bin Chicken

Jon

I looked at my watch. I was early – but that didn't matter. It was a glorious autumn afternoon, and I had a fresh cup of coffee and time to spare. Finding a bench in the warm sun, not far from the bus stop, I decided to sit for a while and go through the notes from my morning class.

A history of literature and the role of scribes, bards and prophets in a study of the great paradigms in human evolution. Thoth, Egyptian god of writing, law, philosophy and magic, depicted with the head of an ibis and the body of a man. His scribal messengers were revered as divine servants. The sacred ibis, incarnation of Thoth, mummified as a sacrifice and immortalized in scriptures and carvings.

My mind began to glaze over. Returning the notes to my satchel, I grabbed my phone and began scrolling through the latest news feed.

Geelong legend stares down death threats in a battle against the Calabrian mafia's fruit and veg racket.

Gender the key to confronting anti-meat movement.

Awkward trend: Dogs with mullets.

Good grief!

Returning my phone to my pocket, I leaned back on the bench, and watched the traffic speed by. Taking another sip of coffee, I heard the unmistakable honk of an ibis. The great white bird glided towards me, flapping occasionally to slow its descent before perching on top of a roadside bin. Its ragged white plumage stained brown from a lifetime of rummaging through refuse. I watched in disgust as the ibis expertly opened the lid, plunging its black beak deep into the putrid mound. It emerged boasting a long, sodden chip, soaked in a cocktail of soft drink and bin-juice.

How could such a vulgar creature ever be seen as 'god-like'? How could such an advanced civilization like the ancient Egyptians worship this as a living incarnation of Thoth, the god of scribes?

Gagging, the bird tossed the sodden chip onto the footpath and dove back into the foul container.

"This was no keeper of sacred knowledge," I thought to myself. "No symbol of wisdom or scripture. This was just a filthy bin chicken."

Pulling my phone out of my pocket, I swiped my thumb over the news feed again.

Disney in trouble from feminist warriors over Snow White kiss…

Talk about rubbish.

Perhaps the ibis *does* symbolize our modern day 'scribe'. Like the ibis, modern society no longer views the writer as someone to be revered or respected.

Are modern writers just a pest? A nuisance? A filthy scavenger digging through garbage, upending discarded waste and selecting only the 'juiciest' morsel to regurgitate?

Is that what has become of our literary knowledge?

Never in human history has knowledge been so attainable. Yet never has it been so devalued and disposable. For centuries, drawings and texts, the knowledge and wisdom of ancient civilisations, were 'carved in stone.' Great care was taken with every line and every shape and every curve - the accuracy of the text, its purpose, its message and meaning studied with meticulous analytical care.

Today our messages are flippant. Click bait. Opinion overrules fact, and accuracy is no longer important – "as long as it leads with a strong hook."

Our history is no longer carved in stone. Instead, it is a 'live' document, open for change and manipulation. Errors can be corrected instantly – or ignored.

"We'll just post an apology or a retraction."

Re-emerging from the bin, the ibis craned its neck and stretched open its mouth. A thick web of mucus and muck stretched across its gaping beak. Spreading its wings, the ibis dropped to the path, nosing around the base of the bin for any hidden scraps. Letting out a repulsive "honk", it picked up the discarded soggy chip and gleefully gulped it down.

Was this my future? After all – as a writer I have accepted jobs and 'cashed the cheque'. I have often been given the task of preparing so-called 'fact sheets' and 'technotes' – instructional pieces designed to inform readers on the latest technologies and research developments. The instructions for these are clear.

Keep it succinct.

Keep it factual.

Acknowledge and verify your references.

Sounds simple? But on top of that there is an expectation that any source material has be 'pre-approved', and any results or recommendations are 'favourable'. In other words, keep you research 'in-house' and cherry-pick statistics that support *their* pre-determined outcomes.

But my role was not to challenge their methods or question their motivations. My role was to present the information given to me in a more palatable form.

So, as a writer, am I a bin-chicken?

I accept not *all* of my writing will be 'scripture,' and I am certainly no artist. Afterall – can an artist truly work to a deadline? Can an artist restrict their ideas according to corporate agendas? Can an artist adjust their work to comply with marketing strategies specified to meet the expectations of a target audience?

Yet even for an artist – at what point does a piece of work transform from being "self-righteous, narcissistic drivel, typical of the self-obsessed nature of a 21st century writer", to a crucial piece of text, "providing insight into the cultural behaviours of a western civilization in the 21st century"?

Are the hieroglyphic of ancient Egypt truly symbols of profound wisdom?

Or were they just graffiti? Nothing more than snapshots of pop-culture from a forgotten world?

I looked over to the ibis. It paused, staring at me with cold, beady black eyes. Its face and neck were bald, its leathered black skin giving it almost reptilian features. I both despised, and admired the bird. Through centuries of co-existence, this creature had established a symbiotic relationship with its human neighbours, adapting from a nomadic, to rural, to urban lifestyle, in order to survive and thrive in this new world.

Perhaps we as writers need to adapt – to redefine our role in society?

I could see my bus pulling around the corner. Rising from the bench, I tossed my empty coffee cup into the open bin. Upset by my sudden movement, the ibis quickly took to the air. Making my way toward the approaching bus, I suddenly felt a wetness down my shoulder.

I stripped off my shirt and swore in disgust at the white defecation streaming down my back, as the 'sacred ibis' flew off in the distance.

22 Things I Have Learnt in 22 Years (Pandemic Edition)

Natalie Power

It has been 22 years, 264 months, 1147 weeks, 8030 days from the day I was born to the day of my twenty-second birthday. When I was growing up, birthdays were always the most special time of the year in our household. Unwrapping gifts we'd spent all year waiting for, blowing out birthday candles and cutting the cake to signify another year passed – and most importantly, getting to spend the day with our most treasured friends and family.

Birthdays always brought forth the best memories, ones that we would cherish for years to come and hope to replicate as the years go by. When we were kids, the most exciting part was, of course, getting spoilt with presents and getting to test out all the crazy new toys we'd been given – fleeting presents that we would enjoy for the first week before retiring them to the top shelf of the cupboard, never to be touched again.

The excitement of being able to say you're ten now, and not nine anymore was a **massive** milestone and one we would talk about over and over again, so excited to be double digits. Then slowly but surely, as we got older, the birthdays started to represent a different kind of change and growth, not only physically but emotionally. It became less about the gifts and more about the experiences. Getting your L plates at age sixteen to graduating to your Ps at eighteen and finally being able to drive unsupervised. To the first (legal) drink and making memories with your friends that you'll laugh about for years to come. To now having all these mixed feelings, excited about becoming an adult and embarking on a life of your own but in some strange way, also beginning to grieve the youthful, innocent version of you that you were only a few years prior.

Your days become less about playing with friends and begging your mum for the newest PlayStation. They become more about trying to figure out if you have time to catch up with your oldest best friend (whom you haven't seen in God knows how long) for coffee during your thirty-minute lunch break, whilst also trying to plan your completely forgotten assignment that's due in two days.

Life looks really different at twenty-two to what it did ten years prior, and you have no idea when you stopped being a teenager. It's like you blinked, and suddenly you've been thrown into this thing called adulthood with no real clue on what you're supposed to be doing and what path you're supposed to be headed on. Well, that's how I feel anyway. Once I turned twelve all those years ago, all I started to think about was when I would turn thirteen, and then fourteen, and then fifteen and so on – we all know how it goes. My teenage years were spent wishing to be older.

When I was eighteen, nineteen and twenty, I spent my time laughing, drinking, dancing and chasing the sun into the early hours of the morning. I lived my life to the fullest and indulged in countless moments, some that I wish I could remember and others that I will never forget.

And then one day, it stopped. I, like everybody else going about their lives, never expected for the world to come to a screeching halt. From what started out as mere whispers and chatter about some virus somewhere in China, to news stories plaguing the tv.

And then it happened.

Life as we once knew it changed completely.

The world stood still.

At twenty, when I felt like my life was finally starting, I had to hit pause, indefinitely. Suddenly, all these plans I had made disappeared in front of my eyes. My twenty-first was the birthday I had been most excited for, the birthday where I could finally 'celebrate becoming an adult.'

Instead, my first overseas holiday was cancelled. Weddings were postponed numerous times. New babies were welcomed into the world via face calls, unable to properly meet people who would love them the most. Children learned from home, missing out on some of the most important years of social development and making friends. Workplaces closed. Curfews. Zoom calls. Phone calls. Press conferences. Restrictions lifted. Restrictions imposed again. Lockdown 1, 2, 3, 4, 5…. I've lost count now.

It wouldn't be forever. That's what they said.

Just a few weeks to 'flatten the curve.' That's what they said.

But a few weeks turned to a few months, which turned into a year and a half, and a year and a half is a long time to sit and think. To try and remember what life was like, pre-pandemic. To reminisce and crave the life you once had.

Grief and uncertainty are the two emotions that have come in waves since this whole ordeal started. It doesn't matter if you're twelve, twenty-two or sixty-two; the grief and mourning for how things once were affects everyone in some way or another. And eighteen months down the track, sometimes it is hard to see a light at the end of the tunnel. Sometimes it is hard to be positive. Will things ever go back to how they were? How do we adjust to all these new feelings and emotions?

Perspective truly is an incredible concept. Looking at situations with a different lens can shine a light in a way you've never considered before. It can make us realise all the things we once took for granted that we never will again – dinners with friends, concerts, sports games and everything in between – and all the things we are truly grateful for.

In this time that the world stood still, I have come to realise many things. I have learnt so much. Pre-pandemic and during.

I have gotten to know myself better, to listen to myself better, to trust myself better. Being twenty-two may not seem very old or experienced to many; but with two decades plus two years of crazy experiences, heartbreaking lessons, and unforgettable memories with a global pandemic on top , you come to figure out a thing or two. In the last twenty-two years, I've learned a lot — far more than any blog entry could ever include. I know there's still a lot I don't know, but these are some things that I do know. I wanted to share those lessons with you all — and possibly my younger self — as a reminder that we're all stumbling through life together, one step at a time.

1. **Life is about the journey AND the destination.**

   Everybody has heard the saying, "Life is about the journey, not the destination." Whilst I understand what this quote is trying to grasp, I believe that it is never that black and white. Life is about the beginning, middle and end. We work so hard to get what we most desire – a job, a relationship, a house or whatever it may be – that I think we deserve to truly celebrate and be proud of ourselves for reaching that milestone. The journey is where we make the memories, learn the lessons and pave the way. The destination is what makes it all worth it in the end.

2. **Our attitude towards life has a huge role in life's attitude towards us.**

   If we want to avoid any semblance of toxic positivity, this lesson has to be taken with a grain of salt. Obviously, things happen in life that are completely out of our control and that can rock our world entirely, but there are other situations where it is important for us to take the reins on our attitude and outlook. In my own personal experience, if I've woken up and thought to myself that it wasn't going to be a good day, nine times out of ten it has turned out to not be a good day. On the other end, if I've told myself that I want to have a good day and I'm going to be grateful for the little things, then typically the day will look a lot different to the previous one. Perspective and attitude can affect our day-to-day lives incredibly.

3. **Things won't always go the way we want them to, and that's okay.**

   This is something I have definitely struggled with over the years. I have always been prone to getting my hopes up and putting all my eggs in one basket, just for it to all come crashing down. And I used to wonder, "Why is this happening to me?" Until I realised, it's happening to everyone. This is life. Sometimes things work out better than we could've imagined it, and other times not so much. And that's okay.

4. **The only people we need to go through life impressing is ourselves.**

At a time where I was sitting at a crossroads in my life, conflicted over a decision between what was best for me and what would benefit someone else and make them happy, someone very close to me told me, "You're the one who has to go to bed with yourself and wake up with yourself everyday. Staying true to you and what you want should always be number 1." That is when I realised that I needed to stop making all my decisions based on what would benefit everyone else and start making decisions based on what I actually wanted.

5. **To succeed, at first you may fail. A lot. But that doesn't mean you won't get there.**

This is one I think everybody knows all too well. I am somebody who struggles with getting things right the first time. If it doesn't work out, I get so insanely frustrated that I quit. Learning manual is one example. Producing multiple pieces for these classes is another. But here I am, still persevering.

6. **Perfection is subjective and searching for it will ultimately waste a lot of your time.**

This ties in very closely to my previous point. A lot of us spend our lives searching for perfection, only to realise it doesn't really exist. There's no such thing as the perfect job, the perfect partner, or the perfect house. Everything has its downfalls, but that doesn't make it any less worthy.

7. **You are the only person responsible for creating the life you want. The power is in your hands.**

Everybody on this planet is busy creating their own lives; they don't have time to create yours. Sure, lending a helping hand never goes astray and kindness is always welcome, but if there is something in your life that you truly desire, you need to work for it and not expect someone else to hand it to you. You will appreciate it more. Don't doubt yourself.

8. **Sometimes saying no is better than saying yes. Sometimes saying yes is better than saying no.**

   This ties in loosely to one of my previous points. At the end of the day, you need to listen to what you want. Don't say yes just because you feel bad saying no and don't say no just because you're afraid of saying yes. Many of us sit inside our comfort zone; for some that is constant people pleasing and saying yes to everyone and everything, and for others it may be that you say no to everything, too afraid to open yourself up to more!

9. **Boundaries are necessary in order to protect yourself and your identity.**

   Boundaries are not there to punish the people in our lives; they're there to keep those people in our lives. Whatever the boundary may be, don't feel guilty for it. Boundaries are necessary to stay true to ourselves.

10. **Stop waiting for the other shoe to drop.**

    You have no idea what is around the corner. It may be either amazing or the last thing you expected, but don't let this stop you from going after what you want or from allowing yourself to be happy where you're at.

11. **What you think of yourself is not only more important than the opinion of others, it's all that truly matters at the end of the day.**

    Your relationship with yourself should be at the centre of your life. You have to live with yourself in your mind, so it's wise to make it somewhere comfortable and happy to be.

12. **Happiness is something you work on every day, not just a milestone you reach and have forever.**

    This one is pretty self-explanatory, I believe. When you have a choice, choose happiness. Every single day.

13. **If it disrupts your peace, it isn't worth it.**

    Whatever it may be, a rude family member or a job you hate, trust me when I tell you it is never worth subjecting yourself to that. If it is feasible and manageable, remove yourself from that situation. Stop wasting your time on things that contribute to your unhappiness. None of it matters more than your mental health. None of it matters in the grand scheme of things. Let go without regret. Be proud of yourself for standing up and admitting that something needs to change.

14. **Not everyone is going to understand or like you, and that's okay. Hold onto the ones who do.**

Also, very similar to a couple I have mentioned. This one has been a very important lesson in the years of being a teenager and growing into adulthood.

There is always going to be someone who doesn't like you, whether there's a reason or not. The greatest thing you can do for yourself is to not care. Don't waste your time trying to make somebody like you. If they can't see the good in you, they're just simply not the right person to keep in your life. Shit happens.

15. **"Don't get so busy making a living that you forget to create a life."**

This is a very famous quote and an exceptionally spot-on one at that. Your work isn't everything. Memories, family, friends – that's what it's all about. You won't be going to the grave wishing you filed those documents differently; you'll be going to it treasuring all the amazing moments you had in your life and the stories you got to share.

16. **Forgiveness is for you, not the other person. Holding onto anger and resentment is like drinking poison.**

There are always going to be people in our lives who will do wrong by us, whether intentionally or unintentionally. Some of these people will want to amend their mistake; others won't. Some of these things may be completely unacceptable, and other things might be easy to move on from. But whatever it is, it is important to forgive. Not for the sake of the other person, but for you. You don't have to let this person back into your life, and you never have to excuse what they did or forget about it. But holding onto it will only eat away at you, and trust me when I say it happens all the time. There are so many people who hold onto this all-consuming anger for years, letting it get in the way of so many things, and the person who wronged them is out living their life undisturbed by it. Let yourself be hurt and mad and upset, and then move forward.

17. **Your life is happening right now.**

Stop. Waiting. For. The. 'Right.' Time. There is no right time. Live your life right now!

18. **Stop living your life out of fear, and live it out of love instead.**

Learning to live in love is not always easy; for many of us we have kept ourselves alive by being controlled by fear. Learning to live in love is always worth it though. Fear is all too prevalent in our life – fear of rejection, fear of abandonment, fear of not being good enough – the list goes on. Fear is very powerful and it has the ability to keep us locked in these tiny boxes of comfort and predictability, never allowing room for growth. Wouldn't you rather live a life where you made decisions based on love, rather than fear?

19. **Things gather dust and take up space. Memories don't.**

A tale as old as time. Possessions are just that, possessions. If holding onto it doesn't bring you happiness, it isn't needed. Spending your time and money on experiences will always be a more worthwhile investment.

20. **It. Will. Pass.**

Nothing lasts forever, even if it feels like there's no end in sight. Just hold on, give yourself some credit and put one foot in front of the other. Reach out if you need it. Time really is the best healer.

21. **Make every day count.**

You never know what day might be your last, so make it count. This doesn't mean every day has to be productive – I can be just as happy having a lazy, self-loving day as I can be on a super-motivated, productive day. Whatever makes you happy.

22. **Hold the people you love close to your heart and remind them just how much you love and appreciate them.**

And like the last point I made, you also never know what day will be the last of those around you. Give love and lots of it. You will never be too cool to love those around you. None of us are here forever.

And there we have it. Just a small, but very important (to me) list of lessons I have learnt in my years of growing, learning, messing up, failing and succeeding. Of course, a lot of these points are personal and subjective. They may differ from person to person, but that's the beauty in it. Throughout our lives, we'll all learn important lessons as we stumble through life, going through all the ups and downs we're bound to come face-to-face with.

And remember, in this difficult and trying time, it is incredibly important to reach out to those around you, for your sake and theirs. We're all navigating each day a little differently to each other, and we can only hope and pray that we see the other side of this ordeal soon.

If you can take one thing from my piece, let it be that you are the number one person in your life and you should treat yourself as a priority, always. Take care of your mind, body and soul – especially, but not limited to, during a global pandemic.

Family gatherings.

Living Well in Bendigo; An Aunty's View

Meg Irwin

Aunty Steff Armstrong, bright eyed, and wearing a yellow dress that accentuates her athletic body, stands in a large circle of year 9 and 10 First Nations students from local secondary schools. They are at a Weenthunga Health Network "Women's Health Day" to learn about medical, nursing and other health careers. Aunty Steff is vivacious. It is surprising to notice the grey in her great halo of hair, but not to learn she enjoys marathon running.

Interviewing her is a treat, but keeping up is a challenge. Her ideas expand and branch unpredictably. She moves over wide terrain, and doesn't slow for corners.

Aunty Steff is a Gamilaraay woman from northern New South Wales. She is the program leader of the Bendigo Weenthunga Health Network, and is involved in many groups in and around Bendigo, including the Bendigo Reconciliation Group. She trained and began her teaching career in Bendigo. For the last 40 years she has taught across Australia; in Broome, Ceduna, the Kimberley, and the Pilbara - and for the last 15 years, back in Bendigo, where she and her husband enjoy living nearer to family in their small community of Eaglehawk.

"From the outside Bendigo looks big, and rich, and ripe." Aunty Steff says. "You've got the fountain and everything - it looks glossy."

But inside, things are less comfortable.

She describes one incident when taking a group of young First Nations women for a run around the lake. A pair of men mumbled a racist slur as the women passed. Aunty Steff was shocked by their overt racism, and wondered, "Did I really hear that?"

She is also unsettled by evidence of unconscious bias, such as a radio interviewer assuming the new Early Childhood Centre at Bendigo and District Aboriginal Cooperative (BDAC) was needed because it would keep Aboriginal people out of jail (BDAC is the local Aboriginal Co-Operative providing health and community services). "It was that perception of Aboriginal people as really still on the outside," she says.

There is, she believes, something foundational affecting Bendigo. "We Aboriginal people know that trauma is passed on. I don't think many non-Indigenous people realise. Initially at colonisation, people were sent out here, away from their own families, and were trying to find their way."

From that trauma, explains Aunty Steff, something constant arose – of people arriving, then attacking the country and its people, maybe through their way of farming or of building. "In Bendigo, it was for gold."

She says the people who came "were not living with or alongside the people" and that created "a country that was pulled apart."

With that pulling apart as a basis, she says, "the whole country changes and the people change. There are all those massacres; the pain and the trauma. It makes it like any other war-torn country. And then, the surge of people continued to come, in different waves over many years."

"I think, for anything to be well now, we need to stop and reflect and think what to do next."

She warns that anything takes time: "It's not going to happen in my lifetime, but what I do in my lifetime will make a difference."

"In Bendigo," she says, "it's hard to find that spirit of change." She says non-Indigenous supporters are cautious about speaking out against racism, and young people did not mobilise around the Black Lives Matter campaign, as they did elsewhere in Victoria.

She acknowledges that pushing too hard may raise "the ugly head of racism that will pull things apart", but she challenges people to be more daring.

For Aunty Steff, letting things be is not an option. "I could easily retire now and sit back, but I come from a strong matriarchal line of Aboriginal women. My grandmother and my mother and my aunties fought and stood up strong, so I have to do that. You're bound by those protocols: it's a way to live your life. My grandmother and my great grandmother; everyone did their bit. It's not what I do in my life. It's adding on, and it's passing on to the next generation and the next."

"Mum had some terrible things done to her through racism", Aunty Steff says, "yet she was always looking for something positive. She had the police officer down when they were working with kids, she had the school principal, all coming and sitting at her little camp, listening to her giving them ideas of what to do next."

"That's how I want to live my life."

She also feels "blessed" to have relationships with many people and communities: "I get that little bit of strength from all of them, and I hope they take little bits from me. That weaving continues, just like a basket, always weaving something much bigger than yourself."

In Bendigo, she has found "some beautiful relationships, and people truly wanting to work together." She admires the Dja Dja Wurrung Traditional Custodians' work with the Council. "They have made a Reconciliation Plan. I think Dja Dja Wurrung will be important going on. When I left Bendigo, they were not visible. They have grown their space and kept it, to be able to be strong, and then to be able to have the conversation with others."

She draws inspiration from her four years traveling with her husband and two daughters when they were young. She experienced "true freedom, with a spirit of adventure, and no fear." It was "a time together as a family, teaching her children "with love", spending time with other family and friends, and being on Country." She found out what it is to live well, and always remembers that.

She understands learning as a "gift" at every stage of life. "When a piece of knowledge is received and used with humility, more learning follows."

Aunty Steff wants a transformed community in Bendigo. "There's an opportunity to work together more optimistically," she says. "We can ask ourselves - how do we live better?"

"Aboriginal people love their Country so much, and want it to be loved."

She wants everyone to learn to listen to Aboriginal people, and to be willing to change and think differently about this country. "When we think differently, we do things differently; thinking of others, thinking of Country."

"But there's much more that we have to do, and a whole lot of work before we get there."

She believes there is a role for Council "to map out" how individual actions can fit together, "to provide leadership", and ensure that, "we're making Bendigo a place where all cultures are invited, where we look to First Peoples for some of what is done."

She says that "when you want something to change, you have to have a vision." She saw an example of this in Broome. Established by the local (First Nations) people, "Mabu Liyan" ("For Good Spirit") incorporates a vision of connectedness and strength. All decisions and plans are intended to align with Mabu Liyan.

And Aunty Steff would love to see leadership like Nelson Mandela's, who, she says, "did all he did for the love of his people and country."

For Bendigo to move forward, Aunty Steff wants non-Indigenous people to have more conversations in families and at work, "to just have a go."

"I know it's hard for the everyday person in the street," she says. "We have these academic conversations, but it's really about trying to have those conversations closer to home; for ordinary people taking small steps; people starting to look at 'what can I do?'. Then that grows."

"People will get energy from this," she says, "they'll change the space they're in, because they want it to be better for everyone." She wants people "to make it part of their life", not just to celebrate NAIDOC week.

For people who want to be "allies" of Aboriginal people, she says it is important to keep working towards "that sense of peace."

She asks a question of all of us: "So, what would you like Bendigo to be? Not just thriving economically and having the biggest buildings. Something more than that: for people to live well; that idea of reciprocity and being respectful for one another, and taking responsibility for what you do."

Why we must support "The Uluru Statement from the Heart"

Meg Irwin

With recent Black Lives Matter protests, and Rio Tinto's notorious destruction of ancient Indigenous sacred sites, Australians can no longer cling to the belief that First Nations people are treated fairly in this country.

The "Uluru Statement from the Heart" offers us a way forward. The one-page Statement was released in 2017, with the authority of a large body of First Nations Elders, after extensive consultation with First Nations communities across the country. This was part of the Federal Government's bipartisan consideration of how to recognise First Nations people in the body of the National Constitution. It is our best chance for national healing, and we must support it.

*　　　*　　　*

The Statement from the Heart calls for constitutional protection of a First Nations "Voice to Parliament" to advise government on laws and policies that impact on Indigenous affairs, and for a "Makarrata Commission" ("Makarrata" is a Yolngu word meaning "coming together after a struggle") to supervise processes of treaty-making and truth-telling. These are summarised as "Voice, Treaty, Truth", which is the 2019 theme of NAIDOC Week.

First Nations participants in the consultations were not satisfied with the government's intention to recognise First Nations people in the Australian Constitution only symbolically. They believed that systemic inequities must also be addressed. They also wanted to ensure that any new body to represent First Nations to government had constitutional protection and could not be overturned at the stroke of a pen, as had happened with other legislated bodies such as the Aboriginal and Torres Strait Islander Commission (1990-2004).

The Statement from the Heart had not been required as part of the tax-payer funded consultations, but on 27 May 2017, Australians woke up to find it across our media. It was a beautifully crafted and moving document, with emotional, yet dignified language "from the heart". It also came from the heart of the country, Uluru. It spoke "heart-to-heart" to all Australians. It seemed in just one page to encapsulate what is wrong and what can be right with our country.

*   *   *

While Australian referendums have seldom led to constitutional change, the so-called "Aboriginal citizenship" referendum in 1967 did so. A direct appeal by First Nations people to ordinary Australians contributed to that achievement. Hence, the Statement from the Heart includes the line, "In 1967 we were counted, in 2017 we seek to be heard".

Soon after the statement was released, then Prime Minister Malcolm Turnbull distorted the meaning of the "Voice to Parliament", calling it a "third house". As the Voice to Parliament was to have only advisory not legislative power, this was palpably untrue. Many First Nations people had put enormous effort into the consultations. They first had to put aside their justifiable distrust of government. The statement specified some of the systemic violence against their people: high incarceration rates, the removal of children and high levels of youth detention. By dismissing the statement, Turnbull continued a familiar pattern of using Australian institutional power (in this case, governmental), to crush a perceived opposing interest. The Statement from the Heart offers a far better paradigm; of equality, and shared sovereignty: 'We invite you to walk with us in a movement of the Australian people for a better future.'

*   *   *

There are five reasons for us to support the Statement now.

First, it is authentic and trustworthy. The Statement arose from the biggest tax-payer funded consultation and consensus so far achieved among First Nations Elders and communities across Australia. Reputable fact checking (by The Guardian, The Age, among others), confirmed what the Statement said about systemic injustice. It is true, for example, that Aboriginal people in Australia are "proportionally…the most incarcerated people on the planet".

Second, the Statement's call is reasonable and generous. The basis of the call for fairness and self-determination for First Nations people is put this way: "Our Aboriginal and Torres Strait Islander tribes were the first sovereign Nations of the Australian continent and its adjacent islands, and possessed it under our own laws and customs … This sovereignty is a spiritual notion: the ancestral tie between the land, or 'mother nature', and the Aboriginal and Torres Strait Islander peoples who were born therefrom, remain attached thereto, and must one day return thither to be united with our ancestors. This link is the basis of the ownership of the soil, or better, of sovereignty. It has never been ceded or extinguished…" That sentence continues, "and co-exists with the sovereignty of the Crown." The Statement from the Heart is inclusive of all of us.

Third, support for the Statement is strong and growing. Across all social media platforms, the Statement is discussed and promoted, with sites, such as fromtheheart.com, posting new messages of support from high-profile First Nations people several times a day. Activist First Nations and Reconciliation Groups continue to promote the Statement. Bipartisan Federal Government committees continue to work towards implementing the Consultation outcomes. First Nations concerns remain in public awareness, with, now, some First Nations Federal Parliamentarians (not all fully supporting the Statement), and several State Governments actively working with First Nations people towards State-based treaties.

Fourth, it's our turn to do the work. The burden of inequality falls most heavily on First Nations people. They have put in the work to make the Statement. It is now up to us and our Parliamentary representatives, to honour and implement it.

Fifth, we will all benefit. If we work in respectful relationships with First Nations people and keep going in good faith, there is hope for healing and for maturation as a nation. We may, eventually, be able to live free of the shadow of dispossession and violence that occurred at colonisation, and that continues in systemic injustice today.

We could continue to accumulate guilt, with more deaths in custody, more destruction of Country, more families torn apart. That choice would leave us hobbled as a nation, in a cycle of violence and lies, which would only harm us further. Instead, let's take the generous invitation of the Uluru Statement from the Heart to walk together into a better future.

Wolves vs Brentford…

We're Not All In This Together; Reflections On The Kung Flu

Simon Wooldridge

Noon, Saturday 18 September 2021. I'm at Molineux, Wolverhampton Wanderers' famous football ground in the English Midlands. I'm here for the lunchtime kick-off game against newly-promoted Brentford – a minor team from the western outskirts of London now punching two divisions above its traditional weight. They're playing in England's top division for the first time since 1947. Imaginative but prudent ownership can go a long way in the volatile world of European football.

I'd been looking forward to the game. Somehow 'awaydays' – games at grounds you visit once or twice a season or even less frequently – are more fun. You're heavily outnumbered by the home fans so getting behind your team and making a noise is a must. The problem was, I felt like shit. And I was going downhill. The night before, I'd been out at a surprise but low-key-ish seventieth birthday party. I hadn't really been in the mood; I thought I was just tired. Getting up at 7.30 a.m. that Saturday, I still felt tired but put it down to a busy last ten days or so. On the train journey from Nottingham to Wolverhampton, I didn't manage to shrug off what I still thought was just a bit of general tiredness and lethargy. I changed trains at Birmingham for the last twenty-minute leg. The train was packed and noisy, with fans of both clubs mixing happily. The walk from Wolverhampton Station to Molineux should have been a breezy ten minutes but turned into a sluggish fifteen.

It can't be, I thought, watching the teams warm-up. *I've been jabbed twice....* Reason told me I was just a bit run down or had a cold building up.

Somehow, despite all top-level English football grounds being all-seater, there's a tradition for away fans to stand throughout a game. Thereby ignoring regulations, stewards' instructions and relative comfort along the way. So I watched the whole game standing up, much of it with the late summer sun bearing down on me. But I had to sit down at half-time; I was going seriously downhill.

Brentford won 2-0 – much to the delight of the 2000-odd away fans in the 29,000 crowd. I walked back to the station. This time the trip felt like it took me half an hour. My feet were leaden, my head was spinning, and my mouth was dry – as though I'd been chewing cardboard or sandpaper.

Back home in Nottingham that evening, I did little beyond sitting in an armchair while trying to focus on something on Netflix or Amazon. It all went over me that evening.

Surely not, I thought. *I've been jabbed twice....*

*　　*　　*

7 p.m., Friday 20 March 2020. I was out for drinks with Bill Dew, the graphic designer who had worked with me on a book I'd just published. We admired, appraised, and generally all-around critiqued a sample copy over drinks in The Dragon, a pub in central Nottingham. It looked good – though I promptly decided not to risk a different colour on the spine to the front cover again. A bit of wiggle room on how the dust jacket gets wrapped could mean a spine with 1-2mm of the cover encroaching on it or a front cover with 1-2mm of the spine intruding. Lesson learnt. It wasn't long

before we were off the subject of books and talking about what everyone else was talking about – the virus that had come out of Wuhan in China. We knew we were heading for a "lockdown" – a word very few of us were acquainted with before early 2020. But since then, it's become one of the most commonly used words in the English language.

The evening was interrupted when the pub manager made an announcement. The government has finally decided to action a national lockdown. The Dragon will remain open for the rest of the evening, but from tomorrow, it, and every other pub in the country, will be closed until further notice. Non-essential shops will be closed. Restrictions on travel will be introduced among a whole raft of regulations and changes.

"Watch the news, read the papers for the full details," said the pub manager. It felt bizarre, surreal – the stuff of dystopian novels and science fiction films. *When I get in this evening… that's it until further notice?* I thought to myself. I ended up drinking far more than I usually would. As did Bill. As, so it seems, did everybody.

*   *   *

Sunday 19 September 2021. I have a splitting headache. I ache from head to foot. I struggle to get out of bed – effectively pulling myself up by trying to grip onto the wall. A few minutes later, with a piece of toast in my hand – liberally covered in raspberry jam – and a half-drunk glass of orange juice on the benchtop, I realise my sense of taste has gone.

I've got it. I must have. But I've been jabbed twice…

Exhausted, despite having about ten hours' sleep, I go back to bed. I sleep until mid-afternoon. I have all the tell-tale symptoms, and I am aware of jabbed people getting it. I'm also mindful of jabbed people getting it who have had it before. In a brief moment of kind of clarity, it makes me further question the wisdom of a possible vaccine passport.

Yeah, I've been jabbed twice. Look at the National Health Service (NHS) app on my phone. Neglecting to mention coming down with it months after the second dose was administered. Pointless. That evening, light-headed and drained, I get online and order the government testing kit. I request it at 8 p.m. on a Sunday night. It arrives at 9.30 a.m. the following day.

*   *   *

March 2020. I live in a flat overlooking a main road – the A60 / Mansfield Road in central Nottingham. In the days after the lockdown was announced, the road quietened down dramatically. Traffic, at a rough estimate, fell by about three quarters. At certain times of the day, the road noise became almost entirely absent. Buses kept coming past, but there was hardly anyone on them.

I took heed of the first lockdown restrictions – venturing out to a nearby supermarket just a couple of times a week. That was it, for months. At first, we didn't have to wear masks. But social distancing was a big thing, and people stared daggers at each other for coming too close in shops or on the street. There was genuine fear in the air. The reports of what could or would happen to you if you caught COVID were horrendous. We all listened, and the vast majority of us did what we were told.

*   *   *

Monday 20 September 2021. I feel like I've been hit by a bus. I ache from head to foot. I struggle to get out of bed. And when I do manage to get out of bed, I have just enough energy to make it to the living room and slump in a chair. I watch Netflix and read. Then go back to bed. I'm running out of Panadol. A couple of hours later, I summon the energy to make a sandwich – mature cheddar with chilli chutney. It would probably be quite lovely if I could taste it. I go back to bed.

*   *   *

Spring 2020. No one knows how long this is going to carry on. I tell myself not to expect to be able to do anything again until at least the end of May. The end of May? Man, that's a long way off, but I pondered it. A few weeks. A few weeks of no football, no gigs, drinking at home and watching Netflix on my laptop. It won't be that bad, I thought. My work as a copywriter wasn't going to be dramatically affected by this. However, I knew I was going to miss actually going out and meeting people for work.

Then they started clapping for the NHS on a Thursday evening. Once was great, but it became tokenistic boring and pointless. It wasn't about showing appreciation for the NHS; it was about showing your neighbours what a good person you are.

*   *   *

Meanwhile, the government introduced the furlough scheme whereby companies could simply stop people from working. The government would cover up to eighty per cent of their wages up to a certain amount. Not a particularly low level, though. This was going to cost billions by the time everything was totted up. Millions of people were furloughed – some reports said up to nine million people ended up on this scheme (with well over a million still taking advantage of it as late as September 2021). Working at home became the primary option for millions of office-based workers. But, key workers and people in essential retail carried on as before. Generally, they were paid some of the lowest wages in the country. Unless they had a lengthy financial history and other qualifying criteria, support for the self–employed was virtually non-existent.

And then, even the Prime Minister caught it.

Despite a widely adopted and often repeated slogan, "we are all in this together," it was soon abundantly clear that we weren't. The government and media lectured people from the luxury of a safe and secure office or studio or from a large home with a lovely garden retreat. While millions of people were confined to terraced houses or small flats on the twelfth or fourteenth floor. Families of five living in two-roomed apartments were told not to go outside unless they were going to work or for some brief exercise or to the shops. Though it was common for their jobs to be generally lower-paid and with a higher element of risk than those of the politicians or media. Many of these people were also holding down more than one job.

The stats – cases, hospitalisations and deaths dominated the news. They were terrible but not as bad as feared or projected. The media seemed to be revelling in it. Their historical doom-mongering talents extended further than they had in a generation. Politicians also seemed to be revelling in it. In 2020 Britain, there were very few people who could remember the Second World War. But it was hard not to imagine that the Prime Minister, Boris Johnson, saw the pandemic as his "Churchill moment". Dramatic daily news briefings were beamed into households across the country every late afternoon. "The science tells us…" became the catch-all. The only thing is that "the science" didn't always accurately predict how things would unfold.

*　　*　　*

Summer 2020. Weather-wise, a lovely summer but a wasted summer as no one really got to enjoy it. I spent most late afternoons and early evenings sitting on my front step, reading a book and necking a beer or three. As the evening cooled down, I came in, got myself something to eat, sat down in front of Netflix, and consumed a bottle or two of white wine. Like millions of others, mine wasn't a healthy lockdown.

It carried on like this for months. The same news, the same daily routine, the stats going up and the media looking for new ways to frighten the public. And then the Prime Minister's chief advisor got busted breaking the travel rules. It ultimately turned out that he was one of several leading figures during this crisis who believed the laws they laid down didn't apply to them. Students barely out of their teens were fined £6000 for hosting a few friends for a night's drinking and revelry, but the PM's advisor predictably just wheedled his way out of it. Bizarrely, through all of this, Britain's borders remained open.

*　　*　　*

Tuesday 21 September 2021. More of the same. Tired. Headache. Aching from head to toe. Dry mouth, no sense of taste. I must've slept for 14 hours.

*   *   *

By late summer 2020, some of the restrictions had been eased. Non-essential shops re-opened. Cafes, bars and restaurants re-opened, but there were all sorts of new rules. You had to check-in, and you had to sit at a table – and it was table service only. You had to wear a mask to and from your seat. Pubs closed at 10 p.m. – and everyone rushed for taxis, Ubers and public transport simultaneously. It wasn't much fun, but it was better than staring at the same four walls. The government introduced a scheme to try to kick-start the hospitality sector. On certain midweek days for a few weeks, people could eat out for half price – the government picking up the rest of the food bill. "Eat Out to Help Out" soon became known as "eat out to kill someone" when the increased level of infections and hospitalisations led to a rise in deaths after a few weeks.

Speculation about when the lockdown would really finish properly was rife. And changeable. Public anxiety grew. People wanted some kind of certainty; it's a natural human need. We had nothing anywhere approaching it. It was all ifs and buts. Are we coming out of this or not? Meanwhile, several vaccines were hastily being invented. We carried on, though I'm not sure we carried on calmly.

The stats rose and rose. The government, its advisors and committees bumbled along while the media collectively rubbed their hands in glee. We were put out of our misery at the end of

October when we went into lockdown again. At first, we had regional variations, shillyshallying around and little in the way of clear direction. Things closed down again. But it was different. I could see and hear the traffic from my place overlooking the A60 / Mansfield Road was just as noisy as before this lockdown and as busy as before the first lockdown. *Aren't people going to take this as seriously as the first lockdown?* I wondered. It was soon apparent they didn't, despite face masks now being obligatory in many situations – which wasn't the case the first time around.

*   *   *

Wednesday 22 September 2021. Not quite as tired. Spent more time in the armchair than in bed. The washing up is piling up and must be starting to smell. No energy to tackle it, though. Headache is not as fierce.

*   *   *

November 2020. An aside. Well, of sorts. Just to compound matters, I was diagnosed with prostate cancer. Christ knows how long I'd actually had it, but it explained a few things. Drug treatment started straight away, with radiotherapy scheduled to begin in March. I'd be going in and out of hospital every day for a while during the pandemic.

*   *   *

Mid-winter 2020-21. The bodies kept piling up at a comparable rate to the criticisms levelled at the government. You could forgive them for the first few months as they navigated unknown territory, but now they were nine and ten months into it; I think we could've expected more. The chopping and changing of rules and the expectation that the public would digest the minutiae of some of the changing regulations was ridiculous. You could sit in someone else's garden and use their toilet if you needed to, but you couldn't go into their house! Places with 900 infections per 100,000 population were ranked as a lower risk than places with 400 infections per 100,000. "Support bubbles", groups of six… I can't even remember the rules, when they came in or when they changed them. It seemed most other people were in the same boat. It was also clear that many people were just ignoring the rules.

I started to wonder. As awful as this thing was (and is), what is the fall-out going to be?

- The cost of furlough. Future taxpayers are going to be hit severely paying that back.

- A significant increase in domestic violence. The tension in some homes would be reaching (and exceeding) boiling point with these changed, pressurised living conditions.

- Mental health issues (now and in the future). Some people are seriously depressed because of their lack of human interaction and concerns about future job prospects.

- Elderly couples are separated in care homes and not allowed to visit each other.

- Interrupted and disjointed education for children – and to a lesser extent, university students (who were still paying full fees for off-campus remote learning).

- The consequences of small businesses going out of business will undoubtedly include suicides.

- Babies missing out on interaction with other babies will surely have a long-term detrimental developmental effect.

- Elderly people are simply terrified to do anything or see anyone. The media did an excellent job on them! Imagine being in your eighties and thinking you might have five years left on this Earth and being quarantined for a quarter of that?

- Delays in treatment for other medical conditions.

- People taking heed of the "protect the NHS" message and not contacting their GP when something is wrong. What would the ultimate human cost of that be?

The list could go on.

And then they backtracked and cancelled Christmas with four days' notice. It's not difficult to think they did some of these things not because they necessarily had to but because they could. I'm no pandemic-denier, but it's hard not to think governments in some way have taken advantage of the conditions of the past eighteen months to see how much they could "test" the general public. They're probably quite satisfied and perhaps even amused by the outcome.

The "testing" of the public – not just in the UK but in France and Australia particularly – has been fascinating to watch. Mainstream media has effectively supported and helped to drive a significant – though seemingly readily accepted – campaign of fear, resulting in a largely compliant populace.

I read that more people in the UK died from cancer and heart disease in one day than people died from the virus in a month. This is a bastard of a thing, but by mid-late 2021 the chances of dying from COVID or getting seriously ill were actually minimal. Suppose the measures introduced to combat this thing were applied elsewhere. In that case, we'd see a total ban on the sale and use of alcohol and tobacco, and driving would be limited to about fifteen miles per hour. Meanwhile, the backlog of people needing treatment on the NHS for cancer, heart complaints, hip replacements and a whole range of other things just grew.

"We need to protect the NHS," we were told. But let's put that romanticised feeling about the NHS to one side for a moment. Taxpayers – individuals and businesses – fund the NHS. And as a proportion, particularly for lower and middle-income people, contribute quite a lot of money. Just because we aren't charged when we visit a GP or hospital doesn't mean we don't pay. (Some people who don't contribute don't get access to the NHS, but that's a wholly different story.) Apparently, the NHS also employs more non-clinical staff than clinical. Again though, a whole other story. We fund the NHS to protect and treat us.

*   *   *

Thursday 23 September 2021. Starting to feel human again. The headache has largely passed, and a vague sense of taste has come back. Not needing quite as much sleep.

*   *   *

March-April 2021. I visited Nottingham City Hospital for twenty radiotherapy sessions to treat my prostate cancer. Everyone was masked, and there were hand gel stations at regular points throughout the hospital. The whole thing went relatively smoothly, even if it did knacker me out a bit.

As 2021 progressed, we were again treated to excess doom-mongering by the media. This was coupled with an indecisive government led by a Prime Minister whose personal popularity seemed to be his priority. And then the Health Minister, Matt Hancock, a beta male of a politician if ever there was one, was caught on a security camera outside his office having a bit of tonsil tennis with an adviser, Gina Coladangelo. Not the first politician to have an away fixture, but it turned out the images the public saw were from a period when intimate contact between two people from different households was against Hancock's social distancing guidelines. Yet another "do as I say, not as I do" message from the government.

Rules were gradually relaxed during spring and summer. They were still confusing, though. The government relaxed the wearing of masks, yet some transport companies (Transport for London for one) continued to make them mandatory, while others "recommended" the wearing of masks. Some places even "invited" you to wear one. A shopping centre near where I live relaxed its

mask-wearing policy and said individual shops within the centre could choose to have their own rules. Hospitals, GP surgeries and anywhere under the NHS flag steadfastly demanded the continued wearing of masks. This suggested they knew something the government didn't. The government appeared to be succumbing to public pressure or realised that enforcing mask-wearing just wasn't going to work. In any event, most people couldn't get anywhere near a GP. This profession had seemingly reinvented itself as a non-contact telephone advisory service.

More chopping and changing. We had what was called "test events." Football's FA Cup Final was played in late May in front of a restricted crowd of around 21,000, which was all that was allowed into Wembley's 90,000 capacity stadium. While on the subject of football, the government and the game's authorities buckled to pressure and allowed thousands of UEFA "guests" and flunkies into the country so England could hold onto the prestige of hosting the Euro 2020 competition final. The football tourists didn't have to go through the standard arrival procedures – testing, quarantine etc., that ordinary travellers had to endure. If you were wealthy and/or connected, different rules were still being applied. Ironic, really, considering it was well-heeled international travellers who brought the first waves of the Kung Flu into Britain in early 2020. So, no, we're clearly not all in this together.

In late June, workplaces opened up fully again. You went to work unless you were isolating or on furlough. Millions of office workers had got used to the idea of remote or hybrid working, and debates raged (ok, they were conducted respectfully online) about the future of office work. Then we had the "pingdemic". Now that millions more were out and about, their phones were being "pinged" when they came into contact with, or were in the same vicinity of, someone who had tested positive. Then that rule was relaxed – if you'd had two jabs, you didn't have to isolate if you were "pinged".

At that point came the announcement that in 2022 national insurance contributions would be increased to help pay for the whole thing. Some people were up in arms; others responded with: "Well how did you think this was going to be paid for?" A reasonable question on the surface until you consider the government's profligacy around the furlough scheme, contracts awarded spuriously to friends and buddies and foreign aid going to countries like China and India. Nuclear-powered, spacefaring nations that are standing very much on their own two feet in the twenty-first century.

And on the subject of China. Well, this whole thing started there – whether by accident or design is another matter. Whatever one's position on that, the international community's response has been curious. I would've thought some kind of questioning of the Chinese as to how the hell this thing happened would've been appropriate, at least. Still, it seems trade and future relations are more important than trying to find out why four million (and counting) people have died.

In August, I get the cancer all-clear; blood tests every six months from here on to keep track of PSA levels.

*   *   *

Friday 24 September 2021. Feeling almost normal again.

*   *   *

Saturday 25 September 2021. Still isolating which is a bummer because I was due to go to London for a sporting doubleheader. I'd planned to watch the Australian Rules Grand Final between Melbourne and the Western Bulldogs in an Aussie expats' pub in South London and then onto Brentford's Premier League game with Liverpool. However, I had to settle for living-room laptop viewing for both.

Monday 27 September – Thursday 30 September 2021. Back working, but not at work. I have to continue self-isolating. I feel better, but not the same as a few weeks ago by any means. I'm also pretty bored. After finishing work on Thursday, I go for a walk. I haven't been out for ten days, and I need the fresh air and relative exercise. Fifty minutes later, I'm back, slumped in the armchair, exhausted.

*   *   *

Autumn 2021. Over the past few weeks, we're still tracking daily deaths on either side of a hundred. But most things really are back to normal. Mask-wearing, to some degree, has continued and will be an ongoing feature of life in Britain. International travel is starting to open up again, but I don't plan to do any until it returns to the regulatory levels of pre-March 2020.

Through all of this, I paid some attention to Australia, particularly Victoria, where I lived for eighteen years until early 2019. "Zero Covid" seemed a lofty ambition for the State Premier to voice so early in the piece. Particularly when he had access to information from other countries indicating that outcome was about as likely as Martians landing on Earth. The on-off lockdowns in Australia – often imposed with barely any notice and due to a single case – baffled me. Though it didn't baffle me as much as the widespread acceptance of these measures and the endorsement of some shocking police behaviour. Leaving litter at places of national importance or urinating around them is not behaviour to be endorsed by any means, but cracking skulls is a response too far. As is police wading, in numbers, into people on beaches for not wearing a mask. Beating the shit out of people to protect them seems a rather cack-handed way of doing things. Yet, it seemed to be not just accepted but applauded.

*   *   *

Saturday 2 October 2021. I'm out and about again and go to a football match at my local club, Notts County – a famous old English club which has fallen on hard times in recent years. The oldest professional football club in the world and a founding member of the English Football League, it now plies its trade in England's fifth tier. It's a rainy, misty, cool-ish day, and Notts lose 4-1 at home in front of a healthy – very healthy for this level – 5807 people. It's good to be out.

*   *   *

Monday 4 October 2021. The first visit to work for over two weeks. It's good to be around people again. I share anecdotes with someone hit much harder than me by the Kung Flu; off work for six weeks and in hospital for part of that. I feel lucky.

This thing is here to stay. It's not going to be "beaten". It needs managing in the same way seasonal flu is managed. People need to be careful. Get jabbed, and then get jabbed again. And when the booster is available, get jabbed again. Wash your hands regularly and wear a mask when appropriate. But don't let this thing scare you or rule your life. Life is short – and for people in many countries, even shorter and also brutal. Our daily existence is full of risks. Every time you walk out the front door, you're taking a risk, every time you walk down some stairs, every time you get in a car or on a bus, every time you eat in a restaurant, every time you walk down the street. One more risk has been added this past eighteen months, but it's one to be considered objectively – and objectivity's not something we've seen a lot of recently.

Shit Happens

Jon

A sickly humid blend of effluent, sweat and straw clings to the air like a thick fog. Engulfed in the pungent haze, I close my eyes, take a deep breath, and smile – I was home.

For me, the agriculture pavilion is an oasis away from the crowds and chaos of the Royal Show. Away from the masses of mullets, muffin tops and camel toes jostling for position in the queue for a carnival ride or cheese-on-a-stick. Away from showbag alley, a place of social distancing ignorance filled with a ravenous sea of Veruca Salts screaming at apathetic parents. "But daddy – I want it! I want it NOW!"

In the agricultural pavilion, there was no chaos or crowds. There were no showbags filled with confectionaries and unnecessaries. Here – children carried buckets of shit.

*   *   *

It is competition day, and the usual tranquillity of the dairy pavilion has been replaced by a hum of activity – hair clippers, blow driers and spray cans. Professional crews busily prepare their cows for competition, as keen bystanders cheerfully debate the latest international bloodlines, sale prices and judging results.

A cow stands proudly in her stall, contently chewing her cud, oblivious to the frantic activity around her. I watch as every strand of hair is meticulously trimmed and styled with a level of skill that would challenge even the best metropolitan salon. Her features are adorned with make-up, oils and shines. Toes manicured, painted and polished. Her udder was filled to perfection. The soft pink skin of her mammary was filled tight with milk, amplifying the intricate network of veins and blood vessels. Enough to fill every fold of skin and exaggerate every curve, but without unbalancing the vessel, straining the attachments, or swelling the delicate glands.

To the general public, this is nothing more than aesthetics and vanity. But for the cattle fitter, it is strategic art, using textures and tones, shadows and outlines to create an illusion of optics. Techniques to draw the eye, exaggerating structural ideals while detracting from structural flaws.

"Who is she?" I ask her handler. I already knew who she was — she was the reigning Champion — Holstein royalty. But it's best to break the ice with a farmer by asking about their animal, and not generic small talk about the weather.

"Dominate Candy," he replies cheerfully.

"You've got her in great form," I said honestly.

"She does it all herself," he smiles, clearly uncomfortable with the praise. "She knows what it's about. She's the professional here."

"Good luck — she's gonna be hard to beat," I said, throwing him another cheeky compliment.

"Cheers," he said back with an embarrassed smile.

It's funny — throw a politician a compliment, and they run with it — gloating. Throw a farmer a compliment and they duck for cover.

*   *   *

Returning from the wash bay, a young handler weaves his gentle beast through a maze of prams, partitions and ignorant onlookers. I step aside to make way as he leads his cow back to her stall, the refreshing smell of shampoo and coat conditioner breaking through the acrid air as she passes. Still damp from the wash, the elegant black and white Holstein strolled calmly behind her master.

"Stop!" A neighbouring exhibitor calls out, leaping to his feet and racing to the back end of the cow.

The handler stops abruptly, calling to his teammates for help. I drop my notes and rush to his aid. Grabbing the cow's tail, I lift it clear as a filthy bucket is thrust in position. A thick stream of shit spews from the cow's rear end, filling the bucket with a greenish-brown sludge. A team quickly gathers, fists filled with paper towel, expertly wiping away any minute fleck of splashback.

The handler smiles gratefully.

"Cheers buddy. Thanks for that."

"No worries," I reply cheerfully, secretly relishing the opportunity for some active involvement.

As he moves off, I look down at the splattering of green on my freshly pressed moleskins. This is what I love about rural life. Whether it be the opposing exhibitor rushing to the aid of his competitor, or the wannabe journalist spoiling his professional attire – we're a community, where everyone leaps to a neighbour's aid without a second thought.

The World's Largest Entertainment Industry is Built on a Foundation of Abuse and Exploitation

Delilah Cornwall

By the end of 2018 the videogame industry had made US$139 billion in revenue. In that same year, the worldwide box office made US$19 billion, the NFL made US$15 billion, Major League Baseball made US$10 billion, the NBA made US$8 billion, and the NHL made US$5 billion for a combined total of US$57 billion, around one third of the videogame industry's year total.

While most industries suffered during the global pandemic of 2020, the videogame industry boomed, raking in a record-breaking profit of US$162 billion. The industry is only projected to continue growing, with profits estimated to get as high as US$295 billion by 2026.

So, with videogames accounting for such a mammoth portion of the entertainment industry's combined revenue, it's worth asking why that might be, and what it means. After all, even if you don't play videogames, or you only play them very casually, you almost certainly have friends, children, a partner or partners that spend a large percentage of their time engaged with the medium. It's in everyone's interests to be informed about the machine that creates their entertainment.

There are several fluffy answers as to why the videogame industry has become the undisputed titan of the entertainment industry and we're going to quickly move through them before we get to the real answers.

Since the 1985 release of Super Mario, the game that heralded videogaming's triumphant comeback after the crash of '83, videogames have embedded themselves deeply into popular culture and become a staple of entertainment on computers, consoles, tablets and phones. New media platforms such as YouTube and Twitch have appeared, allowing "Let's Players" (people who record themselves playing games and post the videos after the fact) and even more lucratively, "streamers" (people who live broadcast themselves playing videogames) to cultivate audiences of millions and make a good living as what is effectively a performer. Some of the most successful of this group even become millionaires themselves.

Esports (the competitive play of videogames in leagues and tournaments) have also taken off dramatically in recent years. Games such as *Starcraft* have been popular in Korea for decades, but lately competitive *Call of Duty*, *League of Legends*, *Dota* and *Fortnite* have become huge, giving out massive cash prizes, and attracting audiences of millions to watch their finales.

But all of that is mere window dressing; symptoms and side effects, not the disease. The foundation of the videogame industry's ludicrous financial success is a systemic culture of companies abusing and exploiting their workers. These are toxic, misogynistic workplaces that harbour and safekeep known sexual predators, and routinely ignore or cover up wrongdoings for years on end. They do this while developing videogames that are increasingly marketed and designed to be invasive, predatory money-pits that exist solely to prey upon the consumer. Consumers such those with gambling issues, or the neurodivergent. Even children.

Activision–Blizzard, Cyclical Layoffs and a Hideously Overpaid CEO

We're going to start by talking about Activison–Blizzard, a company that will be the most reoccurring villain in our cast of bastards throughout this article.

Activision–Blizzard is the largest videogame company in the industry with a market cap of US$70 billion. If you're unfamiliar, this is the company behind *World of Warcraft*, *Overwatch*, *Candy Crush* and *Call of Duty*. You're familiar with at least one or two of those names, I'm sure. Activision–Blizzard's success is built on cyclical lay-offs and a massive wage gap between its lowest paid workers and its CEO, who is regarded as one of the most overpaid CEOs in the US, period.

By the end of the 2018 fiscal year, Activision–Blizzard had made a record setting US$7.26 billion in sales (compared to US$7.16 billion in 2017). In February 2019, Activision–Blizzard laid off 800 employees, a full 8% of its staff. Of this situation CEO Bobby Kotick said: "While our financial results for 2018 were the best in our history, we didn't realize our full potential." However, despite these supposedly disappointing sales figures and the layoffs, Activision–Blizzard then expanded the workforce of three of its flagships, *Call of Duty*, *Overwatch* and *Candy Crush* by twenty percent.

This is standard practise for Activision–Blizzard and the industry at large: fire a huge swathe of workers and then hire new ones when crunch (the topic of the next section) demands it. And then lay them all off again. How do we know this is cyclical? Because it happened again the very next year. In 2020, a year where most industries suffered but videogames boomed, Activision–Blizzard made a profit of US$8.1 billion, a huge jump since 2018. However, just before their major press-event Blizzcon 2021, Activision–Blizzard announced that they were laying off as many as 190 staff members, this time with the added insult of including a US$200 gift voucher to Battle.net, the company's online store, as part of their severance packages.

All of this while two other facts are a constant reality at Activision-Blizzard. First, Activision-Blizzard pays many of its employees less than they need to make ends meet; many staff reported being unable to afford eating in the company's own cafeteria, and some are delaying having children or deciding not to have them at all because they are struggling financially. Second, Bobby Kotick, the company CEO, is one of the most drastically overpaid men in America. Kotick made US$28 million in 2019, earning him the 45th spot on Fortune's most overpaid CEOs list in America. In 2020, he made 30 million dollars, upping him to the 16th rank on that same list. Kotick has this year in 2021 elected to take a 50% pay-cut, though it should be noted that this is only due to pressure from the board of directors and is not in any way going to the employees who are still so drastically underpaid. In fact, Kotick is still set to take home a huge round of bonuses this year due to the impressive profits of 2020. All while already being worth US$8 billion and with Activision-Blizzard gearing up to hire as many as 3000 new employees for 2021, to begin the cycle again.

The cherry on top? Activision-Blizzard doesn't pay taxes. In 2018 Activision-Blizzard's tax rate was -54%. Yes, negative. Not only did Activision-Blizzard not pay any taxes but they were in fact given a tax refund of 243 million dollars despite not having paid taxes in the first place.

Crunch, and Crunch Culture

Crunch is the term used within the videogame industry to refer to the near ubiquitous practise of periods of intense development over weeks, months or even years. During crunch employees are required to work 80-to-100-hour weeks, including official or unofficial mandatory unpaid overtime. Indeed, official, or unofficial "optional" overtime is also common, wherein if you don't do it, some other poor bastard will be forced to, or the game won't get made and you are likely to be ostracised from the rest of the company. Such demanding workloads result in complete isolation from one's friends, family and loved ones.

Crunch is everywhere in videogame development from the largest "AAA" (the term used to refer to the biggest most prestigious companies in the industry) developers to the smallest independent developers. In order to paint you a clear picture of it, I'm going to briefly touch on four of the biggest stories of unmitigated crunch in the videogame industry in recent years; the cases of Rockstar's *Red Dead Redemption 2* released on October 26th 2018, Bioware's *Anthem* released on February 22nd 2019, Naughty Dog's *The Last of Us: Part II* released on June 19th 2021 and CD Projekt Red's *Cyberpunk 2077* released on the 10th of December 2020.

Red Dead Redemption 2 is widely considered a masterpiece making US$725 million in its opening week. But the human cost was immense. There are reports of employees working 100-hour work weeks to get it done, with some employees crunching for over a year. Others were made to sign waivers disavowing their right to only work eight hours out of every 24. Many current and former employees have spoken up, some publicly and some anonymously, about the "culture of fear" that pervades Rockstar; how if you weren't putting in these hours you would be judged, spoken down to and abused by other employees and management. You would be repeatedly told that working for this company, in this industry was a privilege and if you couldn't handle the conditions there was a long line of people ready and willing to replace you. Many who spoke anonymously did so because they feared reprisal from the company.

It is also worth mentioning that *Red Dead Redemption 2* is not the first time Rockstar has been accused of crunch. During the production of *Red Dead Redemption* (2010) the previous game in the franchise, a group of employee's wives accused the company of forcing their husbands to work 12-hour days, every day in the months leading up to the game's release. This claim was backed up later by the employees themselves, several of whom talked about an internal company laundry service popping up to help employees stay at the office longer. *L.A Noir* (2011) was said to have a similarly brutal work schedule and several employees who worked on *Max Payne 3* (2012) described the experience as a "death march".

Next, Bioware's *Anthem* – which wasn't even supposed to be called *Anthem*. The development team already had tee-shirts printed calling it *Beyond*, but a week before it was publicly unveiled it was decided that getting the copyright on something as broad as *Beyond* would be too difficult. The name was changed at the last minute. This is a good indicator of how mismanaged the game was during the period of constant crunch. From the beginning, the game was plagued with a lack of direction, changing its core concepts and ideas throughout development. Workers would crunch 60-to-100-hour weeks for months on end only to see all their hard work thrown out as what the game was even supposed to be was suddenly changed, everything they'd done scrapped to make room for something entirely new. The project bled staff. Veterans of the company who had worked at the company for decades in leadership positions, to new employees who burnt out early under the demanding load, left Bioware in droves. Many employees talked about the manipulative language used by managers to encourage them to work well beyond their limits, explaining that it would all come together in the end in a phenomenon they called "Bioware magic" Bioware had done this before, but the "magic" was persistently absent as deadline after deadline passed. Many developers spoke of PTSD, severe anxiety and suicidal thoughts during this period. In the end, the game that was *Anthem* was rushed out the door in less than 18 months, looking nothing like what most the people who ever worked on it thought or wanted it to look like, just to meet their final deadline. The game received widespread derision from players and reviewers.

Naughty Dog's *The Last of Us: Part II* is a deeply divisive game. Some think of it as the defining videogame masterpiece of all time and others think of it as trash and a waste of time. What can't be denied are the game's absolutely incredible visuals or the equally incredible amount of crunch required to obtain that level of quality. Naughty Dog employees were not given permission to speak to the press (which is obviously something any innocent company would do) but according to many anonymous sources, the company has an unsustainable culture of perfectionism where everyone is expected to work incredible hours and get the job done no matter the cost. Like Bioware and Rockstar before them, this is not the first time Naughty Dog has used crunch. During the production of *Uncharted 4* (2016) the company, like Bioware, bled staff, burnt out as they were by the insane work hours and the midway scrapping and starting again of the entire project. *The Last of Us: Part II* was no different, more 100-hour work weeks, mismanagement and remaking parts of the game over and over led to massive demoralisation and mental health issues, long delays, short deadlines and a sense of obligation to suffer to get the job done.

Finally, CD Projekt Red's *Cyberpunk 2077*. You should know what I'm going to say by now, but that's my whole point. After studio leads at the company promised concerned fans and members of the press that they would not crunch to make their game, it came out that even as that was being said some staff had already been working 70 plus hour weeks for over a year. The game was hit with numerous delays as elements were thrown away and burned and then rapidly replaced in a mad dash leading to all sorts of mental health issues for employees as they, as is standard, worked long, uncompensated overtime for huge stretches of time before the game was finally released - totally and completely broken. The game was unplayable on the Playstation 4 causing huge controversy and demands for refunds.

My purpose in this incredibly brief cook's tour of these games and the companies behind them is not to say that Rockstar, Bioware, Naughty Dog and CD Projekt Red are worse than other developers, far from it. My goal here in repeatedly hammering home the same points about these company's similarly horrible conditions is to emphasise just how universal crunch culture really is. All these games were in production simultaneously and released within two years of each other. These four companies are not the worst the industry has to offer in terms of abusive and exploitative working conditions, but they are the norm. And I shouldn't have to tell you that that's worse.

Cultures of Harassment, Assault and Misogyny

Now you and I, dear reader, are going to talk about another widespread issue in the games industry. The prevalence of sexual harassment, assault and misogyny in some of the industry's biggest companies - and how hard these companies work to cover it all up.

Riot Games, most well-known for its incredibly popular and expansive MOBA (multiplayer online battlefield arena) game *League of Legends* came under fire in 2018 when a ground-breaking article detailing the culture of misogyny, sexual harassment and gamer-bro, frat-boy in-crowd culture was released. Women in the company were routinely passed up for promotion, placed on lists of "most to least fuckable" by male employees, had it implied that they only had their jobs because of their looks, told they weren't gamer enough, accused of having too much ego or being ladder climbers and had comments made about how their children and husbands must miss them while they were at work. The company adhered to a culture of extreme gatekeeping, particularly towards female hires, who were extensively grilled by male staff about whether they were "core" (as in hardcore) enough gamers to work for them, an attitude pervasive amongst gamer-bros that women who don't play the same games as themselves aren't "real" gamers.

In 2018, all this and much, much more prompted the first walk out strike in videogame history. After events at Activision-Blizzard - which we will get to - the California Department of Fair Employment and Housing begun an investigation into the toxic culture of sexual harassment at Riot Games, which Riot has reportedly been deliberately delaying and obstructing by not telling its employees about their right to talk to the investigation.

Meanwhile, over at Ubisoft, developers of the *Assassins Creed*, *Far Cry*, and *Rainbow Six* (in fact the developer of all Tom Clancy branded games), the family owned and operated business was protecting abusers and burying accusations through the use of a very complicit HR department. The accusations against them included sexual harassment, verbal assault, physical assault, racism, and both threats of, and actual, rape.

These accusations have only come to light recently. Allegedly, Ubisoft Vice President, Maxime Beland, while at a work party, put his hands around a female employee's neck and proceeded to choke her. This accusation prompted more than a dozen women in what we can now call the first wave to come forward using the #metoo movement in order to tell their stories and name names, claiming a culture of severe sexism often accompanied by racism.

Ubisoft Executive Tommy Francois was accused of and is apparently well known for frequently pressuring female staff to have sex with him in front of other employees and frequently attempting to kiss and touch them without permission. The company allegedly spent years covering up this sort of behaviour and simply moved abusive staff members from one division of the company to another when things got too hot. Such behaviour has earned Ubisoft a dubious nickname in some circles: "the Vatican of the games industry". Ubisoft CEO Yves Guillemot gave a brief statement, hardly acknowledging any of this, before immediately moving on without saying how much he knew and when he knew it. Despite recent claims that "big strides" have been made, as many as forty percent of Ubisoft employees, when asked, still feel unsafe going to work.

Finally, the most recent big event in sexual assault and harassment in gaming: the recent lawsuit levied by our old friends the California Department of Fair Employment and Housing towards our old enemies at Activision-Blizzard.

Along with sharing almost all the horrific culture of Riot and Ubisoft, Activision-Blizzard is the only one of these companies with a confirmed kill count. A female employee, who had been subject to intense sexual harassment for months - up to and including having naked photos of her passed around the office - committed suicide whilst on a "work trip" with a male supervisor.

The details are this bad across the board. Widespread discrimination. Sexual assault. Violence. Female employees passed up for promotion whilst doing twice as much work as male employees who play videogames on work hours and make constant jokes about rape. Male supervisors 'hitting on' female employees, female employees being derided for becoming pregnant or for having to pick their children up from school or day care. Woman being kicked out of lactation rooms so that male employees could have meetings, systemic deadnaming and misgendering of trans staff, it goes on and on. If you've been paying attention to the news at all for the last few years, then you are aware of the fact Bill Cosby is a rapist - and so the fact that there was a "Cosby Room" at Activision-Blizzard with a massive, framed picture of him on the wall should be enough to horrify you.

Activision-Blizzard employees staged a walkout recently as yet more details of the toxic culture of misogyny continue to surface.

All three of these cases are ongoing. All three of these companies are under investigation and all three of these companies are being sued. It's not nearly enough. The actions taken by the companies themselves do not go nearly far enough in taking responsibility for this nightmarish culture, and the steps to prevent it all from happening again in the future have been laughably minimal. None of the victims have been compensated or received any justice at all. And while its likely none of them ever will, what with how rich and powerful these companies are, it is a stone-cold, undeniable, heartbreaking and utterly enraging fact that there is at least one former Activision-Blizzard employee who will never, ever get the justice she deserves.

Loots boxes, Microtransactions and Games Designed to Prey on Players

Finally, Activision-Blizzard makes one last appearance alongside a newcomer to this article, the well-known and well-hated money leeches, Electronic Arts.

Whereas up until now I've talked about how videogame companies exploit their workers, loot boxes and microtransactions are the way in which videogame companies are increasingly exploiting their *players* too. A loot box is, as an EA representative explained to the UK's parliament, a "surprise mechanic". The gist is you pay real world money for an in-game box, you open the box and get a number of random in-game items ranging from common and boring to rare and cool. The catch is the rare and cool items are incredibly rare and so players are encouraged by the game to spend as much money as possible. If that sounds like the pokies down at your local RSL, you're right. That disgusting little "surprise mechanic" line was given in an oral evidence session during the UK's ongoing investigation into loot boxes as a form of gambling, something Brazil has also picked up on in recent months.

Microtransations are almost old news at this point but no less greedy: they are simply small in-game purchases you can make. You spend five real world dollars and you get a specific item that you paid for in-game. But let's put both loot boxes and microtransactions in context. You pay here in Australia anywhere from $60 to $100 dollars for the base version of a new videogame, not accounting for special or deluxe additions that slice of parts of the game for those who pay more. Once you've done this, companies like EA and Activision-Blizzard (who dramatically increased the popularity of loot boxes with their 2016 smash-hit *Overwatch*) deliberately encourage and funnel players to spend more and more money.

The clearest example of this is the Ultimate Tournament mode in EA's *FIFA* series – FIFA being the worldwide soccer association responsible for running the World Cup.

FIFA and EA have a longstanding partnership wherein EA makes the videogame version of the World Cup, and every year millions and millions of copies of its yearly *FIFA* release are sold. Ultimate Tournament mode is basically Fantasy Football; you can put together a team made up of players from every team in the world and play other players using these teams - but with the catch that all these players must be bought with FIFA Ultimate Tournament Coins. These FUT coins are an evil-genius layer of obfuscation: you spend real money to buy fake money, which you can then use to then spend on loot boxes. Such loot boxes have a 0.1% chance of turning up the most valued players in the game. EA is on record saying multiple times that their goal with the FIFA franchise is to funnel as many people to this game mode as possible in order to find the "whales"; people who will spend thousands upon thousands of dollars on as many loot boxes as possible.

These whales are almost always children, people with problem gambling issues or the neurodivergent. EA, Activision-Blizzard and Epic games (who makes *Fortnite* - a game almost exclusively played and loved by children) - know this. It's a deliberate part of their business model and they keep doing it over and over, creating predatory economies which trap the vulnerable into paying huge sums of money.

What To Do?

Overthrow capitalism. No really, that's the only long term and complete solution. The rot at the heart of the videogame industry runs deep, all the way to the core and increasingly people are starting to take note and get angry about it. I only covered videogame developers and publishers in this article, another article could easily be written about the gamers themselves and another about the videogame journalists and journalism and how these groups deal with the industry. The short answer is badly in both cases, but the latest ongoing situation at Activision-Blizzard has caused at least a small shift. Some gamers are swearing off Activision-Blizzard titles for good, while some journalists and big names in the communities surrounding some of Activision-Blizzard's biggest titles have put up their hands and said they won't cover or have anything to do with any of Activision-Blizzard's games until the situation is properly redressed.

But the people with the most power to make change in the videogame industry are the workers themselves. After the situation at Riot was brought to light, employees staged the first walkout strike in videogame history. The situations at both Ubisoft and Activision-Blizzard have prompted strikes, walkouts and letters demanding justice and improved conditions. The topic of unionisation in the videogame industry has been talked about and has been slowly gaining momentum for years, through the efforts of groups like Game Workers Unite. Notably, the lawsuit against Activision-Blizzard is being headed up by a union.

Ultimately, though, even the strongest union is a band-aid solution. Because the beast itself, that economic and social system that allows industries like the videogame industry to become the monsters that they are, is capitalism and capitalism will always be at odds with what's best for both workers and consumers (a totally capitalist term in and of itself).

The events shaking the videogame industry should look to you like a warning. A canary in the coal mine for how bad even supposedly "soft" jobs might become under unregulated capitalism. If you're looking at all this and saying. "So what, All this happens at my work and worse!" then congratulations, the company you work for, and capitalism is screwing you over too. And you should really be upset by that.

The Real Hugh Glass: His Life and Death

Zech Elliot

In 2015 a film was made called *The Revenant*. Directed by Alejandro Gonzalez Iñárritu it starred the 90's heartthrob Leonardo DiCaprio. This film was inspired by the 2002 novel of the same name written by Michael Punke.

Many people are only aware of Hugh Glass through the film adaptation of Punke's novel, but most of the events that occurred in the film did not actually happen to the character in real life, such as crawling inside a horse to seek warmth and shelter. Nor did he have a half native American son.

While the film is more of a redemption story than a tale of revenge, Hugh Glass's life wasn't quite as dramatic as Hollywood makes it out to be. The real Hugh Glass was born in Pennsylvania in 1783. Little is known about his early life. He was mainly recognised in the 1800s as an American frontiersman.

In 1823, Glass was not aware that the expedition he was about to sign up for was a journey that would nearly cost him his life. The mission led by General William Ashley, which Glass didn't join until much later, was…

After departing from St Louis, Glass and his men headed to the Missouri River where they caught up with General Ashley and his men in the month of June. Together they ascended the river but were attacked by native Americans from the *Arikara* tribe. Glass was wounded in the leg as a result of this conflict. After retreating down river with many of the men injured Glass, General Ashley and several others set out on a scouting mission to the Grand River in South Dakota. The purpose of this mission was to…

While scouting for game the unthinkable happened. Glass encountered a grizzly bear with two cubs. Although the bear was killed with the help of the company, Glass suffered serious injuries and most of the men, including General Ashley, believed he would not survive. Glass appeared to be nearing death. The men carried the injured Glass for two days before expedition leaders finally announced who would be staying behind to keep the wounded man company until he died.

Initially, John Fitzgerald and Jim Bridger stayed at camp to watch over Glass. Feigning innocence, they took flight and later claimed Glass was dead when they re-joined their party. Somehow, Glass miraculously recovered from most of his injuries and set off in hot pursuit of the two men who had previously left him for dead. It is rumored Glass allowed maggots to lick his wounds to prevent the onset of diseases.

After a long arduous journey and being attacked several times by Native Americans, Glass finally arrived at Fort Henry. At first, he was intent on exacting revenge. Reunited with Bridger Glass decided to spare the young man because of his age. He also found a note saying General Ashely and the group were stationed at a new camp where he learned about Fitzgerald rejoining the army in Nebraska. Glass later met up with and forgave him too but was given money as compensation.

Later in life, Glass returned to South Dakota as a fur trapper and was even employed by the US army as a hunter. Several incidents occurred with the Native Americans in this time. On one occasion Glass was shot in the back with an arrow during an attack. But it was in another altercation in Montana where Glass finally met his fate after in confrontation with Indians.

The legend of Hugh Glass lives on in poems, novels, television, films and even songs.

Gold Rush

Rhys Allen

After four months of retirement, I figure dad would surely have found time to buy a new shirt. Every time I see him now, he is wearing his oil-stained XXL yellow high-vis; torn at the top pocket and draped over the rotundness of his frame. Its dulled florescence counterpoints his sun-burned face.

Time for a new shirt old fella.
We're in the bush mate, don't want to get shot.
Fair point.

His detector - a Garrett – is a top-of-the-line gold-hunting machine. It squawks and it warbles like a sick bird as he waves it back and forth across the leaf litter and quartz so common to the Victorian Goldfields. It is a strange landscape. On the one hand, the red earth and soaring gums are redolent of an ancient history, of a time before boots and picks and spades. On the other, every inch of ground has been ripped and churned, over and over and over, during the gold seeking frenzy 150 years earlier. It is clear that not a single natural line now remains.

*   *   *

High in the sun-drenched branches of tangled eucalypts, confused magpies attempt a conversation with the mineral hunting device.

Warble
(Warble)

Ground iron I reckon

Dad might have said this, studying his contraption intently.

Have to balance it out.

I watch, not replying, a miner's spade in hand. What do I know about metal detecting? Dad pulls himself to the top of a mullock heap.

Deep.

He says this - mostly to himself - as he stares intently at the long-abandoned mineshaft.

Watch your step.

He pokes the detector into the side of the heap, and it immediately chatters, excited by something hidden in the tan dirt. I lift an eyebrow. It is a new sound this time, higher-pitched and much clearer than before. I see his body tense as he checks again.

Warble (Warble)
Over here.

His directive is short and concise. I stroll over, brush away a fly, and experience a flash-back to the last time I followed him through a heat baked bush, miner's spade in hand. Thirty years? Were we closer then? I can't remember. I am hungry.

I've seen a lot of Dad since he retired. He speaks less about work now than he did, but it still dominates the conversation.

I knew this bloke, Johnno, about your age. Good worker, but you'd never loan him your tools. Split up with his missus. Restraining order.

I make the appropriate noises in response.

Oh, too bad, that's rough.

I plant the spade into the spot he is indicating and take out a shovel-load of topsoil and grit.

Cheers.

He moves the detector carefully over the freshly dug soil.

Warble!
(Warble)

He splits the pile in half, checking each mound for the signal.

(Warble)
Warble!

He continues dividing the pile until it is clear that he is now holding whatever it is that is exciting the Garrett. As he sifts through the dirt I noticed the hairs on his hands are still ginger, not turned to ash and grey as the hair on his head long since had. I might have remembered that hand, thirty years younger, as it swung towards my face in a moment of anger, but it isn't the same hand. It doesn't matter anymore.

A bit of lead.

He seems pleased.
Now he knows.

We're rich.

He might have laughed at this, might have placed the dingy lump of metal safely into the torn pocket of his high vis shirt. I look at him again. I smile. He might even be happy.

Make up your mind!

Dan and Mark, ~~Gladys~~ Dominic and Annastacia, Steven and Peter.

Sandgroper Abroad

BENDIGO, **Wednesday 15 September 2021.**
"Lockdown restrictions will be lifted in regional Victoria from tomorrow night, [Thursday 16 September 2021] following advice from Victoria's Chief Health Officer," says Dan Andrews.

Okay. Apart from the fact, the most impactful restrictions will still be in place, I'm good with that, but why now? There are more than two hundred new positive test results in Victoria today. Dan, what happened to your long-held policy that "even one person in the community while infectious is a risk to public health"? Make up your mind, Dan!

"Make up your mind!" Nowadays, that's a more frequent catchphrase than a state premier invoking, "we're all in this together." Get on the beers, get off the beers, get on the beers. Study on campus, study at home, study on campus. Mask off, mask on, mask off. Five to a funeral, fifty in black, then back to five. Or was it four plus one? Contradiction, thy name is 2021.

Remember a couple of weeks ago when New South Wales faced similar infection numbers to Victoria's today, Dan? You pompously "slammed" the NSW Premier, Gladys Berejiklian, saying, "I just remind you all we had a ring of steel around Melbourne last year, and it didn't just protect country Victoria, it protected the whole country." You boasted, "We are avoiding a NSW style lockdown where we lose control of cases; we've avoided that."

But then you were "forced" to extend your "short, sharp lockdown" (again) when cases in Victoria climbed to six the next day. *Six*!

Working from home…

Yet today, it's okay to "ease restrictions with 221 new infections detected?" What happened to, "I make no apology for following the advice of the chief health officer," when you banned kids from playgrounds a couple of weeks ago?

You implemented your silly playground ban when Victoria recorded 22 positive test results and then lifted it hours later on a day with 120 new cases recorded. What the fuck? Make up your mind, Dan!

I don't think I was alone when I laughed out loud as you solemnly announced, "Only one carer can attend [playgrounds with kids], and adults should not remove their masks to eat or drink." No winter-warming lattes for Mum or Dad then, not unless they suck their frothy-coffees through their masks.

Was that meaningless restriction part of the "detailed plan" you fan-fared a few days later? I remember you telling us during your interminable media conference. "I do want to be very clear with the people of Victoria – this will not be Freedom Day; it will not be an opening-up type day. It'll be modest changes that hopefully can be meaningful in people's lives."

We got that, Dan, yup. We got that. Pffffttt. Make up your mind!

I wonder if it was the ridicule echoing around the state as you lost control of "the optics" that forced you to recognise the same reality the Federal and NSW governments accepted months ago.

The Delta variant of the coronavirus has walked all over communities from New Delhi to Caracas, from Bonn to Birmingham. Lockdowns don't seem to "stop the spread" anymore. Curfews don't work. Masks worn during jogs along bush tracks don't slow the rate of infection. The slightest breath shared between people passing in their local Coles – masked or un-masked – is enough to break your curfews and rack up another "case".

The Delta bug now travels around the globe via truck drivers, ships' crews, cricketers, wedding guests, removalists, drug dealers and airline cabin staff. It infects everyone now, including children, but it still doesn't kill most, especially those of us who jumped at the chance to squeeze some AZ or Pfizer into our arms months ago.

Statistics from the great COVID experiment in Britain, and Australia's experience in NSW and now Victoria, show it has become a plague of the unvaccinated. We're told our society can gradually open up again as the jabbed reach seventy to eighty per cent of those eligible for vaccination. With the vulnerable now protected, Dan, your iron boot can finally be removed from our necks. Have you made up your mind, Dan, or are you looking for an excuse to prolong our agony?

But why am I still blood-hot and bitter? Why does the prospect of easing COVID restrictions in Victoria not wreath my face with smiles? I'm vaccinated; my wife's vaccinated. We will momentarily be able to hug our daughter in Melbourne again. Time for a jig!

But no, it's not. There is still the tear-pricking disappointment brought on by the realisation the rest of my family continues to be trapped and unreachable behind WA's "Iron Border." Mike McGowan has made up *his* mind!

Dan has been dragged kicking and screaming to COVID

realpolitik. But, WA's paralyser-in-chief, Mark McGowan, is clinging to his border blankie.

"What we have said is between 80-90 per cent," he preached on Monday. Not the seventy to eighty per cent safety belt of the eastern states for McGowan. For him, it's ninety per cent of WA

Double-vaccinated expat-sandgroper.

vaccinated before he will allow even a double-vaccinated expat-sandgroper to cross the Nullabor.

"I expect that [opening WA borders] will be some time next year," he struts. "At that point in time, we would set a date. That may be two months from then. That would allow everyone who wanted to get vaccinated to get vaccinated."

So not Christmas, January, or February, but maybe March or April 2022 before McGowan may, perhaps, let me arrow along Highway One to my home state.

Despite the AFL Grand Final being played in Western Australia between planeloads of South Australians and Victorians with their bubbled WAGs. I can't repatriate to my state of origin at Christmas to cherish my children and grandchildren.

McGowan says he "understands" because he hasn't seen his brother in a while. Pfffttt! But, the word is he's just blowing smoke to conceal how dilapidated and non-COVID-ready his state's medical system has become. Apparently, McGowan's "iron border" has been welded shut to hide a crippled health system, not to protect my home state from Delta.

Media reports tell us every major hospital in Perth now calls "capacity code-yellow" emergencies multiple times a month. Medical professionals in the West inform us that a code-yellow crisis is only declared by a hospital with severe infrastructure or other internal hospital emergencies. They explain that a capacity-related code yellow means a hospital cannot treat more patients in its emergency department.

"We've got patients, critical patients, who are supposed to be in the emergency wards, and they're being kept alive in ambulances and in the corridors of the hospitals. That's disgraceful," WA's AMA President, Dr Honey, said.

He said the state's health system is in crisis despite WA having no COVID cases.

How did this happen, Mark? A handful of Delta cases and your hospitals will have to shut their doors. WA is awash with record iron ore, gold, nickel, bauxite and now lithium royalties, as well as soaring gas sales, and has been for years. Its mining sector started a second "boom" just before your Government was elected four years ago. Mining industries are rocketing, officially hiring more people than at the peak of the first mining boom in 2013. Tens of billions of dollars are flooding into the state's treasury, and you haven't had to support crippled businesses and workers, as have NSW and Victoria. So why are the state's hospitals starved of staff and operating funds? Why are they in code-yellow crisis?

No answers from Mark. Just bluster and projection. He points accusatorially at other state premiers and the Federal Government. Blaming them for his intransigence. Ridiculously signalling fault like the bony finger of a hooded Mr Death standing over stricken dinner guests in a Monty Python sketch, as a voice quavers, "it was the salmon mousse." It's another trait he shares with Dan.

But his local hashtag supporters adamantly back him. Then dismissively suggest "Zooming" as a substitute for warm embraces.

Pfffttt.

I've recently endured two significant life events via Zoom, and I'm not Robinson Crusoe in this respect. Initially, the wholly unsatisfactory experience of "giving away" the first of my three daughters to marry. I couldn't see, hear or be heard as the digitally fractured image of the ceremony was streamed via an intermittent smartphone connection.

Glitch. A sea breeze buffets my daughter's words away as she turns to grasp her husband's hands. *Glitch.* She's wearing a wedding ring on the beach at Yallingup. *Glitch.* Blurred faces square across my screen as strangers peer at me from Dublin and the United States. *Glitch.* Then she's gone. *Glitch.* A patch of sky. *Glitch.* I'm asked to rate the experience in stars out of five.

Then, at the other end of life. Barry was my Regimental Sergeant Major and guide for the final few years of my career in green. He retired not long after I ended my contract with the Queen and I returned to jeans and a T-shirt at Channel Nine. In later years, he and his wife regularly welcomed me into their home when I visited their city. As the saying goes, "he'd give you the shirt off his back."

I was shocked to receive an email from one of our "Band of Brothers" a few days ago. It announced Barry's difficult death after a couple of years of declining health. I knew he'd passed his best years, but he always brushed sympathies aside.

So I sat locked down in my home-office chair wearing a sombre jacket and clicked the link to activate the memorial-service stream. Unlike my daughter's wedding, the video and audio were crystal clear. But the pristine vision of a "five-allowed-at-funerals" group sitting on empty pews before a flag-draped coffin in an echoing chapel was almost sadder than Barry's death.

The service was one-way. I couldn't see or hear any of my brothers in arms online. Barry's family of three leaned on each other as they briefly and alone celebrated his meaningful life. I felt like a distant fly on the wall as 4K-sharp faces recited quiet words.

And then, like the wedding, they were gone. Nothing left but an amplifier hum. No condolences or war stories, humorous or sad. Just a logo on a blank screen. "How do you rate your experience?" asks white on red text.

Pfffttt, Zoom. I don't.

As I said, I'm not Robinson Crusoe. My experience pales into insignificance compared to the heartache caused by Queensland's cruel banning of a grieving daughter from attending her dad's funeral and Victoria's refusal to allow a fully vaccinated Sydney mum to visit her cancer-stricken daughter.

…avoiding a NSW style lockdown.

Epilogue.

The Lancet is a respected international medical journal. It publishes peer-reviewed scientific papers authored by scientists from across the globe. A recent article is titled: The next pandemic: Impact of COVID-19 in mental healthcare.

The paper opens with: "Since the COVID-19 pandemic was declared by the World Health Organization (WHO), countless investigations performed worldwide have demonstrated the impact of COVID-19 in global mental health. Isolation, less income, symptoms of anxiety, fear, sadness, and mourning have been widely reported during this period. These stressors have been associated with an increased incidence of mental disorders and worsening of pre-existing psychiatric conditions. In this sense, it has been suggested that *concurrent to the COVID-19 pandemic, there is a psychiatric epidemic with wider, longer, and still unexpected consequences* [emphasis added]."

Recently state premiers appeared to agree on a national plan to transition Australia's COVID-19 response. The scheme gave millions of Australians hope. Its measures to minimise cases in the community without lockdowns and ongoing restrictions of movement across state and international borders heralded a return to a long-promised "new normal". But the plan is already in tatters as state premiers equivocate over what 70 per cent and 80 per cent "fully vaccinated" *really* means for their ~~detainees~~ citizens.

So, make up your minds, Dan and Mark, ~~Gladys~~ Dominic and Annastacia, Steven and Peter, but beware, your decisions are likely to be the Wuhan of the next pandemic. We are tired. Not just from the stress and anxiety caused by the threat of COVID-19, but from the anger and now bitterness caused by the menace of your unending "short, sharp lockdowns" and perpetual border closures.

REGENERATION

Instagram

Q Search

Michele_Douven_ ✓

Fresh Canvas

Deep dungeon, despair
Black walls surround, isolate,
A bubble of stone.

Liked by PW1956 and 425 others

5 HOURS AGO

Add a comment...

Post

Instagram

Q Search

Michele_Douven_ ✓

The cell door, opens.
A tunnel upward, spirals.
Escape toward light.

Liked by PW1956 and 425 others

5 HOURS AGO

Add a comment...   Post

Instagram

Search

Michele_Douven_

Tree walls enclose, shroud.
Night crowds, envelops, swallows.
No path, no escape.

Liked by PW1956 and 425 others

5 HOURS AGO

Add a comment…   Post

Michele_Douven_

Dawn light, pierces night.
Darkness recedes, furls shadows.
Trees part, a way opens.

Liked by PW1956 and 425 others

5 HOURS AGO

Add a comment...   Post

Instagram

Search

Michele_Douven_

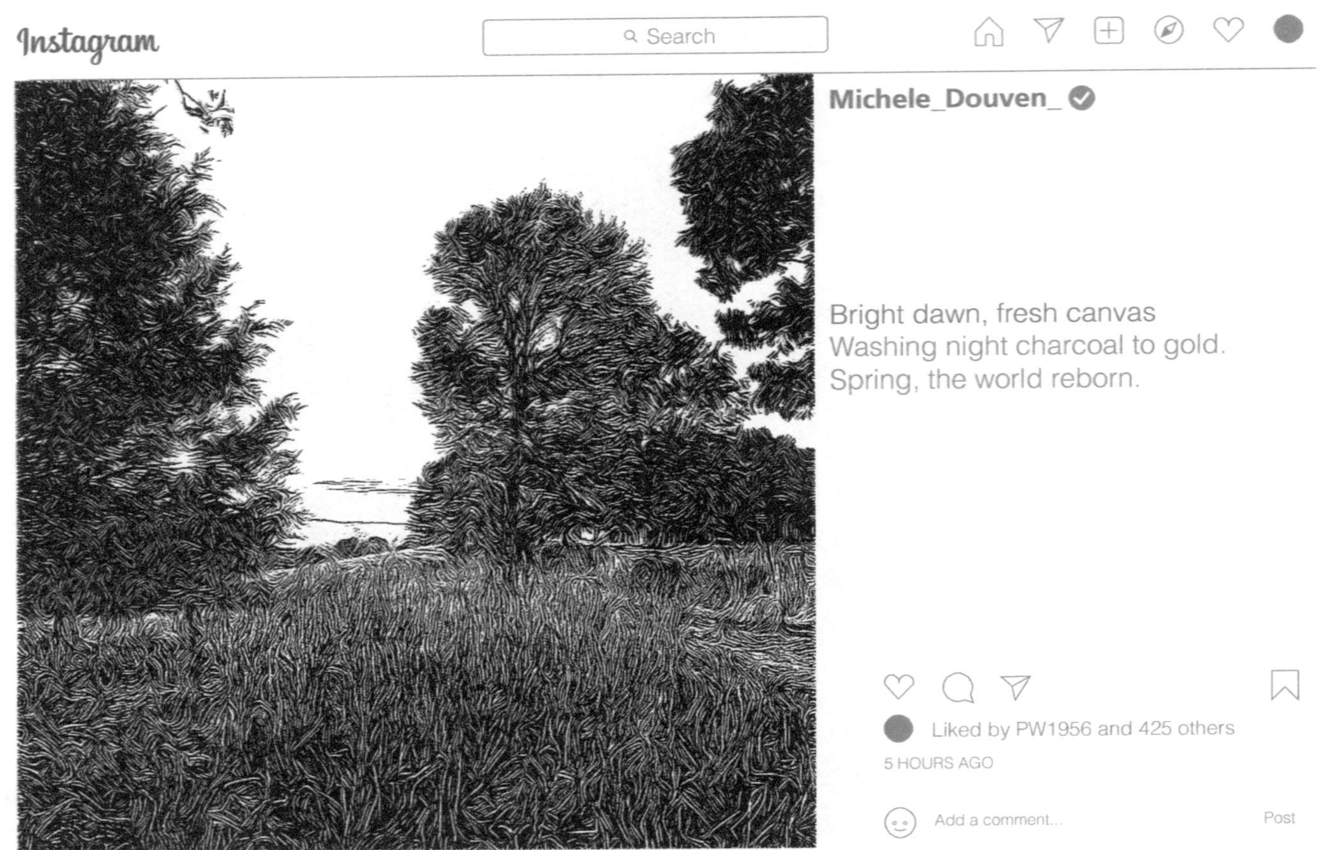

Bright dawn, fresh canvas
Washing night charcoal to gold.
Spring, the world reborn.

Liked by PW1956 and 425 others

5 HOURS AGO

Add a comment...   Post

The hair of the dog
Meg Irwin

You were always careful about red-backs and white-tails. Your slippers, lined with black faux-fur, were a particular risk. Before you put them on, you always checked, feeling with your bowing hand. (A bite, even a small one, on your fingering hand could have serious repercussions.)

But one night, there was an itch on your foot that quickly became sharp pain. When you ripped off the slipper, there was a three-centimetre hair sticking up from inflamed red skin in the middle of your sole. The black hair was as strong as wire. It seemed to be growing there.

On closer examination, you saw the hair's sharp tip was embedded in your foot. With a painful wrench, you pulled it out. It was one of your dog's hairs.

Like nearly everyone, you'd got a dog during the pandemic - about the same time as you'd got the slippers. Both suited your new home-bound lifestyle.

It was not an ordinary dog. She was a beauty – a purebred with the imposing posture of a champion, abandoned after bearing maybe five litters in her short two years. When the pound rang after three weeks for their post adoption follow-up, you told them, "She's a terrific little dog," referring to her excellence, not her capacity to inspire terror.

Early on, she showed herself a great protector. She'd bark if anyone approached the house. She'd vie with you to be the first to check around a corner, each of you taking responsibility for the other. You called her "DD", short for Defender Dog. All your life you had protected others. You felt a new peace in having a protector of your own, so you let her have her way.

DD's black hairs were everywhere. They were strong, like silk. They caught and held in the carpet and were difficult to vacuum up. Your slippers were always full of them. So were the cushions you sat on, the clothes you wore, and the sheets you slept between.

You adjusted. No one could visit anyway, so the vacuuming didn't matter. The inflammatory response when hairs stuck in your skin subsided. You developed immunity. *The hair of the dog,* you thought – a kind of inoculation against the fear and loneliness of the pandemic.

You focused on other things; feeding yourself and paying the rent with no income, the friends who were sick or dying, your music, and books which you read for hours every day. You borrowed library books, and bought more at the op shop when it was open. You developed a new interest in dystopian fantasy, which met the strange conditions of your life.

Summer came and you dispensed with the slippers. Everything had gone online, and, after long resistance, you agreed to a concert. You needed the income and there was potential for an international audience. Practising took all of your attention.

In the kitchen, you slipped on the lino. Then it happened again. You wondered if your balance was playing up or if something neurological was going on. Then, one day in the shower, you felt a weight and drag on your feet. You discovered mats of black hair on each sole.

When you looked at your (never shaved) legs, it seemed the hair was a little darker than usual. So was your facial hair, and there was more of it. But now was not the time to seek medical attention. The concert was approaching and the hospitals were full and dangerously infectious.

Like a feather-foot, you thought, transgressively, I will leave no tracks. It was how you always aspired to play your music – leaving no trace.

And so you played. The online reviews were admiring. "The

howls of both instrument and musician captured the pain and possibility of our time." said one. "The strange effect of slobbering into the instrument while playing has never before been heard," said another.

And after your concert, you hung up your instrument because there was no one to throw it for you to chase. Dropping onto all fours, you strolled out of the house, with DD in the lead and no more restrictions.

VISA
CASIO ALARM CHRONO
TII 2
21:5843
WATER WR
ALDI

The regenerated list
Peter Wiseman

"Testicles, spectacles, wallet and watch." It was a mantra I sometimes muttered during my teens. A checklist of the essentials needed for a "big-night-out" in the seventies. I don't remember where it came from, and it hadn't entered my mind for decades until the other day.

I heard myself repeating it under my breath as I was attempting to get out of my front door. I say attempting, because as I recited the list, I kept discovering additional, absolutely-must-have-items to stuff into my crowded backpack.

I wasn't going far; Dan said I couldn't. I was just off to Aldi for a "big shop." Tossing my keys to the keyless car in the mug holder, I was reaching awkwardly around for my seatbelt when my *lockdown-illegal* passenger – my wife – ventured, "Got a mask?"

"Yup, you?" I squirmed as the bloody belt refused to find its way into the buckle hidden under my hip.

"Yup. Got enough bags?" the *interrogation* continued.

"Y E S. I have enough bags."

"Got a trolley token?"

Fuck. I don't have anything in my wallet these COVID-days. Not money anyway. No one takes cash anymore. I use a virtual card on my phone to pay for purchases. The phone even has my rewards cards in its digital wallet and a vax certificate in the check-in app.

A revised big-night-out list flashes into my mind. *Testicles, spectacles, phone and watch.* Nope, it doesn't have the alliteration which rolled off my teenage tongue.

"Testicles, spectacles, smartphone and watch." *Maybe.* "Testicles, spectacles, Android and watch." *Nope.*

"What are you doing? We'll be late," the interrogator again.

We pull into the Aldi car park and start looking for a space, a smugly supplied trolley token nestling in the cup holder with the keyless car's keys.

"There's one," I'm told as an empty space slides into the rear-vision mirror. "You missed it." Smugness again.

Winter rain splatters hard across the windscreen and I hear my internal song-like voice reciting the list again, *Testicles, spectacles, wallet-phone, watch, trolley token and puff jacket.* Except the jacket isn't in the car. It's lost next to the front door, hidden by the first list.

*   *   *

Alcohol slimed jelly-hands shiver as my wet T-shirt, goosebumps, mask-fogged glasses and I wait beside the chilled-meat section. I'm fumbling my sticky, but sanitised phone, "favouriting" Aldi in my Service Victoria QR Code app. *Testicles, spectacles, wallet-phone, puff jacket, watch, mask, hand sanitiser, shopping bags, trolley token, QR code app.*

I peer out of my mask and glasses cage, "Cheese, don't forget the cheese!" I'm the one feeling smug now, until I look down and see two blocks of Cheddar weighing down the tight plastic stretched over lamb leg-steaks.

Elbows wedged over the trolly handle, I follow my guide and pass along my most anticipated aisle. Its stacked goods sing through my peripheral vision: foreign-sourced screwdriver bits, wooden toys, pickled cabbage, 3D printers, watercolour painting sets, Cape Curry Sauce, marzipan...

Rounding a corner, I spy the "lockdown juice" section. Another list begins its song, *Tamova vodka, Highland Earl, Captain Morgan, Darley's London Style Gin...*

*   *   *

The queue for checkout one is spaced halfway along the bread aisle, so I lean onto the handle again, eyes defocussing. *Testicles, spectacles, phone-wallet, watch, mask, bags, trolley token, QR code app, Covid safe app, vax certificate, photo ID with address, hand sanitiser, blood-pressure tablets, Endone, Buprenorphine sub-linguals, phone charger, USB cable, headphones, spare mask, spare-spare mask, TAFE swipe card, USB stick, tissues...*

I pause; with the new corona-virus necessities of life, the list grows ever longer. But is everything a "big-night-out essential" in 2021?

At that moment, I remember a Chinese doctor's small hands deftly lifting tiny "ductus" twenty-five years ago. Then offering them like a minuscule sacrifice to my "Steven's tenotomy scissors" wielding wife. The "snip" because my *interrogator's* continuing health is my number-one concern.

List clipped, I triumphantly restart the song. *Spectacles, phone-wallet, watch, face mask...*

The Black Horseman

Sha James

The Black Horseman of the Apocalypse
Threw the world into dark despair
His malevolent viral eclipse
Unleashing a crown of fear

Nation upon nation divided
Families rendered apart
Children confused and confounded
Loved ones torn limb from heart

Grey clouds gathered over the lands
People free no more to roam
Prevention resting in human hands
Forced to retreat into their homes

Livelihoods tattered and torn
Businesses crumble all around
Earth wretched as everyone mourns
Cherished dreams run into the ground

Where governments begin to falter
The burden too great to bear
No home, no roof, no shelter
Respite transforms scorn into care

Big business comes to the rescue
Local heroes born from our tears
Citizens waiting in lieu
Closed borders adding to the fear

Out of the ashes of great undoing
Sprout seeds of hope and faith
The human spirit regrouping
Revealing superhuman traits

Diversity turned to Unity
The human spirit once again soars
With new-found solidarity
The monster met with a roar

No mountain too big to climb
No depth too deep to plunge
With godlike strength and time
We strive to overcome

The battle not yet over
Lessons still to learn
Preserve and protect humanity
The prize for which we yearn

Secrets of the Moor Part Two

Bev Amy

Two friends, Susie and Julia travelled to Ireland for a long overdue vacation. Julia was committed to completing the novella she was writing.

Susie needed a rest from the pressures of her job back in Melbourne. She read, reminisced and wandered The Moors, enjoying the fresh cold air.

On one of her ramblings, Susie discovered a dark cave and while exploring the many forks she found a small statue of the Goddess Ana, with an Afghan Hound tucked in the folds of her skirt on each side. Ana or Anu is the Goddess of Mother Earth.

Strange other-world experiences took place and Susie was awakened to her role in her world.

The two women arrived at Dublin Airport to fly to Melbourne. They were confronted with anxious, angry, panicking crowds yelling, shoving and desperate to get on flights home.

They heard the words… corona… covit…whahoon…

Part One of Secrets of the Moor can be read in the 2020 Edition of Painted Words.

We glean a small amount of information from the man sitting next to Julia on the plane. He has cancelled his appointments and is heading home to Melbourne before the international borders are closed. We stare at him in horror.

"What on earth do you mean?" gasps Julia.

"What I am saying is that five weeks ago a Coronavirus outbreak erupted in Wuhan, Mainland China. It came from bats in the Wuhan Wet Food Market and has now transferred to humans. It is rapidly spreading to the rest of the world and we are anxious to get home before we can no longer travel."

"I find it hard to believe that a virus is going to close down world travel," retorts Julia.

"Well, I have family in Melbourne and I am not prepared to risk it," he replies, and buries his head in his book. We shake our heads with an eye-roll at each other.

Much later, I awaken from a troubled dream-filled sleep. Ana and her Hounds are restless locked in the hold. I begin to worry that I have caused more trouble than just a few lambs in another time zone not taking their milk. What if I have contributed to this disaster by removing Ana from her sanctuary and from Ireland?

While on holiday we avoided the news and internet. Now it seems we should have been keeping up to date with world affairs. It is pitch black outside the small window as the plane drones on through the night. I pull out my mobile phone and hit search, Coronavirus, Wuhan. What I discover does nothing to allay my growing anxiety. People are dying in the thousands. The hospitals are flooded, and something about flattening the curve, whatever that's supposed to mean.

Hundreds of news items and postings from ordinary people are all saying the same thing. Get home now before your country closes its borders on you. There was one from an English couple stranded in Spain who were finally allowed to drive straight home across the continent to enter England via the Channel Tunnel. There were eerie photos of the huge auto-routes void of traffic. The borders were closing behind them.

China has expelled all visitors, closed its borders and locked people in their homes and apartment blocks - *This is madness, it can't be happening.*

I quietly signal to the air steward for a glass of white wine. I rarely drink alcohol but this is all too much to take in and I am reluctant to disturb Julia, sleeping with her head on the man's shoulder in ignorant bliss.

Another seven hours pass before we touch down at Tullamarine, Melbourne's International Airport. I am exhausted after relaying to Julia all the information from the search. Her dark eyes are huge, staring at me in disbelief from her deathly pale face. I give her a hug and brush her crumpled hair from her face as we stand to collect our overhead baggage. I will carry on as planned, I am more determined than ever to put my ideas into action. Even if my contribution is small in the grand scheme of things, I owe it to Ana to fulfill my promise.

*   *   *

The following day I start to put my plan into motion, but not before I unwrap my splendid find. Ana and her Hounds look at me questioningly. I explain we are now in Australia, home, and from today onwards I am her servant to do whatever is necessary to heal as much of the damage done to our Mother Earth as I can. I will educate myself in all things environmental and find the right people to help us in our task. As I sit her on my kitchen window ledge and gaze out at the grey day, she tilts her head and smiles up at me.

First, I need to see my area manager, my immediate superior in the jewellery company where I have worked for the last thirty years. We organise to meet for dinner that evening. Peter, looks distinguished, as always, in a light grey suit with a deep blue tie, the colour perfectly matching his smiling eyes. He stands to hug me when I arrive. I am Godmother to his three children, and Peter's wife Jenny is my other very close friend.

"Susie, we have all missed you, I do hope the holiday was wonderful and you are recharged for another thirty years?" I laugh with him and, during a superb three course vegetarian meal, I outline my ideas of repairing my childhood home, restoring the food-bowl and bringing back the local flora and fauna. I carefully omit to mention my Goddess. I explain my wish to keep as much land as possible from being over-developed. He is politely sceptical and refuses to accept my resignation, until finally I agree to continue to mentor the two hundred staff under his watch.

"You will not have to come to the stores, it can be done remotely via Zoom, a computer program like Facetime, which is being utilised to help the 'work and study at home where-possible' policy. We have had to adapt to these changing times extremely quickly, and our online business is growing exponentially. So, more training is needed in many areas. As well, we've had to have constant counselling to address the impact – due to conspiracy theories and other concerns about this viral out-break - on our people's mental health." He was amazed how completely Julia and I had cut ourselves off from the world. He explained everything patiently.

Now that Peter still had me on board with the company, he was happy to listen more carefully to my project.

"I will talk with the Directors regarding funding for your project," he said. "We have environmental personal on staff and the marketing department can do your promotions and when Julia puts a photographic book together, we will fund the printing. I am sure the others will agree to work with you on this." He laughs. "We have never forgotten you, as the determined young woman so incensed when you discovered the ivory jewellery we had in our stores. It took you two years, but we finally gave in to you and removed the offending pieces from sale."

I smile at the memory, "I sometimes think it would have been easier to just fire me."

Paul laughs again, "And miss out on all your good work and the profits you have made for the company! No, you are an asset not to be lost. I will have the lawyers write up a new employment agreement and start the ball rolling with your Malmsbury restoration mission. A new fun chapter! Jenny, who always trusts your instincts, will be excited when I tell her. You can bet she and the children will be your first volunteers."

The next day I phone my real estate agent, bank manager, accountant and solicitor. After this, things move rapidly. The old family home in Malmsbury is purchased, for considerably more than I had hoped, but I want that particular house. Nothing else feels right. We also acquire surrounding land - as much as the owners will let go and my bank manager will agree to.

Every evening I sit quietly with Ana and keep her informed as to our progress. She listens intently as I tell her of our land purchases and the efforts to replant and regenerate the many acres which had lain fallow, due to drought and neglect. The house and a small shop outlet is coming together as I envisioned.

My Zoom sessions are intense and exhausting. As light relief I explain my new venture to my colleagues, who are enthusiastic and want to help. It is during these conversations I discover many hidden talents which I can utilise in and around the house. We set up a roster around days off, and when the weather and COVID-19, as this deadly virus is now called, permit, we meet at the house in Malmsbury. I am astonished by people's range of skills and, under the watchful eye of my architect friend, the old house is transforming into a huge beautiful light-filled homestead. A past owner, after my family sold it, had the grand idea of exposing the brickwork inside to show what a brick nog cottage looked like. I hate it and we insulate and re-plaster. We extend out the back to the ancient plum tree, which is pruned and fertilized, for maybe the first time in its life. The plums are delicious fresh or as jam or sauce, and will sell in our small road-side shop.

An enormous new kitchen-dining area and separate pantry, with high airy sunlit-flooded ceilings, fills the interior verandah. Homemade produce soon overflows on the wooden crafted pantry shelves. The kitchen is alive with happy energy and the rich aromas of freshly baked bread and bubbling soup.

A large bathroom is built at one end of the house and the bedrooms are painted and refurbished with stylish beds, desks and chairs, made or restored by my helpers. Bright blankets, curtains and cushions arrive by the car load. The lounge with a roaring fire is a peaceful resting place.

The gardens are beginning to take shape. We replant Mother's cottage garden with everything we can source that is colourful and flowering. Trees and roses line the drive and pathways. I find clumps of agapanthus still surviving in a damp corner of the yard. These go in beside the roses along the front path. My favourite playing area as a child, amongst the elm suckers out the back gate, is transformed into a hide-away and curving maze for the children to explore while we are working.

By this time, the townsfolk are taking an interest. A Town Hall meeting is called by the local historical group. I tell them, "This is my small contribution to counter the effects we, as humans, have had on our precious Mother Earth. This house was my childhood home. It is where I belong. I intend to restore the food bowl my father established, replant the pine forest. We will set up a nursery of plants, including forgotten and endangered species. A seed bank will be established in the cellar. We will grow commercial quality organic food, and our proceeds will go towards purchasing more farms and land to keep safe from developers, especially in the wetlands beyond the reservoir, my first concern. I have put an offer in, and by re-establishing this area and the plant life, we will see the birds, small animals and frogs return to their habitat. We have built a cold-store, storage sheds and a research facility."

Some of the folk leave, shaking their heads, others smile and ask questions, a good number offer to help.

They start work in the acres of fallow land I have purchased. Some of them are experienced in growing fruit, vegetables and herbs and over the next few months this tired old soil is brought back to life. "Plant trees and the rains will come," my mother used to tell me.

A potter and his family move in to a picturesque stone cottage near the cemetery and he joins our efforts to reclaim the land and recreate the township's former glory. Closely following are bee keepers, herbalists, trades-people, artists and writers, all looking for a more sustainable lifestyle with like-minded folk. We are becoming known overseas and hundreds of requests for information means Julia and I update our blog on a daily basis.

People are keen to leave the big cities where outbreaks of the deadly COVID-19 virus are increasing at alarming rates. Whole communities are being locked in their houses for days, weeks and even months. Travel is restricted to within five kilometres of home. The elderly are especially vulnerable and isolated due to "lock downs", as we now call them. It is frightening, and we do our best to continue safely in this unknown environment.

It is not plain sailing in other ways either. I often cry when I tell Ana about our continuing journey and the difficulties I face from the councillors and developers. There is more money for their coffers in developing the land, than preserving it. A new strategy for funds is required, and Peter launches some serious online fundraising events and jewellery auctions to supplement my bank balance. I sell my Melbourne apartment and move permanently to Malmsbury. Ana and her Hounds are delighted with this change.

Julia works tirelessly to complete her first coffee table book, a pictorial history depicting the origins of the house, the "before and after" of our venture. Peter, as promised, has it printed and distributed in record time.

I continue my Zoom sessions and my jewellery staff love their weekend stays in the house. Julia and Jenny and the children visit often.

I start to relax. My job is almost done. Sometimes I stir in my sleep to see Ana sitting with the Hounds curled at her feet. She is smiling.

Years pass -

When the house is particularly crowded with weekend guests, I carefully place my Goddess in my red jacket pocket, wrap my red shawl around my shoulders and escape through a side door. I walk down the hill to my childhood friend, Rupert. We make large mugs of tea and coffee and curl up in comfy old armchairs on his top floor balcony. We watch the stars. We overlook the valley of Malmsbury and gossip. Rupert knows every dwelling and every occupant. He has never left the family farm. We watch house lights twinkle out and the sky turn dark.

We awaken from dozing when the sun's rays appear over the distant hills. Covering us are soft, warm blankets made by the local women from Rupert's wool.

I know Ana and her Hounds have brought the blankets to us to keep off the nights chill. Rupert scoffs at me, but he has no other answer.

Instagram

Michael_Sidwell_ Some of my earliest memories are of casting a line with my father, just as he had with his own father, before the world changed. Whether out in a little tinny, bobbing atop the bay's choppy waves, or on the brown-water banks of King Parrot Creek - fishing was always there. Catch and release, catch and release, just for the fun of it. Unless it was a big one - perhaps a giant perch, or a rainbow trout. Maybe a full bucket of flathead. These might make it to the dinner table. I recall the quiet moments of introspection as I stood apart from the others. Sometimes, I fished alone.

Liked by PW1956 and 425 others

5 HOURS AGO

Add a comment...   Post

Instagram
Search
Michael_Sidwell_ Watching clouds drift across an endless sky, bluer than any ocean, as bees float and hum between yellow-faced flowers. Talking to my father as he did with his, asking questions about the world, learning to bait a hook, or how to catch a flathead without catching my thumb on those horribly stinging spines.
Liked by PW1956 and 425 others
5 HOURS AGO
Add a comment...
Post

Instagram

Michael_Sidwell_ It used to be a community then, down on the pier. Lines of people chatting, leaning against the rails, asking how each other's day was. How their catch was. I remember the laughter as I cast with a tremendous whip-crack; the line snapped and my hook, bait and sinkers sailed out into the blue. Good-natured laughter, applause, and "…there she goes!" I felt part of it all, not pushed out or aside, but a part of this great community.

Liked by PW1956 and 425 others

5 HOURS AGO

Add a comment… Post

Instagram

Search

Michael_Sidwell_ Will we ever see it again? Will it ever come back? Those salad days of camaraderie, of buying bait and hiring boats. Of laughter and boasting and home after dark, maybe with a big, hard-fought fish, and a story of the battle to tell my mum.

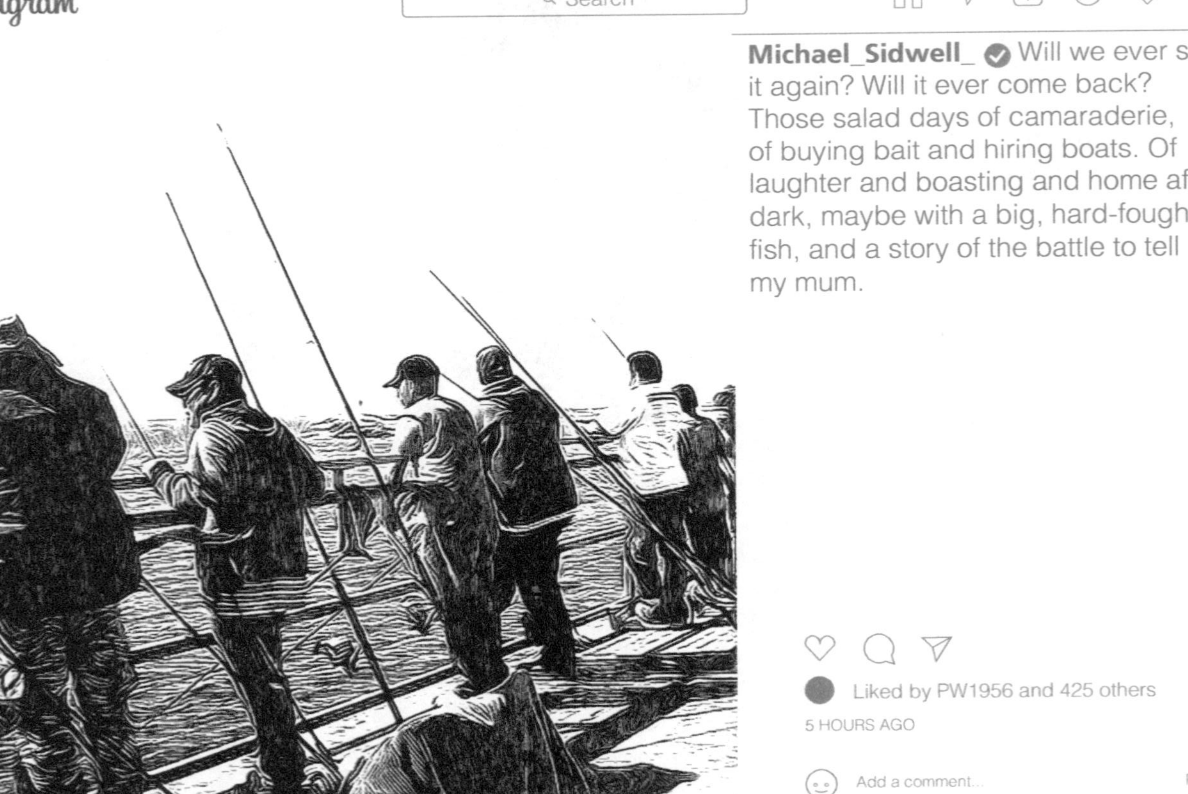

Liked by PW1956 and 425 others

5 HOURS AGO

Add a comment...   Post

Instagram

Q Search

Michael_Sidwell_ Will I ever stand on the shore or wade knee deep to cast a line into the curling waves with my child? Will we ever sit, legs dangling, over the lip of a high riverbank and drop a line into that burbling, brown stream? There in the glow of dawn, or twilight dusk, watching for the tell-tale jiggle of the rod, that tantalising tug of the line. We stand together, watching the dip and rise of floats, bobbing with the water and the hope of a bite, as we hope for the world around us. COVID variants, vaccines, lockdowns, travel rules and gathering limits; each jiggle of a line promising that catch.
Liked by PW1956 and 425 others
5 HOURS AGO
Add a comment...
Post

Instagram

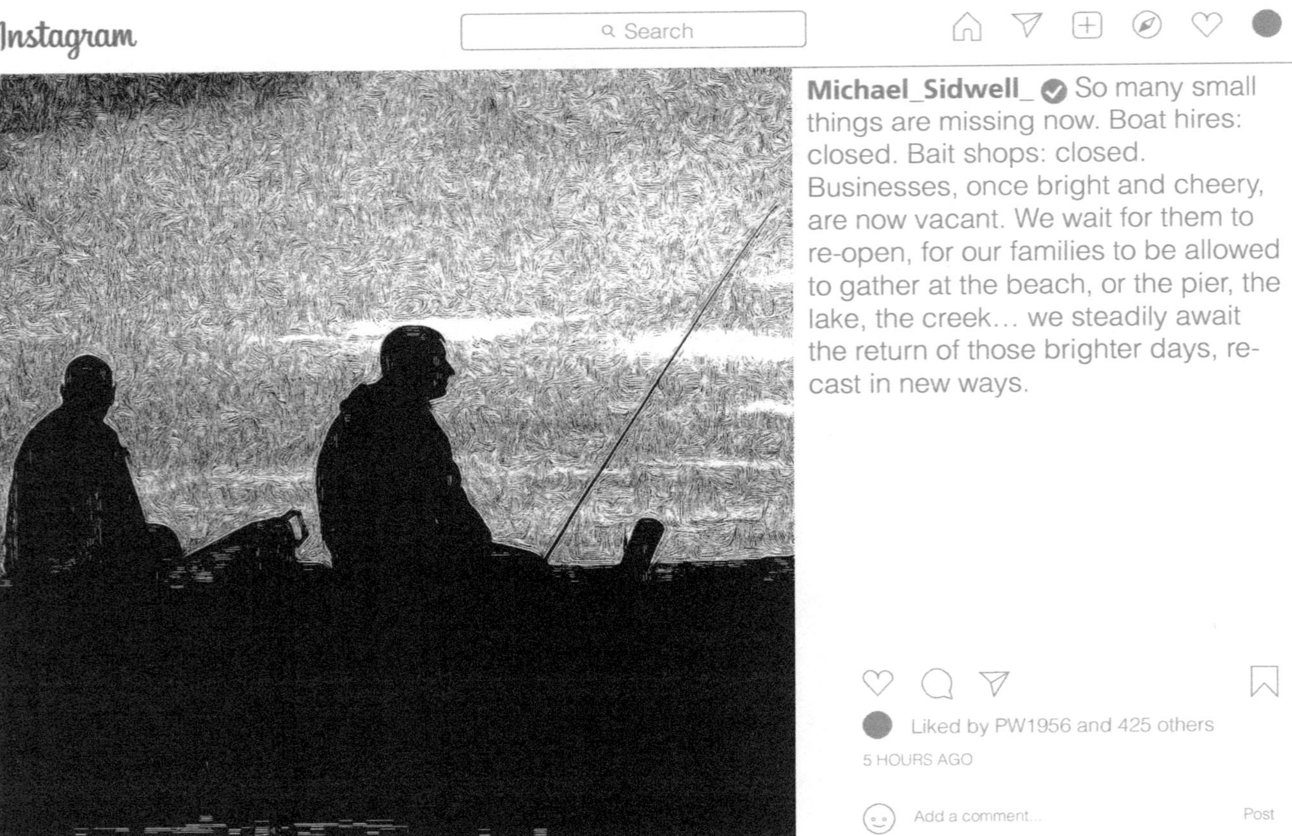

Michael_Sidwell_ So many small things are missing now. Boat hires: closed. Bait shops: closed. Businesses, once bright and cheery, are now vacant. We wait for them to re-open, for our families to be allowed to gather at the beach, or the pier, the lake, the creek… we steadily await the return of those brighter days, re-cast in new ways.

Liked by PW1956 and 425 others

5 HOURS AGO

Add a comment…

Post

Instagram

Search

Michael_Sidwell We live with it now, the world slowly accepting a new normal. Maybe. It will never be the same as it was, but we'll make do, as people have always done. There have been and always will be those who have gone through worse. They made their lives and lived on, as we will also do. We can cower in fear for future generations, or we can stand and face this new way of living; accept the changes, and gather our strength. The world goes on, and so do we.

Liked by PW1956 and 425 others

5 HOURS AGO

Add a comment...

Post

Instagram

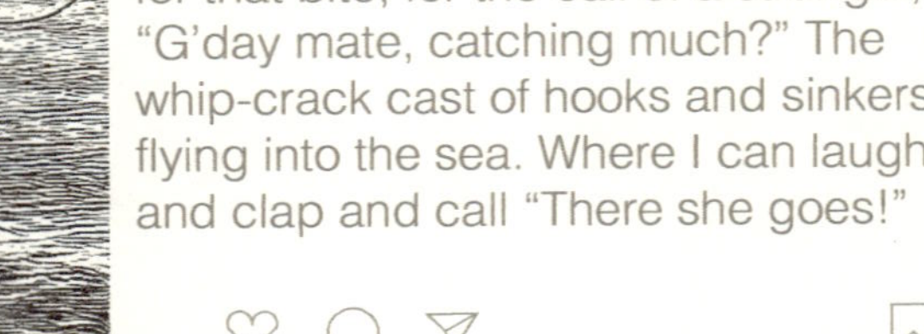

Michael_Sidwell ✓ The ocean is still there, and the sun still rises. We've had our shots and the ones after that and will have the ones still to come. Vaccines are improving, fighting variants, day by day, that's how we do it. And as we return to our hobbies and our old ways, we find our lifelines. This one is mine, cast into the watery-blue, where the sun-gold paints a trail to the edge of the world. And I wait, like we all wait, with hope for that bite; for the call of a stranger, "G'day mate, catching much?" The whip-crack cast of hooks and sinkers flying into the sea. Where I can laugh and clap and call "There she goes!"

Liked by PW1956 and 425 others

5 HOURS AGO

Add a comment...   Post

Sprout
MJ Douven

Green fingers reaching,
Promise of new life, of hope,
Spring children blossom.

www.ingramcontent.com/pod-product-compliance
Lightning Source LLC
Chambersburg PA
CBHW020539120726
47903CB00001B/39